Katrina Mae Leuzinger

THE
FAIRY
THIEF

Loblolly Press, LLC
Kill Devil Hills, NC

Names: Leuzinger, Katrina Mae, author.

Title: The fairy thief / by Katrina Mae Leuzinger.

Description: Kill Devil Hills, NC: Loblolly Press, 2022.

Identifiers: LCCN: 2022921502 | ISBN: 979-8-9873222-0-8 Subjects: LCSH Fairies--Fiction. | Los Angeles (Calif.)--Fiction. | Fantasy fiction. | Love stories. | BISAC FICTION / Fantasy / Contemporary. | FICTION / Fantasy / Urban Life. | FICTION / Romance / Fantasy. Classification: LCC PS3612 .E89 F35 2022 | DDC 813.6--dc23

For Brandon

Trigger warnings for The Fairy Thief can be
found here:
KatrinaMaeLeuzinger.com/TriggerWarning

Read safe, my loves.

Chapter One

As she poured the creamer into the antique crystal bowl, Petra wondered if she'd gone insane.

Sane people took a normal, logical approach when they lost their car keys. They retraced their steps, checked their coat pockets, and muttered ineffectual platitudes like, "It's always in the last place you look."

Petra's boss was fond of asking, "Did you look for it like a man or did you look for it like a woman?" Her theory was that women actually lifted things up or moved stuff out of the way when they were searching, whereas men simply glanced around before declaring the object hopelessly lost.

But Petra had looked for them like a woman. She'd retraced her steps, moving systematically through each room in the creaky old house. She'd upended her purse and turned all her pockets inside out. She'd even checked in the refrigerator. As she moved aside the Coffee-mate, she remembered what her grandmother would say when something went missing around the house.

Oma said that fairies stole them.

"But why do they steal things?" Petra had asked her.

It was one of Petra's earliest memories. She couldn't have been more than four years old. Oma had trusted her to carry the antique crystal bowl out to the garden. Her hands had been sweating as she clutched the bowl and took slow, deliberate steps across the foyer to the back door. The sunlight refracted through the bowl, dotting her pink sneakers with little rainbows. Oma had waited patiently for her, holding a carton of cream, her ice blue eyes twinkling out of her wrinkled face, long white hair blowing in the breeze.

"Oh, viele Gründe," Oma had said. "Lots of reasons."

Oma spoke perfect, albeit heavily accented, English, but she always insisted on speaking German to Petra. She was determined that no granddaughter of hers would grow up without knowing the mother tongue. "Mostly, they're just mischievous."

"What's *mischievous* mean?"

"It means they like to play tricks on people. They think it's funny."

"But isn't stealing bad?" Petra's little brain struggled to reconcile the happy image of fairies painted for her during bedtime stories with this new, contradictory information.

"They don't mean to be bad," Oma assured her. "Most of them are good; they just like shiny things and playing pranks. They don't know any better."

Petra stared out the kitchen window into the garden and felt a pang of guilt. When Oma was alive, the garden in the backyard had been the envy of the whole neighborhood. Oma didn't grow her roses in orderly little rows like snooty Mrs. Mason next door did. Oma's roses grew on vines which crept up the swing set and the branches of her pear tree. After spring, the tiny white flowers on the pear tree would begin to blow off in the wind, scattering white petals on the mushrooms that grew near the roots. There were watermelons in the summer and pumpkins in the fall, their yellow blooms springing up between the fragrant rosemary and basil plants. She never used any of those overpriced synthetic fertilizers the other ladies swore by, and yet it was always Oma's pumpkins that took the blue ribbon at the Fall Festival every year. Oma's pumpkins were big enough for Petra to crouch inside, and made the best Blachinda in the world.

When she had inherited the house last year Petra had tried, really tried, to keep the garden growing... at least for awhile. But work always kept her busy. No matter how great her intentions, the plants had started to wither from neglect. Now all that remained of Oma's roses were the brown vines, barely visible against the bark of the pear tree, a tree that had produced only a few, mealy pears this year. Weeds had crept in, choking out those prized pumpkins. Other plants had gone wild in Oma's absence, like the little rosemary shrub that had morphed into a towering presence, slowly consuming the rest of the garden.

Not for the first time, Petra gazed at the tangle of weeds and dead flowers and considered hiring a gardener. That's what busy working people did, right? Pay someone else to grow their flowers? Or was that just what busy working people with money did?

"The hell are you doing?"

Petra dropped the jug of Coffee-mate in surprise, splattering it all over the blue tile floor. Her boyfriend, Brad, laughed at her and ducked into the laundry room for the mop. Brad had slept over again last night. Based on his Superman pajama bottoms, he was in no hurry to depart today. His light brown hair, usually stiff with product, currently lay soft and flat on his head. Lately, he'd been sleeping over on the four days a week he didn't have his part-time job at the law firm, playing video games and lifting weights while she was out.

"I got called in to work," Petra said.

Brad chuckled as he emerged from the laundry room and handed her the mop. "Yeah, that's definitely not what I was asking about."

He pointedly eyed the bowl. Petra flushed and tried valiantly to come up with an explanation that did not make her sound like she'd gone crazier than a squirrel on the 405. She wiped the splattered creamer off the side of the bowl.

"Promise you won't make fun of me."

Brad laughed again. "I'm not sure anything good ever follows those words."

He busied himself making breakfast, setting a skillet down on the stove. "No promises." Brad switched out the coffee maker plug for the toaster and pulled some eggs out of the fridge.

"I can't find my keys," Petra said.

"What's that got to do with the creamer?"

Blushing crimson, Petra stared at her feet as she rushed to get the words out. "My Oma used to leave a bowl of cream out in the garden for the fairies."

Brad nearly dropped the egg carton.

"Well, that's totally reaffirming that your grandma was a crazy old coot," he said with a chuckle. "It's not the genetic kind of crazy, right?"

Petra's ice blue eyes narrowed as she stared down her boyfriend through a film of red.

"Don't make fun of my Oma!"

"Sorry." Brad raised his hands in surrender, cowering under her glare.

"So, you're putting that out in the garden because somehow this will help you find your keys, since that's what your in-no-way-crazy grandma used to do?"

Petra sighed and sat down at the table across from him. When he said it out loud, it felt even more superstitious than it did when the idea had popped into her head.

"You're think you're dating a lunatic, don't you?" she said.

"Hey," he protested. "Give me some credit. I can be open minded."

Petra looked up at him hopefully. His expression was completely serious.

"What I was thinking was, do you really think the fairies like coconut?" His grin cracked through the veneer of mock-seriousness. "Or should you maybe pick up something classic like hazelnut flavor?"

He burst out laughing, unable to contain himself anymore. Petra snatched the bowl and stomped out of the kitchen.

Brad called after her, still laughing, "Come on, it was just a joke, babe!"

His "joke" was still ringing in her ears as she crossed the garden. She realized with dawning horror that she was actually considering the question. Was flavored coffee creamer good enough, or did it have to be real cream like Oma used to put out?

Feeling like more of an idiot by the minute, she gingerly stepped over the bramble of rose vines and into the perfect ring of mushrooms. No matter how overgrown the garden got, those mushrooms always remained. They were red with white spots and grew single file in a circle two yards wide, as if they'd been planted that way. Oma had always called it the Feenring, the fairy ring.

Petra carefully knelt and set the bowl down in the middle. A cool breeze whipped her hair as she stood up, sending her long blond curls flying out behind her. With the breeze came an earthy smell, like rich soil and lavender. Petra clutched her shawl closer to her against the chill. She glanced back through the kitchen window to make sure Brad wasn't watching her before she whispered to the ground, "Bring my keys back... please?"

When Petra came back inside, Brad was sitting on the couch waiting for her, dangling the keys from one finger.

"Look what I found," he boasted.

Petra took them from his hand and rewarded him with a lingering kiss.

"Where were they?"

"You left them in the refrigerator. How did you not see them when you got the creamer out? You must be blind."

Petra stared at the keys in her open palm, and tried to think back to when she had searched the refrigerator earlier.

"Yeah," she agreed, shaking her head. "I must have just missed them."

Chapter Two

B *ut I looked in the refrigerator,* she thought
again as she crossed the foyer. She held
an egg sandwich in one hand while she rooted
for the phone at the bottom of her purse with
the other. How her phone could be so hard to
find in a bag so small was beyond her. She'd
just pulled it out when it rang in her hand.
The sound of a foghorn blared out as loud
as the iPhone could manage, the characteristic
WHEEEEE-OOOOOH echoing off the vaulted
ceiling. Petra answered it without so much as
glancing at the screen.

"Hey, sorry. I couldn't find my keys, but I'm on
my way now..."

"Cool. Can you bring coffee? I'm out." Del's low
voice came through the phone and Petra winced.

"Like, I love my kid, but I'm not gonna make it through a Kindergarten musical about the wonders of recycling without coffee," Del continued.

Shit. Gloria's show...

"Listen, Del..." Petra began as she swung open the door to the garage.

The door opened to the half of the garage Petra had converted into a studio. Bins of old paintings and art supplies lined one wall. The rest of the studio space was taken up by an armchair and an empty easel. In the other half of the garage, where she had expected to find her Jetta, was a candy-apple red Mustang.

"Hang on," Petra said. She pulled the phone away from her face and shouted back into the house. "Really?!"

"You have a two-car garage and three bedrooms!" Brad yelled back. "There are better places for you to pretend you still paint!"

"Es ist mein Haus, du Scheißkerl!" She slammed the door for emphasis and punched the garage door opener before bringing her phone to her ear again. "I'm back."

"You know, the impact is kinda lost when you yell at him in a language he doesn't understand."

"Yeah, no. If Brad understood the things I call him, we'd have broken up at least two years ago."

Sunlight glinted off the hood of the gray Jetta parked in the driveway. Petra's heels clicked on the pavement as she raced toward it.

"Look, I um..."

Del sighed. "You're not coming, are you?"

Petra tossed her purse and egg sandwich into the passenger seat and cranked the noisy, diesel engine to life. Her silence spoke for her as she threw the car into reverse. The awkward quiet persisted all the way out of the driveway and halfway down the street.

"Will you tell Gloria 'Tante's sorry'?" Petra finally said. "Get her some flowers from me? I'll pay you back."

"It's okay. I didn't tell her you were coming," Del said in a tone which suggested it was definitely not okay. "I didn't want her to be disappointed when you flaked."

Petra was torn between guilt and gratitude that Gloria wouldn't know Petra had promised to see her "niece" make her thrilling stage debut as a laundry detergent bottle.

"There's no one else to cover the front desk," Petra protested. "Hope called out because her baby's sick, and Sylvia has to get to her second job and–"

"And the Hammond Executive Hotel will crumble to the friggin' ground without you."

Petra's guilt soured into annoyance. "No, but I might get *fired*."

"Good," Del shot back. "You hate that job anyway."

Not wanting to argue the point, Petra swallowed her retort, apologized again, and said her goodbyes, promising to make it up to her later.

The truth was Petra did not hate being the Front Desk Manager of the Hammond Executive Hotel. Maybe she didn't love it either. Hotel management wasn't exactly a childhood dream. But she loved having business cards with her name on them. And how great she looked in a tailored suit instead of that uniform polo she'd worn when she started there. She loved having a job that was a couple promotions past entry level; one that would inevitably keep promoting her as long as she didn't screw up.

Mostly, she loved that she was good at it.

Breakfast was still being served in the open dining room adjacent to the lobby when Petra arrived, so there were plenty of guests milling around. The Hammond was a stone's throw from LAX and rented rooms by the week, making it popular with business people, although they still got the occasional vacationing family. One such family sat in the middle of the dining area. The three kids were somehow managing to produce 90% of the noise in the room. Stern looking, middle-aged men in business suits glared openly as they sipped coffee and checked their emails.

Petra offered the front desk girl, Sylvia, a wave as she ducked behind the counter. Sylvia returned it with a smile. The younger woman covered her other ear as she continued to take a reservation on the phone, casting a meaningful look at the rambunctious children. Her purse and the uniform for her other job sat next to her, ready to run out at the door as soon as she got off the phone.

Quick as a flash, Petra removed a stack of coloring pages and crayons from a drawer and strode across the lobby with them. The kids were making laps around the dining room, running full tilt and shouting at each other. Petra intercepted them as they rounded the coffee station.

"Heeey, you guys like coloring?" Petra asked.

The two girls accepted the shiny new distractions with smiles and plunked down where they stood, voices immediately dropping to a much more tolerable volume.

Works every time.

Their older brother looked less convinced. He scowled at the butterfly-winged fairy on the first page.

"Fairies are for girls," he protested.

"Oh yeah?" Petra asked. She took the coloring pages and began to flip through them. "Have you ever heard of the Elbkönig?"

The boy shook his head. Petra handed him a page with a skull-faced creature in a tattered cloak lurking in the forest.

"They live in the darkest part of the woods, where the trees groan and the birds refuse to sing," Petra said, dropping her voice to the same spooky undertone Oma used to use. "Elbkönig hide in the shadows just off the path, waiting for prey to wander into their midst."

She let the words hang for a moment while she busied herself fixing three coffees– one no cream and three Sweet and Low, one six sugars and three creams, and one two creams two sugars.

"Mostly..." Petra said as she popped a lid on each cup, "they eat children."

When she turned around again the boy's eyes had grown rather wide.

"Yeah, but they're not real... right?" he asked.

Petra's mind returned to the fairy ring in her garden.

"Probably not," she answered. "But make sure you stay on the path anyway, okay?"

He nodded emphatically and plopped down to color with his sisters.

"Do you have any idea how much money I spend here?!" The angry shout from the other end of the lobby turned Petra's head, and everyone else's, that direction. One of the guests, Mr. Clark, leaned over the front desk, too close to Sylvia for comfort.

Jesus, what now?

"Good morning, Mr. Clark," Petra called out as she made her way back to the desk. She pulled out her phone and quickly Googled last night's baseball scores. "Did you catch the White Sox game?"

Mr. Clark turned his attention to her with a bright smile. Sylvia shot a grateful look at Petra over his shoulder.

"I had to work through most of it, but I came in at the 7th," he said. "My God, that suicide squeeze!"

"I know!" Petra responded with neutral enthusiasm, unsure if a suicide squeeze was a good thing or a bad thing. "So... is there a problem I could help you with?"

He jerked his thumb at Sylvia. "Your new girl says you don't have a room for me next week. My secretary put in the reservation Monday."

"System says 'sold out,'" Sylvia said in a half-whisper.

"Actually..." Petra stepped behind the desk and logged into the computer. "Martha never called this week. I was planning to catch you today and check if you needed a room."

"Martha didn't...?" The wind went out of Mr. Clark's sails.

Petra clicked away on the reservation system as Sylvia watched.

"And Sylvia's right, we are sold out," Petra continued. "But don't worry. I always keep a few rooms on hold for important guests."

In truth, she had one room, and it was out of order. Petra checked the notes and then shot a message off to Devon in Maintenance, telling him to get on that A/C repair stat.

"Oh, well... thanks for taking care of that." Mr. Clark shuffled his feet and looked up at Sylvia. "Sorry for... Obviously I didn't *mean* to snap at you."

Sylvia had a look that said she was not yet prepared to accept Mr. Clark's half-assed apology with any degree of grace. Petra interceded and thanked the guest for her before grabbing his confirmation off the printer. Mr. Clark walked away dialing his phone, probably to yell at his poor secretary.

Petra handed the diabetic coma-inducing coffee to Sylvia. "Thanks for covering till I got here."

"Thanks for making that asshole say 'sorry,'" Sylvia said. She snatched up her things and headed for the door. "Bye, Boss Lady."

After a quick look around to make sure no other guests needed her, Petra carried the remaining coffees into the back offices. She passed through her own office– a small space she shared with the Head Housekeeper– and gave a cursory knock on the open door before walking into the connecting office.

"Coffee?" Petra offered, holding out the no cream three Sweet and Low to her boss.

Beth accepted the cup with a grateful smile and motioned for Petra to sit. Petra took the seat across from Beth's cluttered desk and sipped her own coffee. Her face reflected back at her in the "General Manager" name plate.

"You handled that well," Beth said. She indicated the bank of monitors on the wall which displayed the feed from the security cameras. Front Desk empty, cooks cleaning up from breakfast, housekeepers smoking by the back door, pint-sized guests still coloring.

Petra tried to mask just how pleased she was to hear that with a joke. "You spying on me again?"

"Take the compliment, Bachman," Beth said with an eye roll. "When did we get coloring pages?"

"Oh. I um..." her cheeks flushed. "They're just doodles. I made some copies and stapled them together. The crayons came out of petty cash." Feeling suddenly unsure, she added, "You signed off on the expense report."

That earned her another eye roll from Beth. "You think I'm going to write you up over crayons? That's hurtful..."

Petra had once seen Beth fire a Sales Manager for not returning a phone call, so getting reamed over a few boxes of knockoff Crayolas didn't seem that far out there. She kept her mouth shut.

"What I should get on you for is Hope not showing up again," Beth said. "What's her excuse this time?"

"Sick baby."

Beth scoffed. "I'm a single mom too. I still manage to get here every day."

Petra managed to stop herself before pointing out that Beth's kids were teenagers. Hope's wasn't even a month old.

"Part of being in charge is making sure you have the best possible team working under you," Beth said. "That's how you get to be where I am; and I think you could get there. Maybe even work for Hammond Corporate. I want you to think about that the next time Hope calls out. Do you think she's the best person you could have working for you, or do you just feel like she really needs the job?"

Petra weighed Beth's words in silence. She had her eyes on the prize, the big desk and the corner office Beth was currently holding court in. Petra was 27 now, and she wanted that promotion to General Manager before she was 30. She could

get there. She only hoped she didn't have to get
there by mercilessly firing single mothers.

"Think about it," Beth advised. She smiled wide.
"That's the kind of thing you'll have to think
about now that you're AGM."

Petra's whole brain stalled. "I'm... what?"

With another toothy smile, Beth reached in her
desk and produced a new name tag and a stack
of business cards. They read, "Petra A Bachman,
Assistant General Manager."

"I thought Hammond Corporate wanted to
transfer someone in," Petra said.

"They did," Beth said. "I told them I wanted
you."

Petra clutched the business cards with shaking
hands. "I... Thank you. Thank you so much. I..."
Her head turned automatically to the monitor as
a guest approached the desk. Petra leapt to her
feet and headed for the door, still babbling. "I
don't know what to say..."

"Say that you'll get your team in order," Beth
said.

Petra nodded and ducked out the door.

Three reservations and a check out later, she
was back in Beth's office talking raises and new
benefit options, her head still spinning. She
called Brad, and he promised to take her out to
his favorite steak house to celebrate. The news
spread fast, and a few coworkers came by to
congratulate her. The cooks even whipped up
a batch of her favorite Black Forest cupcakes,
which only Beth had the willpower to resist.

"You're missing out..." Petra teased Beth as she sunk her teeth into another chocolatey bite.

"Just wait till you're my age," Beth said. "You can't eat cupcakes and still have a waist like that forever."

Petra cast a self-conscious glance down at her belly, which seemed well contained by her pencil skirt for the time being. Brad was always bugging her to eat better too. She had a tendency to graze on snacks instead of bothering to cook and sit down to a real meal.

"Did you get that school group straight?" Beth called out.

Sometime after lunch yesterday Beth had dropped the rooming list on her desk and asked her to figure out the room number assignments for a sixth-grade field trip. The lengthy list of specifications turned the room assignments into a nightmare game of Tetris. No boys and girls on the same floor. Chaperone rooms evenly spaced between the kids' rooms. Kids clustered around their particular chaperone. No kids in rooms with balconies– they'd learned that lesson the hard way after some surprisingly determined boys had climbed the balconies to get to the girls' rooms. And no other guests anywhere near the noisy hordes of children. Not to mention making those 86 rooms fit in around all the other reservations. She'd spent hours trying to work it out while dealing with near constant interruptions. Ultimately, she had had to bring it home and finish it there.

"Yes!" she declared with triumph. "Let me grab it."

She walked back to her own desk, retrieved the stack of papers from her laptop case, and began sifting through them.

"Well?" Beth asked her after some time.

Petra went through the stack for the third, frantic time.

"It's not here," Petra said with dawning horror.

"Did you look for it like a man or–?"

"Yeah, I looked like a woman."

It should have been right there. Petra remembered pouring herself a glass of Shiraz to celebrate finally slaying that particular dragon, then taking the paper and putting it in her laptop case. She remembered that clearly. So clearly.

"Someone took it out of my case," Petra said, and even as the words came out of her mouth, she didn't quite believe them.

Beth had moved to the doorway between their offices.

"Are you sure you didn't put it somewhere else?" Beth asked her with some bemusement.

"No!" Petra insisted. "It was here!"

She had walked back to the kitchen table with the glass of wine in her hand and slipped the paper into the case right at the front of the stack just as Brad had walked in and asked her if she was finally finished.

"But... why would anyone take that?" Beth posited.

"Maybe it was..." Petra stopped herself before finishing the thought. And yet, unbidden, she recalled the smell of lavender wafting through the fairy ring this morning.

Beth was still waiting for her answer.

"I don't know," Petra said.

The remainder of her work shift was spent redoing the rooming list for Albert Einstein Middle School. She wasn't entirely sure that Beth believed she had done it in the first place. At least it went a little faster this time, with some of the details of what she had done before returning to her as she worked.

She was beginning to doubt her own recollections. Had she really put the paper back in her laptop case?

Had she really looked in the refrigerator for her keys?

Chapter Three

It was after dark when Petra got home, and the very first thing she did was walk straight over to the kitchen table and look for that rooming list. There was her wine glass from last night, with a tiny ring of dried red wine at the bottom. No rooming list.

"Hello to you too," Brad called out from the den.

She'd been in such a rush to get to the kitchen she'd blown right past him. Petra walked back through the curved archway into the living room. Brad was stretched out with his MacBook on the carved antique sofa. The decor and furnishings were dated, but Petra couldn't find it in her to change a thing. The old sofa was beautiful despite being in desperate need of reupholstering. Lace doilies adorned almost every surface, and a large brick fireplace dominated the room.

Family photos covered the walls: Oma and Opa's wedding; Oma holding her newborn daughter in the hospital, her sister there to hold her hand since Opa had passed; a strangely similar picture of that baby all grown up– Liese smiling for the camera, Oma next to her and Petra swaddled in a pink blanket; Liese pushing Petra on the garden swing; Liese helping Petra blow out the candles on her sixth birthday.

Petra's mom wasn't in any of the pictures after that.

The wallpaper was so old that the pictures had become a fixture. Removing any of them left behind a perfect rectangle of un-faded paper. Usually, one such large, landscape rectangle stood out like an eyesore over the mantelpiece. Today, that eyesore had been replaced with a different one– a Thomas Kinkade print of a cobblestone bridge.

Brad stood from the couch and wrapped his arms around her from behind. He had to crane his neck up to kiss her cheek. At six feet even he was an inch taller than her, but with her black leather knock off Manolo Blahnik heels, she closed the gap and then some. Petra kept her gaze trained on the print, certain that if Brad saw her face it was going to betray her.

"Wow," Petra managed.

"Just 'wow'?" Brad asked with a chuckle. "No, 'Thanks Babe. That looks way better than an empty wall.'"

Petra tried to put on her best poker face and spun in his arms.

"Sorry," she said. "Thank you. It's just um"—*an over-priced piece of shit hot off a printer, covered in a few brush strokes by slave-wage artists in third world countries so that it vaguely resembles real art*— "expensive," she finished. "You don't need to spend that kind of money on me."

"I know. I wanted to congratulate you for getting promoted, and it's perfect for us, right?" he said with a self-assured smile. "Reminds me of the stuff you paint. You know, that twee kind of fantasy and flowers and shit."

Petra swallowed the impulse to yell at Brad for calling her paintings twee. Whether she liked it or not, the man had just spent upwards of a thousand dollars on a present for her. She leaned in for a kiss that Brad met with a small scowl at her high heels. Not wanting to get into it, Petra kicked the shoes off, lowering herself down to just shorter than he was. This time he returned the kiss, grasping her hips and urging her closer.

"It would look really great in your bedroom with all those blue tones..." Petra suggested when the kiss broke.

She knew it was a bad idea even as the words were coming out of her mouth. Brad untangled himself from her arms, clenching his jaw into a hard line.

"Yeah, because God forbid, I change one thing in this house," he snapped.

"It's *my* house–"

"I know!" Brad cut her off. "You have made it abundantly clear it is *your* house."

Petra had a moment of whiplash from the turn in the conversation. She stared back at Brad's sour face in near-total bewilderment. "Do you *want* it to be your house?"

Brad let out a bitter laugh and turned away from her, stomping off towards the couch.

"Jesus, Petra. We've been together almost three years," Brad said. "I sleep here four nights a week or more. What the fuck do you think?"

He sat down on the couch in an angry huff. Petra wrung her hands, trying to think of the right thing to say.

"You could have asked," she offered.

Brad looked up, his expression softening as he met her eyes. "I was going to ask you to move in with me a year ago." He sighed. "But then..."

Petra took the middle seat on the sofa, her thigh resting against his.

"Oma died," she said quietly.

Brad put an arm around her shoulders. "I get why you want to keep the house. It's in rough shape and the commute sucks, but it's a good neighborhood." With a wistful smile he added, "Good schools..."

One year. That meant that while Brad was getting ready to ask Petra to move in, Petra was getting ready to break up with him for what felt like the hundredth time. But then he'd been there to hold her when she lost her only remaining family on this continent. He had helped her plan the funeral, called acquaintances with the bad news...

At some point, breaking up with Brad had fallen off of her "to do" list.

Now she was trying to picture what it would be like for the two of them to start filling up those empty bedrooms.

"It doesn't feel like my house," she said slowly. "It's Oma's house."

Brad chuckled. "It would probably help if you ditched the needle point throw pillows."

Petra smacked Brad with one of those pillows and then lay her head down on his shoulder.

"Oma would flip her shit if I let a man I wasn't married to move in here," she said.

It sounded so silly out loud Petra was sure Brad was going to tease her. Instead, he stared off into the middle distance, his brow furrowed.

"What if we were engaged?" he asked. "Would your Oma still roll over in her grave?"

Petra's throat went dry. "Um... I think that would be okay."

Brad smiled and pulled her in closer, kissing the top of her head.

"Okay then," he said, a conspiratorial tone in his voice. "Good to know."

They sat together in silence for awhile, the weight of the conversation hanging in the air.

"Does this mean the painting stays?" he asked.

Petra's eyes roved over the mass-produced print, which for some reason was a thing that Brad thought she would like. Never mind how many times she'd ranted to him about idiots wasting their money on Kinkaid prints when they could support real artists instead.

Petra swallowed everything she wanted to say and nodded.

It was nice at night this time of year. Petra walked through the garden barefoot, a lace nightie and an old shawl sufficient to chase away the chill. Even withered from neglect, the surviving night-blooming flowers and untrimmed trees were beautiful in the moonlight. A beam fell down to the fairy ring like a spotlight, illuminating the empty crystal bowl.

She should have been upstairs in bed with Brad. Instead, she was out here in the middle of the night, refilling the bowl. She'd stopped on the way home from work for a carton of real cream.

Yup. It's official. I've lost my mind.

Petra sat down on the swing. It was much too late to be calling Del, but she dialed the phone anyway. It only took seconds for Del to accept the call. It was a fair bit longer before she'd woken up enough to make words.

"This better be like, threat-level seven or at least," she muttered with a yawn.

"I got a promotion and I sort of got engaged," Petra said in a rush.

It took even longer for Del to make words this time. Crickets chirped in the garden.

"Are you going to say anything?" Petra asked.

"Naw, I'm just trying to decide which of those things is worse."

"Caldelaria Lupe!"

Del laughed it off like she was kidding.

She definitely was not kidding. "I'm sorry. Congrats. I'm happy if you're happy." Del paused. "Are you happy?"

Petra pushed her feet forward and tucked them back again, coaxing the swing into motion. After a few moments, she had enough momentum to feel the wind on her cheeks; blonde curls blowing wild behind her.

"How was 'The Wonders of Recycling' show?" Petra asked.

If Del could sense that Petra was rooting for a change of subject, she let her have it without protest.

"Gloria botched it," Del said. "Forgot her one line."

"Oh no..." Now Petra felt even worse for not making it. "Is she okay?"

"She's fine. She's decided that acting isn't her chosen career path after all. Now she wants to be an Olympic luger."

"She..." Petra had to take a moment to get her laughter under control. "Like, that sledding-type thing?"

Del couldn't stop laughing either. "She says it's just like sliding, and she's really good at slides. Only Olympians get paid to slide, and they get to be on the YouTube."

A horned owl swooped out of the pear tree with a hoot of annoyance, off in search of quieter gardens.

"Your kid is fucking great," Petra said. "I want six just like her."

"You sure you want 'em with Brad?"

"Yes!" *Maybe...*

"Then why are you out on the swing in Oma's shawl?" Del asked.

Petra dropped both feet to the ground, halting the swing mid-arc. She tugged the shawl back up over her shoulders.

"I'm not," Petra said. "I'm fine."

Del snorted. "Can I go back to bed then? Since you're fine?"

Petra sighed, closing her eyes and resting her head on the chain of the swing. It was cool against her cheek.

"Look, I'm worried about you," Del said. "Even Brad's worried about you. You work all the time. You don't go out. You don't paint anymore."

A twig snapped– loud as a gunshot in the quiet garden. Petra's eyes flew open. The backyard was empty. No sign of opossums or burglars or...

Something besides the bowl in the fairy ring was catching the light.

Del kept ranting in her ear as Petra stood up– something about how you shouldn't keep making a mistake just because you spent a lot of time on it. Petra walked slowly toward the mushroom circle. She knelt down and reached for the little glint of silver half-hidden in the clover.

It was a hairpin. Carved driftwood with a tiny silver dragonfly on the end. Petra turned it over in her hands, and a phrase echoed in her head, coming through in Oma's voice.

"Nimm keine Geschenke von den kleinen Waldwesen an." *Do not accept gifts from the fae.*

But that was silly. There were no fairies leaving presents. It had to have come from somewhere.

Petra put it back down. Then picked it up. Then put it down again.

"I miss her too, you know," Del said. "I know she wasn't really my grandma, but she always treated me like family. I know how you feel."

Petra grabbed the hairpin and stood up.

"You're right. She wasn't your grandma." Petra grasped the hairpin so tight the little dragonfly bit into her palm. "You've still got three of them, and one of them lives a whole block away from you in the same house as your grandpa, your mom, and your stepdad. You have no idea how I feel!"

The call waiting beeped and Petra pulled the phone away to glance at the screen. Hammond Executive Hotel—probably Sylvia with some question about the Night Audit reports. "I gotta go," Petra said. "Work on the other line."

"Hang on. Let's talk—"

Petra hung up on Del and put Sylvia through, already walking back into the house for her laptop.

Petra spent the following week fueled by a new sense of determination. She was going to be the perfect Assistant General Manager and the perfect soon-to-be-wife too.

The new job was going well. Petra helped Hope apply for a low-income childcare program so she could have a more consistent sitter for the baby on work days. Low and behold, Hope stopped calling out all the time. Beth was so impressed she put Petra in charge of banquet staffing and hiring a new Front Desk Manager.

Things with Brad were not as smooth.

"Did you seriously HIDE my shoe?" Petra screamed from the top of the stairs.

Brad popped his head into the foyer and looked up at her in confusion.

"Why the hell would I do that?"

Brad had gotten up before her and jumped in the shower early. He had his part-time job today and was smartly dressed in freshly pressed black slacks and a button-down shirt. His necktie was draped around his shoulder, ready to be tied.

Petra was going to hang him with it.

"Why would you do that? I'll tell you why. Because you're an insecure little Arschgeige who can't handle his girlfriend being taller than him!"

"You are not taller than me!" Brad shot back.

Petra stomped down the stairs, clutching the remaining pump in her hand.

"Why don't you just go marry someone shorter?!" she shouted, resisting the urge to throw the shoe at him. "That scrawny little co-worker of yours, what's her name? Justine. What is she, five foot nothing? Go ask her out! At least she won't have to worry about you STEALING HER SHOE!"

"I did not STEAL YOUR SHOE!" Brad shouted back.

Petra crossed her arms and glared at him.

"I took them off last night and left them in the corner of my room. This morning, one shoe's right where I left it and the other one's gone. I know you took it!"

"Maybe your damn fairies took it! Did you think of that?" he yelled.

Petra paused; the wind knocked out of her sails. She uncrossed her arms. Brad started laughing. It wasn't a friendly laugh or an attempt to relieve the tension. This was a laugh that firmly came at her expense.

"My God," he said. "You're actually considering it. You're certifiable, you know that? Maybe I should go out with Justine. At least she's going places."

"What the hell is that supposed to mean?" She was trying to sound angry, but hurt was creeping into her voice.

"I mean, she has real career aspirations, like me," he said.

"You only work three days a week," Petra countered. "I work my ass off and earn twice as much as you do."

Brad scoffed at her. He leaned against the banister. "Yeah, sure I work part time for now, but only because the job market sucks. While you were off playing starving artist, I was going to law school. You don't even have a Bachelor's. I'm smart, I graduated top of my class, I'm bilingual—"

"So am I," Petra said.

He scoffed at her again. "Yeah, you speak German. In *Southern California*. You really think that's a marketable job skill?"

Petra felt the tears spring into her eyes and cursed herself for them. She did not want to cry in front of Brad. She especially didn't want to cry because of Brad.

"I literally just got promoted," she said as even as she could manage. "I have career goals."

He smiled at her as if she had said something cute. "Yeah, sure you do. And I'm proud of you, babe. Really. Your backup plan turned into a pretty solid this-side-of-entry-level job. But your little hotel thing... that doesn't even compare."

The tears spilled over. "Get out," Petra said between clenched teeth.

Brad reached for her. "Babe, come on. Don't be like that."

"Get out!" she shouted. "I want you gone! And take this twee piece of shit with you!"

Petra pulled the Kinkaid print off the wall so fast the nail came with it, dropping to the wood floor with a ping. She threw it full force, aiming for Brad's head. He managed to catch it, much to Petra's annoyance. He stumbled back, swearing.

"I think I will ask Justine out," he said.

"OUT!" Petra screamed, throwing the shoe after him for good measure. It bounced off the wall.

Brad stormed out and slammed the door behind him hard enough to send one of the little framed pictures crashing to the ground. The anger drained out of Petra as soon as the door was closed. She retrieved her shoe and set it on the mantle next to the clock, then righted the fallen picture. It was an old photo of Petra, Oma, and Del at Disneyland, posing like tourists in front of Sleeping Beauty's castle.

Petra sat down on the couch and allowed herself to cry, just for a few minutes. She had to leave for work soon, and she supposed she'd be doing it in those old worn-out heels in the back of her closet.

Wiping the tears from her eyes, she got up and went to the refrigerator. Petra carried the cream out into the garden. The crystal bowl, now empty, was right where she had left it in the middle of the fairy ring. She knelt, being careful not to dirty her stockings, and poured a generous amount of cream into the bowl. Then she stood up, and stared into the distance, arms crossed and lines of mascara streaking down both cheeks.

"Bring my damn shoe back!" she demanded. "What the hell do you want with one shoe anyway?"

And maybe it was because Brad wasn't there to witness her, but she didn't feel foolish this time. She felt angry. She felt like the universe owed her some explanations.

Petra tromped back inside and returned the remaining cream to the fridge. She glanced at the clock to see just how late she was going to be today. There was the back leather knock off Manolo Blahnik high-heeled shoe, to the right of the mantle clock, just where she had left it.

To the left, was the other shoe.

Chapter Four

T hree hours later, the shoe was still there.

Petra was sitting on the couch across from it, staring at it suspiciously and starting in on her fourth glass of wine.

She'd called in sick to work, a mere hour before her shift. Beth was not pleased. Not only had she given insufficient notice, but Beth wasn't at all convinced she was really sick.

"You're never sick," Beth had argued.

"Everybody gets sick," Petra countered.

She had stared at the shoe the whole time she was on the phone, eyeing the way the overhead light cast a small white glare on the surface.

"Not you," Beth said. "You don't even sound sick. What's really going on? Did you have another fight with your boyfriend?"

"He's not my boyfriend anymore," Petra had responded without thinking.

"So, it is about Brad. How long are you going to stay broken up this time?" Beth had said with satisfaction.

Petra's mind had wandered, still staring at the shoe, and she wondered dimly if she should consider apologizing to Brad.

Because Brad had most definitely not stolen her shoe.

"What's really going on?" Beth had asked. "You can tell me."

Petra had snapped her focus back to the conversation.

"You want to know what's really going on?" she asked.

Fairies. Honest to God, Oma's bedtime story fairies. Fairies that steal keys and shoes and drink cream and smell like lavender.

"I'm really sick," Petra said.

After ending the phone call with Beth, she went over all the possible, rational explanations. Brad was the first one she seized on. Brad was being an asshole and gas-lighting her. Brad had stolen the shoe. Then, after their fight on the stairs, Brad had snuck back in while she was in the garden and placed the shoe on the mantle. This made so much sense that for a moment relief flooded through Petra in a way that was palpable. Her world, which had just turned completely upside down, momentarily righted itself. "Brad is an asshole" was a much easier pill to swallow than "fairies stole my shoe, then returned it because I left them a bowl of cream and asked for it back".

She'd actually laughed then, at how simple, clean and obvious it was, and breathed a big sigh of relief. She'd even picked up her phone to call Beth back and tell her that her crazy, paranoid ass would make it to work after all.

But then that terrible, nagging little voice in her head spoke up.

But wasn't Brad already gone?

She'd heard him pull away, his red Ford Mustang screaming out of the driveway. She hadn't stopped to watch, but she'd still been able to hear it. The window was open in the living room, letting in the sounds of chirping birds and passing traffic. She'd heard the car drive away as she'd picked up the fallen shoe and returned the picture to the wall. The sounds of the engine had faded as the car became more distant, and by the time she'd sat down on the couch to cry she couldn't hear it at all.

That doesn't matter, calm, rational Petra reasoned. *He must have come back.* She was out in the garden for at least a few minutes. Maybe five at the most. It wouldn't have left much time to spare, but it was absolutely possible that during that window, Brad could have turned around, pulled back into the driveway, come inside, placed the shoe on the mantle, and left again, backing out of the driveway and down the street before she returned to the living room.

But... wouldn't you have heard him from the garden?

The property wasn't that large, and you could clearly hear it from the backyard when a car pulled into the driveway. When she was little, Petra used play on the swing set while listening for her mom to get home from work. At the sound of the car engine, she'd run into the house and out the door into the driveway, meeting her mom there before she'd even have time to get out of the car.

Well, maybe the minivan was louder? Logical Petra speculated desperately. *Sure. Mama's minivan was louder than Brad's Mustang. That's incredibly likely.*

Her mind searched desperately for an alternative, logical explanation, and, finding none, the room began to tip sideways.

It was then that Petra resolved to get drunk.

Very, very drunk.

After finishing off the last bottle of wine, Petra wandered back into the kitchen in search of further refreshments. She found an old plastic bottle of gin in the back of the pantry that would do nicely.

Stumbling a bit already, Petra fixed herself half a cup of coffee sweetened with lots of cream and sugar. She then filled the remainder of the coffee cup with gin and carried it with her back into the living room.

The shoes were still there on the mantle, on either side of the brass clock. Petra plopped down on the couch and continued to stare at them.

She wasn't sure why she was staring exactly. She only knew that the shoes were suspicious, damn suspicious, and if anything else was going to happen, then goddammit she would see it this time. Although her vigil would have been a lot more effective if she didn't keep getting up for more booze.

As she fixed herself her fifth gin and coffee, she realized that she was going to need more cream. She'd emptied the carton into her last drink and, of course, most of the cream had gone into the bowl in the garden this morning. For reasons that no doubt stemmed from her increasing intoxication, Petra found this to be deeply funny. She laughed so hard she had to clutch the edge of the kitchen counter to keep from falling over, and then she fell anyway, laughing as she went crashing to the ground.

She lay on her back, bottle of gin still clutched in one hand. From her vantage point on the ground, it was easy to admire the beautiful ceiling tiles. She wondered why nobody put ceiling tiles in houses anymore.

The house had been built in 1880, an old classic Victorian some doctor had constructed as a summer home, then abandoned when his wife left him for another man. It had sat abandoned for years until her grandfather had bought it. Oma and Opa were childhood sweethearts. They'd grown up during World War II, and when the war ended, they found themselves living on the wrong side of The Berlin Wall. It took years for Opa to scrape together the money and the right connections, but he eventually found someone willing to smuggle him and Oma over to West Berlin in the back of a delivery truck.

From there they'd made the long journey to California (this time by plane, and not by hiding in a crate).

Opa was a carpenter, which was fortunate because the house was quite literally falling apart when he bought it. The oak tree in the front yard was growing through the wall on the second floor, and the house was full of rats, roaches, and one particularly persistent possum.

Slowly, the two of them had restored it to its original glory, recreating some features from old photographs of the property. Opa had hand-carved a good third of those ceiling tiles up there, replacing the ones that had rotted out and matching them precisely.

Petra stared up at the tiles, trying to pick out which ones Opa had carved and which ones were original. There were fairies carved into them.

Of course, they had fairies carved into them. There were fairies on the light fixtures too, and a fairy door on the north side of the exterior. And, apparently, fairies living in her fucking garden.

Petra climbed to her feet, slipping once and dissolving into another fit of giggles. She shambled her way out of the kitchen and into the living room. For a few minutes she stood staring at the shoes again, swaying slightly.

She took another swig of her drink — now much more gin than coffee — and lamented that it was so very acidic.

"It needs cream," she said aloud.

And then a funny little idea seized her. She could go steal the cream out of the garden. She chuckled at the notion of stealing it back from the fairies. Still laughing, she wandered into the foyer and out the back door.

The air had that orange tinge to it that it gets right before sunset. When had it gotten so late? Everything in the garden seemed to glow, including the fairy ring, the red and white mushrooms resembling a ring of hot coals. Petra stumbled into it, accidentally kicking over a mushroom as she did. She tried to bend down to pick up the bowl, but the movement made her feel sick. Instead, she plopped down on her butt in a way that the small, still sober part of her brain registered as something that would hurt tomorrow.

Petra scooted close to the crystal bowl in the middle of the ring, eager to slosh the cream into her mug and keep drinking.

The cream was gone. Petra held the bowl upside down and watched one white drop pool and then splash out onto the green clover.

"You drank it already," she said. "You can't share? Greedy shoe stealing bastards."

Petra lay back on the grass. It was soft, much softer than grass was supposed to be. *How can grass be this soft?* she wondered. Her eyelids felt heavy.

"Greedy shoe stealing bastards..." she mumbled again and shut her eyes.

At some point during the night, still drunk and only half conscious, Petra awoke. Her skin felt like ice in the cool, night breeze. Someone was laying Oma's shawl over her like a blanket. It was warm and it still smelled like Oma's perfume. And Petra smelled something else too. Something like lavender and fresh turned soil.

"Shhhh...." a man's voice said. "Go back to sleep."

Drowsy and confident she must be dreaming, Petra closed her eyes.

It was sunrise when Petra woke up again. The first morning rays of light were just starting to filter through the trees. One perfect beam was reflecting off the empty crystal bowl, casting little rainbows on the back of her hand.

Petra squinted against the light. She had a cheap-gin headache that felt like elephants playing the symbols. She sat up and the shawl slipped from her shoulders, pooling in her lap. The flickering, dream-like memory from late last night came back to her. She waited for her brain to register shock or disbelief. For everything to spin the way it had when she found the shoe on the mantle. But everything was already spinning from the hangover, and she'd gotten all the shock and disbelief out of her system yesterday.

Petra made the conscious decision to just roll with it.

With that, she scooped up the shawl and the crystal bowl and padded barefoot through the garden and into the house.

First order of business was to make coffee. She helped herself to Brad's pretentious single origin

Fair Trade organic whole beans and poured them into the silver grinder, wincing at the sound it made. While the coffee brewed, she washed the crystal bowl and set it on the drying rack.

Her stomach churned unpleasantly. Petra took a moment to consider never drinking ever again.

She was still wearing the button-down blouse and pencil skirt she had intended to wear to work yesterday, now wrinkled and covered in grass and dirt. Petra walked into the laundry room and stripped off the dirty clothes, tossing them straight into the washer. She wasn't sure how exactly she had managed to get a grass stain on her shoulder, but she was certain it was never going to come out. Sighing, she fished an old pair of cotton shorts and a tank top out of the dryer and slipped them on.

Petra fixed her coffee with sugar and reminded herself that she needed to pick up cream later.

The next order of business was breakfast. Something with lots of grease. Dirty fried eggs with bacon and toast was her usual hangover breakfast. It was also, more or less, the only thing she knew how to make.

Petra opened up the refrigerator.

No eggs. No bacon. Her refrigerator was stocked exclusively with condiments, a half bag of baby carrots, and some questionable leftover Thai takeout.

Going out to breakfast was probably out of the question. That would involve niceties she didn't quite have the energy for, like showering.

Petra sighed, grabbed some chopsticks out of the drawer, and proceeded to dig into the pad Thai.

She was just about to sit down at the kitchen table when she realized with horror that she hadn't checked her phone in almost 24 hours. By now she'd probably missed at least eight work calls.

Petra made her way across the kitchen to the archway that led into the living room and stopped dead in her tracks.

There was a man in her living room.

At least, he looked like a man.

His hair was copper colored, but not just that reddish-gold shade that copper has when it shines. There were also streaks of colors in oxidized copper– shades of teal, greens, and darker browns. He towered over her, standing at least six foot six, and had a lithe, but muscular frame, like a dancer, with a narrow waist and long, graceful limbs. His sharp cheekbones emphasized his lips, which were currently curved into a mischievous smile. He wore tight-fitting pants, no shoes, no shirt, his chest intersected by the strap of a satchel at his side.

When Petra walked in, he was shoving her mantle clock into it.

Petra dropped the take-out box. The chopsticks clattered down with it, and one rolled to a stop right in front of the man's foot. He bent to pick it up and twirled it with effortless grace between his long, thin fingers.

"Well, this is embarrassing," he said. He had the voice of a tenor, with an almost musical sound to it that mesmerized Petra.

"You weren't supposed to come out of the kitchen yet," he chided her, as if she were the one who had done something wrong.

Petra stayed rooted to the spot, unsure if she was capable of moving or speaking. It occurred to her dimly that she should probably scream, or call 9-1-1, or kick him in the balls or something.

Instead, her dumbstruck brain managed to blurt out, "You're stealing my clock."

"Oh," he said, and glanced at it almost in surprise, still twirling the chopstick in the other hand. "What's a clock?"

The clock he was so casually holding at his side between his thumb and two fingers weighed at least 30 pounds, with its hefty marble base and sides. It wasn't incredibly heavy, but Petra still had to use both hands whenever she lifted it off the mantle to dust.

"It tells you what time it is," she said.

"Why?"

"So... you know when to... wake up and eat and go to bed."

He laughed. A big, riotous sound that filled the room. "Well, why do you need a thing to tell you to do that? Don't you just eat when you're hungry and sleep when you're tired?"

Petra's eyes darted around the room, looking for a weapon. She spotted the fireplace poker, but instead of lunging for it, she found herself asking, "Who are you?"

He smiled and stood a little taller. "You have the pleasure of meeting Raiker the Rogue, swindler, plunderer, and housebreaker extraordinaire, at your service." He bowed dramatically, with much twirling of his hands. Then he righted himself and slipped the clock into his bag. "Now, I should probably be going before you get brave enough to try to hit me with that stick."

He was standing a good seven feet away from her, but then in an instant he was *not*. He had disappeared and reappeared an inch away, looking straight into her eyes. She could see every fleck of copper in those teal-colored eyes. For the first time since she'd walked into the living room, Petra felt afraid, her brain slipping into a spiral of panic like it had when she saw the shoe on the mantle, faced with something impossible and struggling to comprehend it.

He handed her the fallen chopstick, which she took from him wordlessly. Then he leaned down, kissed her cheek, and whispered in her ear.

"Goodbye, Petra Adelina Bachman."

And he vanished on the spot, taking the mantle clock with him.

10 minutes later Petra was still standing there, holding the chopstick and reminding herself to continue important functions like breathing. She could still feel the exact place where he had kissed her cheek, like it was warmer than the rest of her

face. Of all the wild thoughts swirling around in her brain, there was one she kept coming back to, which seemed silly in the grand scheme of things.

That was NOT how Oma had described fairies in her bedtime stories.

Little humanoid creatures the size of her thumb with gossamer wings, sipping cream from the bowl in the garden like hummingbirds, that's how Hans Christian Andersen described them in *Thumbelina*. Not like the six and a half foot tall shirtless Adonis that had just graced her living room and nonchalantly stolen her clock.

Although there was one detail from Oma's stories which tracked with Raiker's appearance: Glamour. Fairies in Oma's stories could glamour—change their looks to whatever they wanted them to be. The man she'd just seen was so beautiful he looked like he'd been photoshopped. Something told her that probably that wasn't entirely natural. And that suspicion naturally begged the question...

Did he make himself look like that for me?

Her mind went to the many fairy tales where mortals were lured away by fae with beguiling smiles and ill intentions. She'd never caught him stealing before. Did she really catch him in the act this time, or was he the one trying to catch her?

Petra put down the chopstick and armed herself with the fireplace poker.

Chapter Five

T he next time Petra saw Raiker the Rogue
   was three days later. She was starting down
the stairs and found him returning the clock to
the mantle. He stared at the space above it, the
perfect rectangle of un-faded wallpaper.

"You brought it back," Petra said, trying her best
to sound casual.

He flashed her a smile that sent a flutter through
her stomach. Petra noted with wonder that his
hair was more copper than teal today.

"What can I say? I have a weakness for beautiful
women who leave me offerings. Just don't tell
anybody. They'll start calling me 'Raiker the
Borrower'. It'd be terribly embarrassing." He
grimaced at the thought and glanced up at her
again. His brow creased in worry. "Why are you
holding a stick?"

Since Raiker's first appearance, Petra had barely put the fireplace poker down. She slept with it under her pillow. She took it in the shower with her. Now she brought it out from behind her back and held it against her side.

"I don't trust you," she said.

Raiker smiled in approval. "Good. You're smarter than I thought you were. That's iron?"

Petra nodded.

"Well... you've got me all figured out, haven't you?"

She could tell by the expression in those copper eyes that he was mocking her. She gripped the poker a little tighter. Raiker continued staring at the wall.

"There's a picture missing," he observed. "Did someone take it?"

"Why? Is there somebody besides you stealing things from my house?" Petra asked.

To her surprise, Raiker's eyes went wide, and he asked her earnestly, "Is there?"

Dear God, I hope not.

Petra was having a hard enough time dealing with Raiker's existence. She didn't think she could handle any additional supernaturally powered thieves.

"It's not stolen. It's behind the TV," she said, pointing.

Raiker turned from her and stepped gracefully from the fireplace over to the TV. Petra hesitated and then chanced a couple steps down the stairs, being careful to skip over the notoriously squeaky third step from the top. He reached behind the TV and produced the missing painting. He smiled when he saw it.

It was a picture of the fairy ring out in the garden, done in oil paints on canvas. It was nighttime, and there were fairies dancing in the ring, their little bodies illuminated by the moonlight. It proudly bore Petra's signature in the bottom corner along with a title: Feenring.

"You painted this," he said. "This is beautiful. Why is it behind the TV?"

Because Oma fished it back out of the trash, Petra thought, looking down at her feet.

Oma had insisted that if Petra didn't want it, she was going to hang it in the place of honor over the mantel "just until you want it back." When Petra had inherited the house, the painting only stayed up a week before she couldn't stand looking at it anymore and stuffed it behind the TV. Occasionally, the thought crossed her mind to throw it out again, but she couldn't quite summon the resolve.

When Petra looked up from her determined gaze at her feet, Raiker was gone. The painting was hanging on the wall. Shaking her head, Petra took it down again and stuffed it back behind the TV.

The following morning, Petra went to the kitchen for a cup of coffee, and by the time she returned to the living room the painting was back on the wall. She looked around warily, gripping the poker a little tighter.

"Raiker?" she called out. Her voice came out weaker than she would have liked.

Silence. Just the sound of the clock ticking, and the low hum of the refrigerator in the next room.

The doorbell rang and Petra almost jumped out of her skin. Muttering a few choice German swear words, she walked to the foyer and looked through the peephole.

Brad.

He rang the doorbell a couple more times while Petra stood there and considered not letting him in. On the fourth ring, she opened the door. Brad greeted her and then strode in like he owned the place. He stopped in his tracks when he saw the painting.

"Damn," he said. "Now I *know* you hated the Kinkaid if you'd rather hang that thing up instead. Or is that up to appease your fairy friends?"

"No," Petra said, hoping it would end the discussion. "What do you want?"

Brad sat down on the couch.

"I want an apology, or, barring that, I want my Xbox and the rest of my stuff."

Petra took a moment to consider.

"Your Xbox is by the TV," she said flatly.

"Come on!" Brad said, standing up. "You accused me of stealing and threw a shoe at my head! You don't think you should apologize for that?"

It's possible that that may not have been her finest moment.

"You said my career wasn't important," she countered.

"Fine," Brad said. "I'm sorry I belittled your career choices."

He put his hands on her waist and smiled expectantly.

"I'm sorry I threw a shoe at your head and accused you of stealing," Petra said with some reluctance.

They made love on the couch, but not until after Petra had put the painting back behind the TV.

For a few days, it felt like things were back to normal. The trouble was, her and Brad's version of normal wasn't something Petra was sure that she wanted anymore. But they had a comfortable routine going, and sometimes it just seemed like staying together was the path of least resistance.

Petra continued to put a bowl of cream out in the garden each morning. It felt less like an offering now, and more like a mob protection racket. Give up the cream or face the consequences. Now and again, she'd catch a whiff of that lavender smell, or a glimpse of copper flecked eyes staring back at her through the bushes.

"You might as well come out," she called to him one day. "I'll introduce you to Brad. Maybe he'll stop thinking I'm crazy."

But Raiker did not appear.

Instead, the remote for the TV went missing. So did her hairdryer, one of her favorite pearl earrings, the spatula, three different refrigerator magnets, and the garage door opener. When her laptop went missing from the bed, she stood in the garden and yelled until it reappeared on top of the refrigerator.

One bright morning she went out to refill the bowl and noticed the flowers. Deep purple tulips had sprung up around the fairy ring, the first she had seen in over a year. The grass was greener, too. The next day, Petra was filled with childlike wonder when she noticed that watermelons were starting to grow on a bright green vine running along the far edge of the garden. There were three of them, each no bigger than her thumb, like perfect little miniatures. She grinned ear-to-ear and glanced from the tiny melons to the bowl of cream in the fairy ring.

Maybe she had finally figured out the secret to Oma's beautiful garden.

Petra rushed back inside, where she found Brad in the living room, eyes fixed on his phone.

"I'm growing watermelons!" she told him excitedly.

"Uh-huh," he mumbled without looking up.

"Come and see!" she demanded.

"Babe, I know what watermelons look like." He rolled his eyes and went back to scrolling. "Besides, we're ripping all that shit out anyway."

Petra rapidly came down from her baby watermelon happy bubble. "I'm sorry, what?"

"Neither of us have time to keep up with all those plants. I talked to a landscaper last week about laying down sod. Think I'm going with Bermuda grass... good drought tolerance. Said he could haul away the swings too."

Brad didn't look up from his phone the whole time he was talking.

"And... were you planning to tell me you hired a guy to tear up Oma's garden?" Petra asked.

Brad scoffed and finally put his phone down. "Christ, is this about the fucking Feenring? Or are you just too stubborn to let go of a bunch of dead roses?"

Petra was beginning to remember why she had kicked him out.

"Wow. Okay," she said.

She took a deep, calming breath, focusing on happy thoughts like baby watermelons. When she exhaled, she was still mad enough to throw him out, but no longer mad enough to toss his Xbox into the driveway after him.

"Here's what's going to happen now," she said. "I'm going to go look at my watermelons. And when I come back inside, you're not going to be here. Take your stuff, get out, and don't come back."

"Oh, come on," he started to protest, but before he could say anything else, Petra walked out the back door.

When she got outside, she went to the fairy ring and stood in the middle.

"Hey, Raiker?" she said aloud. "You think you could work on the roses next?"

Brad was gone when she got back in the house, just as she had ordered. After a few hours on her own, Petra found that she did not miss him.

But the man had never been particularly good at taking "no" for an answer. The texts and phone calls started that evening and persisted for days. Petra ignored every one of them, stopping just short of blocking his number. Then he sent flowers to her at work. Hope took the delivery and carried them back to her office, beaming. Two-dozen red roses in a tall glass vase. The card read, "I miss you. I love you. I want to see you."

It immediately struck Petra that the words "I'm sorry" were conspicuously absent.

Beth emerged from her office.

"You broke up with Brad again?"

"Yup," Petra confirmed.

"Are you taking him back again?"

"NO," Petra said with every ounce of conviction she could muster. And with that, she removed the little card, tore it in half, and threw it in the trash. She gave the roses to one of their regular guests, passing them off as a birthday gift from the hotel.

When she got home that night, the couch throw pillows had gone missing, but out in the garden the most beautiful spray of light pink roses, far more beautiful than any florist's arrangement, had sprung up next to the fairy ring. Petra leaned in close, taking a deep breath.

The scent of roses followed her back into the house as she smiled and hummed to herself. Her smile vanished when she walked back into the living room. The "Feenring" painting was back on the wall.

Curses replacing the song that had been on her lips, Petra reached up to remove it.

"You're wearing my gift," Raiker said from somewhere behind her.

Petra's whole body jolted and she spun around, heart pounding. Raiker perched on the back of the sofa like a bird, watching her curiously.

"I didn't mean to scare you," he said.

His smirk said that was an absolute lie.

Petra fought to get her heart rate back under control. One hand went to her chest, and the other self-consciously reached for the dragonfly hairpin holding up her bun.

"Du verrückter Hurensohn..." Petra swore under her breath.

Raiker laughed. "Do you like it then? The hairpin?"

Do not accept gifts from the fae.

"I... didn't know it was from you," Petra said uncertainly. She forced a laugh. "Does this mean you're gonna steal me away to Fairyland and enslave me?"

Raiker gave her what was surely *meant* to be a reassuring look. "I wouldn't do that to you." He giggled. "And it's Arcadia, not Fairyland. Your realm is called Alius."

"Good to know."

Christ on an everlasting bike when did this become my life?

Petra turned back to the wall and reached for the painting again.

"You never told me why you want the painting behind the TV," Raiker said.

"If I tell you why, will you stop putting it up?"

"Yes," he answered quickly.

Petra regretted the offer almost as soon as it left her mouth, but she sighed and honored her end anyway, turning to face him.

"I did this one a little after high school," she said. "Most of my friends went on to college. Not me. I was going to be an artist. I got a shitty job cleaning hotel rooms and an even shittier apartment."

"Shitty?" He repeated the word slowly, as if he wasn't sure what it meant.

"Yeah... you know. Cockroaches. Rust in the oven. Maintenance guys that always seemed to 'accidentally' come in while I was in the shower."

"And what's college?"

Petra shook her head and laughed. "Never mind. It's not..."

She paused, transfixed as Raiker reached into his satchel. Out came one of her missing throw pillows. The pillow was slightly larger than the bag.

"... important to the story," she finished. "Anyway, there was this artist I really admired– Mirko Maggiore."

Raiker pulled three more pillows out of the satchel, listening with rapt attention.

"I met him after a seminar and he asked to see my portfolio," Petra said. "Told me he wanted to show my painting at his gallery in Newport Beach. *This* painting. Only um..." nausea churned in her stomach, "when I brought it to the gallery, he came on to me."

Raiker cocked his head.

"Sex," Petra clarified, her cheeks coloring. "He wanted sex."

Raiker let out a bark of laughter. "Of course, he did. Have you seen you? Everyone you meet wants to have sex with you."

Petra's breath caught in her throat, condensing into a lump she couldn't swallow.

"Don't pretend you don't know that," Raiker teased. "The way you dress? Those skirts that hug every curve on your body put those long legs on display? No one wears clothes like that and doesn't want attention."

Petra's hands went to the hem of her pencil skirt. She tugged on it, bringing it down a half inch closer to her knees. Tears welled up in her eyes.

"You're an asshole," she said, and she walked out of the living room. Petra took off her heels by the backdoor and went out to the garden. She kicked the crystal bowl over, spilling cream all over the fairy ring, and sat down on the swing. Tears fell down her cheeks and she furiously wiped them away.

She heard the back door open and shut again.

"Go away!" she shouted without looking up from her lap.

Soft footsteps approached, bringing the scent of lavender with them. The swing set groaned as he took a seat on the other swing.

"I've upset you," he said.

"Yeah, no shit." Petra sniffed and dragged her thumbs under her eyes. They came away black with mascara. "Just go." Her voice was tired. "Take whatever you came here for and get the fuck out of my house."

Raiker didn't move from the swing.

"I don't understand," he said. "We were talking, and now you're crying, and I don't understand why."

He sounded so earnest that Petra looked up, her blue eyes meeting his copper ones. Worry lines creased his forehead.

"What's there to understand?" Petra asked. "I thought that this really talented artist thought I was talented too. But he just saw me as a piece of meat."

The worry lines deepened, and Raiker raised one quizzical eyebrow.

"But... he *did* think you're talented," Raiker said. "He wouldn't have wanted your painting in his gallery if he didn't."

Petra let out a bitter laugh. "He didn't want me in his gallery unless it was on my knees."

She needed a drink. A bottle of wine, two sleeping pills, and a blissful night of blacked out rest. And in the morning, she was going to line the friggin' perimeter with fireplace pokers.

"Wait..." Raiker said slowly. "Wait, wait, wait." He hopped down from the swing and paced a few times, then whirled to face her. "You're saying it was *conditional*?"

"Huh?"

"He wouldn't show your painting *unless* you went to bed with him?"

"Yeah," Petra said. "Did you not get that before?"

"No! I did not get that before! That's horrible! It's..." Raiker seemed to struggle for a word that was bad enough. He settled on a string of words that weren't in any language she'd heard before. The sound of it matched his accent.

Petra watched him stomp around her backyard and swear awhile longer. She was beginning to rethink her plan about surrounding the house with iron.

Raiker plopped back down into the swing. He raked his fingers through his hair. When he turned to her again, he'd arranged face into a not-so-convincing mask of calm.

"What did you say his name was?" Raiker asked.

"Why? You gonna go cut out his eyeballs or something?"

Raiker shrugged. "It isn't as if it's difficult. You just need the right spoon..."

The hair on the back of Petra's neck stood up. She shifted her body just a little further away from him.

Yeah, okay. Fireplace pokers. I'm gonna need a lot more fireplace pokers.

"Raiker," Petra said, trying to fill her voice as much authority as she could muster, "please do not scoop out anyone's eyeballs on my account."

"But he wronged you," Raiker protested. "You stopped making art because of him."

"No." Petra almost wished that were true. "No, I made *more* art because of him. I worked my ass off, because I was going to prove him wrong. Only that meeting with Mirko Maggiore was the closest I ever got to success. And then I got promoted at work, and I got promoted again and... I got busy."

Raiker scrunched up his nose like he'd smelled something bad. "Those don't sound like good reasons to quit."

Petra opened her mouth to tell him she hadn't quit, but Raiker interrupted her.

"How do you make it go?" he asked. He grasped the chains of the swing, shifting his weight experimentally.

"Um..." Petra chuckled. "You pump your legs out and in, like this..."

She moved her own legs to demonstrate, bringing the swing into motion. Raiker copied her movements, picking up the concept quickly. With a delighted, infectious giggle, he pushed the swing higher, and higher still. Petra brought hers higher too, until the groan of the rusted beams nearly drowned out their laughter. A child-like impulse seized her, and on the next arc forward she leapt off. Raiker made an incoherent sound of alarm, which shifted to joyful whoop when she stuck the landing. Her feet hit the ground to one side of the fairy ring, and her knees were quick to remind her that she was not six years old anymore. Grinning ear-to-ear and coursing with adrenaline, Petra turned to watch as Raiker copied her.

Raiker didn't jump. He drifted up and down through the air as if on invisible wings. A slow, graceful arc that ended with him standing in front of her, so close their toes nearly touched.

Petra had to remind herself to keep breathing.

"If you don't like looking at the painting... may I have it?" Raiker asked.

Too surprised by the question to really think about the answer, Petra nodded. Raiker smiled broadly and reached for her hand, placing a small kiss on her knuckles.

"Thank you, my lady," he said.

And then he was gone, and when Petra returned to the living room the painting was gone too.

The next morning, she awoke to the, "WHEEEEE-OOOOOH" sound of a foghorn blaring out of her phone. She expected the screen to say "Hammond Executive Hotel" for what felt like the hundredth time, or "Brad" who had been calling even more often. Instead, the screen said "Del". With a pang, Petra picked up the phone, already launching into an apology.

"Okay, I hate not talking to you. I'm sorry I snapped and I'm sorry I missed Gloria's show and—"

"Yeah, yeah," Del cut in. "Grovel later. Channel four news, now. Go turn it on."

Curiosity prompting her to move faster, Petra hauled herself out of bed and raced down the stairs. The remote was still missing, so she used the buttons on the old TV to click over to channel four.

The banner at the bottom of the screen read, "RACCOONS INVADE NEWPORT GALLERY." Based on the footage, calling it an invasion was not an overstatement. There were easily over a hundred of them packed into Mirko Maggiore's gallery– shitting on the floor, tearing up the furniture, and scaling the paintings, tiny claws leaving shredded strips of canvas in their wake.

There was a raccoon giving birth in Mirko's office chair, and two more making new baby raccoons on top of a $10,000 still life. The cameras cycled through footage of the chaos before circling back to Mirko himself, being interviewed in front of the gallery.

"They growl! Did you know they can growl?!" he said, eyes wide. An angry, red slash of claw marks stood out on one of his cheeks. Another had torn through the shoulder of his designer shirt. "I walked in and they just... attacked! Those things have it in for me! How did they even get in?!"

It took Petra several minutes to pick her jaw back up off the floor. Once she did, a grin began to slowly spread across her face, getting bigger and bigger until it evolved into a full-blown laugh.

"What do you wanna bet that douche pissed off the wrong person this time?" Del said.

"Yeah," Petra agreed, laughing so hard she could barely talk. "Karma's a bitch."

Brad was still refusing to give up. A few more texts, calls, and bouquets later, he turned up at her house unannounced. Petra sighed when she saw him through the peephole. He was bearing a bottle of wine, a box of chocolates, and a contrite expression.

"Go away!" she yelled through the door.

"Come on, babe. Don't be like that."

Petra turned to walk away from him.

"I'm sorry!" he yelled, and she stopped.

There it was.

"That's what you wanted to hear, isn't it?" he continued. "Let's talk. I love you. I'm sorry. Let me in."

I'm over him, she reminded herself. *I'm not taking him back this time.*

But he's sorry... muttered the weak little voice in her head. But he made her miserable. She would be happier without him. She was sure of it.

Almost sure.

Not incredibly sure.

She did love him.

And he was sorry.

Hating herself, Petra opened the door. Brad smiled and hugged her, pulling her body close to his. He moved his lips towards hers. Time froze as Petra considered if she was going to let him kiss her or not. She shouldn't. She should just ask him to leave. Make a clean break. But the words stuck in her throat and his lips were coming closer and—

"Are you coming back to bed?" Raiker's melodic voice called out.

Petra broke away from Brad's embrace and whirled around just as Raiker came strolling down the stairs and into the foyer. His hair was mostly copper today, with just a little shock of red falling down in front of his eyes. As usual, he didn't have a shirt on, leaving his gloriously sculpted chest exposed.

Only this time, he'd also opted to forgo pants.

Chapter Six

P etra's eyes bugged out and some kind of
small explosion happened in her forebrain at
the sight of this naked, supernaturally powered
cat burglar leaning against the banister. Her
cheeks flushed as she took in every inch of him,
and then she immediately attempted to avert her
eyes (and only partially succeeded). Brad, too,
flushed red and then started to turn a color more
closely resembling purple. Raiker simply stood
there and smirked as if him being naked was
the most natural thing in the world (and Petra
supposed maybe to him it was). Finally finding his
voice, Brad rounded on her.

"Who the HELL is this?!" he demanded.

Raiker did one of his flourishing bows.

"You may call me Raiker the Rogue, swindler, plunderer, and housebreaker extraordinaire," he said with a smile. "And you must be Brad."

In one step of his long legs, he moved right in front of Brad's face, standing between him and Petra. Brad took a stumbling step backwards. Raiker stared down at him.

"Petra Adelina Bachman isn't happy when you're here," he said to Brad.

"You had sex with this freak?" Brad demanded, looking at Petra over Raiker's shoulder.

"Yes," Raiker said, before Petra could answer. He moved forward again, invading Brad's personal space. This time Brad was backed into the wall, trapped between it and the crazy naked man towering over him. Raiker put one hand flat on the wall next to him, boxing him in completely.

"I have bedded your former lover many times, in many different ways, all of which she found infinitely more satisfying than any experience she'd ever had making love with you," Raiker continued in a pleasant, casual tone, as if he were discussing what he had for dinner last night.

Brad ducked under Raiker's arm and wrenched open the front door.

"You fucking whore!" he spat at Petra as he stormed out.

Raiker stood naked in the open doorway and continued to yell after him.

"She also likes that I'm taller and have a larger phallus!"

To her horror, Petra noticed old Mrs. Porter from across the street staring open mouthed at the scene. Petra waved at her meekly over Raiker's shoulder, then grabbed him by the arm and dragged him inside, slamming the door shut. Raiker laughed uproariously as he wandered off into the living room. Petra followed him on unsteady legs, trying not to notice how much his butt looked like it had been carved out of marble.

Raiker's satchel was in the middle of the living room floor. He scooped it up, still laughing.

Finally, Petra managed to find her voice.

"What was that?!" she yelled.

"You're welcome," Raiker said, still laughing.

He turned around to face her again, and Petra averted her gaze, staring determinedly at the ceiling.

"Could you put your pants on please?" she hissed.

"Why?" he said. "What's the point of pants? You like looking at me with no pants."

"Raiker, PANTS!"

Raiker sighed. He held his hands at his shoulders, and then in a sweeping gesture brought them across his chest and down to his knees, trailing his long fingers along his body. As he moved his hands, clothes appeared. He was now wearing a pair of black jeans and a dark blue button-down shirt; exactly what Brad had been wearing, right down to the Abercrombie logo stitched on the breast pocket.

"Does this please my lady?" he asked.

Before she could answer, he moved towards the wall and started taking pictures down.

"Why did you lie to Brad?" she asked.

"You're welcome," he said again. "That's what humans say when they do someone a favor, right? You are welcome. Funny phrase. Bit presumptuous, isn't it? You don't seem welcome for the favor at all." He proceeded to slip the purloined photographs into his satchel. "You didn't want to be with him, but you were going to anyways. So, I made him want to leave. It was funny, wasn't it?" He giggled like a child that had just pulled off a successful prank.

"Okay," Petra said. "That's it." She crossed the room and grabbed the poker from its rack next to the fireplace. "I want you gone," she demanded. "No more taking my stuff, or spying on me, or walking around naked."

Raiker turned and took a cautious step toward her. He kept a casual smile plastered to his face, but it didn't quite meet his eyes. Those teal-blue eyes were wary.

"Petra Adelina Bachman you don't scare me with that," he said, eyeing the fireplace poker. "I could take that bitty stick from you faster than your poor little human eyes could blink."

Despite his words, his gaze remained apprehensive. Petra gripped the poker tighter, holding it in front of her like a broadsword.

"Go ahead then," she dared him.

For a moment they both stayed frozen, three feet apart, eyes locked together. Then Raiker shifted his weight to one foot, and Petra didn't wait to find out if he was going to lunge for the poker. She charged forward and swung it in his direction as hard as she could. Raiker leapt back gracefully, so that the tip of the poker just barely grazed his stomach instead of whacking him in the ribs. The poker made a loud hum and left a bright, glowing blue trail.

Something happened to Raiker in that split second. His handsome face shimmered and was replaced by something inhuman. A long hook nose, a pointed chin, and pointed ears stuck up out of a mop of brown hair. The clothes vanished, leaving his oddly proportioned, too skinny body naked. His skin was covered in light green scales. Petra would have described him as ugly if not for the staggeringly beautiful, huge, gossamer wings that had appeared on his back. They looked like a dragonfly's wings, almost sheer and capturing the light in the room like a prism, casting dancing rainbows everywhere.

Petra screamed and dropped the poker.

The alien features contorted into a distinct pout.

"I worked hard on that glamour," Raiker whined. And he vanished.

After the incident with the fireplace poker, Petra didn't think she was going to see Raiker again. She stopped putting the bowl of cream out in the garden. A few weeks later, the tentative tendrils of green that had sprouted began to brown again. After some hesitation, Petra sold a few things clunking around the attic so that she could hire a gardener. He managed to maintain things, but it wasn't nearly as beautiful as it had been when Oma had tended it.

Or when the fairies had tended it.

Petra avoided going into the garden whenever she could, preferring to observe the swelling watermelons from the kitchen window while she sipped her morning coffee.

The phone calls, flowers, and surprise visits from Brad had stopped cold. Her only news of him was when Del called with an update Petra didn't really want.

"You, uh... been on social media much lately?" Del asked.

Petra mentally braced herself. "Why? What's Brad been saying about me?"

"He said right after you got engaged, you cheated on him with some asshole that tried to beat him up."

Petra clutched her coffee cup so tight her knuckles turned white.

"I didn't cheat," Petra said defensively. "And—"

"Oh shit. So, there is a guy?"

Fuck.

Petra rooted around for a plausible explanation. "It was a one-night stand. I picked him up *after* Brad and I broke up, not before."

Del went quiet. Finally, her voice came back through the speaker, concern etched into every syllable. "Since when do you have one-night stands?"

She should have known Del would question that. Maybe she should have told her friend something a little closer to the truth. Unable to turn back now, Petra tried to laugh it off. "Since when are you so judgy?"

"I'm not judging, I'm worried. It isn't like you to have casual sex."

A tiny voice came through in the background on Del's end. "What's casual sex?"

"Cállate, Gloria. Go clean your room!" Del responded.

Petra couldn't help but laugh. "You know she's not going to drop that."

"Yeah, I know, and don't change the subject. Why'd you break your rule for this guy?"

Petra groaned and hopped up on the kitchen island. "I don't know. He's... hot." That didn't seem a strong enough word. "He's got cheek bones you could cut glass with and he's um..." Her gaze wandered to the swing set out the window. "He's playful. And enigmatic. I never know what's coming out of his mouth next." Petra shook her head cleared her throat. "Is that all Brad's saying?"

"Uh... he's also got a new girlfriend already. Some tiny woman who looks like she was born with a silver spoon up her ass."

That had to be Justine. Petra realized that actually bothered her and was annoyed at herself for it.

"You sure you're okay?" Del asked. "Did this mystery man ghost you, or did you really mean for it to just be a hook up?"

"It was a hook up," Petra insisted. "I don't have any interest in seeing him again."

And see him she did not, but Raiker's continued presence in her house was obvious. Work papers went missing so often that she stopped bringing them home, preferring to stay late at the office and get everything done there, rather than risk them in the house. Jewelry routinely vanished, along with anything else shiny like silverware and wine glasses. One day, she came home to find that half the doorknobs inside of the house had been carefully removed and pilfered.

Petra acknowledged these disappearances without complaint. Or rather, she made a point of never complaining out loud. The last thing she wanted was to reopen communication with Raiker. Not that she was at all sure Raiker wanted to talk to her anyway, not after she had forced him to reveal his true face. So, whether she was mad at him, or he was mad at her, they didn't see each other.

At least not until her locket went missing.

The locket was made of gold, with a single ruby set in the front and the name "Petra" in elegant script. Inside, there was an old photo of her, Oma, and her mom standing in the garden on one side, and a photo of the grandfather she'd never known on the other. Petra kept it safely tucked in the jewelry box on top of her dresser, sitting in its own little crushed velvet lined drawer. She didn't wear it very often, afraid that something might happen to it, but that day she'd selected a blood-red pencil skirt to wear to work, and she found herself thinking about how the ruby in the locket would match. So, she'd opened the little drawer... and it was gone.

Stupidly, Petra shut it and opened it again, as if that would somehow make it reappear, like opening the refrigerator over and over expecting there to be something you want to eat.

But of course, the drawer was still empty. The locket was gone.

Tears sprung into Petra's eyes.

Summoning her resolve, she marched down the stairs and towards the door to the backyard. She paused at the door, then turned, grumbling, and headed to the kitchen instead. Cursing herself the whole time, she pulled the crystal bowl down from the shelf and splashed some hazelnut Coffee-mate in it.

Petra carried the bowl outside and set it in the center of the fairy ring.

"Look," she said. "I need you to bring my locket back, okay? Please Raiker?"

There was no answer. No familiar breeze carrying the scent of lavender or the flash of his bright teal eyes.

Still, she hoped the message had been received.

Petra tried her best to drive the locket from her mind for the rest of the day. Work was crazed. They were under goal for the previous month, and their brand scores had dropped. Now heads were clearly going to roll and Petra just hoped hers wasn't on the chopping block.

To add to the mess, they had a particularly unpleasant guest in 204. Sharon Holly seemed to have made it her mission in life to make things as difficult for everyone around her as possible. She had begun her stay by arriving at 10a.m. on a Saturday and demanding that she be allowed to check in immediately. The 3 p.m. check-in time apparently only applied to lesser mortals. After Petra tactfully explained to her, several times over, that they'd been full last night, and checkout time was not until 11 a.m., and therefore she could not check in now, she'd demanded to know how long she would have to wait. A few minutes after Petra finally convinced her to leave the desk, she got a call from Martina in housekeeping. Martina had left a room door propped open while she went to get a vacuum. She had returned to find that Ms. Holly had decided that that should be her room, despite it costing twice as much as the standard room she had booked. Ms. Holly refused to leave, not even to come down to the front desk and actually check in.

Then she called down to complain that her room had not been vacuumed.

Things really didn't get any better from there.

Which is why Petra found herself in Beth's office, face down on her desk, begging, "Can I just kick this bitch out?"

Beth laughed at her. "That's not a very Assistant General Manager thing to say."

Petra sat up and plastered a smile on her face.

"Okay," she said. "I'm fine. I've got this. I am not going to murder Sharon Holly. I'm going to go apologize and send someone to vacuum her room."

"That's my girl," Beth said, already turning back to her computer. "We can't afford another bad Trip Advisor review."

Petra dragged her feet out of Beth's office and towards the front desk. Before she could make it to the door, Hope stepped through. She was grinning ear-to-ear and holding a gorgeous bouquet of wildflowers tied with a piece of twine. Hope held them out to her.

Petra cringed. "Don't tell me those are from Brad."

Hope shook her head, still grinning.

"There's a man here asking for you. He says you know him."

Sylvia popped through the door and asked in an undertone, "Can I know him?"

With dawning realization and a growing pit of dread twisting in her stomach, Petra pushed open the door.

Raiker was standing at the front desk, drumming his long fingers on the counter. He looked like he'd stepped out of a Fred Astaire movie. He was dressed in an old-fashioned, perfectly tailored tuxedo, complete with a white waistcoat that accentuated his slim frame, and a shiny black top hat. He even had a black cane with a silver dragonfly on the handle, which he had casually laid across the counter as he waited. His eyes were copper-colored today, nearly human looking, but his hair stuck out in bright lurid teal underneath the hat. When he saw her, he bowed and tipped his hat to her.

Petra froze in terror.

"What...?" she managed.

She had probably meant to say, "What are you doing here?", but instead what came out of her mouth was, "What are you wearing?"

Raiker actually looked affronted.

"I thought you'd like it," he said, pouting. "You're the one who insisted I wear pants."

Behind her, Hope and Sylvia giggled.

Blushing bright red, Petra grabbed Raiker by the hand and dragged him away from the desk.

"I thought I was supposed to wear a suit to where you work. You wear suits. It's formal. This is what people wear to look formal," he protested.

Petra dragged him down the hall towards a vacant room.

"Yeah. That's what people wore about 70 years ago," she said.

Raiker's expression was puzzled as she used her master key to open the door and shove him inside. She slammed the door shut behind her and threw the deadbolt.

"Wait..." Raiker said. "What year is it?"

"2018," Petra snapped. "What are you doing here?"

Raiker continued to look perplexed.

"How old are you Petra Adelina Bachman?" he asked.

"I'm 27," she said. "And call me Petra. You sound weird when you use my full name. People don't talk like that."

Raiker twirled the top hat in his hands and sat down on the bed. As he did, the dapper suit vanished, replaced by his usual faded black pants.

As if he was doing away with all pretense of playing human at the same time, his ears grew into points and his wings appeared in an instant. The dragonfly wings were just as dazzling as they had been on his true form, at least six feet across and catching every light in the room.

Sometimes when she saw him it was easy to forget what he really was, looking perfectly human, aside from his wild colored hair and eyes. Petra was reminded with a jolt that he was anything but.

"Petra," he said slowly, like he was testing it out. "Just 'Petra', really? Are you sure about that?"

"Yes," Petra said, recovering from her shock. "You have to leave. You can't just show up at my work."

"If you want me to leave, why did you drag me into a bedroom?" he asked with a wicked grin.

"Stop flirting!" she demanded. "And stop stealing my stuff. Get out of my life!"

"But I came to tell you something important," Raiker protested.

Petra sighed. "Okay. Then tell me and get out."

Raiker stood and crossed the room to stand next to her. He put one hand on her shoulder and stared into her eyes.

"Petra," he said, and there was no humor or flirtatiousness in his expression then. For once, he seemed deadly serious. "I didn't take your locket."

Of all the things Petra thought he might have said, that certainly wasn't one of them.

She was about to ask at least a dozen follow up questions when a faint sound like a bell interrupted them. Raiker reached into his pocket and removed a small marble that was glowing bright blue. He curled his fist around it and closed his eyes.

"I have to go," he said.

He vanished on the spot, leaving Petra standing alone in the hotel room, wondering if Raiker didn't take the locket, who did?

Or what?

By lunchtime that day, Petra's gentleman caller was the talk of the hotel.

"A vintage tuxedo. Like the ones in Titanic. With a cane! And a top hat! And he had blue hair!" Petra overheard Hope whispering to Beth.

"That's one way to rebound," Beth whispered back with a chuckle.

The many hotel guests who had been milling around the lobby at the time had not failed to note Raiker's arrival either.

"Some kind of costume thing going on?" Mr. Clark asked when he stopped by the desk to extend his stay.

"Was that hot guy your boyfriend?" A couple little girls from Albert Einstein Middle School demanded.

It got so bad Petra decide to take a rare lunch out, ducking out of the hotel for an hour to go to the coffee shop on the corner. She got a turkey sandwich and a cappuccino and sank happily into an armchair, finally away from the prying eyes and whispers. Here, there were just the pleasant sounds of classic rock on the radio, punctuated by the occasional hiss of the milk frothing wand. Petra settled in, and thought perhaps she'd read a few pages of that overdue library book tucked into her purse.

"WHEEEEE-OOOOOH!" The ringing cell phone cut through her brief moment of tranquility. Petra rooted in her purse for it and answered.

"What is it?"

"Did you go out to lunch with your new man?" Sylvia asked.

Petra groaned.

"Tell me you didn't call me just for that."

"Sorry, boss lady. I called because Ms. Holly said that you told her we'd take 30% off her bill because her room wasn't clean when she checked in. I wanted to be sure that was actually true before I did it."

"Sylvia, you can tell Ms. Fucking Holly that I said no such thing, and that she can take her 30% discount and shove it up her ass," Petra snapped.

The idle chatter in the coffee shop stalled as everyone turned to look at the crazy woman yelling obscenities into her phone. Sylvia had also gone quiet.

Finally, with a small giggle, she asked, "You want me to use those words exactly, boss?"

Petra stared longingly for a moment at the half-eaten sandwich and the open Neil Gaiman novel.

"I'll talk to her," Petra said. "I'm on my way back."

The rest of the day passed in a blur of paperwork, phone calls, and forced smiles. By the time Petra headed for home, she'd been at work for the last 14 hours. It was fully dark when she pulled in the driveway. It was the night of the new moon, and swirling cloud cover blocked out the glow of even the brightest star, leaving everything outside the beams of her headlights pitch black. Petra noted with dismay that the porch light was burned out.

Petra decided to leave her car in the driveway. She shut the door behind her, temporarily almost blind after the glare of the lights inside the car, and stumbled her way towards the front door. She walked up the steps and stopped to examine the porch light as her eyes adjusted to the dark. The lamp was a newer addition, with two bulbs that pointed out in either direction. Both of them were dead.

It didn't take Petra long to discover why. As soon as she stepped inside and flipped the light switch in the foyer, she realized the power was out. Petra opened the front door again and gazed over to the neighbor's houses. Mrs. Mason had her lights on, and she could just make out the glow of Mrs. Porter's television across the street.

Just me then.

It wasn't an altogether uncommon occurrence. The house was old and prone to faulty electricity. You couldn't run the coffeemaker and make toast at the same time without blowing a fuse. Oma used to keep candles and kerosene lamps all over the house for just such an occasion.

Praying she still had a lighter by the fireplace, Petra slipped off her high heels and made her way into the living room, using the flashlight on her cell phone to guide her. The house was eerily quiet, and full of those particular creaks and groans old buildings are famous for.

Petra jumped when she heard one such creak from upstairs.

It's just the house settling, she reminded herself, echoing the voices of her mother and grandmother that had reassured her thousands of times as a child.

But didn't that creak sound remarkably like footsteps?

There was a cadence to it, first one small creak, then another, as if someone were taking tentative steps across her bedroom floor.

Petra opened up the little wooden box on the corner of the mantle where the lighter and matches were kept.

Empty.

Of course, it was empty.

"Raiker you bastard..." she mumbled, and then froze as the distinct sound of a door creaking drifted down the stairs.

Someone was in her room.

Petra had the phone in her hand, ready to dial the police and bolt for the door. She was a second away from calling when she realized with a rush of relief what it must be.

Raiker. Raiker was in the house again, maybe returning her locket or more likely helping himself to more of her jewelry. Her sense of relief was so powerful she actually laughed a little.

Petra turned from the empty box and made her way to the stairs. She took them two at a time, calling out to him as she did.

"Raiker, how many times do I have to tell you to—"

Petra froze in the doorway to the bedroom, gazing in terror at the thing that was standing next to her bed.

She was beautiful, almost too beautiful to look at, with the soft, pale features of a young woman. She had jet-black hair that hung down to her waist, and was clothed in an ornate white gown that stopped just above her knees. Her skin emitted a strange glow that illuminated the room ever so slightly, and she had huge wings, with a span almost four times that of her petite body. Her wings reminded Petra of a moth's wings. They were off-white and looked soft to the touch, like antique lace.

The ethereal beauty stopped where the dress ended. Instead of legs, she had long talons like a bird. They were black, hideously scaled, and bent backwards as if she were waiting to spring. The talons ended in deadly sharp claws that left long scrapes in the wooden floor as she moved, claws which were stained with something that looked horribly like blood.

The creature looked up at her and smiled. "You're pretty," she said. "So very pretty. Do you think you're prettier than me?"

Petra's eyes darted from that face to the bird feet. She took a step backwards towards the stairs.

"N-No," she insisted, her voice shaking.

The creature frowned.

"I think you might be," she said. "I think I should rip you up so you aren't pretty anymore."

The thing lunged for her, springing forward on those horrible legs. As it did, it let out an unearthly bird screech, loud as a clap of thunder.

Petra turned and fled for the stairs. Her stocking feet slid out from under her on the slick wood floor as she rounded the corner, sending her careening down the steps. Petra tumbled to the bottom, knocking her head and her flailing limbs on the way down in an explosion of pain. She landed on her back, looking up at the top of the staircase. The creature crouched there, head cocked the way a bird's will as it considers a worm it's about to devour. It slowly started towards her. The claws dug into the stairs with each step making an awful shredding noise.

Petra scrambled backward, willing her aching limbs to move. Her vision swam and her head throbbed, but all of that seemed distant and unimportant compared to running from the monster.

Petra's eyes darted to the fireplace poker in the living room. Could she make it there in time? Would iron even work on whatever this thing was?

She pulled herself to her feet and ran flat out towards it. She could hear the creature gaining on her, shrieking and tearing across the room.

It struck her from behind. One claw shredded a long line down her back, ripping through her blouse and then her skin as Petra screamed. It brought a foot down on her back, pinning her in place, and then flipped her over. Petra was forced to stare into its cruel, beautiful face as it smiled down at her. Petra screamed again, her heart beating so fast she thought it might burst out of her chest. The realization hit her that she was going to die.

A flash of blue light burst through the darkness and the creature flew off of her with a flap of its great white wings. Raiker had appeared next to Petra, wielding a huge sword with a silver hilt and a blade covered in blue flames.

"Get behind me!" Raiker shouted at her, and Petra did not wait to be told twice.

The creature hovered a few feet off the ground, suspended by a slow, rhythmic flapping of its wings. Her long hair swayed in rhythm with the wings. She eyed Raiker's sword with apprehension.

"You are not a part of this, pixie. Run along," she said.

Raiker held his ground. The light from the sword was almost blinding, casting shadows all around the room.

"I'm not going to let you hurt her," he said. "Go! Get out of here, you ugly jealous wretch."

The creature hissed at him. Raiker raised his sword higher.

"I mean it!" he shouted. "Go!"

She landed on the ground, folding in her wings behind her. Her claws clicked on the wood floor. "Are you telling me this mortal is under your protection?"

She said it like a taunt, her words loaded with significance that Petra didn't understand. She said it like the only possible answer he could give was no. For a moment Petra thought he was going to do just that — lower his gleaming sword, stand aside, and allow this terrible and beautiful thing to tear her to unrecognizable shreds. Petra could see him weighing that decision in his eyes.

"Yes," Raiker said, the word heavy on his tongue. "On my honor as Raiker the Rogue, swindler, plunderer, and housebreaker extraordinaire, this human is under my sworn protection."

The creature looked surprised.

"Very well," she said. "I'll be sure to tell the rest of the Unseelie seeking the key."

The creature faded slowly and then vanished. As she did, the lights in the house suddenly flickered back on, like the glowing dawn after a storm.

The rushing adrenaline drained out of Petra in one great whoosh, and just as fast she felt her knees give out

Chapter Seven

P etra was covered in bruises from the tumble
down the stairs. It felt like she might
have broken her wrist. The room wouldn't
stop spinning, making her suspect she had a
concussion as well. The long scratch on her back
bled profusely, staining her torn clothes.

"Let me help you," Raiker said.

He held out his hands, and the tips of his fingers
glowed softly as he ran them over her body. It felt
like stepping into a warm bath. With each pass
of his fingers, warmth spread through her and
the bumps and bruises faded. Raiker murmured
assurances as he worked. Petra couldn't find
the words to respond, like her ability to speak
had stalled out in the aftermath. He started at
her head, stopping the swimming instantly, and
ended at her toes, healing everything in between.

Everything, that is, aside from the gash on her back. It began at the base of her neck and ran all the way down to her lower back in a single perfect line parallel to her spine. Raiker tried for several minutes, touching his fingertips to her bare back as Petra held what was left of her shirt against her chest, but instead of that warmth she felt only a prickling, tingling feeling, and the wound remained open.

"I'm sorry," Raiker said. "I can't fix that. That was from her claws, right?"

Petra nodded.

"But it's not very deep," he assured her. "You'll be alright. Do you have any bandages?"

Petra pointed to the guest bathroom and waited on the floor for him to return. Briefly, she considered asking him to drive her to the hospital. She stopped when she thought of what she would say when they asked her what happened, and how badly Raiker driving her car was sure to go.

Raiker returned with the first aid kit and opened it up. He stared blankly at the contents.

"What do I do?"

"You have to clean it with the alcohol, and then bandage it with the gauze and the tape." Her voice was hoarse. Mechanical.

Petra wondered what he was used to treating wounds with. Or maybe he'd never seen a cut he couldn't heal before? That thought wasn't a comforting one.

Raiker poured the alcohol onto a cotton ball and touched it to the gash. Petra cringed from the sting. Raiker drew his hand back immediately.

"But it hurts you," he said.

"I'll be okay," she insisted, and tried to manage a smile. "I'm tough."

Hesitantly, Raiker began again. Petra tried her best not to wince.

"Is it going to heal?" she asked him. Each word came a little easier than the last one. The room around her was shifting back into focus. "It isn't poison, right? That thing..."

"They're called anguanas," he said. "They're a type of fairy. And, no, they're not venomous. Dangerous, violent, and petty, yes, but not venomous. It will heal the slow way."

Petra let out a small sigh of relief and then cringed again as Raiker continued to clean the wound.

"Fairy isn't a species then? It's more like a genus?" Petra asked, mildly impressed with herself for remembering a term she hadn't used since 10th grade biology.

"It's a what?" Raiker said.

Apparently, fairies didn't have 10th grade biology.

"What type of fairy are you?" she asked.

"Oh. I'm a pixie. Or sometimes we're called dryads, but that's a bit old-fashioned."

"Nature spirits," Petra said. There were a lot of dryads in Oma's bedtime stories.

Raiker chuckled. "So, you do know *some* things."

Not nearly enough.

Petra felt as though she was facing one hell of a learning curve.

"Why did she want to hurt me?" she asked.

"Because you're stunning to look upon," he said in a matter-of-fact way. "Anguanas are beautiful, aside from the bird feet or some other flaw. Naturally beautiful. It's not a glamour." He hesitated and then added, "Not like me."

As he cleaned the wound, he laid the used, blood-soaked cotton balls in a stack next to her. Petra tried not to look at them.

"They don't like that part of them is ugly, and they get a little crazy when they think someone is prettier than them."

Raiker put down the peroxide and started bandaging the cut. Petra didn't really think that he had answered her question precisely.

"But why was she here?" Petra asked. "Why are you always here?

"Come on. Surely, you've figured it out by now?" Raiker said.

When Petra didn't answer, Raiker stopped what he was doing, halfway through dispensing another piece of medical tape.

"Look, it was one thing to play dumb before, but I'm not the only one trying to steal the key now," he said. "Why don't you just give it to me? It's not doing you any good. I can sell it for a pile of gold, and everyone else that's looking for it won't bother you anymore once they know you don't have it."

He finished with the tape and walked out of the room. When he returned, he had a bowl of warm water with a washcloth floating in it, along with a tank top and pants he must have pulled out of the dryer. He began to carefully clean off the blood-streaked skin of her back with the washcloth. It wasn't long before the water in the bowl was tinged pink from the blood.

"It's really the best thing for everybody," he insisted.

"It sounds like it," Petra agreed. "There's just the small problem that I don't know what the hell you're talking about."

"Of course, you do," he insisted. "'Petra Adelina Bachman has the key.' That's written. It can't not be true. Now tell me where the key is, and we can be done with all this mess."

He stood up and held the fresh clothes out to her. "Here. Put these on."

Petra climbed to her feet, taking advantage of Raiker's outstretched hand to help her up. She took the clothes from him and changed into them gratefully, but not before insisting that he close his eyes. She watched his face closely as she took her clothes off, and when she was finally satisfied that he wasn't going to peek, she let her gaze drift past him to the wall full of pictures behind him. She stared at a picture of Oma as an idea dawned in her head.

"Raiker... what did you mean when you said that it was written?" she asked as she gingerly pulled the tank top over her head, wincing as it slid across her back.

"There's an old fae language that hardly anyone speaks. It's the oldest language, the one all other tongues come from. It's the one that everyone's true name is written in, because everything said in that language has to be true. And it's written in the old tongue that Petra Adelina Bachman has the key. So, you have to have it."

"You can open your eyes now," Petra said.

Raiker opened his eyes and locked them onto hers.

"Just *tell me where it is*," he said. "This will all go away. I'll even split the gold with you. 60/40."

Petra found herself desperately wishing she could. Instead, she asked, "Raiker, do you know *when* this was written?"

"Why?"

Petra pointed at the photograph of Oma on the wall.

"Because I was named after my grandmother."

In the past month, Petra's view of the world had expanded exponentially. She'd accepted that the fairies she'd learned about in bedtime stories were real. That some of them were dark things with sharp claws that wanted to hurt her. And that somehow, her grandmother had been mixed up in all of this. Because of what amounted to a data error, now all these things were after her, and this key that they thought she possessed.

Petra had somehow made room in her mind for all of that, and yet Raiker seemed incapable of grasping that two people could have the same name.

"But how can you both be named Petra Adelina Bachman?" he asked for what felt like the hundredth time.

"My mother named me after her mother," Petra said. "It's not that weird."

From the look on Raiker's face you'd have thought Petra had just suggested that recreational dental surgery was not that weird.

"Not that weird?" he repeated, flabbergasted. "Not that weird? Do you have any idea the cosmic ramifications of two beings having the same name?"

"Are you trying to tell me that no one in fairyland–" she paused and corrected herself, "No one in Arcadia has the same name as anybody else? There is only one fairy named 'Raiker the Rogue'?"

Raiker scoffed at her. "Raiker's not my true name. You think I would just tell you my true name? I barely know you. Why would I give you that kind of power over me?"

Petra sat in the armchair next to the couch and watched Raiker pace back and forth across the living room.

"This is bad," he said finally, continuing to pace. "This is very bad."

Pacing gave way to flying as his feet lifted off the floor. He flew slowly from one end of the room to the other, back and forth, his wings humming softly.

"Because I don't know where the key is?" Petra ventured.

"Exactly," Raiker said. "And clearly, I'm no longer the only one who's been hired to find it. The Unseelie—"

"The who?" Petra interjected.

"The... dark fairy court. The Nasty Ones. They think you have it. And they'll all know it now. Believe me. Never trust an anguana to keep her mouth shut. Terrible gossips, the lot of them. They're all coming here to find it now and they won't stop. And... and..."

"And you told them I was under your protection," Petra said.

Raiker stopped in midair and looked at her in despair.

"Yes," he said. "I did."

"What does that mean exactly?"

"I means that in all likelihood I am going to die."

Raiker flopped onto the couch face first.

"I'm too young to die," he moaned. "I'm only 2,876 years old. My mother always warned me, I'm a sucker for a pretty face, and that one day it'd be the death of me, and she was right."

He continued to lay there, her hero from an hour earlier that had fearlessly defended her from the monsters, reduced to a quivering lump on the couch. Petra got up off the chair and stood over him.

"Okay. What if we found the key? This is Oma's house. I inherited all her stuff. It has to be in here somewhere. If I can help you find it, you can tell everyone you took it and sold it and this all goes away, right? My life can go back to normal."

"Sure," he said. "Assuming we can find it before The Unseelie brutally murder us both."

"Oh well, assuming that, of course." Petra said, in her best attempt at being glib.

Raiker sat up and looked at her strangely.

"I like you Petra Adelina Bachman," he said.

He laughed and then sprang to his feet.

"Alright," he said. "First, we need to do something about your fortifications.

Whatever Petra had imagined fortifying the house might look like, it was nothing like what Raiker proceeded to do. He started by demanding that she go shopping, producing a list that looked more like what you might find at a medieval market, and much less like things that could be purchased at Walmart.

Petra squinted at the items and tried to come up with 21st century human alternatives.

"I can't afford to buy all this," she said.

"Oh," Raiker said. "Not a problem. Here."

He reached into his satchel and produced a fat stack of hundred-dollar bills. Petra's eyes went wide when he handed it over.

"Just be sure to spend it in the next half a day or so," he instructed.

"What happens after that?" she asked.

"It disappears," he said, grinning. "Neat, right?"

It was pretty neat. She'd read about "fairy gold", but she didn't know it could also look like hundred-dollar bills.

Petra stopped just before she walked out the door, frowning. "Hey, when you said you'd split the gold with me when you sold the key..."

"You know, I need to go do a thing in the garden. Very important thing," he said, disappearing on the spot and neatly dodging the question.

She started out in the kitchen section of Walmart, loading her cart up with every cast iron pan, pot, and waffle iron she could find. Then she pushed all that a couple aisles over to house wares and bought every single fireplace poker set, ultimately needing two separate carts to haul all of it.

"It's for an art project," she told a curious onlooker, trying to sound as convincing as possible, before stopping to ask an employee if they possibly had any more skillets in the back.

The horseshoes were a bit trickier to acquire. She could buy them online all day long, but suspected the situation might be a tad too urgent to wait for Amazon two-day shipping. After calling several small equestrian centers to ask where they get them, she finally got a tip on a tiny animal supply store in old town San Dimas. She asked the man behind the counter for three, but when he asked if she preferred iron or aluminum, she amended her order to: the entire case of iron horseshoes. The old man behind the counter of the mom-and-pop store was rather gratified by the sale total. With a small pang of guilt, Petra handed him her emergency credit card instead of the fairy gold.

Raiker couldn't touch most of what she had packed into her Jetta, so that left a lot of the heavy lifting to her. He set her to work digging and refilling small holes all over her front and side yards, leaving behind a patchwork of brown spots in the lawn. After assuring her that the neighbors could only see him if he wanted them to, Raiker followed Petra outside, wings and pointed ears on full display. The grass grew back wherever he passed. He hovered over her, sometimes literally, critiquing her work.

"That's too much dirt," he said, again.

Petra had a vision of hitting him with a giant fly swatter. She threw down the shovel.

"I give up," Petra said. "It's late. I've been doing this all day. I'm going to bed."

"You should put the horseshoes over the doors first," Raiker insisted. "It'll keep burbers out."

Petra sighed. "What happens if a burber gets in?"

"Well," Raiker said as flew over another bald spot in the lawn, "If you're very lucky, it will just kiss you and drain all of the blood out of your body through your mouth."

Petra felt her skin go cold.

"And if I'm not lucky?" she asked with some hesitation.

"If you're not lucky, it will make you fall in love with it, and you'll be so consumed with love that when it leaves you, you'll go mad and waste away until you die. And if you're very, very unlucky, it will possess you and force you to brutally murder everyone you know and love, while they scream and spend their last moments wondering why you've chosen to hurt them."

Petra took a moment to process all that and tried to remember to keep breathing.

"Right," she said. "Horseshoes first."

She retrieved a hammer and some nails from Opa's old workbench and stood up on a ladder to hammer the first nail into the wall just above the garage door. She managed to get the nail halfway in without banging any additional holes in the wall, and then hung the first horseshoe up on the nail. The other two entrances were both in the foyer. Petra folded the ladder back up and struggled to carry it into the house, holding the door open with her foot. Raiker stood on the other side of it in the foyer, watching her and smirking.

"You mind giving me a hand?" Petra snapped at him.

"Certainly," he said. "Put the ladder down and come here."

Petra hesitated in the doorway, eyeing his gossamer wings. Heart beating a little faster, she set down the ladder and approached him, holding the hammer, nails, and iron horseshoes.

"Do not touch me with those," he said, suddenly surprisingly stern.

Petra nodded and Raiker grinned at her. He stepped behind her and slipped his arms around her waist, pulling her in closer to his body than seemed entirely necessary. His bare skin was warm against hers, almost feverish.

Petra's breath caught in her throat as her feet left the ground with a flutter of his wings.

Flying. I'm flying.

He flew across the foyer to the front door, hovering just above it. Petra held the point of the nail against the wall, and it was only then that she noticed how badly her hands were shaking; bad enough that she scratched the wood paneling.

"I won't drop you," Raiker teased.

Petra looked down at the floor a yard below her dangling feet. Falling wasn't really much of a concern.

"That's— That's not why," she stammered.

Raiker unwrapped his left arm from her waist, holding her against him with only his right (it did not appear to cause him any additional strain). He took the nail from her and held it steady, leaving her to hammer it in.

She could feel his breath on her neck.

"Do I make you nervous?" he whispered in her ear.

Petra aimed for the nail and hit Raiker's thumb instead. He let out a long, loud string of fae curse words and quickly descended to the ground.

"Verzeihung! Sorry! Oh my God, I'm so sorry!" Petra said.

Grimacing, Raiker brought his other hand to the bruised thumb and healed it with a pass of his glowing fingertips.

"No harm done," he said.

Raiker ended up hammering the nails in himself, while Petra apologized several more times. He then lifted her up again to hang the horseshoes, completing the job.

As soon as she returned to solid ground, Petra felt the pull of exhaustion claim her. Yawning, she turned and started for the stairs, then paused. The staircase was still gouged all over from the anguana's sharp talons. Petra knelt and ran one finger down the scrape, tracing the ridges. She shivered. When she looked up again, Raiker had landed on the steps in front of her.

"I'm not going anywhere," he assured her. "I won't leave you alone until this thing is over."

Petra had never been the type to feel like she needed a man to protect her. She wasn't afraid of the dark, she didn't mind living alone, and she could watch scary movies without holding anyone's hand. Yet her relief that Raiker was going to stay here with her was so great it was almost palatable. That was probably because for the first time in her life, there were literal monsters lurking in the shadows.

"Do you sleep?" she asked.

"All living things sleep," Raiker said. "I'm no exception."

Petra raided the linen closet, pulling down sheets, pillows, and blankets to make up one of the guestrooms.

"You can sleep in here," she called down the hall to where she'd left Raiker. The little bedroom had been hers growing up. It had a single bed in the corner by the window. The walls were still covered in the sky-blue paint she'd picked out as a little girl. The room was just across the hall from the master bedroom, to the left of the staircase. She spent a few minutes making up the bed, yawning again as she tucked the sheets into the old mattress. Petra started counting up how many hours it had been since she'd slept. She'd got up for work at 6 a.m. this morning... no, *yesterday* morning, so it'd been at least... 38 hours.

She'd finished making the bed and Raiker still hadn't appeared.

"Raiker?" she called out.

Petra walked out of the room. She found him in the master bedroom, crawling into her bed.

"I made up the bed in the guest room," she protested.

"No," Raiker said. "I'm sleeping in here. That's too far away from you. I wouldn't be able to get to you fast enough if something happens."

Having seen Raiker teleport across a room in an instant, Petra doubted this very much. She eyed him warily, unhappy with this arrangement, but much too tired to protest.

"Fine," she said. "But we're just sleeping, okay?"

"What else would we be doing?" Raiker asked, feigning puzzlement.

"Right," Petra said.

She crawled into bed next to him and reached over to turn out the bedside lamp. Petra found herself peering into the darkness, her eyes playing tricks on her. Every shadow seemed to be something malevolent, lurking and waiting to pounce. She tore her gaze away and found Raiker's eyes instead.

Raiker reached out one hand and touched her face. His eyes remained locked on hers, heavy with concern. When he spoke, there was an odd cadence to his voice, as if each word carried weight.

"*Petra Adelina Bachman,*" he said, "*You're safe. Go to sleep now.*"

And instantly, she did, drifting off into a peaceful sleep, where she dreamed of dancing fairies with gossamer wings.

Chapter Eight

W hen Petra woke up, she discovered that she'd snuggled up to Raiker in her sleep. She was spooned against him, her body curled into his with his arm draped over her stomach. As her drowsy mind shook off sleep, the cozy feeling she'd had waking up in his arms was replaced by a growing sense of awkwardness, laying so close to this strange man she'd just met. Petra carefully attempted to extract herself from his embrace. When she tried to sit up, his arm tightened around her, pulling her body close to his again, like a child clinging to a teddy bear.

"Raiker..." she said, nudging him gently.

He continued snoring. She made another attempt to escape and succeeded only in rolling over to face him.

"Raiker!" she tried again, shaking him this time.

Raiker's eyes opened.

"Good morning, my lady," he said. "Did you have good dreams?"

He stroked her face tenderly, moving a stray curl out of her eyes. Petra quickly wiggled out of his arms, sitting up. Her eyes narrowed as Raiker hopped out of bed, bearing a smug expression, like he was proud of himself. She was developing a strong suspicion about how it was that she had fallen asleep so suddenly and slept so deeply.

"You did something to me, didn't you?" she said.

Raiker's face contorted into a pout.

"Don't be angry," he said. "I gave you a little push, that's all."

Oma had never called it a "push", but the fairy ability to make mortals do their bidding or control their minds was something that featured heavily in her stories. In one of Petra's favorite tales, a fairy comes upon a group of people gathered in a church and makes them dance all night. Priests and nuns, commoners and nobles, all dancing together with abandon.

But now that she knew this sort of mind control was possible, Petra immediately began to think of far more sinister applications.

"So, these bad fairies, the Unseelie, they could make me do whatever they wanted?"

Raiker stepped closer to her and looked her up and down as if he were sizing her up. He put one arm around Petra, pulling her body close to his. It was almost an embrace, but there was nothing warm about the gesture. Petra was keenly aware of how strong he was, and how helplessly he had her pinned in place. As if to emphasize that point, he used his other hand to tilt her chin upward, forcing her to stare into his eyes. His irises were bright red today and disconcertingly inhuman.

"*Petra Adelina Bachman,*" he said, his words heavy with importance, "*Take off your clothes.*"

The words felt like a weight on Petra's brain, and with them came a slightly woozy feeling reminiscent of being stoned. For just a moment, taking her clothes off seemed like a perfectly reasonable, even enjoyable thing to do, and she found herself reaching for the bottom hem of her shirt to pull it up over her head.

Then several thoughts occurred to her at once. She remembered that he was trying to push her. She also remembered that there was no way in hell she actually wanted to strip down in front of this lecherous cat burglar. Upon coming to these realizations, the fog cleared from her mind almost immediately. The weight of the words lifted, and in their wake, they left a feeling of being seriously, royally pissed off. Petra slapped Raiker across the face.

Raiker released her and backed away a respectable distance. He laughed and flashed her a grin that was one-part amusement, one-part respect.

"See?" he said, "Don't worry about it."

He bounded out of the bedroom then, and after a moment, a somewhat confused Petra went after him.

Raiker skipped the stairs, preferring to gracefully vault over the banister and float down to the living room below on his wings. He landed just in front of the wooden arch way that led into the kitchen, folding his wings in to fit as he passed through it. Petra took the longer route down the stairs and headed into the kitchen after him.

She walked in to find Raiker drinking her cream straight out of the carton while standing in front of the open refrigerator.

As if he sensed that she was going to require a better explanation than whatever the hell that was, Raiker sighed and addressed her again.

"Pushing someone is a tricky thing, and not all types of fae can do it," he explained. "And there's a lot of things that can make it easier. Knowing someone's true name, eye contact, if the person isn't expecting it or, better yet, doesn't even know it's possible. Which is why it's incredibly difficult for a fairy to do it to another fairy."

He put the cream back and began to help himself to a jar of strawberry jam, licking the jelly off one long finger.

"It helps if their inhibitions are already lower, like if they've had too much mead or they're tired or injured."

He eyed her almost empty refrigerator with a frown and then moved on to the pantry, which Petra was certain would also disappoint him.

"And some people are just more susceptible than others. Their will or sense of self are a little weaker. Or they're stupid. You do not seem to have those problems."

Raiker munched on a few stale crackers as he searched the almost empty pantry.

"But most importantly," he continued, "The less the person wants to do something, the harder it is to push them into doing it. If an Unseelie told you to gouge your own eyes out, it's unlikely you would actually comply. Which incidentally means you are disappointingly set against undressing for me."

He chuckled and shook his head as he shut the pantry door behind him.

"I'll be right back," he said, vanishing on the spot before she could respond.

Petra, who had *almost* stopped being surprised whenever he did that, busied herself making coffee.

When he reappeared a few minutes later he was holding an elegant china plate of French toast in each hand.

"Breakfast for my lady," he declared. "French toast made from brioche stuffed with sweetened orange mascarpone and fresh berries, courtesy of Café Le Mourd."

He set the plates down at the kitchen table and then vanished again. He reappeared 10 seconds later holding a small china carafe.

"Forgot the syrup," he said as he sat down at the table, perching on the extreme edge of the chair to leave room for his wings.

"You stole this from a five-star restaurant?" Petra asked, bemused.

Raiker shrugged.

"I'm a thief, not a cook," he said, pouring an ungodly amount of maple syrup over his French toast.

Petra sat and helped herself to a bite as well, knowing that this purloined breakfast probably cost at least two days salary. It tasted like it did too.

"Raiker," Petra said with some hesitation, "If you had been able to push me, would you have actually let me take off my clothes?"

Though she felt like the question needed to be asked, she almost regretted it when she saw how hurt he looked. He stopped eating and took her hand, his ordinarily playful expression faltering.

"Of course not," he said. "I wouldn't dream of it."

Petra looked down at her food, unable to meet his wounded eyes. But when she looked up again, that familiar wicked smile had returned to his face.

"When you take your clothes off for me, it will be because that's what you want to do," he said, and he slowly stroked one finger across the palm of her hand.

Petra scowled at him and yanked her hand back. She chose not to comment on his use of the word "when", preferring instead to continue eating her magnificent gourmet breakfast.

She managed one more bite before the muffled sound of a foghorn drifted over from somewhere in the kitchen.

"WHEEEEE-OOOOOH!"

"Oh... shit," Petra said with dawning dread.

"Oh, right," Raiker said, "It wouldn't stop doing that, so I put it in the cookie jar."

With a groan, Petra rose to her feet and darted to the blue ceramic "Kekse" jar on the kitchen counter. She grabbed the phone out just as it stopped ringing.

There were 27 missed calls and 14 voicemails. With growing trepidation, Petra hit play.

"Hi Petra," Hope's voice chimed, "Got a question. Could you call me back?"

"Listen," Hope said on the next message, "We've got four rooms left, but when I try to assign the reservation, it says there's no rooms. Not sure what I'm doing wrong. Please call me."

"Bachman," Beth began on the next message, "You know you need to be available to answer your phone. Hope called me after you wouldn't pick up. You better have a good explanation."

"You know," Raiker called to her from the kitchen table, "You really ought to have cookies in your cookie jar."

"Quiet," Petra hissed.

"Petra, Mr. Baker says he has a company profile set up, but I can't find it. Call me back," Hope said on the next message.

"Petra," Beth's voice intoned, "that's the second phone call from Hope I've gotten tonight. Call me back *now* and tell me why it is you aren't answering your phone."

"It's just teasing, really," Raiker continued to grumble, "to have a jar labeled 'cookies' and no cookies in it."

"Shut up!" Petra snapped.

She stopped listening to the whole messages after that, getting the gist from the first few words.

"Bachman, if you don't call me back in the next five minutes—"

"Petra, at least assure me that you're going to be in tomorrow—"

"Petra, your shift started 30 minutes ago. You missed the morning meeting—"

"Petra, I'm not even mad anymore. I'm worried—"

"Okay, now I'm really worried. This isn't like you—"

"Petra, I've called two hospitals now, and I called Brad. Where are you?"

Petra finally put the phone down and hung her head.

"I have to go to work," she told Raiker.

"Will you bring home cookies?"

Petra thought about calling on her way in, but she didn't know exactly what she was going to say. One excuse after another ran through her head and almost all of them seemed like they would get her fired. She even found herself wishing for a traffic jam just so she could have that much longer to formulate an excuse, but it was already past 10 o'clock. The morning commuters had long since arrived at their destinations. Cursing the total absence of LA traffic for the first time in her life, Petra pulled up in front of the Hammond a mere 40 minutes later.

She was still trying to dream up an excuse as she walked through the front doors, so nervous she didn't realize she'd walked straight past Beth until she called out to her.

"Petra, what happened to your back?" Beth asked.

Petra hadn't given it much thought when she'd thrown on the loose fitting, gray sleeveless blouse she was wearing. It was cut down just below her shoulder blades, leaving a good five inches of the bandage covering the anguana's claw mark exposed. She'd intended to throw a suit jacket on over it, but it was so hot out Petra hadn't put it on yet.

"I was..." Petra began.

She quickly ran through the options in her head, trying to decide which one best matched the wound.

...in a car accident.

...jogging and I slipped and fell on a knife.

...attacked by a hawk.

"...mugged," she finished, just as Sylvia and Hope came darting across the lobby to meet her.

"Mugged?" Beth repeated.

"A homeless man jumped me walking back to my car. He had a knife and..."

Sylvia had moved around to look at her back. Never one to put much stock in personal boundaries, Sylvia lifted up the back of Petra's shirt, exposing more of the bandage. She inhaled sharply.

"Oh my God, Petra," Sylvia said, horrified. "It goes all the way up your back! You must have been so scared. Did you go to the police?"

Unbidden, the memories from the Anguana attack crept into her head. The way that terrible creature had looked at her as it had held her pinned to the floor. The searing pain as its claws had ripped into her back. The helplessness of knowing she was going to die and that there was nothing she could do to stop it.

In spite of herself, tears sprang into Petra's eyes and ran down her cheeks.

"Okay. That's enough. Everybody give the woman some space," Beth barked. "Hope, get her a cup of coffee and something unhealthy to eat. Sylvia, go watch the desk."

She put her arm around Petra and steered her towards the back office, away from the prying eyes of an increasing number of staff and guests. Petra was both ashamed of her emotional outburst and grateful for the leeway it was obviously affording her.

"He must have taken your phone," Beth said.

"Yes," Petra said, seizing on the suggestion.

As subtly as she could manage, Petra reached inside her laptop case and turned her phone off.

"But I should have called anyway," Petra insisted. "I'm sorry."

"It's okay. I'm just glad you're alright." With a dark chuckle, Beth added, "And I'm glad I don't have to replace you."

Petra couldn't recall ever previously having a workday where everyone was this nice to her. Beth did the occupancy report for her and volunteered to go talk to Ms. Holly when she came down to complain about their latest "ineptitude" (She had put a "Do Not Disturb" sign on her door, but insisted that it was no excuse for not cleaning her room). Sylvia did all her side work without being asked and also emailed Petra several just-this-side-of-safe-for-work pictures of shirtless men holding puppies. The cooks made her bratwurst with Black Forest cupcakes for dessert and snuck a healthy splash of brandy into her coffee. The beautiful bouquet of wildflowers on her desk didn't hurt her mood either.

But she did have a lot of work to catch up on, and it was well after dark by the time she felt she had made enough of a dent to go home. The news of her "mugging" had spread throughout the hotel, and Devon in maintenance had insisted on walking her out to her car, lecturing her all the while on the merits of various self-defense products, concealed weapons, and alarm systems that he couldn't believe she didn't own. Petra didn't mention that she had a six and a half foot tall supernaturally powered guy with a sword waiting for her at home. That probably wasn't the sort of security measure Devon had in mind.

Petra had almost made it home before she remembered that Raiker asked her to bring home cookies. Deciding that it was also probably past time that she filled the refrigerator with something resembling food, she steered her Jetta into a narrow parking space in front of Stater Brothers.

It wasn't so much that Petra didn't know how to shop for groceries. It was just that everything she cooked tended to involve either the toaster or the microwave. Anything more elaborate than that and Brad usually took over. He used to tease her that if he ever left, she'd clearly starve, subsisting solely on a diet of tortilla chips and wine. Much as

Petra hated to admit it, that might not have been far from the truth.

Petra wandered the aisles listlessly, passing an array of fresh meats and vegetables before finally filling her cart with foods a little more in her comfort zone: Lean Cuisine dinners, frozen veggies, chips and salsa, and booze. She threw in some cream and Chips Ahoy cookies for Raiker and then decided to get a bag of oranges too, just so she could say that something in her cart wasn't frozen or processed.

The bag of oranges and two out of five wine bottles went back after she saw the checkout total, and then she was on her way home.

Petra had to admit she was relieved to see the kitchen light on as she pulled up in front of the house. No strange beasts lurking in the dark this time. Just Raiker, waving through the window before returning to removing all the cups from her kitchen cabinets. He was shirtless again, and Petra was starting to wonder what the mostly elderly neighbors must think about her new gentleman caller. At least he'd remembered to conjure up some pants this time.

Petra let herself in through the garage door and stepped into the darkened foyer, her eyes blinking furiously to adjust from the floodlights in the garage. Shadows danced as she made her way into the living room and towards the kitchen, struggling with the heavy grocery bags clutched in each hand.

A low growling noise pierced the quiet and Petra dropped the bags with a gasp. The wine bottles smashed. Petra spun to face the sound coming from the darkened stairs.

"Raiker!" she yelled as she backed away from the staircase, where she could just make out two eyes staring back at her, reflecting the light from the kitchen.

Raiker was there in an instant, putting himself between her and the thing on the stairs with his flaming blue sword at his side.

"What is it?" he demanded.

"There— there's something there..." Petra stammered as she pointed at the stairs.

Raiker slowly advanced on the bottom step, the glow from his sword shining onto the staircase and illuminating... a puppy. At least, Petra's initial thought was that it was a puppy, but on closer inspection it seemed to be a fully grown, ludicrously small dog, with curly black fur and brown eyes. He was no bigger than a cat, but he growled at Petra with all his might, doing his level best to look scary and failing miserably.

Petra let out a breath she hadn't realized she was holding in, torn between relief and confusion. Raiker laughed.

"Oh, that's just Shitpoo," he said, as if this would explain everything. "Shitpoo, come on down here. She won't hurt you."

The dog immediately stopped growling and padded down the stairs, coming to a stop at Petra's feet. He began to lick the puddle of wine that was now seeping through the bottom of the grocery sack on the floor. Petra scooped him up before he could slurp up any more, wondering vaguely how much alcohol was too much for a 10-pound ball of fluff.

"You didn't tell me you have a—" Petra broke off as the dog started licking her face. There was cheap wine soaked into his muzzle. "Do fairies keep pets?"

"He's not my pet," Raiker said. "I stole him for you. He's here to scare away hobyahs."

Petra carried the dog into the kitchen and set him down in the sink.

"Okay, one, I can't take care of a dog," Petra protested as she rinsed the wine out of his fur.

"Sure, you can," Raiker said. "He's perfectly well behaved, and he likes you."

"Two," Petra continued, "He doesn't look like he can scare away much of anything."

"Hobyahs don't like dogs," Raiker explained. "Even diminutive ones. They won't come near the house as long as Shitpoo's here."

"I suppose I don't really want to know what happens if a hobyah gets in the house?"

"Well, normally they murder all the adults in the home and cart off the children in a burlap sack to eat them later. But since it's just you and me here, it would probably start by tearing off your—"

Petra held up her hand to stop him.

"I think I get the picture."

With his fur soaked from the sink and pressed against his skin, at least half of the little dog's mass seemed to vanish. He shook himself off, flinging water droplets everywhere.

"Three," Petra said, "Where is it you stole him from exactly?"

"I took him from a woman in Palo Alto who was breeding dogs in her backyard."

Raiker produced a towel and swaddled the wet dog in it affectionately. He lifted him out of the sink and cradled him against his chest like a baby.

"She wasn't very nice to the dogs," he explained, and his usual playful expression was replaced with a dark look. "I wasn't very nice to her either."

Petra took a moment to decide if she was going to ask if the puppy mill lady in Palo Alto still had both her eyeballs. She settled on filing that under the category of things she'd prefer not to know, along with whatever part of her a hobyah would slice off first.

"But before I... did that, she said his name was Shitpoo," Raiker continued.

Petra looked over the shaggy, brown-eyed dog cradled in Raiker's arms.

"Okay, I think 'shitpoo' is a breed, not a name," Petra said. "Like, shih tzu/poodle mix. It's sort of a joke."

Raiker shook his head.

"No, it's his true name," he insisted. "It's what he answers to. Isn't it Shitpoo?"

Shitpoo barked as if in confirmation, tail wagging furiously from inside of the rapidly unraveling dishtowel swaddle.

"I can't keep him," Petra made one last attempt to protest. "I'm at work all the—"

"Brad stopped by earlier." Raiker said, making an obvious effort to change the subject. "He seemed to be under the impression that you might be dead."

Oh God. I forget that Beth called Brad looking for me...

"Uh... How did that go?" Petra asked, dreading the answer.

"It went well."

There was mischievous glint in his eyes that Petra didn't like. Raiker put Shitpoo down on the floor, scratching the little dog behind the ears before letting him scamper away.

"I assured him you were not dead," Raiker continued in a casual tone. "He called me a 'fuck boy' that had stolen the love of his life. I told him you not being in love with him had naught to do with me, and then he punched me in the gut."

"That... that doesn't sound like it went well," Petra stammered.

"Oh, I'm getting to the good part. The boy can't throw a punch to save his life. But he did start the dual, so it was perfectly honorable for me to retaliate by knocking his front teeth out."

"You punched out his teeth," Petra repeated.

Raiker stood a little taller. "Knocked him out cold too. I peeled him off the driveway and left him on the seat of that roofless car of his."

Petra took a moment to consider whether or not she actually cared before asking, "Is he okay?"

Raiker shrugged. "Seemed to be. The sun turned him a bit pink. He spent some time looking for his teeth in the grass and then he drove off."

Raiker pulled something out of his pocket and tossed it into the air. Two small, white objects fell into his open palm, and he closed his fist around them, grinning.

Petra's voice jumped a full octave. "You stole Brad's teeth?!"

Raiker laughed and tossed them in the air again. "Oh, I'm going to have a lot of fun with these. We could make him–"

"Nope!" Petra cut him off and held out her hand. "Whatever you're planning, don't. Gimme the teeth."

Raiker grudgingly put them in her hand. Petra walked to the sink and threw them down the garbage disposal. The motor protested loudly. A thought occurred to her as she listened to the blades grind.

THAT'S why I wasn't allowed to leave my teeth out for the Tooth Fairy.

"Spoil sport," Raiker teased over the noise.

Petra switched off the disposal. In the sudden silence she heard glass tinkling in the living room. "Dammit. Shitpoo, no!" She ran back to the foyer, where she found Shitpoo lapping up more wine. "No! Shitpoo, sit! Stay!"

Shitpoo did not sit or stay, and Petra was having serious doubts about Raiker's assertion that the dog was well behaved.

"*Shitpoo, don't drink that,*" Raiker said as he walked in.

Shitpoo stopped, sat down, and proceeded to lick himself.

"You're pushing him!" Petra shouted in realization.

Raiker laughed at her. "Guilty."

"That's completely unfair," Petra mumbled. She brought the dog back to the sink, grumbling curses the whole way. She could feel Raiker's eyes on her and she washed wine out of the dog's muzzle for a second time.

"Did I do something wrong again?" he asked.

Petra turned to look at him. It was hard to stay mad with that earnest look in his eyes.

"You... scare me sometimes," she admitted. "Just... don't hurt anyone else on my behalf, okay? I don't want that from you."

Raiker's shoulders slumped and his wings closed in behind him.

"I didn't mean to scare you," he said in a small voice.

He looked so crestfallen Petra almost felt bad for saying anything. She wrapped the dog up in a dry dishtowel and handed him to Raiker.

"Here," she said. "Keep an eye on this little wino."

Petra grabbed a mop and broom out of the laundry room and returned to the foyer, intent on cleaning up the puddle of wine and grocery bags full of broken glass. But instead of a puddle on the floor, she found a small cloud of wine droplets suspended in midair. Raiker was sitting on the bottom step in front of it, conducting the cloud with his hands like an orchestra. At his prompting, the wine cloud drifted away, past where Petra stood in the archway and into the kitchen, where she watched the large, red cloud split itself into eight little clouds, then rain down into eight of the coffee cups sitting on the kitchen counter.

Raiker grinned at her, clearly pleased with himself.

"I didn't want it to go to waste."

Petra grabbed two of the coffee cups off the counter and brought one to Raiker, sitting down on the step next to him. Shitpoo nosed at her ankle until she scooped him up into her lap, rubbing his belly. The wine was now more of a red blend than the individual bottles of pinot noir, merlot, and cabernet they had started out as, and Petra supposed it was at least partially contaminated with whatever dirt and debris was on her floors. But it tasted just fine.

"I didn't know you could do that," Petra said, eyes wide in wonderment.

"I can do a lot of things," Raiker replied. "Not all of it scary."

He smiled at her and she smiled back, her unease already slipping away.

"Would you like to see some more?" he asked.

Chapter Nine

P etra was on her third coffee mug of floor wine, sitting on the garden swing, watching Raiker talk to the fireflies. Shitpoo snoozed on the grass next to her feet, his little paws batting frantically at the air as he chased squirrels in his dreams.

At Raiker's whispered bidding the lightning bugs formed themselves into a straight line. Then the line bent into the shape of a heart, and the lights blinked on and off in perfect synchronicity. Petra clapped in appreciation, and Raiker took a bow.

"They just do whatever you tell them to do?" Petra asked.

"They're a lot less stubborn than you," said Raiker.

He whispered to them again, and this time
the fireflies began to form letters, spelling out
R-A-I-K-I ...the remaining bugs formed just the
first stroke of the letter E, and there were none
left for the remaining R.

"Raiki?" Petra giggled.

"I seem to be a little short on bugs," Raiker said
with a frown.

He reached out and cupped one in his
hands, whispering a series of instructions before
releasing it again. The bug whizzed off into the
night.

"My mother used to weave tapestries from
spider webs," he said. "She could push the spiders
to make the most beautiful pictures. Fae traveled
from all over to watch her work."

"Used to?" Petra asked.

The firefly returned. Trailing behind him
was a small glowing cloud of his compatriots.
Apparently Raiker had sent him out for
reinforcements. Now Raiker was able to form the
rest of the letter E and the R, spelling out his
name in glowing lights.

"Used to," Raiker said. "She died when I was
young."

"I'm sorry," Petra said. "Mine too. Car accident."

His eyes met hers then and Petra found herself
mesmerized by the way the glow from the
lightning bugs made the flecks of gold in his irises
shine.

"So, you know then," he said simply. "What it's
like."

"I do."

Raiker watched the fireflies blinking his name on and off for a moment.

"It wasn't just skill; she had such artistry for it." He waved his hand at his own creation. "What I can do is... just good enough to charm beautiful women." He flashed her a smile. "Is it working?"

Petra rolled her eyes at him. "Do you ever stop flirting?"

A murmur from Raiker and the fireflies shifted formation, reforming into the letters N-E-V-E-R. Petra snorted.

"You know what I mean though. You're an artist," he said. "Anyone can pick up a brush. That doesn't mean they can paint."

As Petra watched, the fireflies shifted into the shape of a Cheshire cat moon surrounded by stars. Then into a simple sailboat floating on a glowing wave. If charming her was truly the goal, Raiker was having more success than Petra was ever going to admit.

"What sort of pictures would your mom make?" she asked.

"Lots of things," said Raiker. "Lovers and landscapes and self-portraits. They were quite insubstantial. Any little breeze could rend them into nothingness." Raiker smiled at the memory, the warmth of his expression tempered by the sadness in his eyes. "I used to ask her to do butterflies. She made them for me over and over again."

"Why butterflies?"

"I don't know. Because I loved them. I obsessed the way only children can. What did you love as a child?"

Petra felt blood rushing into her cheeks and looked down at her feet.

"Fairies."

When she looked up again, the fireflies had swarmed around her. At Raiker's bidding the cluster split in two, moving to either side of her, and then split again, stretching out in two long lines on either side of her before finally settling into the shape of wings; radiant, golden dragonfly wings extending out from her back, just like Raiker's. The individual fireflies blinked on and off randomly, making the wings look as though they sparkled. Petra stood, grinning ear-to-ear. The wings moved with her, and then began to open and close slowly as if they really could lift her off the ground.

Raiker stood facing her, his own real wings lining up just above the ones he'd made for her.

"They suit you," he said.

Petra found herself staring at Raiker's wings, and the way each little scale reflected the glow from the fireflies. Impulsively, she reached out her hand to touch them.

Raiker snapped his wings shut, jerking them violently away from her hand. As if his concentration was broken, the fireflies scattered, her luminous false wings dissolving into a cloud of lights around them.

"I'm sorry," Petra said quickly, withdrawing her hand. "I shouldn't have—"

"No. No, don't be sorry." With a nervous laugh, Raiker unfolded his wings again. "You startled me, is all. You're so human. A fairy would never..."

"Is it like, an etiquette thing? Do fairies have etiquette things?"

"We have a lot of etiquette things. But that's not... It's more like when something gets too close to your eyes and you shut them, even if you don't mean to."

"You mean it's instinctive? To protect them."

"Exactly. They're... fragile. Precious." He took a step closer to her. "But you can touch them if you want to."

Tentatively, Petra reached her hand towards him again. For just a moment, his wings fluttered out of her reach, and then with a deep breath Raiker held them still. The scales were cool and smooth under her fingertips, almost the same temperature as the night air, like little panes of glass. Each scale was set into a framework of copper-colored lines, as fine as string, and Petra suspected that the frames were some kind of veins. They felt warmer than the scales did. She let her hand trace the lines up to the top of the wing, where a larger, ridged vein started at his back and narrowed as it reached the wing tip. She moved her hand to the space where the upper one met the lower and Raiker laughed, sending a vibration through the wings.

"That tickles," he said.

Petra withdrew her hand apologetically.

"What's it like to fly?" she asked him. "I mean, really fly. More than three feet off the ground."

Raiker grinned down at her.

"Hold on to me," he said.

"What?"

One second, she had both feet planted firmly on the ground. The next, Raiker put one hand behind her back and the other behind her knees and swept her up into his arms. And before even the rest of that second managed to pass they were rocketing upward, leaving the ground far, far beneath them. Petra shrieked and clung to Raiker's neck as tightly as she could. She watched the garden shrink below her. Shitpoo stood in the middle of the fairy ring, barking up at them they as they disappeared into the clouds. The cold night air whipped at her skin; the G-force pressing down on her in a way that felt horribly like she'd be ripped right out of Raiker's arms and plummet to her death at any moment.

"DU VERRÜCKTER HURENSOHN! PUT ME DOWN! SCHEIßE!" Petra screamed.

"That is not a very nice thing to say about my mother," Raiker chided her.

He stopped his ascent, hovering in midair with a gentle humming of his wings. Petra didn't know how high they were now and she refused to look down and find out.

"Alright, just breathe," he reminded her. "Deep breaths. Come on. You're safe. I've got you."

Petra was not convinced of that. She made the mistake of looking down and shrieked again.

"*Petra Adelina Bachman!*" Raiker commanded, his gold-flecked eyes fixed on her blue ones, "*You are safe. You are not going to fall. I've got you. You can trust me. Breathe."*

There was some part of her that realized she was being pushed. The rest of her brain was just grateful for the reassurance that she wasn't going to die. She embraced the hypnotic suggestion with open arms. Petra inhaled deeply and exhaled as her heart rate slowed from hummingbird speed to resting.

"I'm sorry," Raiker said. "I think I scared you again."

He didn't sound sorry this time. In fact, he barely managed to stifle a laugh. Now that she had relaxed her grip slightly, Petra noticed she had dug her fingernails into Raiker's neck, leaving long rivulets of blood. Served him right.

"You're full of shit," she said.

"Yes, well, we're not good liars as a rule. And it was pretty funny."

"It was *not* funny."

"It was at least a little funny."

Petra scowled up at him.

"Hey, we're flying," he reminded her. "Don't be angry with me. Marvel at the flying."

Now that she had calmed down, it *was* something to marvel at. They were much too high now for Petra to pick out which house was hers in the sea of city lights below her. Above, the sky dazzled with stars which would ordinarily be lost to light pollution, but from her vantage point up here she could see every one. Cloud cover swirled just below their feet, obscuring part of the city as the night wind pushed it along. It was colder than it had been down in the garden, too cold for the thin pencil skirt and tank top she was wearing, but at least Raiker's skin was warm against hers.

Slowly this time, he flew forward, carrying her across the sky. Petra spotted the fairgrounds below them, the little illuminated Ferris wheel barely bigger than her thumb.

A moment later, Petra watched as a glowing ball of light streaked up from the fairground towards them and then exploded with a great BOOM several yards below their feet, trailing flaming streaks of red in all directions. Petra was in awe of the shift in perspective, looking down at the fireworks outlined against city lights instead of up at them against the black sky.

Raiker shot upward.

"They're shooting at us!" he yelled. Now it was Petra's turn to laugh at him. "How do they even see us?!"

"Calm down. They're not shooting at us," she said. "It's just fireworks. They're supposed to be pretty."

"Pretty?! They're exploding!"

"Relax," she told him. "Just watch. And, um, stay out of range."

Raiker watched a few moments longer, shuddering every time another firework boomed.

"No," he said. "Not pretty."

Raiker zoomed off, well away from the fireworks before descending and landing on the flat roof of an apartment complex.

"Firing explosives into the air for fun. Humans are insane..." Raiker mumbled as he set her back on her feet.

Her legs felt a bit wobbly after their flight across the night sky, and Raiker grasped her shoulders to steady her.

"You're freezing," he said, with sudden concern. "Wait here."

He vanished, leaving Petra laughing and wondering what the hell else she possibly could do but "wait here".

A few minutes later he returned with a bottle of amaretto in one hand and a gorgeous light blue coat in the other. Petra accepted both gratefully, comforting herself with the assumption that whoever he'd taken the Prada coat from could probably afford to replace it.

They sat together on the rooftop, sharing the bottle of candy sweet liqueur. Raiker reached over and rested one warm hand on her knee.

"I should have stolen you a longer coat," he said. "Your skin feels like ice."

"Yours doesn't," she said. "Are you ever cold?"

"Not this close to the equator."

His hand slid slowly up her leg, fingering the hem of her skirt, and Petra knew that the warm feeling that spread through her then had little to do with magic, or their position relative to the earth's equator.

"Raiker... what are you doing?" Petra said; her voice a warning.

"Warming you up. I don't want you to freeze."

Petra reached down and moved his hand back to his own lap.

"I'm good. Thanks."

Raiker's face contorted into a pout.

"I let you touch my wings," he whined.

"That's not really the same thing as letting you feel up my skirt."

Raiker laughed. "I don't think it's as different as you think it is."

They returned to the house high on life and more than a little tipsy. Petra locked herself in the bathroom and slipped into her warmest flannel pajamas, the soft fabric chasing the rest of the chill from her skin. When she emerged, Raiker was already asleep, sprawled on her bed and snoring. His wings fluttered with each exhalation.

But Petra wasn't tired. Petra felt like the adrenaline surging through her would never leave. She left the room and went back downstairs, carefully skipping over the squeaky step. She stood in the foyer where the TV and her laptop waited to her right.

Petra went left instead. She walked into the studio, sat down in her favorite arm chair, and began to draw.

Chapter Ten

I t was her day off, and Petra was determined to
use it finding this damn key. She woke up early
and started in on the cupboard under the stairs,
sifting through a stack of old board games and
jigsaw puzzles.

"I don't even know what I'm looking for," Petra
called out through the open door.

There was no answer. Petra poked her head
back out of the closet. "Raiker?"

"In here!"

Petra followed the sound of his voice through
the door to the garage. She found him perched on
the back of the armchair, holding her sketchbook.

"This wasn't out before," he said. "Did you make
art?"

"I made a sketch. I'd hardly call it art. Give that
back."

Petra tried to grab the sketchbook, but Raiker held it over his head and then fluttered up to the ceiling, leaving her eyes level with his kneecaps and the sketchbook well out of her reach. Raiker flipped the book open to the drawing she'd been working on last night. His mouth dropped open. Slowly, he floated back down to the floor, his eyes fixed on the picture.

In the drawing a beautiful fairy woman with dragonfly wings stood holding a spider in the palm of her hand, lips pursed as if she were whispering to it. A single strand of web trailed out of the spider's abdomen and over to a giant spider web hanging from a tree branch. But not just any web. This web had been woven into the shape of an intricate butterfly.

On the floor next to the woman's bare feet, a fairy child with unruly hair sat cross-legged watching his mother, his little hands clapping in appreciation. There was a butterfly perched on his shoulder.

Petra was just beginning to feel deeply apprehensive about his reaction when Raiker broke into a grin. He reached out to touch the picture, and then pulled his hand back again, as if he were afraid of damaging it. Tears spilled out of his teal green eyes.

"This is..." he seemed to be struggling for words, "It's so... joyful."

"That's the feeling I got when you described her," Petra said, a little taken aback by his tears.

"It is. I mean, it was. Joyful. Only..." Raiker trailed one long finger over the picture.

"Sometimes all I can remember is what happened to her. And then I forget there were moments like this before."

Petra reached her hand up to his face, wiping away one tear with her thumb.

"What happened to her?" she asked.

"She... It doesn't bear repeating."

Raiker shook his head and snapped the sketchbook shut.

"Does this make me your muse?" he asked, his expression defaulting back to libidinous. "I like being a muse. I could pose for you. I mean, I was hoping to get *you* naked, but if you want me to take my clothes off for you that feels like the wind's the right direction."

As far as attempts to change the subject went, it wasn't the smoothest transition, but Petra was inclined to let him have it. She was less inclined to go so far as to actually let him keep unlacing the cord that bound the fly of his pants. After only a moment's hesitation, Petra reached her hand down to still his.

"How about we keep looking for the key instead?" she suggested.

"You're no fun," he pouted. "Besides, I've been looking for the key while you've been off wasting your life at that inn."

"You mean working?"

"I stand by my words."

Raiker glanced around the dusty garage.

"I haven't searched this room properly yet though."

Petra glanced from the dusty studio space to the car parked on the other side of the garage.

"I take it the key doesn't really look like a key?" Petra asked.

"No, it does," Raiker said. "It just doesn't necessarily look like a key here. Well, it might, but I already stole all your keys."

"I noticed," Petra said, rolling her eyes. "So how do you... remove the glamour from the key? Am I saying that right?"

"That's right. Mostly right. It's a... I don't know how to say it in your language. It's a really tricky glamour. It can't be removed while it's still in your realm. I have to take it back to Arcadia with me first."

An hour later the two of them were up in the cramped attic, digging through old boxes. Oma had been many things, but organized was not one of them. She also seemed to have been incapable of throwing anything out. Petra had already found six boxes of *Reader's Digests*, a bag of power cords that belonged to unknown appliances, and every piece of her mother's first grade homework.

"I don't suppose you can magic away dust?" Petra asked, after wiping the sweat from her forehead and leaving behind a smudge from her dirty hands.

"I could, but that sounds exhausting. Yours or Oma's?"

Raiker held up an impossibly 80's purple sequin covered jacket.

"Mama's, actually," Petra said, before turning back to a box of broken oil lamps.

Raiker slipped on the purple jacket, preening in front of a dingy antique mirror propped against one wall.

"What do you think?"

The jacket hit him about at the midriff, but otherwise fit surprisingly well.

"I think shoulder pads should never come back," said Petra.

"But look how shiny it is when the light hits it! Can I keep it?"

Petra laughed. "Sure. Why not?"

Raiker beamed at her and then went back to preening in front of the mirror. Petra opened another box. Yellowed newspapers, piles of embroidery thread, and an antique clothes iron. Petra picked up the iron, her hands coming away orange with rust.

Could be useful.

She warned Raiker not to touch it and set it aside.

Behind that box was an old, leather-bound steamer trunk, about three feet across. A huge, rusted metal lock held it shut. Petra had never seen it before. Raiker wandered over to look.

"Where's the key?" he asked.

"Don't know," Petra said.

Raiker reached a hand out towards the lock and then withdrew it quickly.

"I'm usually quite good with locks, but iron can be tricky," he said. "They just take a little more persuasion, if I-"

"Move over."

Raiker moved away and Petra slammed the sledgehammer she'd retrieved from the corner down on the lock with all her might. It took a couple whacks, but on the third try the latch broke off the front of the trunk, taking the lock with it.

"Whoa," Raiker said. "That works too."

They opened the trunk. Inside was a treasure trove of photographs, letters, and old-fashioned women's clothes. Petra picked up one of the yellowed black and white photos. In the picture, a stately looking gentleman was standing in front of the framework of a house still under construction. Petra flipped the photograph over. Someone had written "Dr. Oscar Greene. May Day, 1899" in neat cursive on the back.

"Who is he?" Raiker asked. "Is that your grandfather?"

"No," Petra said, flipping the photo over again. Only now did she begin to recognize the shape of the building that was then still in progress.

"No, this is the guy that built this house. This was decades before my grandparents bought it. My Oma told me a little about him and his wife. I guess this is how she knew. All this stuff."

Petra sifted slowly through the stack of pictures, watching her house come together in black and white.

"The fairy ring was there already," Petra noted with wonder, staring at an image of her backyard. It was mostly being used to store lumber then, but there was that perfect circle of mushrooms, still untouched after all this time.

"The fairy ring has always been there," Raiker corrected. "Well, long as I can remember at least. They do move sometimes."

"They move? On their own?"

"They..." Raiker smiled at her, "You don't really know what they are, do you?" He pointed at the mushrooms in the picture. "There's a sort of wall between my world and yours. A powerful fae can cross through it anywhere, but most of us have to look for a place where it's just a little bit more... permeable."

"And my garden is permeable?"

"Your garden is incredibly permeable. Or, it was before I warded the daylights out of it, lest more Unseelie decide to come calling. Nothing can pass through there now unless I let it. Probably. In theory."

Petra picked up a portrait of a pretty young woman with dark hair wearing a corseted dress. The handwriting on the back told her that it was Mrs. Lillian Greene, taken around the same time the house was constructed. Mrs. Lillian Greene was notably much younger than her husband, and Petra supposed that might have been one of the reasons Lillian went on to ditch hubby for another man.

"I think they knew about the fairy ring," Petra said. "Or suspected something at least. They're fairies carved into the kitchen ceiling. They're in the ironwork on the chandeliers. There's a fairy door around the side of the house."

"There's a drawing of a pixie on the wall of your guest bedroom behind the nightstand, too."

"Oh, no that one was me," Petra said with a smile. "Oma grounded me for a week for 'defacing the walls.'"

Petra paused on a photo of the oak tree, which nearly 120 years ago was already a sprawling, towering presence. Lillian was resting in the shade of the tree, reading a book.

"First time I came through here... was it 1,000? ...No, 1,500 years ago. There wasn't a house here then, but there was this sort of shrine. The humans thought I was a god." Raiker sighed dramatically. "No one ever mistakes me for a god anymore."

Petra was beginning to suspect that the Greene's owned a camera, which must have been an extravagance for the time. Many of the pictures were posed, but some looked surprisingly candid, like the one of a stern looking Dr. Greene reading his morning newspaper in what was then a formal dining room, now Petra's kitchen. There'd been another building with the kitchen and servant's quarters back then, about where Mrs. Mason's house was now. Petra looked at the familiar carved ceiling tiles and wondered if Lillian had taken this particular photo herself.

The last picture in the stack was out of order with the rest. Here the house was once again just a framework. Dr. Greene stood posing in the center of the shot wearing a long coat, slacks, and a top hat. He was holding a hammer, as if he too were building the house, and looked about as convincing as a child wearing Daddy's tool belt. A few actual construction workers stood around in the background. Lillian was talking to one of them, a handsome young man with a clean-shaven face and a broad frame. The pair of them stood awfully close together.

Petra pointed the couple out to Raiker.

"Maybe this was her secret lover," she said.

Raiker's eyes went wide as he snatched the picture out of Petra's hand.

"I know him," Raiker said. "Knew him. Well, not *knew him* knew him, but knew of him, of course. I did dance with him once."

Petra took the picture back, studying the young man's face.

"Are you saying this guy flirting with Mrs. Greene is a fairy?"

"That 'guy' is King Oberon the All-Knowing, ruler of the Seelie Court. And he was not flirting with Mrs. Greene. He was bound to Queen Titania."

Petra snickered. "Is 'bound' like married? Because it doesn't look like that's slowing him down any. Lillian Greene was married too and that obviously wasn't slowing her down."

"Yes, well when fae swear a vow it actually means something."

Petra scowled at the overwhelming condescension in his tone.

"Wait... back up..." she said as a thought occurred to her. "You said 'Titania and Oberon.' Like *Midsummer Night's Dream* Titania and Oberon? Was Shakespeare a fairy?"

Raiker chuckled. "No, but he was fathered by one."

"No way!" Petra said, grinning.

"Oh yes. His father, Amity the Benevolent, brought him to court once. He, uh... wasn't welcome back again after he wrote *A Midsummer Night's Dream*. Queen Titania did not care for it. Small wonder she didn't have him flayed for the insult."

Petra's mind was spinning.

"Fairies can have babies with humans? How many half-fairy mutant children are running around out there? Could Shakespeare do magic? Is he even really dead?"

Raiker burst out laughing.

"They're not..." He was laughing so hard he couldn't finish the sentence for a full minute. "William Shakespeare was *human*. Fae/human children take after their mothers."

Petra found herself surprisingly disappointed by that answer.

"Like, completely human? Not even a little different?"

"Eh... sometimes they're a little more creative or charismatic. It's how you end up with a lot of your musicians in Alius..." With an apologetic frown he added, "Maybe a few dictators."

"So... when Lillian Greene ran off to have Oberon's babies, those were human babies?" Petra said with a smirk.

"They were *not*..." Raiker sighed in exasperation as Petra laughed at him. He pointed to the picture. "You see the ring on his wrist?"

Petra looked at it again. At first glance she had thought that Oberon was wearing a slim bracelet on his left wrist, but on further inspection it appeared to be tattooed on his skin.

"Queen Titania's true name was seared into his skin, and his onto hers. Then obscured, for obvious reasons. When we bind ourselves to someone else it's for life, and we can live a very, very long time. Queen Titania and King Oberon were together for over a hundred millennia before he died."

A hundred millennia. I guess that does make Raiker young by fairy standards.

Petra found herself wondering what sort of ills fae were vulnerable to. Old age did not seem to be one of them.

"What happened to him?" Petra asked.

"Nothing happened," Raiker said. "He decided to end his life."

Petra clapped her hand to her mouth. "I'm sorry. That's awful."

Raiker frowned at her reaction.

"It's... it's not uncommon. Especially for the very old ones. They tire is all." He looked away from her, like he couldn't meet her eyes and then added. "There's no shame in it."

That sentence was delivered with such conviction Petra wondered which of them he was really trying to convince. Maybe this was just one of those cultural differences she wouldn't be able to reconcile.

"Do you think Titania will... tire?" she asked. "Especially with Oberon dead?"

Raiker chuckled, and Petra was relieved to see him smiling again.

"Oh, I think Queen Titania the Almighty is going to live forever," he said. "She's started taking lovers now that he's gone. Had a child even. But she'll probably never bind herself to anyone else again. It's very rare to meet a fae with a second ring."

Petra chanced a glance at Raiker's wrist, which was currently obscured by the purple sequin jacket. Raiker grinned when he caught her looking and pulled back the sleeve, revealing his bare, tawny wrist.

"You know there's nothing there," he said. "I wouldn't be trying to get you in bed with me if there was."

"Actually, I was wondering if that was something you can glamour away."

Raiker shook his head and laughed.

"You don't understand. *Fae don't break vows.* Seelie or Unseelie. We're only worth as much as our word. If we vow to stay committed to someone, we do not stray from them until death. I vowed to protect you, and that means I will lay my life down for yours and repay anyone that causes you harm in kind."

So *that's* what it meant when he said she was under his protection. Petra wasn't sure she liked the sound of that at all. She was glad to have someone protecting her from the things that went bump in the night, but she didn't like the idea of anyone dying for her. She especially didn't like the idea of Raiker avenging her if she was already dead, and possibly losing his own life in the process.

Raiker put one warm hand on her cheek and turned her face towards his. They were almost nose-to-nose now, crouched there together in the tiny attic. His long fingers wound through her blonde hair.

"Tell me why you care if I'm bound to anyone," he said.

"WHEEEEE-OOOOOH!"

Petra tore her eyes away from Raiker's and pulled the ringing phone out of her pocket. She breathed a sigh of relief at the interruption, genuinely unsure what she would have done without it. *Probably Raiker. Raiker's what I would have done.*

"Hi. What's up?" she said.

The sigh died on her lips as Del's voice came through the phone. Del was sobbing, babbling something completely unintelligible through the tears.

"Whoa, slow down," Petra said, standing up. "What's wrong?"

"Gloria," Del choked out. "Gloria's missing."

Chapter Eleven

P etra upended her purse on the kitchen counter, scattering lipsticks, tampons, and crumpled receipts everywhere.

"Raiker, where the FUCK did you put my keys?!" she screamed.

"It wasn't me!" he protested, hovering behind her. "Well, it wasn't me *this time*..."

With a growl of exasperation, Petra shoved past him and charged into the living room. She ripped the cushions off the couch, tossing them behind her. There was a tightness in her chest, as if there wasn't enough air in the room.

"Do you have anything with her blood on it?" Raiker asked.

"No! Why- why do you think that's a thing I would have?!"

She stumbled away from the couch, nearly tripping on the discarded pillows, and ran towards the foyer.

Raiker stepped into her path and grabbed her. He trapped her in a tight, inescapable hug.

"Lass mich gehen!" Petra shouted, struggling to get away.

Raiker didn't let go. "Listen to me, Petra," his voice was calm and authoritative, "we will find her. Now, I can move a lot faster than your car can. I need you to take a breath and tell me where to start looking."

Petra drew in a long breath that exited her lips as a sob. She crumpled into Raiker's warm chest.

"She's *six*, Raiker..." Petra cried in a small voice.

Raiker shushed her and stroked her hair. Abruptly he stopped, turning his head towards the window.

"Is Del coming here?" he asked.

"No. Why—?"

And then Petra heard the car too. A nondescript black sedan pulled into her driveway. The door to the backseat opened, and out bounded a little girl with dark brown pigtails and a pink backpack.

Petra ran out of the house so fast she nearly banged the front door right off its hinges.

"Tante!" Gloria shouted, smiling through her missing front teeth.

Petra swept the girl off her feet and into a hug. Relief flooded through her so fast it made her dizzy. Her arms shook with it.

"Tante... you're crushing me..." Gloria complained with an over-dramatic groan.

Petra put Gloria back on her feet and knelt down to her level. She clutched the child's slim shoulders, checking her over for bruises or God knows what.

"Are you okay? What happened?" Petra asked.

"Mom and Dad were fighting so I ran away from home. I wanna live with you now." Gloria craned her neck to look behind Petra. "Who's the weird guy on your porch?"

"I'm gonna kill her," Del swore to Petra over the phone. "I'm gonna ground her till she's 40, and then I'm gonna kill her."

Petra hopped up on her kitchen counter, cradling the phone against her shoulder. "On the plus side, your kid's a genius."

"She stole her dad's phone and called an Uber. That's not genius, it's criminal."

"At least she's safe."

There was a squeal and a crash from the other room. Petra ran to the foyer in time to see Raiker and Gloria come screaming down the staircase riding a trashcan lid like a sled. It flipped as it hit the bottom step, sprawling them both onto the hardwood floor. Raiker took the brunt of the impact, with Gloria landing on his stomach.

"How did we do this time?" he asked.

Gloria held up her dad's phone and shook her head solemnly. "6.8 seconds. Not fast enough."

"Hmmm..." Raiker stroked his chin. "We're getting too much resistance. What if we lined the bottom of the luge with fabric?"

"Ooo! There's sheets in the closet! Come on!" Gloria grabbed Raiker by the hand and raced back up the stairs. She stopped and purposely jumped up and down on the squeaky step. The old wood made a noise like a howl.

"Say, 'hola lobito!'" Gloria demanded.

"*Hola lobito!*" Raiker repeated obediently. He jumped on the stair himself and then scooped Gloria up, carrying her over his shoulder the rest of the way to the linen closet.

Petra stood at the bottom, trying to decide if she should intervene.

"Nope," Del said. "I'm gonna kill her, and I'm gonna kill her dad for not having a better password on his phone, and then I'm gonna kill that fucking pig at the police station!"

"What'd the cop do?" Petra asked.

"Said she had to be missing at least four hours before they could direct resources to finding her."

Petra's hand clenched into a fist, false nails digging into her palm. Later, she was going to have a suggestion for Raiker about the next person who deserved to have raccoons invade their work place.

The voice of Gloria's dad, Joe, cut in in the background. "Jesus, Del. Not everything's a racist conspiracy."

"Naw, fuck that," Del shot back. "You know if it was a little white girl gone missing her face would have been all over the news."

The would-be-lugers returned to the landing at the top of the stairs. Raiker started duct taping a tablecloth to the trash can lid under Gloria's supervision.

Del stopped yelling at Joe and returned to the phone. "This *pinche de madre* got an injunction to stop me from visiting my grandma."

"You can't take my daughter out of the country and not tell me!" Joe yelled.

"Out of the–?" Del swore. "TJ is two and a half hours away, *with traffic!*"

Petra's call waiting beeped. She told Del she had to put her on hold for a sec, although she didn't think Del even heard her.

"I need you to come in. We're swamped," Beth said by way of greeting. "Someone called a bomb threat into the airport again. Good news is, we're definitely making goal this month."

"Bad news is, we're all gonna blow up and die," Sylvia yelled in the background, her words momentarily drowning out the sound of ringing phones.

Petra muted the call as Raiker and Gloria made another screaming run down the staircase. The sled bit it on the bottom step, propelling the occupants into the air. Raiker grabbed Gloria and rolled in midair, putting himself between her and the floor again. It wasn't a maneuver that seemed entirely keeping with the laws of physics.

"6.2!" Gloria declared. She stepped on Raiker's stomach as she climbed back to her feet. "Were you watching, Tante?"

Petra took the call back off mute and nodded at her niece enthusiastically.

"Beth, I um..." Petra looked at Gloria racing Raiker up the stairs and summoned her resolve, "I can't today. Family emergency."

"Bachman, I've got 106 check in's we didn't have an hour ago. *That's* an emergency," Beth snapped. She paused and sighed. "I'm sorry. Is everything okay?"

"Yeah. But I gotta go. I'll tell you about it later."

"Hang on, what family?" Beth asked. The contrition in her tone was replaced with suspicion. "Aren't they all in Germany?"

"Bye," Petra said, and hung up on Beth.

There was a moment where she stared at her phone, unsure if she'd made the right decision. Then she looked at Gloria, smiled, and put Del back on.

"—two drive by shootings, *and* a woman was found decapitated in an alley," Joe ranted. "And that's just the news from Tijuana *last week*."

"Look, Del," Petra cut in before Del could come up with her next retort. "You and Joe obviously have some things you need to... work out. And Gloria's not ready to accept that she has to go home yet. Why don't I watch her today? I'll have her back by bed time."

Del exhaled a long breath. "You don't have to work?"

"No," Petra said. "I've got nowhere to be but here."

Petra said her goodbyes to Del and then headed out to the garage. There was some old plywood behind the workbench. If she leaned it against the staircase, she was pretty sure they could get that luge run down to five seconds.

Petra returned Gloria with a belly full of In-N-Out and tiny Olympic rings painted on her nails. When Del opened the door, Gloria rushed into her mother's arms and told her she was sorry. Del held on to that kid like she might never let go. She surreptitiously wiped the tears from her eyes before she finally released her. She looked a mess, her dark hair sticking out every direction and puffy circles under her eyes.

"Can Raiker come over and play some time?" Gloria asked.

"Who's Raiker?" Del asked.

"Tante's new boyfriend."

"He's not," Petra interjected, her cheeks coloring. "He's um... he's a friend."

Del raised an eyebrow.

"We'll talk about it in the morning," Del said. "Go brush your teeth." She ushered Gloria inside and shut the door behind her. She turned back to Petra with a small smirk. "So, is this the naked kind of friend?"

"No! Well... *he'd* like to be. And..." the words spilled out of her in a rush. "I don't know. Maybe I do too, but I don't do hook ups." She remembered the lie from weeks ago and amended her statement. "I mean, I don't usually do hookups. And Raiker can't be more than a hook up because..."

He's a 2,000-year-old magic immortal being straight out of Oma's bedtime stories.

"Because he's Raiker," she finished.

Del laughed. "Normally, I'd invite you in to drink wine and drill down into whatever the hell *that* means, but," she yawned, "It has been a fucking day."

"Yeah, no, you should go to bed," Petra agreed.

"Screw my bed. I'm putting down a sleeping bag in front of Gloria's door."

Petra laughed and Del laughed with her. The sound came out slightly strangled, and after a moment Del's laughter shifted into the tears that were just under the surface.

"Am I a bad mom?" she asked.

"No!" Petra pulled her into a tight hug. "You're a great mom. Just... maybe try not to let Joe get under your skin while Gloria's around."

Del nodded and sniffed. "Thanks for being there today."

Petra gave her friend one last hug. "I'm sorry I haven't been there more."

Petra took the elevator back down to the parking garage, so lost in thought she nearly forgot where she had parked. She doubled back and finally found the Jetta in row E, next to a van that was so far over the line she couldn't open her door. Narrowly resisting the urge to key the minivan, Petra walked over to the passenger side.

"Hello Petra," a rumbling baritone voice said.

Her head snapped up, and she spotted the figure leaning against the hood of the car across from hers. A pixie, like Raiker, with dark skin and long dreadlocks studded with beads that caught the flickering overheard lights. Where Raiker was lean and svelte, this one was broad, with a hugely muscled chest like a bodybuilder and a massive wingspan. Another flicker of halogen bulbs and Petra realized he was also armed. A matching set of U-shaped blades, one strapped to each hip.

The creature followed the direction of her gaze. "Oh, you like these?" He unsheathed one and held it up. "I mostly use them to cut off limbs." He looked her up and down, as if he were trying to decide which limb to amputate first. "Don't worry. As long as you give me what I want, I won't hurt you."

"O-Okay," she said. She couldn't keep the tremor from her voice. The tremors seemed to have taken over her whole body– wobbling her knees, pounding in her heart, and stuttering her thoughts. She wanted to run. Instead, she forced her legs to take a stumbling step closer. "Y-You can have the key just... just put that away, please?"

A sparkle of amusement lit up his gold eyes and he sheathed his weapon. Petra made herself take another step and began to rummage in her purse. She still had the car keys in her other hand.

"It's in there?" he asked, indicating the purse.

Petra nodded and slipped her fingers into the brass knuckles.

He made a grab for the purse and Petra let him have it, pulling her hand free. She brought her knee up between his legs and then threw her whole weight into the punch, aiming for his nose. It glanced off his cheek instead, as he doubled over and dropped the purse. Petra whirled around to the passenger door, already frantically hitting the clicker to unlock it. She yanked the door open and tried to jump in, but a hand grabbed the back of her shirt. The fabric ripped as he pulled her back, slammed the door shut, and then slammed her into it. Her face smashed into the roof of the car. Petra tasted blood in her mouth.

The pixie yanked her head up by the ponytail and he brought his blade to her neck. Petra froze, breathing hard. Each exhale came out as a panicked whine. His weight pressed into her, pinning her in place.

"Do not try that again," he spat between gritted teeth.

He took the brass knuckles and the car keys from her hands, flinging them to the other side of the garage. Then he turned her around and forced her chin up so that she met his eyes.

"*Petra Adelina Bachman, where is the key?*" he demanded.

Petra could feel the weight of the push in his words, that irresistible pull to do what he had asked, but she didn't have the answer he wanted.

"I don't know!" she cried. "I don't know anything!"

He left out a long sigh. "I don't have time for this."

Petra felt a sharp pain as he cracked the pommel of the blade down on her head, and then everything went black.

Chapter Twelve

When Petra woke again, it was to a screaming pain in her head that seemed to pulse every few seconds. Her eyes fluttered open and, unable to comprehend what it was she was seeing, she shut them and opened them again, blinking slowly in the dim light. She was looking at something brown and slightly porous that let in a filtered amount of the sunlight outside. The muscles in her limbs ached. Something was... pulled over her face? Like a blindfold maybe?

Petra looked down, and realized her arms and legs ached because they were pulled tight against her. She was curled into a ball, and she could see the rest of her body, so it wasn't a blindfold she was looking at it was... it was...

I'm in a bag.

She had been stuffed into a scratchy burlap sack. The pulsing throbbing in her head was matching the cadence of the footfalls of the thing that was carrying her, slung over his shoulder with her back pressed against his. It was putting a terrible pressure on the cut down her back, but the bandage still seemed to mostly be in place. Her long hair was caught up where the sack was gathered into a knot at the top, tugging every so often and sending the pain in her skull into overdrive. Petra tried to reach up to pull her hair down, but she couldn't move her upper arms more than an inch from where they were pinned to her sides. If she really tried, she could just barely reach her forearms up and feel the back of her head. She couldn't stretch up as high as the wound, but she could feel the sticky blood that had matted into her hair. Feeling a little sick to her stomach now, Petra lowered her hand again.

It was then that the thing carrying her began to sing, and Petra recognized the deep, booming voice of the fairy from the parking garage.

"No care and no sorrow,
A fig for the morrow!
We'll laugh and be merry,
Sing neigh down derry!"

"Hello?" Petra said, tentatively.

"You're awake," the fairy said in a friendly, almost conversational tone.

"Could you put me down please?" she asked as nicely as she could manage.

The thing carrying her did not slow his stride.

"If you don't tell me where the key is, I'm going to put you down on the wrong side of a waterfall," he said.

Petra realized that she could hear water, a dull roar somewhere in the distance.

Where the hell is there a waterfall in L.A.?

It was cold too. Petra suspected she should be sweltering inside the burlap sack, but instead the scratchy fabric seemed to be providing a thin layer of protection against the elements. Bright sunlight pierced through, so either she'd been unconscious all night or...

Toto, I don't think we're in California anymore.

"Okay, how about you let me out of this bag and we can talk about that?" Petra suggested.

The thing laughed at her.

"Nice try, little girl," he said. "Don't think I don't know about your friend."

"My friend?"

"The fae that warded your house and closed off the fairy ring there. You obviously have some powerful allies. But they won't find you now. This sackcloth was woven by Calceo the Clever himself. Even the most powerful fairy won't be able to trace you here."

Petra took a moment to let it sink in that she was entirely on her own and then proceeded to claw helplessly at the side of the sack until the nail on her index finger broke off. The roar of the waterfall was getting louder, and the fairy raised his voice to sing over it.

"O'er hill and o'er dale,
So happy I roam,
Work light and live well,
All the world is my home."

"Hang on, I know that song," Petra said. "That's from 'Hans in Luck.'"

"It's from what?"

"*Kinder- und Hausmärchen.* Um, *Grimms' Fairy Tales.*"

The pixie grunted at her.

"Never heard of them."

Petra had a well-worn German copy of *Grimms' Fairy Tales* on the shelf next to her bed. It was an old edition, too old to even have the copyright information in the front of the book. Oma used to read her the stories at bedtime. It was only when Petra grew old enough to read herself that she realized how many embellishments Oma had added to those archetypal tales.

I'm in a fairy tale.

This was exactly the sort of thing that happened to people in fairy tales. Unsuspecting humans met malevolent fairies, got tricked into magic sacks, and tossed over waterfalls.

How did they usually get out of this in the stories?

"Hey!" Petra said a few minutes later, "How about we make a bet?"

The fairy stopped walking.

"What sort of a bet?" he asked, sounding intrigued.

"I bet that I can tell you a riddle that you can't solve."

There was a long pause as he considered her. "What do I get if I win?" he asked.

"I'll tell you where the key is."

Seeing as how she didn't actually know where it was, that seemed like a pretty safe thing to gamble with.

The fairy snorted. "You're already going to tell me where the key is. Once you get a good look at how far down your little flightless body is going to fall, you're going to become a lot more forthcoming."

"Okay," Petra said, trying to keep her voice from shaking. "What else do you want?"

Petra wasn't entirely sure she wanted to hear his answer. Based on everything Raiker had told her about the Unseelie, she figured there was an even chance this one wanted to eat her or worse.

"You can ask me one riddle, and if I can guess the answer, you have to tell me the true name of the fae that warded your house."

"Five riddles," Petra countered, "And I don't know his true name, but I can give you his second name and... What else do you want?"

"Three riddles. And I'm getting ready to throw you over a waterfall. I'm not sure how much more you have to offer me."

"Right. About that–"

"I assume if you win, you want me to not throw you over the waterfall. His second name, and current location."

"Second name, the last location I saw him in. And if I win, you have to let me go... somewhere *safe*, not the wrong side of a waterfall. And you will never do me any harm– wait, do me or any of my descendants harm for as long as you live."

He laughed. "That's a lot of caveats, Petra. Are you sure you've worded them carefully enough?"

Petra took a moment to genuinely consider the question before answering.

"Yes."

"Then we have a deal."

"No. Say it back to me. Swear it."

He grumbled and set the bag down on the ground. Petra was happy it wasn't pulling on her hair anymore, but otherwise being set down didn't provide much relief.

"Petra Adelina Bachman," he said, "You can ask me three riddles. If I can answer all three correctly you will give me the second name and the last known location of the fairy that warded your house. But if I cannot answer one or more of your riddles correctly, I will release you from this bag somewhere safe. And I will never maliciously cause you or any of your descendants physical harm for as long as I live. This I swear, on my name, Follium the Unwavering, artisan healer and heir to the Marquisate of Lightwood.

"And when we're done with this nonsense, I'm going to start by cutting off your eyelids. Hurry up and ask me your riddles so we can get on with it."

Now she just needed to remember some riddles.

"What can you hold in your right hand but not in your left?" she asked.

"Your left hand," he answered with barely a moment's hesitation.

"Shit."

Follium laughed at her. "What else have you got, little girl?"

Petra racked her brain.

"How's that one go? Ummm... Okay. I am the first on earth, second in heaven. I appear twice in a week, though you can only see me once in a year. What am I?"

Follium paused.

"Say it again," he said slowly.

"I am the first on earth, second in heaven. I appear twice in–"

"The letter 'E.'"

"*Shit.*"

He laughed again.

"Only one more try now," he reminded her. "Better make it a good one."

How did they usually get out of this in the stories?

Usually, they *cheat.* In "The Riddle" the prince asked the princess "What slew none, and yet slew twelve?" a query she couldn't possibly know the answer to, because she hadn't been with him to see 12 men die after eating a poisoned raven. Bilbo Baggins asked Gollum what he had in his pocket. What could she ask this fairy that he wouldn't ever know the answer to?

"A guest comes in and asks for a Junior Executive Suite for two nights. There's one vacant, unreserved Junior Executive Suite left in the hotel, but when the front desk clerk goes to book it, the computer reservation system tells her that the vacant room is unavailable. Why?"

Several seconds of stunned silence followed.

"*What?*"

Petra allowed herself a triumphant smile. "You need me to say it again?"

Follium began to mumble furiously under his breath. They weren't words in a language that Petra understood, but if she had to guess from his tone, she was pretty sure he was cussing her out.

"What's a computer?" he said finally.

"Nope," Petra said. "If you wanted hints, you should have negotiated for hints. Your lack of knowledge about basic human technology is not my problem."

She was laughing now, no, giggling, nearly giddy. Positively bursting with overconfidence and the satisfaction of knowing she had bested this thing that by all accounts should have been the death of her. She was vibrating with it.

After another minute's hesitation and quite a lot more swear words, Follium untied the knot at the top of the sack. It fell down at her sides and Petra collapsed backwards onto the ground, laughing so hard now there were tears in her eyes. She stretched out her arms and legs, groaning as her cramped muscles screamed in protest.

"The room was available the first night but not the second, and the guest wanted it for two nights," she said between giggles.

By way of response, Follium only grunted and muttered darkly.

Petra was looking up at a canopy of evergreen treetops partially shrouded in mist, no doubt from the nearby waterfall which continued to roar somewhere to the left of her. She was lying on a bed of snow, and it was rapidly seeping into her thin, torn clothes. Petra stood up on wobbly legs, teeth chattering.

Her captor looked much more comfortable in tight pants, a vest, and a long, blood red coat with flowers embroidered in silver. It wasn't an outfit that would be appropriate for snow by human standards, but he seemed nice and warm in it.

At least until he took the coat off. He shivered and held it out to her with one hand. Petra stared at it, sensing a trap.

"Just take the damn thing," Follium snapped.

Petra took the coat. The moment she slipped it on it shrunk, tailoring itself to her shape. Petra buttoned it up with shaking hands, grateful for the warmth it provided. But the cold air still sliced through the back of her wet shirt, and it took her a moment to realize it was because there were two long slits sewn into the back of the coat. Holes for his wings.

For the very first time, it occurred to Petra that maybe Raiker almost never wore a shirt because putting one on was a pain in the ass.

"Thank you," Petra said.

"You can repay me by promising not to tell anyone I lost a bet to a flightless human," he said. "Even if you did cheat."

Next to them was a raging stream at least six yards across, the water moving too quickly in most places to freeze over. It ended in a 300-foot drop into a partially frozen lake below.

"Where are we?" Petra asked.

"Uh... I believe you call it... India," he said.

Well, that's a new passport stamp.

Petra swallowed hard and scanned the forest for any signs of civilization. She was already starting to lose feeling in her feet, the snow seeping into her Chucks. If she had to walk until she found someone... *if* she found someone...

"I said let me go 'somewhere safe'," she said. "You have to take me home. You can't just leave me here."

"You don't need to worry about that," he said.

The fairy unsheathed the u-shaped weapons at his side and her disquiet only increased. Petra backed towards the stream, nearly losing her footing on a patch of ice.

"Hey, you don't need the sword-thingies," she said in a shaking voice.

"Arakhs," he corrected. "And I'm not an oathbreaker. I said I wouldn't hurt you."

"Then what do you need the arakhs for?"

Follium plunged the blades into the ground and then stepped back several yards, leaving the emerald-crusted hilts sticking out of the snow.

"Whoever you belong to is no doubt coming for you shortly, and I wouldn't want him to get the wrong impression of the situation once he arrives," he said. "If he doesn't show up, I'll take you home. Promise."

Follium leaned back against a tree and crossed his arms, shivering against the cold. He produced a flask from his pants pocket and took a long swig of whatever was inside.

"You're really just gonna stand there and wait for him?" Petra asked after some time.

"Why? Is there something else you'd rather I be doing?" he asked. "If you've anything to trade I could take a look at that wound on your back."

Petra fingered the top of the bandage covering the anguana's claw mark.

"No thanks," she said. "You can't fix it anyway."

Follium smirked.

"You mean the fairy you belong to couldn't fix it. You've no idea what I'm capable of."

He took another sip of his drink. There was no sound save for the roar of the waterfall. Petra stretched, trying to work out the cramps in her muscles.

Suddenly, Raiker appeared next to her, his flaming blue sword clutched in his hand.

"Petra! You're alive! Oh, thank the gods you're alive!"

Before she could say anything, Raiker turned from her and advanced on Follium, standing tall and menacing with his sword held high.

"I am Raiker the Rogue, swindler, plunderer, and housebreaker extraordinaire!" he roared. "This human is under my protection, and if you lay a hand on her again, I will destroy you!"

"You're a little late," Petra said.

Follium's broad face broke into a grin and he laughed. Raiker looked from him to Petra and back again, confused and still clutching his sword.

"Are— are you not in danger?" he stammered.

"Not anymore," Petra said. "He lost my bet, and I made him swear he wouldn't hurt me."

"Oh. Well... well, that's good then," Raiker said, sounding surprised, and possibly even a little put out.

"Duplicitous shrew," Follium said, scowling. "You said you wouldn't tell anyone."

Raiker rounded on him.

"You do not speak to my lady that way," he said in a dangerous voice.

"Raiker, let's just go," Petra said.

Raiker ignored her and advanced on Follium again.

"Apologize," he demanded.

Follium smiled at him.

"Sure," he said. "Just as soon as you apologize for roping me into that bar fight in Eastbend."

Raiker froze.

"Follium?" Raiker said.

And, much to Petra's indignation, Raiker lowered his sword and embraced the fae that just tried to murder her like an old friend.

Chapter Thirteen

"How long has it been?" Raiker said as he broke the hug. "Three decades?"

"Three and a half at least!" said Follium.

"Too long! I haven't seen this form before."

"Oh, this is just one I've been using the last few years or so."

"I like it! It's so broad. And long hair suits you."

"HEY!" Petra shouted.

They whirled to face her. Raiker seemed taken aback by the rage on her face.

"He tried to kill me! I think I have a concussion."

Raiker rushed over to her, taking stock of her injuries for the first time. He turned back to Follium.

"You broke her!" said Raiker. His voice came out in a whine, like a petulant child upset someone had smashed his favorite toy.

Follium snorted. "She gave as good as she got. Kicked my balls so hard they just about landed in my throat."

Raiker's eyes sparkled with amusement.

"Here, I can fix her," Follium said.

He reached his hand out toward Petra and she smacked it away.

"Don't you fucking touch me!" she snapped.

Follium laughed and retreated a respectful distance.

"She's feisty, this one. And strong willed. Is she even really human?"

"Oh, she's definitely human. She's just impressively stubborn," said Raiker.

Raiker's fingertips began to glow with that soft white light and Petra was relieved to feel the pain leaving her aching head as he ran them over her.

As he worked, he asked Follium, "What's got you out playing mercenary? This isn't exactly your line of work."

"500,000 crowns is what's got me playing mercenary." He chuckled. "The client said they'd hired someone, but he was working too slow. That'd be you then?"

Raiker nodded as he ran his thumb over the bruise on Petra's cheek.

"I understand they've extended the offer to myself and quite a lot of other parties since," Follium said.

Petra saw the worry flash in Raiker's eyes before he turned away from her.

"How many other parties?" Raiker asked.

Follium shook his head. "You shouldn't have taken her under your protection, old friend..."

Raiker shifted uncomfortably. "I like this one," he said. "I can keep her safe."

Petra snorted and scowled at the both of them.

"Will you *please* apologize already?" Raiker asked.

Follium kneeled in front of Petra, adopting an expression of contrition that wasn't incredibly convincing.

"My lady, I apologize for the distress I caused you," Follium said. "Please be assured that I never actually intended to kill you."

Petra's scowl deepened.

"So, threatening to toss me off the waterfall, that was just a bluff?"

Petra felt Raiker's hand tighten on her shoulder, and this time Follium looked genuinely guilty.

"If I had known she was yours I would *never* have..."

Follium's voice trailed off, and the silence hung there for a few seconds before Raiker adopted a smile that didn't quite meet his eyes.

"Water under the bridge, old friend," Raiker said.

Petra shoved Raiker's hand off her and stalked away from them, swearing under her breath. She walked to the edge of the cliff and leaned over slightly, watching the water rush down into the icy lake below. There was a great hole where the waterfall hit the surface of the lake, and everything beyond that was frozen. Even small parts of the waterfall itself were frozen.

Petra shivered. With a better coat and better circumstances, it would have been beautiful. After a few minutes Raiker walked up behind her and reached for her hand. Petra twitched it away.

"Please come away from there," he said.

Petra was surprised to hear something like fear in his voice. She supposed he didn't put a lot of stock in her human levels of coordination and was worried she'd stumble right off the edge. With some reluctance, she allowed him to lead her back over to the trees where Follium waited.

"I should get her home. It's too cold for her here. Too cold for me too," Raiker said, rubbing his hands over his bare arms.

"We'll catch up later," Follium said, and he hugged Raiker again.

Raiker broke off the embrace, but kept a hand on Follium's wrist. He eyed his friend nervously.

"She *is* under my protection..." Raiker said.

Follium swore.

"You can't be serious."

"Come on, be reasonable."

"I didn't even hurt her that badly."

"You still hurt her."

"*Fine.*"

Follium held his arms at his sides in a position of surrender. Raiker twirled his sword in his hand and caught it by the blade. In one quick motion, he swung it and whacked the hilt on the side of Follium's head. Follium staggered and clapped his hand to the injury. It stopped bleeding a moment later.

"I did not hit her that hard!" Follium protested.

Feeling slightly less angry now, Petra allowed Raiker wrap his arms around her. He hesitated before doing whatever magic would transport them back home.

"I've never done this with a human before," he confessed to Follium.

"Just keep a good grip on her," Follium said. "She'll be fine. Although I hear for them it can sting a little... You were alright on the trip here, right?"

Petra was pretty sure she had been blissfully unconscious on the "trip" here, but at least she could say for sure that it hadn't killed her. Feeling apprehensive, she clung to Raiker's neck as he wrapped his arms tighter around her waist. The nervous look in his eyes was not terribly reassuring.

"Here goes nothing," he said.

Later, Petra would tell Raiker it had felt like someone was tearing her limbs from her body, but on further reflection she'd come to decide the pain was greater than even that. It was worse than having her limbs torn off; it was more like every single *molecule* of her tore apart and disintegrated. She lost all sense of where she was, or even who she was. She was only pain. Blinding, all-encompassing pain.

And then a second later it was over, and she was still clinging to Raiker exactly as she had been before, only now she was doing it in her living room. Petra felt her legs give out, and if it weren't for Raiker holding her she would have fallen. A moment later she did fall when she retched, and he dropped her a split second before she would have vomited all over him. Petra's knees hit the ground. She threw up all over the floor, shaking and drenched in sweat.

"Sorry!" Raiker said. "I didn't mean to drop you!"

Raiker kept babbling apologies as Petra threw up again. She continued to heave, sob, and shake until there was nothing left in her.

"Never... *ever*... do that again," she said finally.

"Yes, my lady," Raiker said quickly, "Never again, my lady. We'll just go the slow way next time."

Raiker helped her to her feet.

"'Sting a little' my ass," Petra mumbled. "What's that feel like for you?"

"Uh..." Raiker pushed a lock of red hair out of his eyes, looking guilty. "It sort of tickles a bit."

"Of course, it does. Fucking fairies..."

Petra stumbled towards the stairs, and Raiker had the good sense to let her go.

After the chaos of the day her bathroom felt like an oasis of blissful normality. Petra turned the knob on the old clawfoot bathtub and let the steaming water pour in as she peeled off the borrowed coat and her wet clothes. She made a point to not look at herself in the mirror, because if she looked even a fraction as bad as she felt, she didn't want to see it. She poured in a cup of Epsom salt and the better part of a bottle of lavender scented bubble bath and sank in as far as her 5'11" frame would allow. She'd run the water too hot, but she let it wash over her anyway. Her skin burned briefly before settling into a comfortable numbness that eased away the cramps in her muscles. The salt stung the open wound on her back, but that stopped hurting after a while too.

When she finally emerged from the tub, she was lobster red and pruney, but mercifully clean. She might have been fooling herself, but for a moment she could imagine that all the things that had happened today had gone down the drain with the tub water.

Petra wrapped the towel tightly around her and opened the bathroom door. The steam spilled out into the bedroom and immediately fogged up the outside of the glass of red wine sitting in front of the door. She smiled as she knelt to pick it up, her fingers leaving an imprint on the steam as she took a sip. This was good wine, or at least she suspected it was. Definitely not the floor wine from the night before.

She took a second sip and noticed the robe that was laid out on the bed. It was pale blue satin with white lace trim and the price tags were still on it. The price tags were in French. After casting a suspicious glance around the room Petra dropped her towel and slipped the robe on. The fabric was smooth and cool against her bare skin.

Petra stepped out of her bedroom and found Shitpoo waiting for her at the top of the stairs. He bounded over and skidded to a stop at Petra's feet, rolling over and exposing his belly expectantly. Petra smiled and scooped the little dog up one handed, thinking he was starting to grow on her as he nuzzled her face. Aside from Shitpoo's excitable panting, the house was surprisingly quiet. No creaking footsteps from Raiker moving around the house. No clanging or thumping as he raided her possessions. No subtle hum of his wings.

What she did notice was a smell; some wonderful aroma of garlic and butter wafting through the house that got stronger as she walked downstairs. She followed the scent to the kitchen, where she found the table set for one. There were candles burning in an ornate silver candelabra she had never seen before, casting a glow on a plate of ravioli garnished with sage and drenched in cream sauce. It was the kind of ravioli you needed at least four bites for each one. Petra sat down and sliced into one, revealing some kind of squash mixture on the inside. She took one bite and then narrowly resisted the urge to shove the rest of it into her mouth.

Three bites later and still the kitchen was empty save for her and Shitpoo.

"Raiker?" she called out.

The moment she spoke his name he appeared. He was perched on the kitchen island, watching her, with his wings folded in behind him and his fingers and toes just hanging off the edge. His eyes were moss green now, and his hair was a shade of gold that almost looked like a color which occurred in nature.

"I'm here," he said, "I mean, I've been here. I didn't go anywhere. I was just um..."

"Hiding?" Petra offered.

Raiker flushed.

"It didn't seem as though you wanted me here." He cast his green eyes down to his toes and spoke again without looking at her. "I'm sorry I failed you today. I took you under my protection and then I left you alone. And I know Follium would never have seriously harmed you, but it could easily have been someone worse than him and then—"

"Hey," Petra interrupted. "Don't beat yourself up. I got out of it okay on my own. I'm not mad at you."

Raiker looked up from his feet and tentatively unfolded his wings. "You're not?"

"I'm not," Petra insisted. "Just a lot of weird happened today. I needed a little... human time."

If she was being honest, Petra would say she was more than a little mad at him still for being so quick to forgive his old buddy Follium, and maybe just a bit mad about the horrendous trip back from who-knows-where India. But she certainly wasn't mad that he hadn't shown up to save her. And as for the rest, the shame in his eyes was making it hard to do anything but forgive him.

Petra pointed at the plate of ravioli. "Did you steal one of these for yourself too?"

Raiker shook his head.

"Well, go get one and have dinner with me," she said. "We can talk about how we're going to find this key before something else stuffs me in a bag."

Raiker didn't seem to find that very funny, but he did flutter down off the counter and vanish to wherever he'd produced dinner from. Petra had just enough time to pour him a glass of the Liber Pater Bordeaux sitting on the table and refill her own before he returned and set his plate down.

"So, here's my theory," Petra said. "We're not getting very far with the limited information we have. Maybe if we knew more about this key, we could narrow the search down from 'everything my Oma ever possessed'. I was thinking maybe you know someone we could ask. Why aren't you sitting down?"

Raiker moved from where he was awkwardly standing next to his chair over to her side of the table and took her hand in his.

"Petra," he said, "I will do everything in my power to keep harm from coming to you again."

"I know," Petra replied, with a smile that carefully concealed her apprehension. She squeezed his hand. "I never thanked you for helping with Gloria yesterday."

Raiker shook his head. "I didn't do anything."

"No, you did," Petra insisted. "She was having a day, and you made her happy." She paused and looked away from his piercing gaze. "You helped me too, when I was scared something had happened to her. You didn't have to do any of that."

She glanced up to find Raiker still staring at her. His eyes seemed to melt into hers.

"Yes, I did," he said.

Petra let go of his hand and cleared her throat. She took a long drink of her wine.

"So... the key..." she said. "Do you have any smarter friends we could talk to about it? Preferably one that won't cut off my eyelids?"

Chapter Fourteen

P etra picked up the next application in the
stack on her desk. Her first major decision
as AGM was finding a new Front Desk Manager
to replace her. This applicant, Charlie Myers,
graduated from UCLA two years ago. He had
a degree in hospitality management, was fluent
in English, Spanish, French, and Mandarin, and
he'd been working at hotels since he was fifteen.

Shit. I'm underqualified.

She took another bite of her sandwich and
flipped through the recommendation letters
attached to Charlie's resume.

"Any good candidates?" Beth asked, stepping
out of her office and into Petra's.

"Mmm-hmm," Petra said through a mouthful
of sandwich.

"Hello?" a man's voice called.

Hope was up in an empty room, using her lunch break to pump breastmilk. Petra had left the door to the back office cracked open, so she could hear if anyone needed her out there. At the sound of the man's voice, Petra started chewing faster.

"I got it, Bachman," Beth said.

Petra nodded gratefully and took another bite of her lunch. She half-listened to Beth checking in the walk-in as she returned to her stack of applications.

"If I could just see your credit card, please," Beth said.

"What's a— What for?" the guest asked.

"To pay for your room."

"Oh. Can I pay with cash? I have cash."

There was a soft thump as something landed on the black granite top of the standing reception desk.

"Is this enough?" the guest asked.

"That's..." Beth seemed to lose her composure for a moment, but then she recovered smoothly. "Yes, Mr. Grimm. It's $210 per night for the room, and if you'd like to pay cash, I just need to hold an additional $200 deposit. And I'll need to see your ID please."

"My ID? Yes. Umm..."

He paused for a moment. "What's your name, beautiful?"

"It's Beth." She let out a slightly startled laugh.

"Yes, I can read that on that thing on your shirt. What's your full name?"

Oh fuck me.

As quietly as possible, Petra opened the bottom drawer of her desk and removed the old-fashioned, cast-iron clothing iron she'd found in the attic yesterday morning.

"Elizabeth Marie Etheridge," Beth answered.

Petra held the heavy iron by the handle behind her back and slowly approached the doorway.

"*Elizabeth Marie Etheridge,*" the man said, "*You already saw my ID. And it had all the... whatever an ID is supposed to have. It was an excellent ID.*"

Petra pushed the door open and stepped behind the front desk. Beth was staring transfixed at a man with tan skin and dark blue eyes. He wore an expensive looking, well-tailored suit, and he was just a little bit too pretty to be believed. The man rested his hand on the counter, right next to a small canvas bag overflowing with hundred-dollar bills.

"Hi," Petra said in her very best customer service voice. "I'm the Assistant General Manager. Is there something I can help you with?"

And then she brought the iron down on his hand.

Beth shrieked as the handsome man who had been standing there a moment before shimmered out of existence, replaced by a fairy with a hooknose and scale-covered skin. His dark blue eyes shifted to a dimly familiar light brown and instead of the tailored suit he was clad only in a pair of faded black pants. He yelped and pulled his crushed fingers close to his body.

"Raiker?" Petra asked.

"*Elizabeth Marie Etheridge, stop screaming,*" he commanded. "Petra, what the hell did I do to deserve that?!"

His voice had been deeper before, but now it returned to its usually high melodic tone.

"How was I supposed to know it was you?!" Petra yelled. "I thought you were going to stuff me in a bag! What are you doing here?"

Beth had sat down on the floor with her hands over her mouth, eyes wide with terror and silent tears running down her cheeks.

"Shit. Is she gonna be okay?" Petra asked.

Raiker fluttered up to where he could see her over the counter.

"I'm sure she'll be fine."

He didn't sound incredibly convincing. Petra watched as he used his other hand to heal his mangled fingers. She found herself staring at the way his fingers ended not with nails, but with short, thick claws. Raiker looked up from his work and met her eyes.

"Could you... could you not look at me please?" he asked.

After a moment's hesitation Petra tore her eyes away and turned around, facing the Hammond Hotel logo on the wall. It was a long time before Raiker told her to turn around again, five minutes at least, and Petra spent most of it worried someone else was going to walk into the lobby and see him. She made a mental note to wipe this afternoon's security footage later. When she finally faced him again, he had shifted back to the glamour with the dark blue eyes and the deeper voice.

"That's better," he said, sighing in a self-satisfied way.

"Why do you look like that?" Petra asked.

Raiker seemed confused by the question.

"I'm sure you'd rather look at this than my true face," he said.

"No, I mean your glamour's different."

"Oh," he said, and then flashed her a mischievous grin. "I'm in disguise. Do you like it? I got the suit right this time, didn't I? I copied it from James Bond."

Now that he mentioned it, there was something about his features that seemed a little reminiscent of a young Sean Connery. Like a blue eyed, Latin American 007.

"You watch James Bond movies?" Petra asked.

"No, but you do. I found a stack of them in your living room cabinet. He's beautiful."

As he spoke, he walked around the counter and crouched down next to Beth.

"No, the last moving picture I saw was... *Nosferatu,*" he continued. "Seems like they've gotten a lot better since then."

"Yeah, we've got talkies now and everything," Petra said. "You should see the new *Star Wars.*"

Raiker turned Beth's face towards his and spoke to her softly. "*Elizabeth Marie Etheridge you gave us all quite a scare.*"

"I did?" Beth said, sounding dazed.

"*You did. You fainted.*"

"I... I did faint," Beth repeated. "And I thought I saw... No, I *did* see..."

Beth closed her eyes and shook her head.

"Tell her it was a hallucination," Petra suggested.

"I know how to do it," Raiker snapped before turning his attention back to Beth. *"Elizabeth... Elizabeth Marie Etheridge. Beautiful, stupid woman, look at me. Focus."*

Beth met his eyes again.

"You fainted and your mind is playing tricks on you because you haven't eaten. Why don't you eat, Beth?"

"I'm on a juice cleanse," Beth said without much conviction.

"That sounds like nonsense. Let's try that again. Elizabeth Marie Etheridge, why don't you eat?"

"Because it makes me feel like I'm in control of my life," she said.

"Alright, well not eating is making you see frightening things and pass out. You don't want that to happen again, do you?"

"No."

"Then you are going to go eat something and after that you're going to find a less harmful way to feel in control. Try creating something. Or having sex."

Beth nodded and then looked at Petra for the first time since she sat down on the floor. She laughed.

"Here I am covering for you, and I just realized I skipped lunch," she said. "You got it from here, Bachman?"

"Of course," Petra said, a little taken aback.

Beth bounded to her feet and wandered off towards the kitchen without so much as a backward glance at Raiker and Petra.

Raiker walked back around to the customer side of the desk.

"Are you going to finish renting me a room?" he asked.

Petra looked at the open reservation on the screen. Beth had been in the middle of reserving an executive suite on the top floor to Mr. Jacob Grimm, checking out one month from now.

"And before you try to argue with me, you should know that it's either this or I stop letting you leave the house. I have to be able to be close to you and you're always here."

Petra watched over Raiker's shoulder as Beth sat down in the dining room with a milkshake glass full of chocolate pudding and a long spoon.

"I didn't know," Petra said. "How did you know?"

Raiker turned in the direction she was looking in time to see Beth eat a big spoonful of pudding.

"Oh. That," Raiker said. "Her body is eating itself. I can smell it. It's not a good smell."

Petra shuddered.

"You know what is a good smell?" he said, "Your scent when you're thinking about all the things you pretend you're not interested in doing with me."

Petra felt her face flush and she hoped against hope he was making that up. She focused her attention on the computer instead, finishing the reservation with a fictive address and phone number.

"Yeah, okay. Let's go back to the part where you said you're not going to let me leave the house, because I am an autonomous adult who can go wherever I damn well please," Petra snapped.

"So stubborn," Raiker chided with a laugh.

"I've been called worse. Now do you have actual money for this room? We don't accept fairy gold."

Raiker returned to the hotel about thirty minutes later and paid for the room using cash he pulled out of nine different wallets and two purses. Petra showed him how to work the television and warned him not to bother her.

That worked for about a day and a half.

"Petra, Mr. Grimm's on line two for you again," Hope said.

Petra sighed and set down the rooming list she was working on.

"Thanks, Hope. Put him through."

The line clicked and the baritone voice Raiker had adopted as "Mr. Grimm" came over the phone.

"Hello? Are you still there?" he said.

Petra was keenly aware of Beth's presence in her office next door.

"What can I help you with, Mr. Grimm?" she asked.

"Petra!" Raiker said. His voice rose back up to its usual octave. "Is it time to go home yet? I've watched all the movies."

Curious, Petra turned to her computer and pulled up Mr. Grimm's folio. So far, Raiker had rung up nearly $50 in pay-per-view movies, including *The First Purge, Incredibles 2, The*

Greatest Showman, and a good six hours' worth of pornography. He had also eaten all the candy in the mini bar.

"Alright, I didn't watch all the 'adult entertainment' movies. They're very... monotonous. And no one in them ever looks like they're having any fun. Why are they having sex if it's not fun?"

Petra stifled a laugh and chanced a glance at Beth's office before answering. Beth was in the middle of a phone call with corporate.

"Well, for the money I assume," Petra said.

"They get paid for that?!" Raiker let out a bark of laughter. "They should at least be better at it then. Someone should pay me for it. I'm very good at it."

"Yeah, most men think they are," Petra replied, rolling her eyes.

Raiker's voice dropped to an undertone.

"I'm not a man, Petra," he whispered. "I can do things to you that men can't."

He let the words hang there as Petra struggled desperately to remember just why it was she kept saying no to him.

"What...What kind of things?" she asked.

"Come up to my room and I'll show you."

Petra heard Beth slam her phone back into the receiver.

"Thank you, Mr. Grimm. Please let me know if you need anything else," Petra said in a nervous rush and she slammed her own phone down before he had a chance to protest.

Petra did not go up to Raiker's room, although she did spend quite a lot of time wondering what other magical things that body of his was capable of.

She didn't get much work done the rest of the day.

When Petra went to cover the desk so Hope could go pump, she found Raiker draped over a chair in the lobby, waiting for her.

"You have to go back to your room," Petra hissed.

"Honestly? I think I might. It's only mildly more interesting down here than it is up there," Raiker said.

He bounded out of the chair and approached the desk.

"Is it time to leave yet?" he asked a just a little too loudly.

"Soon," Petra promised. "And please keep your voice down."

"Good. Because I made contact with someone who might know something about the key, and I promised we'd meet them at dusk."

"Meet them where?"

"At the park down the road from here."

"Oh," Petra said, trying not to sound too disappointed that they wouldn't be going to Arcadia.

"Everyone here is miserable. Even the air is miserable," Raiker whined. "The only green thing I can see is that big trash bin out the window,"

Petra gazed around the lobby, which was primarily populated by old men in business suits hunched over their laptops, not talking to each other. Mr. Clark was talking to his wife on his cell phone, reassuring her that he was not having an affair as vehemently and as quietly as possible. Another guest was Skyping with the children he hadn't seen in three weeks.

"They're not all miserable," Petra insisted, although she couldn't manage too much conviction.

"She is," Raiker said, pointing.

Petra cringed inwardly as she watched Sharon Holly charge across the lobby straight towards her.

"I don't know what kind of establishment you think you're running here, but I expect much better for the amount of money I'm paying you," Ms. Holly snapped.

Raiker looked from Ms. Holly to Petra and raised his eyebrows. Petra tried to ignore him as she pasted on a smile and addressed the irate middle-aged white woman standing in front of her.

"I'm so sorry, Ms. Holly. Was there something specific wrong with your accommodations?" she asked.

"I found this on my pillow," she spat.

Ms. Holly set a disposable shower cap down on the desk. Curled inside it was a single hair. Petra glanced up from the strand of bottle blonde hair to the bottle blonde angry woman leaning on the desk.

"Is it... possible that might be your hair?" Petra asked as delicately as she could.

Ms. Holly glared up at her.

"No, it's not my hair. It's that incompetent Mexican girl that cleans my room. Don't you make the help wear hair nets?"

Petra kept her smile fixed in place as she turned to her computer and looked up the housekeeper assigned to Sharon Holly's room. It was Martina, who incidentally had hair so dark it almost looked violet in the right lighting. It was also worth noting that Martina was in her forties, probably about the same age as Ms. Holly and hardly a "girl".

And Petra managed to keep all that to herself, but either because Raiker's smirk was distracting her or because she was just that tired of Ms. Holly's shit, she couldn't quite stop herself from saying, "Actually, she's Chilean-American."

"She's what?" Ms. Holly said.

"Martina's family is from Chile, not Mexico."

Ms. Holly scoffed. "Whatever. It's basically the same place."

"No, it's literally a different continent. In fact, the United States is a lot closer to Mexico than Chile is, but you probably wouldn't like it if I called you a Mexican."

"Why would you-?" Ms. Holly sputtered. "You're not even making sense! What does that illegal being from Chile have to do with anything?"

"She's not illegal. Her family's actually been in this country longer than mine has, but for some reason nobody ever asks me about my immigration status."

Some small part of her brain tried desperately to remind Petra she should stop talking.

"Whatever," Ms. Holly snapped. "I want her fired."

"She's worked for us for 10 years."

"Then you should have fired her 9 years ago."

"Oh!" Raiker suddenly interjected, addressing Petra. "I know this word. Almost know this word. What was it again?"

Ms. Holly rounded on him.

"Excuse me, who the hell are you?"

"Raiker the—" Raiker stopped short and cleared his throat. "Mr. Jacob Grimm."

"Well, Mr. Grimm," Ms. Holly said, "Do you mind—"

Raiker ignored her and turned back to Petra.

"Racist! That's the word, right? She's a racist."

It took every ounce of composure Petra had to not let out a snort of laughter.

"*What did you just call me*?!" Ms. Holly screeched.

"Racist. Am I using that right?"

He turned to Petra expecting an answer. Petra tried to avoid his eyes, because if she looked at him now, she was pretty sure she was going to lose it. Instead, she focused on Ms. Holly, who was clutching the shower cap and turning beet-red. She seemed to have momentarily lost the ability to make words and had begun sort of sputtering in indignation instead.

"You know," Raiker said, "You would be a lot less miserable if you didn't waste so much of your energy trying to convince other humans you're better than them. I could probably get you to stop. What's your full name?"

"Please don't," Petra interjected.

Raiker rolled his eyes before returning his attention to Ms. Holly.

"You should try focusing on something positive. Take a walk. Laugh with someone you like. Dance," he said.

Ms. Holly finally found her voice again.

"*Dance*?!" she choked out.

Raiker smiled that sly, roguish smile and backed away from the desk.

"Dance," he repeated.

Raiker glanced up at the ceiling.

"Where's that music coming from?"

A monotonous jazz XM radio station played through the lobby speakers at low volume 24/7. Now with a flick of his index finger and a small crackle of electricity the stations started to cycle through, shifting from jazz to classic rock to top 40 pop hits.

"What are you doing?" Petra demanded, eyes wide.

"How is he doing that? Is this some kind of trick?" Ms. Holly said as she backed towards the other side of the lobby.

With another little flick and a spark from his finger the radio station changed to some bombastic swing number with a brass band. Raiker grinned and with another flick raised the volume loud enough to shake the whole building. Louder, Petra strongly suspected, than the speakers were actually capable of. The base notes passed through her like a vibration.

The music did not escape the attention of the guests milling about the lobby and dining room. Nor did it escape Beth's notice. She came charging out of the back-office shouting about how the radio had gone crazy. More employees quickly came out of the woodwork. Martina froze halfway into the elevator and Devon came running down the stairs, no doubt rushing to the radio in the office.

Petra couldn't hear what he was saying anymore, but she could clearly see Raiker mouth the word "dance" again. He raised his arms out to either side of his body and sparks shot out of his fingertips. Those electric blue sparks went every direction and struck the people around them. Every person, it seemed, except for Petra. She watched one fly into Ms. Holly and strike her in the sternum. Ms. Holly's eyes widened briefly, but then she smiled. Her stance softened, and she began first to sway in rhythm with the music and then move with abandon. She moved her feet and spun across the lobby, dancing in time with the music and grinning as if she didn't have a care in the world. The other guests were dancing too. Laptops lay abandoned and broken on the floor as they dropped them in their rush to get to their feet. They danced alone, together, sometimes in unison. Their bodies entwining and then separating again. More guests and employees poured down the stairs and spilled out of the elevators, joining in the revelry.

Raiker stood in the middle of it all, smiling with his blue eyes locked on Petra's. He bowed to her and then held out his hand in an unmistakable invitation to dance.

Petra looked from him to her boss, who was currently being lowered into a surprisingly graceful dip by Mr. Clark and giggling. Deciding she was somewhere past the point of getting in trouble, Petra crossed the lobby and took Raiker's outstretched hand.

"How are you doing this?" Petra shouted to be heard above the din as Raiker slipped his arm around her waist.

"Magic," Raiker whispered into her ear, and then he spun her at dizzying speed.

Petra was a fair enough dancer herself, but it was all she could do to keep up as Raiker led. He put both hands on her waist and lifted her into the air, spinning her until the room was spinning too and her shoes fell off. She would have fallen when he lowered her back to her feet if he hadn't held her close. It was the first time she noticed that this glamour was shorter than the other one. With her shoes off they were just about nose-to-nose.

Lips-to-lips...

And before she could think too hard about that, he spun away from her in a perfect on pointe pirouette. A few people turned to watch him, but mostly they were too caught up in their own dance.

Or caught up in each other. Beth had been traded out for Mr. Ramirez as Mr. Clark's dance partner, and the two men were dancing in a way that certainly would have given their respective wives pause. Hope and Devon had moved past dancing to making out on the lobby couch.

Petra watched as Raiker moved with the grace of a ballet dancer, leaping through the air before pirouetting back to her and taking her in his arms again.

"You're amazing," Petra said.

"I'm alright," Raiker shrugged, his voice dripping with false modesty.

The music slowed and they swayed along with it like kids at the prom.

"You're good, too," Raiker said.

Petra laughed. "Yeah, maybe for a human."

They were no more than an inch apart now. She could feel his breath on her face, and smell lavender on his skin.

"You're exquisite," he said, and he leaned in to close the gap between their lips.

Chapter Fifteen

The kiss was soft at first, and surprisingly reserved. But there was nothing tentative about the way his lips lingered on hers before withdrawing oh so slowly, hovering there just a breath away. It was more like he was trying to make the moment last. To make her want more.

It was working.

When he allowed their lips to meet again, it was with that same gentleness, but he let it build this time, slowly parting her lips with his tongue as he wound his fingers through her hair. The kiss deepened until he was devouring her, right there in the middle of the hotel lobby surrounded by people dancing, and nothing, *nothing* mattered except that he did not stop.

When he finally did break away, it was only to move his lips to her ear, where he gently reminded her, "*Breathe, Petra.*"

She hadn't realized that she wasn't.

She sucked in a breath of air that quickly turned into a sigh as he nibbled gently on her earlobe and then kissed the space just below it, sending goose bumps down her arms.

"I suppose there is one redeeming quality to this place," he whispered to her. "It is an entire building filled with beds."

His hands slid around to her abdomen and toyed with the button on the front of her pants.

Oh my God, what am I doing?

If her apprehension showed on her face, it was probable that Raiker missed it, because he was busy planting a line of kisses along the curve of her neck. It sent a fresh wave of sensation through her, but wasn't quite enough to distract from the growing feeling of panic.

What am I doing? What am I thinking? He's not even human.

"S-Sunset," Petra stammered. "It's sunset. We have to go. We have to meet your friend."

"My friend can *wait*," Raiker growled. "There is absolutely nothing I want right now more than this."

Their bodies were wound together tight enough that Petra knew *exactly* how much Raiker wanted this. And any moment now she was going to put some distance between them again.

Maybe.

Raiker moved to kiss her lips again, but he frowned when he saw the panic etched into her face.

"You look... scared," he said.

"No," Petra insisted, and then she almost immediately backpedaled. "Maybe. Not scared. I'm just nervous. I..."

Raiker backed up a respectable inch or so and stroked her hair, his other arm still wound around her waist.

"Petra, what's wrong?"

"I just don't think we should be late!" Petra snapped. She wasn't totally sure why she was yelling. "This is important. I just want to find this damn key so things can go back to normal and I can get all of this crazy shit out of my life!"

Raiker let go of her and backed away, a mixture of surprise and deep, ugly hurt in his eyes.

"That's all I want too," he said.

It was meant to sound cold, but the little break in his voice betrayed him, and Petra found herself recalling when he told her that fairies are not good liars.

She was regretting what she said more and more by the millisecond.

"Raiker, I didn't–"

"It's fine," he cut her off curtly. "You don't mean anything to me either. Let's go."

He turned his back to her and stalked off towards the front doors. After a moment's hesitation Petra put her shoes back on and darted after him, leaving the dancing people in the lobby behind.

She had to run to catch up, and by the time she rounded a corner and spotted him again he had shifted back to his usual human glamour, looking very conspicuous charging down the street shirtless and barefoot with flaming red hair. Wordlessly, he slowed his pace to match hers when he saw her struggling to keep up.

"Are they gonna be okay back there?" Petra asked.

Raiker shrugged. "They'll find some mundane explanation to wrap their little brains around. Probably blame the Devil, or funny mushrooms."

"That's a not good enough answer," Petra said.

"I don't give a damn about your stupid human friends, Petra!" Raiker snapped.

Petra stopped in her tracks, momentarily more shocked than angry. Raiker stopped too. He stared down at his feet and sighed deeply.

"I'm sorry," he said quietly. "That was... That was rude. I..." he sighed again, "I don't know what's wrong with me."

He paused a moment and then added, "They really will be fine. I wouldn't let anything bad happen to people you care for."

"Apology accepted," Petra said. "Raiker, I'm sorry too. I didn't mean—"

"The park's just up here," Raiker interrupted.

He turned from her again and walked down the street. Petra followed him to the park, feeling as though she should say something else, but not quite able to find the words.

It was an old, mostly derelict playground. The kind that was more popular with kids who dealt drugs than kids who still played on slides. It was empty save for a young mother who looked uncharacteristically well dressed for her surroundings. She was pushing a baby in an old-fashioned pram.

"Alright," Raiker said, "I've got 50 gold crowns for the information. Try not to promise anything else."

"You want *me* to talk to her?" Petra asked.

"No. Why don't you talk to him while I keep the mother distracted?"

"Say what?"

But Raiker had already walked up to the mother and struck up a conversation, using some combination of pushing and good old-fashioned flirting to keep her attention solely focused on him.

Tentatively, Petra approached the pram. Sticking out from under a crocheted blue blanket was a bald, six-month-old baby. He looked up at her curiously with his big brown eyes while he sucked contentedly on a binky.

"Ummm... Hi... baby," Petra said.

The baby spit out the binky.

"Shit, is that Raiker the Rogue talkin' to my old lady?" the baby asked.

He had a deep, man's voice that seemed freakishly incongruent with his tiny newborn frame. He didn't even look like he should be physiologically capable of forming his lips to make those sounds.

"Last time I saw that young son of a bitch he stole my mead and my woman right out from under me. What's the matter? He don't wanna talk to me himself?"

"H-He... he thought he should..."

Petra spent several seconds floundering for words.

"You're a changeling," she finally blurted out.

"Heeeey, hundred points for the pretty lady," the baby said. "Sorry, I watch a lot of daytime TV."

"Where's her baby?!" Petra demanded.

"You mean the baby she used to leave alone in the house for hours at a time and hit with her shoe whenever he wouldn't stop crying? That baby? He's fine. He's chillin' out in Arcadia suckin' on beautiful fae titties. He don't have a care in the world."

Petra glanced back at the woman in the designer clothes and felt a hot coal of anger ignite in her gut. She convinced herself that feeling was 100% due to the woman being a child abuser, and had nothing to do with the way Raiker was staring at this woman like she was the last strawberry glazed at The Donut Man. Petra pulled her attention back to the potty-mouthed infant.

"You... you stole her baby to save him?" she asked.

"Sure, sure."

The baby took a moment to lift the handmade blanket out of the pram and drop it into a nearby mud puddle before continuing.

"And because that bitch put an in-ground pool in where a fairy ring used to be. We don't let an insult like that go."

Not that she'd planned on doing so, but Petra made a silent vow to never ever pave over the Feenring in her backyard.

"So, you didn't just take the baby. You're punishing her," she said.

"Hell yeah, I'm punishing her."

The changeling answered in a man's voice, but then giggled like a baby, and the combination of the two was highly disconcerting.

"Last night, I cried for 12 hours. Not straight through. Naw, I stop every 30 minutes or so just long enough for her to think maybe she can finally get some sleep. Then I start again." He rubbed his little hands together as he gleefully recounted his psychological warfare.

"Oh and hey, check out this bad boy I'm workin' on." He opened his mouth wide, revealing the sliver of a tooth poking out of his bottom gums. "Later when she's feeding me, I'm gonna bite her right on the nipple. Then I'm gonna squirt shit out the top of my diaper all over me, her, and the $9,000 sofa, *while* spitting up into her face simultaneously. You should stick around. It's gonna be a fuckin' riot."

Okay. Mental note: Don't piss off the fairies.

"I think I'll pass," she answered.

"Your loss. So did you want somethin' from me, sugar tits?"

Petra scowled. "Okay, first of all, it's Petra. Actually, to you it's *Ms. Bachman.*"

The changeling smiled at her slyly and then let out a high-pitched peel of laughter. "Oh, you're a special kinda stupid, aren't ya? You'da been a lot smarter to let me keep callin' you 'sugar tits' than tell me your true name. Especially when there's a lot of folks lookin' for you, Ms. Petra Adelina Bachman."

Petra took a step back from the pram and cast a worried glance in Raiker's direction, but he was quite engrossed in conversation with the pretty brunette child-abuser.

"Aw, don't worry about me, mama. I aint gettin' myself caught up in all this shit. I wanna live to see another millennia. Just sayin', be smarter next time you're talking to a fae. You're way too fine to end up some Unseelie's dinner.

"Anyway, Ms. Petra Adelina Bachman, you have the honor of addressing Orrian the Orator, collector of folklore and curator of histories."

"And snatcher of babies," Petra added.

Orrian shrugged his shoulders in his "Mama's little angel" onesie.

"Everybody needs a hobby. So, I'm guessin' you're here to ask about that Key of yours."

They were interrupted by a loud fit of giggles as the mother laughed at something Raiker said. Orrian snorted.

"He thinks he's some hot shit, don't he? I mean, sure, he can charm the pants off of humans. But the only reason fae ever give him the time of day is 'cause his mom was famous."

Petra was torn between feeling strangely compelled to defend Raiker and curiosity.

"She was an artist, right?" Petra asked. "Was she really that famous? Even after..." Petra quickly did the math in her head. "I mean, she died over 2,800 years ago, right? Still famous?"

"Oh yeah. The great Desidae the Spider Charmer." He chuckled in an unfriendly way. "More like Desidae the *Flightless*."

Petra wasn't sure if that was meant to be some kind of joke, but it sounded more like a slur. Orrian must have noticed that Petra was not amused at any rate, because he stopped laughing and there was a hint of contrition in his tone when he spoke again.

"Hey, just havin' a laugh, uh... Maybe don't tell your boyfriend I said that. Let's talk business. This info's not gonna come cheap."

While most of what had been going on in her life lately was well beyond her abilities, haggling was quite comfortably within Petra's wheelhouse.

"I can offer you 25 gold crowns for everything you can tell me about the key," she said.

"Yeah right. Hot as this is, I wouldn't do it for a hundred. What else you got, sugar tits?"

Petra recalled Raiker's warning not to promise him anything else before tentatively asking, "What is it you want?"

Those big brown eyes looked her up and down appraisingly before he answered. "I'll do it for some milk."

"Like... from a cow?"

"No, from those."

He pointed one chubby finger at her breasts and licked his lips. Petra flushed and crossed her arms over her chest, her skin crawling.

"I'm-I'm not... I don't lactate," Petra sputtered.

"Sure, not now. I can wait to collect. You're gonna plop out some babies eventually, right? It'd be a crime not to with those hips."

Petra reminded herself again how much they needed the information. Yet she still couldn't quite believe the words coming out of her own mouth when she said, "How much milk?"

"Let's say four liters. I'll take it in installments."

Petra tried to remember how big those bottles of pumped milk were that Hope stored in the break room mini fridge. They were maybe eight ounces? And she'd watched Hope pour some in her coffee one day when they ran out of creamer, so possibly four liters wasn't a totally insane quantity.

"One liter," Petra countered, and then quickly added, "From a BOTTLE, not from... the tap."

"Deal," he answered so quickly that Petra began to worry she should have started lower.

He held out his tiny fat hand, and Petra took it between her thumb and two fingers, shaking on it.

"By anybody's account the Key's way older than recorded history," Orrian began. "Much older than any fairy alive, at least. And you gotta understand, you go that far back, you're lookin' at oral histories, and they can get a mite..."

"Hyperbolic?" Petra offered.

"Yeah. That there's the word. Bit more legends than facts."

"But the Key is definitely real, isn't it?"

Orrian shrugged and offered a dimpled smile. "You have it. You tell me."

When Petra didn't answer, Orrian continued. "The story goes that there were other creatures in Arcadia before the fae came. We call 'em the antea. Then, dependin' on which version of the story you ascribe to, they were all wiped out by the Beast. The first fae, Henosis, showed up in Arcadia and defeated the Beast. He put the Beast in the Cage, and he locked the Cage up with the Key."

"What's the other version of the story?" Petra asked.

Orrian paused before answering. He leaned out of the pram and looked to either side, as if he was worried someone might be listening.

"In the other version, Henosis the First *created* the Beast. Then he used it to wipe out the antea so the fae could have that rock instead."

"I guess history is written by the genocidal victors."

Orrian let out a low whistle and put his face in his hands.

"You have got to mind that tongue of yours if you wanna keep it, mama," he said, but it sounded less like a threat and more like friendly advice. "You don't talk about a folk hero like that."

"*You* do."

"I'm a historian. I got a perspective on things that's a little more nuanced than the drinkin' songs. You gonna let me finish this damn narrative, Ms. Bachman?"

"Sorry," Petra conceded.

"First proper written mention we get of the Key is from about 300 millennia ago. Back then Mab had it."

"Mab?"

"Wow. You really don't know shit. Yeah, Queen Mab, ruler of the Unseelie Court. Word is that's how she got to be queen. Used to wear it 'round her neck. Now, nobody ever says they saw the Beast in person back then, but Mab was doin' some... scary big magic.

"But she lost the damn thing. Or it was stolen. We don't know when exactly, 'cause she wasn't really advertising to her enemies that she didn't have it no more. And then nobody knows where it went. Well, 'cept maybe you, sugar tits. Because four decades ago, somebody worked a piece of magic so powerful it etched 'Petra Adelina Bachman has the Key' into the earth."

His tiny brow furrowed, an expression that almost didn't work with his baby smooth skin, and he looked her up and down suspiciously.

"Hey... how old are you?"

"So, the Key can unlock the Cage," Petra said, changing the subject, "What does this Beast do once it's unleashed?"

"Y'all got a Beast legend too, doncha? How's yours go?" he said.

"You mean, like, in the Bible?"

Orrian nodded, and the familiar Revelations verse rang through her mind in Oma's voice.

Und ich sah ein Weib sitzen auf einem scharlachfarbenen Tier, das war voll Namen der Lästerung...

"It..." Petra started uncertianlly. "It ends the world."

"Yup. Y'all got that story from us. It goes about the same when we tell it."

Chapter Sixteen

"**I** should have asked for more money."

"THAT'S your takeaway?!" Petra shouted.

Raiker shrugged and plopped down on the living room sofa.

"I mean, the asking price for the Key was substantial, but not power-to-destroy-the-world substantial," he said.

Petra stood over him, glowering.

"Right. Someone's trying to get a hold of the thing that could destroy the world, but obviously the more important part is that you weren't getting paid enough to hand it to them!"

Raiker wilted under her glare.

"Do you really think so little of me?" he asked in a small voice.

As if he sensed his distress, Shitpoo hopped up onto Raiker's lap and licked his face. Raiker scratched him behind the ears.

"I'm sorr—"

"Of course, I care," Raiker interrupted. "If someone like Queen Mab got her hands on that thing..."

He left the thought unfinished, but the dark look in his eyes said all that Petra needed to know. Petra shuddered and sat down next to Raiker, clutching her wine glass. Shitpoo licked her face too and then nosed at her wine, before settling down in between them. Petra reached over to scratch his ears and found Raiker's hand resting there already. Impulsively, she took it in her own. Raiker looked at her curiously, but he didn't comment on the gesture. He didn't pull away either.

"Would she really end the world?" Petra asked.

"Queen Mab? Probably not. She's evil, not self-destructive. She might end Queen Titania. Or every fairy in the Seelie Court. And someone crazier than her might just burn it all down. Maybe burn down your realm while they're at it."

Raiker shuddered and snagged the rest of Petra's wine with his other hand, knocking it back in one big gulp.

"How come you don't know who hired you?" she asked.

"Because when someone offers me that much gold, I don't ask a lot of questions."

Petra snorted.

"Well, for what it's worth, I'm seriously reconsidering that policy now," he said. "Honestly, anonymity is fairly common for my buyers. They used a bit of transmittal magic."

"I don't know what that means," Petra interjected.

"It's a grammarie that..." Raiker started to explain and then seemed to think better of it. "We never met face-to-face. I was supposed to make contact again when I had it and then they'd give me the location to leave the Key and pick up my gold."

"Like a dead drop?"

"I don't know what that means."

Petra sighed and went to lean back on the sofa, but she was impeded by Raiker's wings. It struck her that most of her house wasn't really designed to accommodate wings.

"We have to figure out who's trying to get their hands on this thing," she said.

"And we have to find the thing before they do," he added. "And honestly, at this point I have no idea how we're going to do that either."

Petra squeezed his hand in hers. "We'll figure it out."

As far as reassurances went, it was a fairly empty gesture, but Raiker smiled at her as if he was reassured anyway.

"You really believe that?"

"Yes," Petra lied. "Anyway, we could be worried over nothing. Maybe Orrian's lying. That guy's a dick-weasel."

Raiker laughed so hard he startled Shitpoo, who climbed off the couch with a disgruntled grumble and went off in search of a quieter place to nap.

"That is a very curious epithet," Raiker managed between giggles.

"You like that one, I'll teach you some German ones later. My people really know how to swear," Petra said, laughing along with him.

It felt good to laugh together after the fight they'd had earlier. Petra wondered if she should broach the subject of the ugly aftermath of that kiss.

"Why do you think Orrian is a dick-weasel?" Raiker asked before she could form the words.

Petra considered telling Raiker about the particular terms of her negotiation with Orrian, and had a horrible vision of him punching a baby.

Thinking it may be the safer answer, she said, "He said something rude about your mom. He called her 'Desidae the Flight—"

"I know what he called her," Raiker cut her off curtly.

Raiker let go of her hand and stood, pacing the living room. Rage twisted his features in a way that Petra had never seen before. It seemed to radiate off him in waves.

"2,862 years since she died. You'd think they'd stop telling that damn joke by now!" Raiker spat.

He drove his fist into the wall with a bang that made Petra jump and left a hole clear through to the wiring. The nearby pictures rattled off and fell, their glass shattering at his feet. Before Petra could react, he vanished, leaving her sitting in stunned silence on the couch.

She found him in the garden, sitting in the grass in the middle of the Feenring with his back to the house. His face was in his hands; his beautiful copper-tipped wings folded up behind him. He stirred when he heard her approach.

"Leave me, my lady. I'm not good company," he said without looking up.

She could hear the tears in his quiet, shaking voice. Slowly, she walked over and sat down in front of him.

"I'm sorry about your wall," he said.

"I don't care about the wall," she said. "I care about you."

She reached for his hand and he allowed her to take it. They sat together that way for a long time, watching the stars come out over the garden.

"You were only 14," she finally said.

It had been some time since he had stopped crying, and Petra decided that now might be the right moment to see if he wanted to talk about it.

"You said you're 2,876 and if your mom died 2,862 years ago..." she continued.

"You have a remarkable memory," Raiker said.

They lapsed into silence again.

Petra had been six when her mom crashed her car driving home from work. As awful as that had been, she suspected it may have been easier on her in some ways because she was still so young. It was hard to remember Mama sometimes. It would be harder, she thought, to have had eight more years like Raiker had. He had real, lasting memories of his mother, and yet he was still just a child really when he lost her. She thought about saying something like that, but it didn't feel like the moment to talk about herself.

"Raiker, what happened to her?" she asked.

She thought that he would dodge the question the way he had before, but this time he answered.

"She was attacked. They..."

Raiker sucked in a breath and closed his eyes, steeling himself before finally letting the words tumble from his lips.

"They tore off her wings."

The finality of his tone left no doubt in Petra's mind that that was not the sort of injury fae could recover from.

"Why would anyone do that?" Petra asked.

"It didn't really have anything to do with her," Raiker said. "Her lover, he did something to insult a small band of Unseelie. They thought they could punish him by harming her." A deep bitterness crept into his voice. "It didn't work. He didn't give a damn about her. That coward wouldn't lift a finger to avenge her."

"Was he your father?" Petra asked.

Raiker merely shrugged.

"I killed them," he said suddenly. "They were stronger than me, but I tricked them. I..." Raiker looked down at his feet, his expression one of uncharacteristic embarrassment. "I seduced them."

No, that's more than embarrassment on his face. That's shame.

"Raiker, that's..." Petra struggled for a word that was bad enough to describe what it must have been like to be a 14-year-old kid and to come on to the monsters that had killed his mom. "... horrific," she finished.

Raiker did not argue with her assessment.

"It was effective," he said simply. "I tricked them, and I trapped them, and I killed them."

Raiker was silent for a long time. So long, that Petra thought that was end of the story, until very quietly, he added, "I hurt them first."

A chill went down Petra's spine. As if he sensed her disquiet, Raiker lifted his eyes to meet hers.

"Do I frighten you now?" he asked.

"No," Petra said, although she wasn't entirely sure if she meant it. She squeezed his hand. "It just doesn't sound like you."

Raiker shook his head and continued staring down at his feet.

"Did it help?" Petra asked after a while. "Did getting revenge make you feel better?"

Raiker looked up at her curiously. "No one has ever asked me that before."

He considered the question for a time and then shook his head.

"Maybe for a moment," he said. "But then she was still gone. And I was still alone."

"You didn't have any other family?" she asked. "No one to take you in?"

His silence was answer enough. Petra tried to imagine what her life would have been like if Oma hadn't been there to raise her after Mama died.

"I got in a lot of trouble over it," Raiker said. "Queen Titania pardoned me. She was fond of my mother and I think she took pity on me. But I should have been banished from the Seelie Court for the torture alone. And I didn't have the Blood Rights for their deaths."

"Blood Rights?" Petra asked.

"Arcadian law says that if you murder a fae, their family have the right to kill you," he explained.

"But she *was* murdered..." Petra said uncertainly.

"Oh," Raiker said, realizing the source of her confusion, "No."

And then Petra finally got the last piece of the story.

"No, she threw herself off a waterfall."

The tears that had been welling up in Petra's eyes spilled down her cheeks. There was such pain on Raiker's face. Petra could almost picture the lost little boy he was 2,862 years ago, when his mother had been brutalized and she had killed herself. She reached her hand up to his cheek.

"She left you alone," Petra said.

That had been the wrong thing to say. Raiker stiffened and pulled away from her, anger flashing in his eyes.

"She didn't leave me. She loved me," he said.

He stood up and paced the garden.

"You're too human," he said. "You can't possibly understand. No one could have lived like that. The shame of it... It would be heartless to blame her for what she did."

Petra climbed to her feet and tentatively approached him again.

"I do understand," she said gently. "Well, I think I do anyway."

She grabbed his arm, bringing his angry pacing to a halt and turning him towards her.

"You believe she went through something too awful to live with. You think she's not responsible for her own death. Those Unseelie that took her wings, the ones you killed, they were responsible."

Raiker softened slightly and nodded.

"But..." Petra said, "It's not that simple. And you know you're allowed to feel complicated about it. You can believe she had no choice and you can feel like she abandoned you all at once. And feeling abandoned doesn't mean you love her any less."

A sob caught in Raiker's throat, but he didn't just look sad now. He looked like Petra had given him permission to feel something he'd wanted to for 2,862 years, and he was relieved and heartbroken for it.

"She left me," he choked out. "And no one wanted me. I was..."

The rest of his words were lost to tears, and Petra wrapped her arms around him. She held him until his sobs quieted and the night breeze dried the tears on his face, and then she held him still, because she didn't want to stop.

They fell asleep lying close together and when
Petra woke up, they were closer still, with her
head resting on his shoulder and his arm
wrapped around her back. The heat coming off
of his body was making her sweat in her thin tank
top, but somehow, she didn't mind. She lay there
and watched the way his eyelashes fluttered in his
sleep, breathing in the lavender scent of his skin.

She scooted up a bit, so that they were
nose-to-nose, and she traced her finger across the
tip of his pointed ear. He twitched and his wings
fluttered slightly, but he didn't wake up. She let
her hand trail down the curve of his cheekbone,
until the tips of her fingers finally arrived at his
soft lips, and still, he didn't wake.

But he did wake up when she kissed him. Her
eyes were closed, but she felt his lips part for her
and his embrace tighten as the kiss deepened.
When it ended and she opened her eyes again,
she found that his eyes were still shut.

"Am I dreaming, my lady?" he asked.

"No," she said.

Only then did he open his eyes and look into
hers. They were almost gold today, with little
flecks of red.

"I didn't think you would allow me to kiss you
again," he said. "You didn't seem to like it last
time."

"I liked the kiss," Petra assured him.

She ran her fingers through his messy red hair.

"I panicked when you said we should go to bed
together."

"We're in bed together *now*," he pointed out with a grin.

Petra shoved him playfully.

"You know what I mean.".

"Honestly, my lady, I'm trying, but I'm not sure that I do."

His fingertips were tracing circles on the small of her back, just to one side of the bandage.

"You want me," he said. His tone brokered no argument, and Petra didn't know how to argue with someone who could allegedly smell her arousal. "But you won't allow yourself to have me. Why?"

"I don't..." Petra wasn't sure if she wanted to explain. "

Just stupid human reasons."

Raiker seemed to take that explanation well enough.

"But you like this," he said as he snuggled against her.

"Yes."

"And you like kissing me?"

"Yes."

"Can I kiss you again?"

"*Yes.*"

"*WHEEEEE-OOOOOH!*"

Petra's phone blared out from where she had left it on her nightstand. She quickly extracted herself from his arms and fumbled for it.

"I am going to break that evil contraption," Raiker grumbled.

"I will break you," Petra shot back before accepting the call.

227

Hope was on the other end of the line asking if Petra could come in for about an hour today because Beth needed to talk to her. Thinking that sounded slightly ominous, Petra promised she'd be there in an hour. Hope did not mention the spontaneous dance party that had erupted the day before.

It took Petra twenty minutes to scarf down breakfast and get changed, and Raiker pouted the entire time. She watched him take flight from the backyard before sliding behind the wheel of her Jetta and cranking the diesel engine to life. Petra looked up for him at every red light and traffic jam, but she never could spot him following her.

Raiker was already in the lobby when she walked into The Hammond, glamoured as "Mr. Grimm" and, as best as Petra could gather from her limited Spanish vocabulary, complimenting one of the cooks on his blueberry muffins. Petra snagged one of them and then fixed three coffees. She could feel Raiker's eyes on her, and she had a sneaking suspicion the two men—

"I'm not a man, Petra. I can do things to you that men can't."

—were talking about her, but the only word she could really pick out was *"música"*.

Hope was on the phone when Petra approached the front desk, but she mouthed the word "thank you" when Petra handed her the coffee with three sugars, three creams. Hope looked nervous, and it did nothing to assuage the ominous feeling curling in Petra's gut.

Petra walked back into the office, where she found Beth at her desk and offered her the no cream, three Splenda's and the muffin. Petra sat down in the chair across from her. Beth looked like she was in the kind of mood that not even blueberry muffins could alleviate.

"So... about the dancing yesterday..." Petra said, awkwardly attempting to broach the subject she was sure Beth had brought her in to discuss.

"We all got a little carried away, didn't we?" Beth said vaguely. "I guess it happens to the best of us."

Petra kept her poker face firmly in place, but she couldn't quite believe that Beth was mentally prepared to write off the whole episode as the entire hotel getting "a little carried away".

"Petra, I called you in because Sharon Holly lodged a complaint against you. She said you were verbally abusive," Beth said.

Petra snorted. "I should lodge a complaint against her for being verbally abusive. That woman is a nightmare."

Beth didn't think the joke was funny.

"She said you called her a racist," Beth said.

Petra took a moment to marvel at the fact that Ms. Holly had blocked out the memory of the mass hypnosis, but remembered the part where Petra had gently suggested that you shouldn't call people "illegal Mexicans" if they were neither illegal, nor Mexican.

"I didn't say that. Mr. Grimm in 2022 did. I was just standing there at the time," Petra corrected.

"So, you didn't respond to her housekeeping complaint by lecturing her about Martina's heritage?"

"I... very politely suggested... She called Martina an illegal," Petra said.

"Petra, I don't care if she called Martina a wetback. You should know better than to talk back to guests."

She didn't think Beth's statement was wrong from a customer service perspective, but there was something deeply flawed about it when it came to basic human decency.

"It won't happen again." Petra conceded. "I'm sorry, Beth."

Beth sighed deeply and looked down at the notes in front of her.

"Am I getting written up?" Petra asked, increasingly worried about the look on Beth's face.

Beth didn't answer her, and the ominous feeling she'd had since Hope had called this morning started to turn to dread.

"... Am I getting *fired*?"

"No," Beth assured her. "I've been on the phone with Corporate all morning swearing up and down that you're an exemplary employee and you just had a rogue off-day. I even told them you were attacked by a hobo. I had to give them some kind of excuse for your behavior."

Beth sighed again before she continued. "Did you know that Sharon Holly is Mr. Hammond's niece?"

"*Hammond Hotel Group* Mr. Hammond?"

Beth nodded. "They wanted me to fire you, but I convinced them to let me suspend you for two weeks without pay instead. And the good news is, Sharon Holly checks out on Wednesday, so she won't be here when you get back."

Petra sat in stunned silence. She was certain she was going to cry, and she was trying very hard to hold it in until after she exited the building. Her voice was strained when she spoke again.

"Beth, I work my ass off for this job. I stay late, I come in on my days off, I'm chained to my phone. I did everything right."

"I know," Beth said. "This just is what it is."

Petra did most of her crying stuck in a traffic jam on the 10 on the way home. She cried and screamed and swore and banged on the steering wheel until the plastic Volkswagen emblem in the middle popped off and fell into her lap.

I did everything right, her brain kept repeating over and over. *I did everything right, and I got screwed over anyway.*

By the time the traffic jam cleared and she pulled off the freeway towards home, she was more exhausted than angry. She just wanted to curl up on her couch and drink wine until the day melted away.

Petra slammed the car door shut and trudged towards her front door.

"Petra! Good to see you dear. How is everything?" a voice called out from somewhere to her right.

Petra turned and looked into her next-door neighbor's yard. Old Mrs. Mason was sitting at the little stone tea table in her front garden with Mrs. Porter from across the street. They were playing cards and drinking tall glasses of iced tea.

"Come sit with us," Mrs. Porter beckoned.

Petra could think of very little she wanted to do less, but her programming to be nice to old ladies overrode it. She sat down at the table with her neighbors and accepted a glass of iced tea.

"We were just talking about your new beau," Mrs. Mason said, gesturing towards Petra's house. "You have to tell us all about him."

Petra glanced back at the house where Mrs. Mason was pointing. They could see Raiker through the dining room window, shirtless and drinking cream straight out of the carton.

"He's younger than you, isn't he?" Mrs. Mason said.

Petra fought to keep herself from laughing.

"No, he just looks young for his age."

"He seems to have moved in with you awfully fast," Mrs. Porter said.

"He's not my, um, he's just a friend. He needed a place to stay for a while so I'm letting him use my guest room," Petra lied smoothly.

Mrs. Porter smirked. "Funny, I never see the lights on in either of your guest rooms. Just the master bedroom. That's where you sleep now, isn't it?"

Petra bit her lip and held back the urge to tell Mrs. Porter to mind her own damn business.

"He goes to bed early. That's probably why you haven't seen the lights," Petra said as evenly as she could manage.

She tried to come up with an excuse to extract herself from the situation. Maybe she could tell them she had to go because she was getting an estimate on a nice, tall privacy fence.

"Oh, there's no sense in lying to us, dear," Mrs. Mason said. "We've known you too long. The number of boys I saw climbing in your bedroom window..."

"No, Dot, that was *Liese*," Mrs. Porter corrected. "Little Petra's always been a good girl, haven't you, sweetie?"

Yup, Petra thought. *I always do everything right.*

Mrs. Mason sighed. "Oh, forgive me dear. I swear my mind is not what it used to be. But you look so much like your mother."

"Spitting image," Mrs. Porter agreed. "And pretty as a picture. I always told Pet she should have put Liese in those beauty contests on TV."

"Pet would have been better off if Liese wasn't so pretty. She wouldn't have had to beat those boys back with a stick," said Mrs. Mason.

"Pretty's got nothing to do with it. Little Petra didn't give Pet any trouble, did you Petra?" said Mrs. Porter.

Petra stood up.

"It's been very nice talking to you," she said in her customer service voice, "But I have some things to do in the house..."

"Oh, please. Don't be rude. You just got here. And you still haven't told us about your boyfriend," said Mrs. Porter.

"She thinks we're being nosey, Dot," Mrs. Mason said with a knowing smile.

"Nosey? Of course not," Mrs. Porter said. "We're just looking out for you, dear. You need to be careful with a man like that warming your bed. You don't want to end up like your mother."

Something inside of Petra snapped.

"Don't want to end up like my mother?" Petra repeated. "You mean I don't want to end up a kick ass career woman who was running her own business with six employees by the time she was 23?"

"Cleaning toilets," Mrs. Porter mumbled.

"Running a housekeeping service," Petra corrected sharply. "That's who I shouldn't end up like? A woman who graduated Valedictorian at St. Lucy's in spite of having a baby when she was 17? An amazing mom who taught me I was capeable of anything I put my mind to? Are those the traits you're worried I might have picked up from my mother?!

"No, you mean pregnant and unmarried, right? Because nothing she ever did after was good enough to make up for that mistake!"

Petra stormed out of Mrs. Mason's garden, leaving the bewildered little old ladies in her wake. She charged into the house, her high heels clanging on the wood floor, and went straight to her dining room window, pulling the curtains shut with such force that it snapped one of the little rings that held them up.

"Petra," Raiker said, "is everything alright? You didn't tell me you were leaving the hotel. I had to locate you to figure out where you went. Lucky I had some of your blood..."

Petra spun around from the window to face him. In three strides she crossed the dining room to the kitchen, ripped her shirt off over her head, and threw herself into his arms. He stumbled backward; actually *stumbled*, something she had never once seen Raiker, so imbued with supernatural grace, do. Taking a little pleasure in the knowledge that she'd thrown him off balance, Petra pushed his hips up against the kitchen counter and plunged her tongue into his mouth.

Raiker broke the kiss off after a few seconds.

"You are acting very unlike yourself," he said, his eyes wide with surprise.

"I know," Petra said, "Now, shut up, and show me those things you can do to me."

She kissed him again while she fumbled with the clasp on the front of her bra. Raiker pushed her lips away from his, and she settled for nibbling on his ear instead.

"I would like to, but..." He broke off as Petra's bra hit the floor, staring at her breasts with hunger in his eyes. "I would really, *really* like to," he amended. "But you said you didn't want to, and I'm concerned you may have been influenced or..."

Petra crushed her body against his and kissed his neck and Raiker seemed to lose track of

precisely where he had been going with that
sentence.

"Just slow down, a little, alright?" Raiker said
between little groans of pleasure. "I just want to
be sure this is what you want."

Petra was not slowing down. Petra was pushing
her skirt and panties down off her hips, leaving
her standing in the kitchen in thigh high
stockings and heels and nothing else. Raiker
whimpered when he saw her and then, after
seeming to gather his remaining willpower, he
took her face in his hands, forcing her to meet his
gaze.

"*Petra Adelina Bachman, slow down,*" he
commanded.

Petra felt the push slide off her like water off
a raincoat. She smiled at him and grabbed him
through his tight black pants. Raiker moaned in
appreciation.

"You can't push me into doing something I
don't really want to do," she said.

"That's... convincing enough for me," Raiker
said.

He finally returned her kiss and then he picked
her up by the waist and spun her around, setting
her on the kitchen counter.

His fingertips emitted a soft glow the way they
did each time he had healed her bumps and
bruises. Only when he had used them to heal
her, her skin had felt warm under his touch. Now,
when he ran one long finger down the curve of
her neck it felt more like a tingle of electricity. A
vibration of energy that shot down her spine and

took her breath away. And the warmth that spread at his touch wasn't where his fingers caressed her skin, but somewhere considerably lower.

"What are you doing to me?" Petra gasped.

He let his fingers trail down from her neck to her collarbone, leaving those little sparks in their wake.

"Does it please my lady?" he asked.

"Hell yes," she answered breathlessly.

It almost undid her completely when his hands found their way to her breasts and he traced his glowing fingertips across her nipples. Petra cried out as she reached for his pants, fumbling helplessly at the cord that laced up the fly. Waves of sensation broke over her at his touch. She couldn't breathe. She couldn't think.

She definitely couldn't figure out how to undo the damn laces on his pants.

Sensing her frustration, Raiker chuckled and moved her hands so he could do it himself.

"Raiker," she asked, "Is it just your *fingers* that can do that or...?"

He flashed her a wicked grin and brought his hands back to her body. The pants remained on.

"Why?" he asked. "Are you concerned my hands aren't enough?" The pad of his thumb teased over her nipple, making her quiver with the slightest touch. "I bet I can make you come to your fall before you can even unlace my fly."

"You're on."

She started working at the knot again as his hand slipped between their bodies, teasing that magic over the exposed skin at the top of her

stockings before sliding his finger inside her.
And then his magic didn't just spark. It flooded
through her; a torrent of sensation so sudden that
when she tried to cry out from it no sound came
out of her mouth.

He was holding back.

Raiker kissed her and magic poured from there
too. It was in his lips, in his tongue. The force of
it made her hips buck and her head bang into the
kitchen cabinet. And all the while she tugged at
that string, desperate to get him naked. With a
growl of frustration, she grabbed a knife out of
the butcher block behind her and sliced through
the cord in one quick motion.

He leapt back and his pants fell to his ankles.
"FUCK!" Raiker stared at the knife through wide,
terrified eyes. His hand clutched his heart.

Petra laughed and tossed the chef's knife into
the sink next to her. Her hungry gaze drunk in the
prize she'd finally revealed– thick and rock hard
in spite of the fact that he seemed to be having a
small heart attack.

"You... You're crazy, you..." Raiker stammered as
he tried to catch his breath, and then he frowned.
"You cheated."

Petra hopped off the counter, putting her hands
on her hips. "Get over here and fuck me already."

Raiker bit his lower lip. "Yes, my lady."

The next thing Petra knew she'd left the kitchen
counter and was eye level with the chandelier.
Her shoes tumbled to the ground. He held her
in the air with his hands gripping her waist. His

need pressed into the gap between her thighs, feverishly hot against her sex.

"Is this what you want?" he purred into her ear.

She felt that buzz of pleasure, first from his head and then in a line that whispered over his shaft.

Petra could only whimper. Her hands went to him as his slid under her thighs, supporting her weight and spreading her legs wider. She watched his eyes as she joined her body with his. That playful glint was gone, replaced with a shudder and a sigh of relief. He whispered her name, his voice as reverent as a prayer.

They moved in unison, languid as first. Their kisses, as he slid in and out of her, were slow too; gentle and exploratory. They held each other as if making love wasn't close enough. Like if they only clung a little tighter, kissed a little deeper, then their bodies could simply coalesce and they could stay this way forever.

The kiss finally broke and they began to move faster. His magic was everywhere now. It was in his lips on her breast. In his fingertips splayed over her back. In his organ as it filled her up and made her moan every time her body slapped against his. She felt it more strongly wherever her skin was more sensitive, and the feel of it in her quim was as powerful as a lightning bolt. Petra didn't just *come* to her fall, she crashed to it, as if her body had plummeted to the earth and cracked open every nerve. Raiker's fall wasn't far behind hers, and he threw back his head and called out her name as he emptied himself into her.

Both of them spent, Raiker rested his forehead against hers, breathing hard. He was soft but she still held him inside her. She didn't want him to go.

"That was..." He started to speak and broke off. "I don't have a word to describe how good that was."

"Perfect," Petra said.

Raiker smiled. "Almost perfect," he corrected. He slid his hand down between their bodies. "Why don't you let me try again?"

Chapter Seventeen

P etra couldn't see out the window from her
vantage point on the kitchen floor, but
judging by the warm orange glow that filled the
room the sun must have been setting over the
garden. The light reflected off the golden colored
flecks in Raiker's eyes, making them sparkle as he
looked at her.

They lay together naked. Raiker was on his side,
allowing his wings to fold up behind him. Petra
rested her head on his outstretched arm, gazing
up at him.

"Do you always do it in the air?" she asked.

Raiker smiled.

"Beds are fine too," he assured her. "I might have
been trying to impress you a bit."

Petra certainly was impressed. In fact, she had
been impressed so many times she wasn't at all

sure her legs would support her when she finally pried herself up.

Raiker let the fingers of his other hand trail down from her breast to her hip, his touch warm and intimate.

"No more tingles?" she asked.

Raiker laughed at her.

"You're greedy."

He yawned and stretched languorously. "No. No more tingles. I need some time to recharge first. Sorry to disappoint, my lady."

Petra giggled.

"Recharge? Like a battery?" she asked. "Is there like, an outlet we need to plug you into?"

Raiker's eyes narrowed, but his expression remained playful. "You know, just because I don't know what half those human nonsense words mean, doesn't mean I don't understand that you're teasing me."

"Sorry," Petra conceded, kissing his lips lightly.

Raiker returned the kiss and then bounded gracefully to his feet. Petra pulled herself to a seated position somewhat less easily. Her body seemed to have just remembered that the cold tile floor was not the most comfortable place to spoon. She watched Raiker fly across the kitchen and hover naked in front of the open refrigerator.

"I only have so much magic," he explained. "If I use too much, I can't use anymore for about a quarter of a day. Right now, I've got enough left to maintain my glamour and that's about it. After that, I'll start drawing from my own life force."

Petra found herself wondering if their previous entanglements were the best use of Raiker's magic, considering there were dark fairies coming to kill them and all. Still, she couldn't quite bring herself to complain.

Raiker gave up on the near-empty refrigerator and walked back over to Petra. He pulled her to her feet and wrapped her up in his strong arms.

"There are stories," he whispered to her, "of fairy lovers that were so caught up in giving each other pleasure that they didn't stop when their magic ran out, spending every last breath in their bodies, until they died, naked and tangled up in each other, lost to ecstasy."

Raiker's lips found hers, and he pulled her into a deep kiss which sent shivers down her spine that had nothing to do with magic.

"Personally though," he said, "I think I'd prefer to live another day."

He kissed her on the forehead and then resumed his sure-to-be-fruitless quest for food in her kitchen.

"I don't remember that one from Oma's bedtime stories," Petra said with a giggle. "But, you know, there are a bunch of stories in *Grimms' Fairy Tales* where human men kiss beautiful fairies and then refuse to ever kiss a human woman again."

"Kiss?" Raiker repeated with a smirk.

"They're children's stories."

Raiker grinned and stood a little taller. "Is this your way of telling me that I've ruined you for human lovers?"

Absolutely yes.

"I'm not answering that," Petra said.

She sat down at the kitchen table smiling. Her smile fell when the logical conclusion of that line of reasoning slid into place in her brain.

"I guess I'm kind of boring for you compared to sex with other fairies, huh?"

Raiker poked his head back out of the pantry and frowned at her.

"I'm sorry," he said, "Did I do anything this afternoon which gave you the impression I wasn't enjoying you immensely?"

Actually, Raiker had enjoyed himself almost as many times as Petra had. The kind of recharging that human men needed did not seem to be a thing for him.

Raiker crossed the kitchen and scooped her back out of the chair and into his arms. "You are extraordinary, Petra," he said. "I think I could stay here with you in my arms forever and I would never want for anyone or anything else."

Something dark crossed his expression then, and his hands tightened around her. But before Petra could ask him what was wrong, he kissed her with a desperation that left her breathless. When they broke away, his playful smile had returned to his face.

"Although," he said, "I would recover faster if there was food in your house."

"Well, put me down and go steal us some dinner then," Petra demanded.

"No magic," he reminded her as he set her back down.

"Oh, right. Okay. Put your pants on. I'm buying you a cheeseburger."

"I don't eat meat," Raiker protested, laughing at the speed with which she was retrieving her clothes off the floor.

"Then I'm buying you Thai takeout. No, wait. Do you still have some of that fairy gold lying around? You're buying Thai takeout. Are we driving or flying?"

They had tofu pad see ew with extra sugar for dinner, and by midnight they were back in Petra's bed, sharing rather more than the kiss they'd shared there that morning. It was very, very late when they finally went to sleep, and Petra was glad that she did not have work tomorrow.

Petra had expected to sleep in well past noon, but it was barely light out when her bladder commanded that she get up and shamble into the bathroom. She stopped at the window on her way back to bed, staring out at the fairy ring; at that doorway to another world which had come crashing into her own. Lost in thought, she lay in bed for over an hour, unable to get back to sleep.

"Hey Raiker?" she finally said. "Are you awake?"

She knew damn well he wasn't, but her voice was loud enough to change that. His eyes fluttered open and then closed again.

"I have an idea," she said, louder still.

Raiker chuckled and spoke through a yawn, his voice groggy. "You're insatiable. Promise me no knives this time."

"Not that kind of idea."

Petra had to laugh at the deep frown of disappointment on his face.

"How about we save the world first and have more sex later?" Petra suggested.

Raiker smiled and opened his eyes. "And how is it you plan to save the world, Petra Adelina Bachman?"

His tone wasn't mocking or doubtful. Raiker looked at her like he really believed she was capable of anything.

"Take me to Arcadia," she said.

Petra's heart fluttered with anticipation as they stepped through the backdoor and into her garden. Raiker flew on ahead of her, landing just in front of the fairy ring. Shitpoo trailed after him and sat at his feet expectantly.

"Are you ready?" Raiker asked.

Finding herself momentarily unable to speak, Petra nodded.

Raiker reached out in front of him and grasped the air with both fists. In a movement that looked strangely similar to opening curtains, he pulled the air in front of him apart as his fists glowed. Behind the "curtains" was a world of green trees and wild colored flowers illuminated by the first rays of dawn. The portal remained open when Raiker let go. He held out his hand, and Petra took it, following him through to another world.

Petra and Raiker stood hand-in-hand in a perfect circle of red and white mushrooms. It looked just like the Feenring in Petra's garden. They were surrounded by green. Gigantic, sprawling trees that were as big around as cars and must have been thousands of years old. Bright green vines with flowers in every imaginable color wound around them and between them, creating foliage that was so thick it was hard to imagine any creature bigger than a rabbit could walk through. Butterflies danced through the air. Petra looked up from the butterflies to the patch of sky above, a perfect blue unmarred by smog. The air smelled sweeter here too. It took her a moment to identify the scent of rosemary, lavender, and fresh turned soil. It was the same scent that always seemed to be on Raiker's skin. The breeze was filled with the sounds of bird song, frogs, and groaning trees.

And behind her, the sound of a small dog whining. Shitpoo stood on the Alius side of the portal, backing away with a suspicious growl.

"It's perfectly safe, Shitpoo," Raiker assured him.

Shitpoo bounded through the portal, sniffing everything on the other side in a frenzy. Petra scooped him up as Raiker closed the door behind them.

"Is it?" Petra asked. "Safe, I mean?"

"It's... more or less safe here. Very safe at my house. But where we're going..." —his wings folded in behind him— "it's not the best place to bring a human." He patted Shitpoo's head and added, "Or a tiny dog."

"It's disputed territory. The Queens of the Seelie and Unseelie courts are having a bit of trouble deciding where the border is of late."

He played it off like a joke, but there was real worry behind that easy smile.

"Trouble like war?" Petra asked.

Raiker shook his head. "We've had peace for 3,000 years. There's been a few skirmishes... a pretty bad one a couple moons ago... but no one's sending out the press gangs yet."

There was no walking through a forest this dense. Raiker took her in his arms and flew up out of the fairy ring. Soon they were sailing over the tops of trees, and Petra pulled her stolen blue Prada coat tighter against the cold wind whipping her skin. Shitpoo snuggled inside her jacket, a warm lump on her chest. Even from her vantage point high in the air, Petra couldn't see where the forest ended. It looked like all that green stretched on forever.

"Where is everyone?" she asked.

She had expected to see buildings, roads, Titania's castle maybe, but all she could see was wild, unchecked nature.

Raiker grinned at her.

"You're not looking carefully enough," he said.

He slowed to a stop and pointed straight down. There was the smallest break in the trees, a clearing much like the one around the Feenring, nearly imperceptible even from the air. Down in the clearing there were three small figures, children perhaps, with pale green skin and flowers in their hair. They were laughing and playing ball in front of...

The first words that occurred to Petra to describe it were "tree house", but it wasn't really a house built in a tree so much as it was a house made of tree. It was as if the massive tree had grown into the shape of a building, leaving rounded openings someone had fitted with a big front door and glass window panes.

The smallest child flew up on feathered wings to catch the ball and missed. The ball hit the house, nearly colliding with the window, bounced, and soared through the air towards the tree line. A dome, like glowing orange glass etched with strange writing, appeared briefly as the ball sailed through it. The other two children started chiding their friend for letting it escape.

Raiker dove to the ground and set Petra down so he could retrieve the ball. He walked it back over to the edge of the invisible dome and left it just outside. The wards glowed where the ball bumped up against them, but the ball didn't pass through. The oldest child landed just next to it on the other side. He smiled and waved at them, but he waited until Petra and Raiker were back up in the air before he reached through the magic dome and retrieved the ball.

"My mother used to give me hell for going out past the wards," Raiker said, and Petra laughed, realizing it was not dissimilar to her own mother scolding her for leaving the fenced-in backyard. They only flew for 10 more minutes, still within a few miles of the fairy ring at most. Raiker brought them down on an outcrop of rock next to a bubbling stream. Teal blue moss crept over most of the stones, making them slick under Petra's feet. Shitpoo slid right off into the shallow water. He climbed out and shook himself off with a disgruntled snort. Raiker fluttered over to a large, flat rock and knelt on it, pressing his hands into the moss.

"Sorry," he said quietly, and his hands began to glow. The moss died under his touch, shriveling as it changed from blue to brown and then became dust. The wind caught the dust and swept it away.

"I hid it," Raiker explained. "Not that it did much good."

The dust swirled around him and cleared, reveling letters that seemed to have been scorched into the stone. Petra carefully traversed the slippery rocks, so she could take a closer look.

The writing was strange to her eyes, a series of swirling characters, each nearly indistinguishable from the next. Reading left to right, it appeared to be one long, unbreaking word, all curves and no sharp angles. The sentence ended with a space, followed by much more familiar words written in the Roman alphabet.

Petra Adelina Bachman.

"I don't know what you're expecting to find that I haven't found already..." Raiker said.

Petra sat down to get closer still and pulled out her phone to take a picture.

"How did you find it?" she asked.

"Dumb luck, mostly. I don't believe it's an accident that this is written near the closest fairy ring to your house. It just so happens to be near my house too."

Raiker kept talking, but Petra momentarily lost the ability to process new information as she stared at her phone. She had four bars. The phone was asking her if she had the wifi password for Klatch Coffee. She thumbed over to her GPS.

"I'm... I'm in San Dimas..." she stammered.

"What's that now?"

"Forget it." Petra switched over to the camera and snapped a few pictures. She traced her finger over the Old Fae letters, beginning to notice the differences between them. There was a looping, reoccurring symbol that might represent spaces. "Is it like Arabic? You read right to left?"

"Left to right."

Petra frowned. "Then it can't say 'Petra Adelina Bachman has the key.' At least not literally. Some other kind of grammatical construction, maybe?"

"Uh... literally it's... It doesn't sound right in English. It's more like... 'Give and receive the key is to Petra Adelina Bachman.' I guess. Well... *sahib* can also be translated as more like *possess* or..." he cocked his head at the rock and squinted. "...*mine*."

Petra was looking at him the same way he was looking at the rock. "You don't know," she realized. "Your English is just about perfect. Is Old Fae harder to learn?"

"English, I pulled from you."

Petra raised an eyebrow.

"It's low-level telepathy magic," he explained. Reacting to Petra's wide-eyed expression, he stressed, "*Extremely* low-level telepathy. I can't read your thoughts."

"Thank Christ..." Petra mumbled.

"But you grew up speaking English and German. It's innate to you, so it's easy for me to borrow... give or take a few idioms and words with multiple meanings. It comes in handy. Never mind Alius, there's at least a dozen languages common to Arcadia. This way we can all talk to each other. Even young ones can manage it."

Petra shook her head and smiled, thinking about the time she and her cousin Lottie tried to take the train home from Prague and ended up in a creepy little town over the Polish border instead. She could think of a few more times being able to "borrow" someone's language would have come in handy.

"Okay, but why haven't you picked up Old Fae then?" she asked.

"Anyone who's old enough for Old Fae to be their innate language is... not the sort of fairy you'd want to go poking around in their head. Not if you want to keep your head, at least.

"No, I learned Old Fae the slow way. Most children learn it in school." He grinned sheepishly. "And to be honest, it wasn't my best subject."

"Do you still have textbooks then?" Petra asked. "Or some kind of diction—"

Raiker clapped his hand over her mouth, his other hand going to his lips. His ears twitched in the direction of the trees behind the clearing. Petra peered into the lengthening shadows, but saw nothing.

Raiker worked fast, his hands glowing and casting a large bubble which looked rather like the orange dome of "wards" she'd seen earlier. Only this one was light purple in color, etched with symbols he drew in midair. As he worked in silence, Petra looked around the clearing for Shitpoo. She spotted him lapping out of the creek and tried to motion him over with her hand. The dog looked at her briefly, then looked up at a dragonfly buzzing overhead. He snapped his jaws at it and chased it towards the trees.

She was about to chase the dog or point out the problem to Raiker, when Shitpoo levitated off the ground. He let out a high-pitched yelp that made Raiker flinch. With a crook of his finger, Raiker sent Shitpoo flying across the clearing and into Petra's waiting arms. As she caught the quivering lump of fur, Raiker waved his hands again. The purple symbols glowed bright and then vanished, and Raiker let out a breath.

"They can't see or hear us now," he said. "We'll be safe as long as they don't walk right into us."

His voice was barely more than a whisper. Either their protective bubble had a decibel limit or staying quiet was an impulse he couldn't shake. Petra found herself whispering too, as she tried to soothe the little dog in her arms.

"Who's coming?" she asked.

Shitpoo's ears twitched the same direction Raiker's had. Whatever was out there was now in the dog's range of hearing too.

"I don't know," Raiker said. He put his hand in hers and held on tight. "But there's a lot of them."

Petra heard the buzzing first. That same hum Raiker's wings made, only much, *much* louder. The noise grew as the minutes slipped by. Eventually, it was accompanied by a new sound– feet marching in step, coming from the woods.

"I know I said 'never again' with the teleporting thing," Petra said, "but..."

"It leaves a trace. Not for long, but if they're strong enough they can find it and they can follow it." He swallowed hard. "We won't get far if we flee."

Petra sat with that disquieting thought in silence, holding Raiker's hand.

The buzzing reached them first. Fairies flying in a tight V formation high over their heads, all of them dressed in black uniforms.

"It's the Unseelie Guard," Raiker whispered.

There were hundreds of soldiers, so many that they blocked the sun like a cloud as they passed. They flew higher, until they became black pin pricks in the sky, a flock of ravens traveling south for the winter.

The rest of the soldiers emerged from the woods, marching two by two. These dark-clad warriors were wingless– dwarves and creatures that were more beast that humanoid. Things that Petra didn't have a name for. They carried weapons that crackled with lightning or burned with deadly fire. The parade went on and on.

A tall figure with a black hood pulled up over his head dropped out of step just in front of their hiding place. His back to them, he took a long pull out of a flask. The creature paused for a moment, then turned in their direction. Where his face should have been, a bleached white skull shown in the sun.

"Elbkönig," Petra whispered.

"Yes," Raiker confirmed without looking at her. His eyes stayed fixed on the monster, one hand holding on to hers much too tight, and the other clenched around the hilt of his sword.

This wasn't like the skeletal Elbkönig Petra had drawn for children at the hotel to color. There was no skin or muscle, yes, but everything below the bones was still there. A purplish grey brain peeking out through a crack in the skull. A half-rotted tongue that emerged its boney jaws to lick an errant drop of wine off the flask. Sickness stirred in her belly watching it, only slightly abated when it turned to go.

"You said that skirmish was two moons ago," Petra whispered as the Elbkönig retreated. "Was that before or after you were hired to find the Key?"

"Before." Raiker looked at her curiously. "What are you thinking?"

"Maybe someone wants the Key so they can win the war."

Raiker watched the troops march by them, close enough to see the whites of their eyes on the creatures that had eyes.

"There's no war," Raiker said.

His hand shook in hers.

"Were you serious about the Seelie Court 'sending out the press gangs'?" she asked.

Raiker looked straight ahead and set his mouth into a hard line. "Duty would compel me to defend my court, not conscription. It would be an honor to serve in the Seelie Guard."

"But you wouldn't have a choice, would you?"

He looked at her, a glimmer of fear in his eyes, and nodded.

The last few foot soldiers passed them, marching into the distance.

"Now what?" Petra whispered.

"We wait until I'm certain they won't hear us, and we get the hell out of here." Raiker looked down at the words scorched into the rock below them. "And I suppose we go find a dictionary..."

It was near sunset when they took flight again, heading back in the direction of the fairy ring. They flew past it until they reached a lake surrounded by rolling hills. For a moment, Petra thought they were descending into the water, but Raiker turned and hovered over a house she had nearly mistaken for an ordinary bunch of trees by the shoreline.

Raiker's house wasn't made from one tree, but at least three. The trunks wove together until they coalesced into a tall, narrow house high up above the ground. Branches grew together and wrapped around it forming a shockingly flat, smooth balcony that looked out over the water and curved around the whole house. The entrance was dominated by a huge front door made of driftwood and towering windows on either side. Above the door was a smaller, stained-glass window. It looked like a web with a spider in the middle.

Raiker put one hand out and muttered something. The sphere of warding around the house shimmered, and then Raiker descended down onto the balcony.

"Did you just unlock your front door?" Petra asked as Raiker set her back down on her feet.

"I, uh, unlocked it for you," Raiker clarified. "You can pass in and out of the wards without trouble now, just like I can."

Feeling a little like she'd just been given a key to her boyfriend's house, Petra smiled and then walked to the edge of the balcony. It was a bit vertigo inducing, particularly without the benefit of a railing, but the view of the pink sky reflecting off the lake was spectacular. Off in the distance, a pair of topless mermaids lounged in the shallow water near the shore. Shitpoo barked at them, and Petra gripped the dog tight, worried he might charge right off the edge.

"What do you think?" Raiker asked.

Petra looked left to right and then peered over the edge of the balcony.

"I think I'm trapped," she said.

It took Raiker a moment to realize what she was talking about. There was no way to get up to the house, or down from it, without wings.

"Oh," he said, and smiled apologetically. "Sorry, I don't usually entertain guests who can't fly."

He crossed the balcony to the front door and held it open for her. "After we sort out this mess, I'll work on singing you some stairs."

"Hang on," Petra said, "Did you say, 'sing' or....?"

She trailed off as she stepped through the doorway and took in the inside of the house. The interior walls were covered in green vines with heart-shaped leaves and purple flower buds. As soon as Raiker stepped into the room the flowers began to bloom, the buds opening to reveal the purple and white striped petals inside. The room was lit by a hovering crystal globe that encased a glowing orb of light. Petra hadn't seen how exactly Raiker had turned the light on. Maybe it just shone for him, like the flowers seemed to bloom for him.

It was a small, round room with an eat-in kitchen on one side and a living room on the other. Her "Feenring" painting hung on the living room wall. Petra stopped and stared at it.

"Would you like me to put that away?" Raiker asked.

"No." Petra smiled a little. "No, it looks nice there."

Shitpoo darted around the room, tail wagging excitedly as he sniffed everything. For a few moments Petra wondered where the bedrooms and bathrooms were, and then she looked up. High above her head there were three doors set into the walls. Raiker noticed the direction of her gaze.

"Ladders..." he muttered, "I'm going to have to add ladders. Unless you want me to carry you to bed every night..."

"I'm sure that'll be really romantic right up until I have to pee at three a.m.," Petra said with a snort of laughter.

"Well, if you do need to, ah, take care of any necessities in the meantime I suppose you could use one of the pots in the kitchen. And I'll get some food while I'm out, but if you're hungry there's always fruit. Just make yourself at home."

"You're leaving?" Petra frowned and turned back to him.

"I need to go to Court. Tell someone what we saw. I'll be back soon," Raiker promised.

He leaned down and kissed her, quite likely in an effort to distract her mouth from forming a protest. Then he was gone, vanishing from her arms, his kiss still lingering on her lips.

And she was pissed he'd left her behind.

But it was hard to be too angry when she could see honest to God mermaids out the window. Petra watched them splashing in the lake for a few minutes, and then shrugged off her coat and turned to explore the house.

The living room was furnished with benches topped with plush, teal cushions and scattered with throw pillows. There were books on a shelf that had grown into the wall, all bearing titles in a script she'd never seen before. Petra pulled one down at random and found another book hiding behind it. It was very battered copy of Shakespeare's *A Midsummer Night's Dream* in its original English, tucked away like contraband.

Petra sat down on one of the benches and started flipping through the book she'd pulled off the shelf. It was written in fairy language, but not the same one from the rock. It looked like poetry, the slanted handwriting clearly shaped into stanzas.

Trying to get more comfortable, Petra lay down on her side and stretched her legs out on the long bench. She looked up from the plush benches in the living area to the short stools around the kitchen table.

No chair backs, she realized. *Furniture built for wings. That's why the doors are so big, too. He doesn't have to fold in his wings when he walks in.*

She laughed to herself and rolled over onto her back, thinking that perhaps she could convince Raiker to "sing" her an armchair as well while he was working on the stairs and ladders.

High above her head there were tree branches extending out from the walls. There was one every few yards or so, growing into the room for a foot or two and then looping back to the wall again, forming into half circles and squares. Petra squinted at them curiously. She had just stumbled on the idea that they looked a bit like frames without pictures when the answer came to her.

That's exactly what they were. Frames. Frames for spider webs. Petra grinned at the revelation. She wished she could have seen them, Desidae the Spider Charmer's tapestries. Though, she supposed she would have had to get a ladder to look at them properly, because they were way up...

She couldn't reach them either. Not after they tore off her wings.

The thought hit Petra with a start. She sat up and clapped a hand to her mouth.

She couldn't get to her bedroom or the bathroom or even make it up to the front door without... Raiker had to carry her.

Tears spilled out of her eyes.

Petra got up and crossed to the kitchen, wiping her eyes and hunting for a glass of water. Shitpoo followed with a worried whine, sensing her distress. Petra found a clay mug sitting on the edge of the sink, filled it up, and took a long, calming drink.

She lowered the mug and then she did a double take, forgetting her sadness as she stared at the sink. The basin was mounted to the wall and the spigot, which was styled a bit like an old-fashioned water pump, was attached to the basin. There was nothing underneath the basin. Petra could see the kitchen floor through the holes in the drain. She turned the water back on and watched it pour down the drain and...

vanish? She crawled under the sink, feeling for invisible pipes and finding none. Where was the water going? Where was it coming from in the first place?

Magic. He has magic plumbing.

The potbelly stove was, apparently, also magic. It was either that or Petra just couldn't figure out how to light it. There was no refrigerator substitute, but she did find a cupboard that must have served as a pantry. There were some dried herbs in it and a small canvas bag half full of sweet potatoes. The next time Raiker gave Petra a hard time about her empty pantry, she was going to smack him upside the head.

He had mentioned there was fruit though, and Petra rummaged through almost every cupboard she could reach before she realized he meant there was fruit outside. She walked back out the huge front door on to the deck, shutting Shitpoo in behind her. The mermaids were gone now, but there was an owl watching her from the trees. He seemed unperturbed by her presence as she searched the branches for low hanging fruit. The round berries were bright blue and just a little bigger than grapes, with fuzzy skin like peaches. Hoping Raiker would have warned her if anything growing out here was poisonous, Petra popped one in her mouth. The insides were more juice than flesh and it burst in her mouth. They tasted like Creamsicles.

She started grabbing down handfuls and gathering them in her t-shirt, happily munching on more as she worked.

When she turned back to the front door, there was a pixie standing in front of it.

Petra gasped and dropped the hem of her shirt, sending the fruit tumbling down and rolling all over the balcony. She automatically took a step backwards, putting some distance between herself and this strange fairy.

"Careful, dearie," the pixie said. "We wouldn't want you to fall."

Chapter Eighteen

T he warning wasn't totally without merit.
Petra tore her eyes away from the pixie and
glanced behind her. She had stepped inches away
from the edge of the balcony.

"Raiker will be home any minute," Petra
warned.

She had no faith whatsoever that was actually
true, and she was looking around wildly for
anything she could use as a weapon.

"Easy now, little love," the pixie cooed as if Petra
were a frightened animal. "I'm not going to hurt
you."

"How did you get through the wards?" Petra
demanded.

The pixie smiled. She had long, dark brown
hair and bronzed skin. She wore a short, backless
white dress with a plunging neckline that left a lot

of cleavage exposed. The look was completed by
a pair of thigh high boots.
"Raiker and I are... neighbors," she said. "I'm
invited through his wards."
Suddenly, Raiker letting her in felt decidedly
less special.
"Neighbors," Petra repeated.
Raiker trusted this fairy enough to let her
through the wards. That meant it was reasonably
safe to assume she wasn't going to hurt her. But
what Petra didn't trust for a minute, based on the
dress and the bottle of wine in her hand, was that
Raiker and this pixie were only "neighbors".
"I keep a home just over there," the pixie
said, pointing somewhere off to the north side
of the lake. "But I spend most of my time at
my vineyard. I've known Raiker since Desidae
plopped him out right over there on her sitting
room rug. His mother was a dear friend of mine."
"Oh," Petra said, more than a little relieved.
"And sometimes I come over and we pleasure
each other until sunrise," she added causally.
Should have stuck with my first instinct.
"Yeah, that's not weird at all," Petra mumbled.
The pixie frowned. "Oh, you're jealous," she
said. "I didn't mean to upset you. Let's be friends."
She sounded surprisingly sincere, and Petra
found herself warming to her in spite of the
circumstances.
"I'm Sessile the Affective, brewer and bottler of
passions. What do I call you?"
It took Petra a second to remember she
shouldn't give out her true name, and then a few

seconds more to struggle to come up with a fake one.

"Uh... Liese," Petra said.

"It is lovely to meet you, Liese. Should we go inside?"

Sessile did not wait to be invited in before walking through the front door. Petra supposed she didn't really have the right to invite her in anyway. It wasn't her home. Shitpoo gave Sessile a mistrustful growl before tentatively approaching and sniffing her boots. Sessile patted the dog and he wagged his tail.

"Yours?" she asked, as she flitted into the kitchen and up to a cabinet Petra couldn't reach.

"Yeah," Petra said.

Sessile retrieved three dusty crystal goblets from the cabinet. She rolled her dark eyes at the dust and began to wash the goblets in the sink. Petra stood awkwardly next to her, painfully aware of how much more at home Sessile was here than she was.

"Where are you from?" Sessile asked.

"California," Petra answered.

Sessile started at her blankly. "Sorry, Alius geography isn't my strongest suit, and I haven't been in ages," she confessed.

"It's in the United States," Petra supplied.

Sessile smiled apologetically.

"North America," Petra added.

Finally, a glimmer of recognition dawned in her brown eyes.

"Oh, you're from the Americas! That's so peculiar. I've never met anyone from the Americas with such pale features."

She tugged on one of Petra's blonde curls playfully.

"You really haven't been to Alius in ages then," Petra muttered with a dark laugh.

Sessile set the glasses and the bottle she'd brought over down on the table.

"So, do we wait for Raiker the Rogue to grace us with his presence, or do we greedily consume the bottle ourselves before he gets here?" Sessile asked with a giggle.

Her laughter was strangely infectious.

"Maybe we should wait," Petra said. "He did say he was bringing home dinner."

"Hmmm... it is really more of an after dinner beverage."

Sessile left the bottle on the table and lay down on her stomach on one of the benches, her long legs stretched out behind her. Petra sat down across from her.

"Hey, since we're friends, maybe you could tell me..." Petra trailed off, uncertain, but Sessile smiled encouragingly and after a moment she finished the question. "Just how many fairies... are invited through Raiker's wards?"

"Oh, don't worry about that, dearie," Sessile said. "He does the wards over so often I can't get in half the time. Every time he brings another shady water nymph home with him, he has to change the locks again."

Sessile laughed until she saw the look on Petra's face. She sat up and took Petra's hand.

"Ah... you poor possessive little thing. That wasn't the question you were trying to ask me at all, was it?"

"Forget it," Petra said, shaking her head.

Sessile patted her hand sympathetically.

"Do you know how much older than you Raiker is?" Sessile asked.

Petra nodded.

"Yeah, I did that math already. I'm 27 and he's 2,876, so—"

"And if you had to guess, how many different lovers do you think you've had?"

"Seven," Petra answered, wondering where she was going with this.

Sessile chuckled. "Wow, you keep count. Alright. So that's about... one every other year since your body matured."

Petra shrugged. "Yeah, I guess that's more or less..."

And then she did some more math.

"*Oh*," Petra said with horror.

Sessile gave her hand another sympathetic pat.

"Oh, dear God that's... that's..." Petra stammered.

"One thousand, four—"

Petra held up her hand to stop her and Sessile smiled.

"Are you alright, Liese?" she asked.

Petra had gone a little pale.

"I think maybe I will take some of that wine now."

Sessile smiled brightly and fluttered over to the table.

"It's actually a melomel, not a true wine," Sessile said.

She poured them each a glass and brought them back over to the benches. Petra took a sip. It might have been the most delicious thing she had ever tasted; Fruity and sweet, but strong. More like drinking schnapps than wine. Warmth spread through her. Petra smiled wide, her concerns about Raiker's bustling love life forgotten, and took another sip.

"This is amazing," Petra gushed. "You made this? You're amazing. What's a melomel?"

Sessile was obviously thrilled she liked it. Her eyes lit up as she happily babbled about her creation while Petra continued to drink deeply.

"Melomel is fermented honey, like mead, except with fruit mixed in as well. I raised the bees for the sage honey myself. You know, Desidae's actually the one that taught me how to push the bees to make honey from the plants you want them to. The trick is to find the queen. I combined the sage honey with juice from fresh julian berries. And then before bottling I added lust, some happiness, and just a little foolhardy."

Petra stopped drinking, but the melomel in her glass was already nearly gone.

"Wait... what were those last three ingredients?" she asked.

That was about the same time she started to giggle and couldn't seem to stop.

Sessile smiled mischievously and opened her mouth to answer, but before she could Raiker appeared in the room, holding a large basket filled with parcels. Petra dropped her goblet in her rush to get to him and it shattered on the floor. She leapt into his arms, wrapping her legs around him and attacking him with kisses.

"I missed you," she moaned softly.

"I noticed," he said.

He shot Sessile a look as he pried Petra off him.

"Sess... What's in the bottle?" he asked sternly.

"Oh, don't be angry with me," Sessile said. "I brought it over for us when I saw your light on. I didn't expect you'd have company. Since when do you keep humans?"

"This one's special," he said.

"You didn't steal her, did you?" Sessile asked, suddenly very serious.

"That was one time! I— "

Raiker broke off as Petra tried to put her hand down his pants. He grabbed on to her wrist.

"But I need it," Petra protested.

"I know, my lady," Raiker said with an amused smile, "Just give me a moment, I need to murder my friend first."

Sessile was laughing uproariously. Petra laughed with her, although she couldn't quite piece together what was so funny. She was probably having trouble thinking because of the way Raiker's abs created a perfect line disappearing into his pants, and she wanted to get down on her knees, rip off his pants, and lick it all the way down. But he stopped her from getting on her knees so she settled for kissing his neck instead.

"What was in the wine, Sess?" Raiker asked again.

"It's a *melomel*," Petra corrected between kisses.

"Be nice to her. I like her,"

"Awww, I like you too, Liese," Sessile beamed.

"And I don't care that you used to sleep with her and Follium and 1,429 other skanks—"

"That's an oddly specific number," Raiker interrupted with a laugh. "How did you—?"

"Because I love you," Petra said, cutting him off.

Raiker had been acting, at worst, annoyed with Sessile, but he veered all the way to anger then. And when Petra tried to kiss him again, he grabbed her face in his hands and commanded.

"*Petra Adelina Bachman, sit down and stop talking.*"

Petra sat down on the bench obediently.

"Love?" he repeated, but he was talking to Sessile, not to her. "You put in love?"

Sessile shook her head vehemently. "It's mostly libido and joy and lowered inhibitions. And a really pure sage honey. Any love she's feeling is all her, I swear it."

Raiker faltered, looking from Sessile to Petra. "But..." he stammered.

Petra just looked up at him and smiled. And after a moment of stunned silence, it sunk in, and then Raiker smiled back.

Sessile stood and thrust her thus far untouched goblet of melomel into his hands. "Try it, dearie. Why don't you see what a little lowered inhibitions makes you say to her?" She gave him a quick kiss on the cheek. "Don't stay away so long next time."

She waved goodbye to Petra and then she vanished, leaving Petra and Raiker alone.

It took Petra's groggy, slightly hung-over brain a minute to remember where she was when she woke up the next morning. The cozy bedroom was almost entirely taken up by an oversized sleeping pallet covered in an intricate handmade quilt. The room faced the lake, and if Petra had woken up earlier, she could have seen the sunrise over the water out of the window that stretched floor to ceiling. Now the sun was high in the blue morning sky, and there were dozens of butterflies flitting through the air.

Raiker was already awake and dressed, sitting up on the edge of the mattress with his sword in his lap, sharpening it with a stone. The rhythmic sound was doing nothing to help her throbbing headache. Petra pushed the quilt off her and found that she'd lost her pants, shoes, and bra at some point last night, but she was still wearing her t-shirt and lace panties. The events of the night before were coming back to her in pieces.

"Oh my God, tell me I didn't actually try to give you a hand job right in front of your ex..." Petra groaned, putting her face in her hands.

Raiker chuckled and turned around.

"Sessile's wines are great fun at parties, but she really should have warned you about what was in it before she gave you some."

He set down the sword and crawled into bed next to her.

"I don't remember coming to bed..." Petra said.

"No, you wouldn't. After Sess left I made you go to sleep. I carried you up here."

Petra spotted her neatly folded jeans and her bra sitting on top of the wardrobe.

"Since when can you push me so easily?" she asked.

"My lady, you were hopelessly inebriated. You would've eaten rocks if I'd told you to."

Petra shifted uncomfortably. "So... we didn't... have sex last night?

"No," Raiker assured her. "Not that I didn't want to, but I was worried you might be angry with me in the morning."

"Hopelessly inebriated" indeed. Drinking Sessile's melomel had felt quite a bit like the time Petra's cousin had offered her a little yellow smiley face pill in a Berlin nightclub. Only the boy she'd gone home with that night hadn't been nearly as concerned about how she would feel in the morning.

Petra leaned in to reward Raiker's restraint with a kiss, then stopped and clapped a hand to her mouth, giggling.

"Oh no, better let me brush my teeth first..." she cautioned.

Raiker grinned playfully and pinned her to the bed. He stole a kiss, his tongue plunging into her mouth. A fraction of a second later he withdrew, making a face.

"Oh, that's foul..." he said.

"You jerk!" Petra laughed and shoved his weight off her. She frowned suddenly. "Shit. I don't have a toothbrush here."

A quick flight and a hop into an alternate dimension, and then they were back at Petra's house. She washed yesterday's make up off her face and brushed her teeth in the master bathroom. Raiker watched from the doorway, looking pensive.

"Do you remember what you said last night?" he asked.

"Oh no," Petra said through a mouthful of toothpaste. She spit and rinsed her mouth. "What did I say?"

The longer Raiker hesitated before answering the more Petra cringed in anticipation.

"Sorry," Petra said, breaking the silence. "Did I embarrass you in front of Sessile or something? I kinda run my mouth when I drink. I'm sure whatever it was I didn't mean it."

Raiker folded in his wings and shuffled his feet. When he met her eyes, it was with a tight smile. "Forget it. I won't embarrass you by repeating it."

Now Petra was even more worried about what inebriated nonsense had come out of her mouth last night. Before she could ask again, Raiker changed the subject.

"I could clear a little space in my bathroom for you... somewhere for a toothbrush and..." His eyes roved over the array of makeup and beauty products littering the counter and he laughed. "Actually, I'd better just get another cabinet for you. I mean..." he fidgeted with his hair, "if that's something you'd like."

Petra took his hands and led him over to the shower, eager to show him just how much she liked that idea. She was overjoyed and she was terrified. She'd had a plan for her future and she didn't know how Raiker would fit into it. Most of all, she didn't know how she could ask him to be with her, when being with her meant he would inevitably have to watch her die.

But she was drunk of the feeling of his skin against hers. He pressed her back into the frosted glass of the shower and slid inside her, and Petra thought that all those things were problems that could wait for another time.

Over breakfast, Raiker told her how he had fared at Court yesterday.

"I knew I should have changed into something nicer first. They wouldn't even let me in the gate," he complained.

"But you did tell the Queen about all those soldiers, right?"

"I did the next best thing. I left a message with the page for Duchess Calantha the Charming." He took a bite of his Fruity Pebbles, made a face, and added more sugar. "She's the Queen's consort. I'm sure her majesty will get the message eventually." He took another bite, and seeming to remember something, he leapt out of his chair. "Oh! And I stole you a gift. Hold on..."

He returned with a canvas sack and produced a long, thin box wrapped in paper. It was a sword with an ornate sheath that fit on her back between her shoulder blades. The sheath and the hilt were real silver, and Raiker could handle it without trouble, but the sharp blade inside was iron.

"I don't know how to use it," Petra said.

"And I don't have time to teach you," Raiker replied. "But you're pretty damn good with your fireplace poker, and this isn't so dissimilar. You shouldn't need it anyway."

Petra swished the blade through the air experimentally, thinking that the likelihood she'd need it was higher than Raiker was willing to admit.

She glanced over at the large canvas bag, still heavy with mysterious cargo. Raiker followed the direction of her gaze.

"You said you wanted a dictionary..." he said.

They moved to the garage and spread out Raiker's old school books, poring over them in turn. There were three of them, and not a one in a language Petra spoke. The first was a hand-drawn picture book that seemed to be the Old Fae equivalent of *See Spot Run*. "Nova wants to fly." "Nova flies high." "Nova flies low." Each watercolor depicted a cartoon pixie with a bright smile. It gave Petra a sense of some of the basic sentence structure.

More useful were the dictionaries, one Old Fae to Raiker's language, Dryadian, the other Old Fae to Elvish. Put together, it gave her broad definition of what each word meant. Too broad, in fact. Sometimes the Dryadian and Elvish dictionaries disagreed with each other. Other times both books would agree, but a word would have two, even three different meanings.

Petra copied the sentence that ended in her name from the picture she'd taken of the rock yesterday. She wrote it at the top of the blank canvas on her easel, and with Raiker translating, proceeded to dissect it.

"I... don't think it says I 'have' the Key," she said several hours later. She cocked her head sideways at the notes scribbled all over the canvas. "I think *sahib* means more like 'own.'"

Raiker looked up at her from his slumped position in her armchair. "*Have. Own.* What's the difference?"

"I..." Petra felt like she was teetering on the precipice of a breakthrough. "I'm not sure."

Raiker groaned. "We've been at this half the day, Petra. We could be looking for the Key or" —he flew over and snaked his hand down to cup her ass— "taking another shower."

Petra batted his hand away, squinting at the words. "Okay, what about this?" She copied the sentence over again, skipping over the word for "Key" and leaving a blank. "Everything written in Old Fae has to be true, right?" She held out the marker to Raiker. "I want you to write... 'blue shoes'. 'Petra Adelina Bachman has blue shoes.'"

Raiker took the pen from her, grumbling. "Alright. I'll play along." He thought for a moment and then filled in the missing words.

Petra took off her blue flip flops and thrust them into Raiker's arms. She looked back at the words on the board.

Raiker raised an eyebrow. "My lady, why am I holding your shoes?"

"They're still my shoes. My possession. But I don't *have* them anymore, do I? *You* have them."

Raiker looked from the shoes to the canvas, a light beginning to dawn in his eyes.

"Okay..." Petra said. "So now, I'm giving you these shoes. A gift from me to you."

Right before their eyes, her name vanished from the end of the sentence. New letters appeared instead, Old Fae letters, written in the same green ink.

Petra grinned. "What's it say now?"

"That's..." Raiker's eyes had gone wide as dinner plates. "That's my true name."

He dropped the shoes and attacked the new letters with the marker, furiously scribbling until his name was obscured. He took a step back, considered the canvas for a moment, and then ripped it off the easel and set it on fire with his hands.

"Mist!" Petra yelped. "War das wirklich nötig?"

She punched the garage door opener. The smoke drifted outside as Raiker dusted the ashes off his hands and clothes.

"Sorry," he said. He turned to her, eyes gleaming with excitement. "You were right. It doesn't say the Key is *in* your possession. It says it *is* your possession. Or the words on the rock would have changed."

"Right!" Petra agreed excitedly. "Which means it might be in the house, but it might be– I don't know. As long as it wasn't given away, it could be anywhere."

Both their smiles faded as those words sunk in. Petra sat down on the floor. "Well, shit," she said. "So, we're even further away from finding it."

She put her face in her hands, sinking into that hopeless feeling. Raiker knelt and then scooped her up off the floor and into his arms. He flew through the door back into the house.

"Where are you taking me?" Petra demanded.

"I'm going to make love to you until you stop looking so sad, and then probably for quite a while after that." He fluttered up and over the stairs.

Petra couldn't help but laugh. "Shouldn't we be looking for the Key?"

"We can search the world over for it tomorrow, my lady." Raiker set her down on the bed and started unbuttoning his shirt. "Tonight, you're mine."

Petra woke much too early. It was still dark and the bed was empty. Even Shitpoo had wandered off somewhere. A moment later, she realized it was Shitpoo that had woken her. He was somewhere downstairs barking, and then with a hissed command from Raiker, he stopped.

Feeling apprehensive, Petra slipped on the satin robe and stepped out of the bedroom. From the top of the stairs, she could see Raiker standing by the little window to the right of the front door. He was illuminated by the glow of his sword, which he held at his side. With his other hand, he was pulling the curtain back just an inch so he could peer out to the driveway. Shitpoo was next to him; his little body posed in an unmistakable attack stance and pointed at whatever Raiker was looking at out the window.

"What's out there?" Petra asked from the top of the stairs.

Raiker jumped at her voice and closed the curtain. He did his best attempt at looking casual while holding a five-foot long sword.

"Nothing. Everything's fine, my lady. Go back to sleep," he said.

"Wow. You really are a crap liar," Petra said as she walked down the stairs.

Raiker gave her a pained look, but he didn't stop her when she approached the window and peeked behind the curtain. A cloud of fog had rolled in, so thick that Petra couldn't see beyond the far edge of the driveway. But the yard appeared empty and quiet.

"They're shielding themselves from human eyes," Raiker said. "Here."

Raiker put his hand over her eyes and muttered something. When Petra opened her eyes again, there were three fairies standing at the extreme edge of her yard.

The first stood about four-feet tall on two legs, but looked as though he would be just as comfortable crawling on all fours on his elongated, rat-like paws. He was covered in gray hair that was matted with mud, and his yellow eyes glowed in the dark.

To his left was a devastatingly gorgeous female pixie dressed in form-fitting leather. Her hair was shock white and tumbled down to her thin waist in a torrent of curls. She was toting an axe that was bigger than she was, but she held it easily at her side as she fluttered on red-tipped dragonfly wings.

And finally, on the far end was what looked very much like a thin, middle-aged man with a long beard. He carried no weapon, and there was nothing inherently threatening about his appearance, and yet just looking at him made Petra's hair stand on end.

"That's a burber," Raiker supplied, pointing at the bearded man. "Pixie, and..."

he pointed at the hairy creature,

"hobyah."

As Petra watched, the pixie turned and looked straight at her. She smiled and then got the attention of her compatriots, pointing out Petra's face in the window. Petra closed the curtain and took a step back.

"My wards will keep them out," Raiker said.

Nothing about Raiker's demeanor suggested that that was actually true.

"Then why aren't you sleeping?" Petra asked.

"...In case they don't," Raiker said.

Petra chanced another glance out the window. The hobyah raised one clawed finger and scratched it at the air in front of him. It made a sound like fingernails on a chalkboard and left a glowing orange line in its wake. But the invisible wall he was scratching at held.

"Your magic isn't back yet, is it?" Petra asked.

"...I have a little," Raiker answered. "I won't need it. If they could get through, they'd have done it by now."

Petra picked up her sword that was leaning against the wall next to the door and unsheathed it.

"The other stuff we did, the iron and horseshoes and Shitpoo, will that stop them?" Petra asked.

"We won't need them," Raiker insisted again. And then after a moment he added, "They'll slow them down."

Petra tightened her grip on the sword and pulled back the curtain. The fairies had turned away from the house and were facing the darkened street. Petra squinted to see what they were looking at. Slowly, a figure began to emerge from the fog, walking towards them with a strange, sluggish gait. It was an old woman dressed in tattered black shawls. The other fairies moved aside to let her approach the edge of the yard.

The old woman didn't have any eyes.

"That's a banshee," Raiker said, and for the first time he sounded not just worried, but scared.

"What's a banshee do?"

The old woman screamed, opening her mouth far wider than her jaw should have allowed and letting out a shriek as loud as an explosion. Petra clapped her hands over her ears and watched in horror as the wards around the house began to fracture. Bright glowing orange cracks started where the banshee stood and quickly branched out like jagged bolts of lighting, until the entire dome structure was a spider web of fault lines. With one last shriek, the structure shattered, the pieces falling to the earth like broken glass. The Unseelie stepped into the yard.

Chapter Nineteen

"Stay inside!" Raiker yelled, and before Petra could protest, he charged out the front door and slammed it behind him. She could hear Raiker roar and then a great clang of metal on metal. Something hit the house with a thud that made plaster dust rain down.

I have to help him.

But before she could, the banshee shrieked again, and this time the sound pierced through Petra. The pain brought her to her knees and made her drop her sword as she covered her ears and prayed for it to stop.

The sound stopped, with a suddenness that suggested the banshee had been made to stop. In the absence of the screams there was a scrambling, scratching noise. It sounded horribly like it was inside the walls. Petra grabbed the sword and sprang back to her feet, whirling to face the living room.

The scratching grew louder, and then the hobyah bounded out of the fireplace on all fours, snarling. He charged at Petra, but before he could reach her, Shitpoo ran at him, barking and putting himself between her and the monster. The hobyah raised his hackles and backed away from Shitpoo. He let out a low, worried sounding whine. When Shitpoo barked again, the thing panicked. He ran for the fireplace, scrambling and failing to climb back up the chimney. He gave up on the chimney, ran across the living room, and leapt from the back of the couch straight out the living room window, shattering the glass.

A breeze from the west blew back the curtains on the empty window frame, and finally Petra could see what was happening in the yard. The hobyah landed safely in the grass next to the crumpled figure of the banshee, who did not look like she would ever get up again. The hobyah kept running and didn't look back.

Raiker was fighting the pixie in midair, but he was drawing the fight towards the ground. She conjured a ball of white light in her hands and flung it at him. Raiker dodged it, drawing her downward until her boots touched the ground. She conjured another ball of light, but it vanished from her hands the moment she landed. Her glamour vanished with it, transforming her into a scale-covered, hook-nosed creature dressed in tattered rags. She screamed in rage and Raiker laughed, dancing around her before taking a swing with his sword. Raiker knew where all the cast-iron frying pans and horseshoes were buried, and the other pixie didn't.

It didn't stop her axe from working though. She swung it in a wide arc that Raiker nearly dodged, but the blade sliced into his stomach and came away covered in his blood.

Petra ran for the front door and yanked it open. The burber was behind it, and he smiled at her. Petra slammed it shut, and a moment later it exploded in a shower of splintered wood. She shrieked and backed away with the sword held out in front of her.

"Petra..." the burber said.

Petra forced herself to look down at her shaking hands, avoiding looking into the thing's eyes.

"*Petra Adelina Bachman, look at me*," the burber said.

Petra didn't look up, but how much she wanted to look up just then terrified her. This thing was much, much better at pushing than Raiker or Follium.

The horseshoe. The horseshoe over the door will keep him out, she reminded herself.

And it seemed that it was working, because he made no move to step over the threshold. She didn't allow her gaze to go any higher than his shoes.

I have to get to Raiker. Raiker's hurt. Maybe if I run for the back door-

"*Petra Adelina Bachman, help me*!" Raiker's voice shouted from the doorway.

Instinctively, she looked up. Raiker was standing in the doorway, staring at her with his shining copper eyes.

"*Petra Adelina Bachman, I love you,*" he said. "*Do you love me?*"

"Yes," Petra answered breathlessly.

"*That's right. You love me. My beautiful, Petra Adelina Bachman, you would do anything for me. Anything I asked of you,*" Raiker said.

"Yes," Petra agreed. "Anything."

Shitpoo growled at Raiker, and Petra looked down at the little dog and frowned.

"*Don't look at him, Petra Adelina Bachman!*" Raiker shouted. "*Look at me!*"

Petra wanted to look at Raiker. She wanted to get lost in his eyes forever. But she thought forever could wait just a moment while she figured out what was wrong with her dog. Shitpoo didn't growl at Raiker. Shitpoo did everything Raiker ever asked him to do because... because Shitpoo is his true name and if fairies know your true name, fairies... fairies can...

"*Petra Adelina Bachman, I'm hurt!*" Raiker cried out.

Petra pulled her eyes away from the dog and looked at Raiker again. There was a huge, bleeding gash slicing through his chest. Had it been there a moment ago? Did it matter?

"*Petra Adelina Bachman, you love me. You have to help me. You have to take the horseshoe down so that I can come inside where I can be safe and we can be together.*"

Petra reached for the horseshoe where it hung on the nail, but found it out of her grasp.

"Stupid ape, you have a tool in your hand! Use it!" Raiker snapped.

His tone made her flinch. Raiker didn't talk to her like this. She didn't like it. She hesitated.

"*I'm sorry, Petra Adelina Bachman,*" Raiker said. "*But you have to hurry. Just reach up with that sword and knock it down. Go on.*"

Petra raised her sword over her head and hooked it on the horseshoe.

Shitpoo charged over the threshold and bit Raiker on the ankle. Raiker reached down and grabbed him, wrenching him free. He could have let him go then, but instead he grabbed the whimpering little dog in both hands. Raiker squeezed until something inside of Shitpoo cracked and then tossed the limp body aside like it was nothing.

Only it wasn't Raiker anymore, it was the burber, and with a scream of rage and anguish Petra drove the sword into his gut. He stumbled back, dragging Petra over the threshold with him. She let go of her sword and fell to her knees on the porch.

And then the sword wasn't in his gut anymore. He had no form anymore. He was a towering column of flames and white light. But something like an arm or more like a tendril snaked around her wrist and dragged her away from the porch. It seared through her skin where it touched her and she shrieked with pain.

A blast of light hit the burber and it let her go, leaving behind a zigzag of bright red on her arm where her skin used to be. Raiker, the real Raiker, had struck the creature. Raiker was bleeding from several ugly gashes, but none of them seemed to be too catastrophic. She could see the other pixie's body draped over a branch of the live oak tree.

Raiker knelt next to her and put up his hands. He conjured something that looked like the wards he had put around the house, but much smaller. A shield between them and the tower of fire. The shield came at the expense of his glamour, and his true form appeared with a hum.

The burber pushed against the shield, splintering it. With a pained cry, Raiker pushed more magic into the shield, filling the cracks back in. He'd barely finished when the burber cracked the shield again. This time, Raiker's whole body convulsed when he used more magic. He screamed as the blood vessels burst in his eyes and every vein in his arms stood out from the strain.

Oh my God, he's killing himself.

Suddenly, another burst of magic hit the burber, knocking it backwards away from the shield. Petra didn't understand where it had come from until Follium landed on the grass in front of them, his twin curved arakhs clutched in each hand. Without a moment's hesitation, he crossed the arakhs in front of his chest. A ball of orange light surrounded him, and then he threw his arms open. The ball expanded out with a great whoosh until it encompassed the whole property, and when it connected with the burber, it shoved the thing right off the edge and into the street again. It left a trail of scorch marks behind, but it stayed there behind the new wall of warding Follium had created.

After a moment, the burber shifted back into the man with the long beard. He pounded his fist against the wards just once, turned, and vanished.

"You're late," Raiker said to Follium in a dazed voice, and then he collapsed backwards onto the grass.

Follium rushed to Raiker immediately, sheathing his blades at his sides and kneeling in the grass next to him. He placed his palm on Raiker's forehead, in a gesture reminiscent of a mother checking a child's temperature.

"Is he okay?" Petra asked.

Agonizing seconds passed before he answered.

"He's fine," Follium said, and Petra cried with relief. "He'll be fine. He just needs rest."

Follium's fingertips began to glow, and he set to work knitting the slashes in Raiker's skin back together.

"Alright," Follium said, looking up from his work, "Let me see that arm."

But Petra had walked away, back towards the front door of the house. It took some time, but she finally found Shitpoo's prone body curled up in the dirt underneath the azaleas. Sobbing, Petra sunk down next to him and pulled the little ball of fluff into her lap with her good arm.

Petra gasped when Shitpoo let out a soft whine. He was still alive, but the poor broken dog couldn't move, or at least he couldn't without great pain. His little pink tongue licked her fingers, and he seemed to take some measure of comfort in her being there to hold him, in spite of the obvious agony he was in.

Petra sobbed and stroked his fur.

"Good boy, Shitpoo. You did so good. You saved me. You..." Her voice broke.

She looked up when she heard Follium swear. He was crossing the yard over to her and having some trouble navigating the minefield of iron buried in it. His body shrunk down from the barrel-chested glamour to a spindly pixie.

"Can you help him?" Petra asked. "Please help him."

Follium looked from her to the dog and sighed.

"I don't have enough magic left to fix him and your arm," he said.

Petra had been trying not to look at the burns, but she stole a quick glance then. She could see a clearly defined edge around it, a drop off where the burn went in perceptibly deeper than the untouched skin around it. Parts of the satin fabric of her robe had melted into it. The burn covered most of her forearm, and the pain was so bad she was shaking, her breath coming out in gasps.

"I'm fine. Help him. Please," she insisted.

Follium looked like he wanted to argue, but he put his hands on Shitpoo anyway. The tips of his clawed fingers glowed. He pressed them into Shitpoo's black fur in the same place the burber had squeezed. Shitpoo's little chest began to rise and fall.

Follium removed his hands and Shitpoo bounded back to life, barking and wagging his tail. Petra grinned and sobbed even harder, joy and relief now mixed up with pain and exhaustion.

Shitpoo darted over to Raiker and licked his face. Raiker's eyes opened. He smiled, patted the happy dog on the head, then passed out again.

"Now I know why he likes you," Follium said. "You're both sentimental idiots."

Petra shivered in the night air. Her skin felt like ice. She couldn't stop shaking.

"Dammit, your heart's beating too slow," he said. "You're in shock."

She couldn't catch her breath. She was trying not to look at the burn again, and she thought maybe she'd stop feeling so dizzy if she could just breathe. It was too cold to breathe, like the way diving into the ocean in the spring takes your breath away.

"Alright, I think maybe I have enough left for this," Follium mumbled.

He took her face in his hands and stared into her eyes.

"*Petra Adelina Bachman, sleep.*"

When Petra woke again there was sunlight streaming through the bedroom window.

Shitpoo snoozed contentedly on the bed next to her. She smiled and kissed the top of his head. He gave her an annoyed little huff at being disturbed and went back to sleep. The whole episode had the feel of a distant dream. Petra looked at her arm. Sometime while she had slept either Follium or Raiker must have recovered enough to heal her burn. The new skin that snaked around her forearm was baby smooth and strangely hairless, without a single freckle or blemish. The little white scar she'd earned climbing the jetty in Corona de Mar was gone, and Petra was surprised to find that she missed it.

The bandage on her back was gone too. Petra climbed out of bed. Someone, hopefully Raiker, had removed the singed blue robe and dressed her in an over-sized Green Day concert t-shirt. She stood in front of the full-length mirror and lifted the back of her shirt. The claw mark had vanished.

Petra slipped on a pair of leggings and headed downstairs. The front door and the living room window had been replaced, although the hobyah's claw marks in the sofa remained. Out the window, the yard looked perfect. No burnt up lawn. No broken glass. No dead fairies.

Follium and Raiker were in the kitchen, chatting while Follium cooked something on the stove that smelled magnificent. They'd both been restored to their usual, ludicrously beautiful forms.

Raiker rushed to her and kissed her as soon as she walked in. She wrapped her arms around him and held on tight. Her eyes misted over remembering how close they'd come last night to never being able to do this again.

"That's enough," Follium teased. "I want at least one meter between the two of you at all times. I'm not risking my life again because you wasted all your magic making your human's toes curl."

Raiker chuckled and then kissed her again with a defiant smirk.

"I should have let that burber eat you both," Follium said.

Petra crossed the kitchen to where Follium was standing by the stove, and after a moment's nervous hesitation, she hugged him. Follium seemed startled by the gesture, but after a few seconds he returned the hug.

"Thank you," Petra said.

Follium chuckled and then turned back to the pot on the stove. He dipped a spoon in and then offered it to Petra.

"Here, you can repay me by tasting this for me. Does it need anything?"

It was some kind of soup with mushrooms, garlic, and overwhelming quantities of butter and cream.

"No, it's perfect," she said. "Do you guys eat anything that's not full of cream or sugar?"

Raiker and Follium looked at each other for a beat.

"I also enjoy good fresh bread," Raiker offered.

"Yes," Follium agreed. "Especially with honey."

"And butter," Raiker added with relish.

Petra laughed and got some bowls down for the heart attack-inducing mushroom soup.

"So, who should I thank for fixing my arm and my back?" she asked.

Raiker pointed at Follium.

"He's the healer. I fixed the door and the window."

"Who got rid of the bodies?"

They pointed at each other.

"Don't dig under your oak tree," Follium advised.

It took Petra a moment to summon the courage to ask what she really wanted to know. "Are they gonna come back?"

The two fairies exchanged a nervous look, as if there was something they didn't want to tell her.

"What?" she said.

"...They're already back, my lady," Raiker confessed, and he pointed at the north-facing window at the far end of the kitchen.

Petra tentatively approached it and then pulled back the curtain. The window faced out to the little strip of yard between her house and Mrs. Mason's. Perched on the top of Mrs. Mason's roof was an anguana with moth wings, a beautiful face, and wispy dark hair. Only instead of bird legs like the one that had torn open her back, this one had a bright green snake's tail. Combined with the wings she looked as though she were half woman, half dragon. Petra let the curtain fall and backed away. She backed into Raiker, who grasped her shoulders reassuringly.

"There's a couple fire-nymphs behind your garden fence, too, and I suspect there may be a dorotabo under the house," Follium said. "But Raiker put his own wards back up behind mine, so they're twice as strong now. And this time your house is warded for banshees."

"In my defense, banshees are exceedingly rare," Raiker said, sounding guilty.

"Call yourself a housebreaker..." Follium teased.

"Breaking wards and putting them up are completely different," Raiker protested and Follium laughed at him.

Petra turned to face the two pixies, although there was something unsettling about putting her back to the anguana, knowing that she was somewhere behind her. Lurking. Watching.

"So... basically we're under siege," Petra said.

They nodded.

"Is there coffee at least?"

"I will make you some, my lady," Raiker promised.

They slept in shifts, taking turns keeping watch, although neither fairy would allow Petra to take one of the watch shifts herself, or even walk out of the house. She spent her waking hours hunting for the Key instead, sifting through the remaining boxes in the attic. For some reason, she kept returning to that old steamer trunk, and the picture of Lillian Greene talking to the late King Oberon. She wondered what other fairies had come here before, and why one of them had given her Oma something with the power to wipe out a species. What would Oma want with that? It occurred to her that maybe the fairy that gave it to her was trying to hide it, but surely there were safer hiding places than a human woman's house. Especially a house right next to a fairy ring.

Every day there were a few more fairies hovering outside of the wards. And each night she went to bed feeling no closer to the Key, or any kind of answers. But Raiker was always there sleeping next to her, and Shitpoo was always snoring at her feet. She would curl up against Raiker and drift off to sleep, breathing in the lavender scent on his skin and simply feeling grateful that they were all still there.

Petra was startled awake by the sound of Follium's booming laughter.

"You'd really never seen fireworks before?" his deep voice asked.

"No, and they were terrifying," Raiker's high, melodic voice answered him. "Stop laughing at me."

The side of the bed next to Petra was cold, save for the tiny patch occupied by Shitpoo. Raiker and Follium's voices drifted over to her through the cracked bedroom door. It sounded like they were in the room across the hall, where Petra had made up the guest bed for Follium.

Raiker laughed along with his friend despite his insistence that the story wasn't funny.

"Lunaria the Libidinous's birthday party. That was the last time we saw each other, right?" Follium said.

"I believe so. I'm not sure how much of that party I can remember."

Petra momentarily considered getting up and joining in the conversation, but she was warm and comfortable under the covers and decided she'd rather try to get back to sleep.

"I do recall Lunaria demanding that you dance for her," said Raiker.

"Well, it was her birthday. I couldn't exactly say no."

"You didn't want to say no," Raiker teased. "You loved it. You had the eye of every fae in the room."

"But I went home with you," Follium said.

Petra's eyes snapped open again.

"You remember that part, don't you?" he continued, his voice dropping to a low purr that was unmistakably seductive in nature.

Petra quietly sat up in bed, now hanging on every word. There was a long pause before Raiker answered.

"How could I forget?" he said.

Follium chuckled.

"It has been... too long, old friend."

The old mattress in the guest bedroom squeaked as they moved—

Closer together?

Further apart?

Back to me? Dammit Raiker, please come back to me...

—and then Petra heard the distinct sound of the two of them kissing. The bed squeaked again and Raiker let out a low moan of pleasure that hit Petra like a punch to her gut.

She wanted to be angry. Anger would have been so much easier than the devastation she was feeling. She wanted to charge in there, scream at him, and throw them both out of her house. Instead, she sat frozen, feeling sick to her stomach as she listened to them making out.

"We can't do this," Raiker said.

The kissing sounds continued even as Raiker spoke, and Petra imagined Follium planting those kisses on his neck, or his lips working their way down his chest.

"Not that I don't want to, I do. You're... tantalizing. But we need to conserve our magic," Raiker babbled nervously.

The kissing sounds stopped.

"I don't need magic to please you," Follium countered.

The bedsprings squeaked and Raiker let out a gasp that dissolved into a desperate whimper.

There were hot tears spilling out of Petra's eyes and she wasn't sure when they had started. What she did know, was that she absolutely could not take another second of listening to this.

Petra stood and picked up her sword leaning against the bed. She wasn't sure yet what exactly she planned to do with it, but it probably involved shoving it up Raiker's ass.

"Stop. I can't. I'm sorry," Raiker said.

The bedsprings groaned as one of them stood and began to pace the room.

"It's Petra," Raiker said, "You know I'm sleeping with Petra."

"And?" Follium said, sounding irritated.

"And you know how prone to jealousy humans are. Their weird obsession with serialized monogamy."

Petra loosened her grip on the sword slightly.

"If she wakes up and finds us together, she won't understand. It will hurt her."

"What do you care what the mayfly thinks?" Follium said.

What the what *thinks?*

"Don't call her that," Raiker said. "She's young. She's healthy. She's—"

"She's *dying*, Raiker. They're all dying." Follium sighed sadly. "Don't do this, old friend."

"Do what?" Raiker asked, his tone defensive. "I'm not doing anything. I just don't want her to—"

"Don't fall in love with a human," said Follium.

"I am not..." Raiker's voice trailed off, and several seconds passed before he spoke again. "Would it really be so bad if I was?"

Petra clapped a hand to her mouth to stifle a small gasp.

"Petra has six, maybe even seven decades left," Raiker continued. "I could spend them with her."

"Binding isn't supposed to last six or seven decades. It's meant to last millennia."

"Except when it doesn't. I've met fae who only had a handful of years with their partner. Things happen. Death happens. We're a lot more fleeting than we like to pretend we are." Raiker paused before he spoke again. "My mother... I only had 14 years with my mother. I could love Petra a lot longer than that."

"Raiker... think about this," Follium said, "Think about what folks will say about you if—"

"To hell with what they'll say and to hell with you!" Raiker snapped, and he stormed out of the guest bedroom, slamming the door behind him.

When he pushed open the door to the master bedroom, he found Petra in bed, lying there with her eyes closed as if she'd been asleep the whole time. The sword was back in its place, and Raiker stepped carefully over it as he climbed into bed next to her.

Raiker stroked her hair, and Petra stirred as though that had been the thing that had woken her. Even in the dark she could see the tears in Raiker's eyes as he looked at her.

"What's wrong?" she asked.

"Nothing," he insisted. "I'm sorry. I didn't mean to wake you. I was just..." He stroked her hair again. "It scares me how much I care about you," he whispered.

Petra reached out to him in the dark, pulling him into an embrace that didn't end until both of them were spent.

No magic required.

Chapter Twenty

F ollium was sitting at her kitchen table
drinking her coffee when Petra came
downstairs. Petra stiffened when she saw him, but
tried her best to maintain her composure.

"Good morning," she said, as cordially as she
could manage.

"Is it?" he muttered with a grumble.

Petra smirked as she poured herself a cup of
coffee and turned back to Follium with a smile on
her face. "I get it. I'm pretty cranky when I don't
get laid, too."

Follium regarded her silently for a moment
through narrowed eyes before managing a dark
chuckle.

"So, you heard us," he said. "Is this the part
where you get strangely possessive and threaten
me if I don't stay away from him?"

Petra shrugged and sat down at the table across from him. "I usually save the threats of bodily harm until after my morning coffee."

Follium laughed and stirred some more sugar into his cup. "Petra, I think I might've liked you under other circumstances."

Petra snorted. "Yeah sure. If only you hadn't tried to throw me over a waterfall and suck my boyfriend's dick. We could have been best friends."

Follium made an exasperated noise. "For the last time, I was not really going to throw you over a waterfall. It was an empty threat."

"It sounded damn convincing to me. And I hear most fairies are bad liars."

Petra had been determined to remain civil, but her tongue was getting the better of her. It was hard to look at Follium and not think about his hands all over Raiker. She stood up from the table and stalked off towards the archway into the living room. Forget breakfast, she was going to wake Raiker up and channel all this rage into doing terrible things to him. Follium could sit down here and drink her coffee and listen to the bed squeak.

"You're going to get him killed," Follium called to her, and Petra stopped. "When they came for you and he didn't have the magic to defend himself he should have fled, but he stayed and he nearly died because you are under his protection."

I'd like to think that's not the only reason he stayed.

"How much did you overhear last night?" Follium asked.

Petra walked back into the kitchen and sat down. "I woke up somewhere around the recap of Lunaria's birthday party."

"Then you missed the part where I had to convince him that the magic he struck the burber with was sufficient retribution for the burns on your arm. He wanted to go after him and avenge you. I think you have some understanding now of how dangerous that would have been."

Petra's hand went to the smooth patch of skin on her arm and she shivered involuntarily. "Thank you."

"I'm very glad you're grateful," Follium said. "Now you can repay me by telling Raiker that he's released from his vow to protect you."

It's that easy?

"I didn't know... Raiker didn't tell me I could do that," Petra said.

"It would be dishonorable of him to suggest it."

They sipped their coffee in silence.

"Do you know what the worst thing you could call a fae is?" he asked her after some time.

"No, but I'm guessing it's what you're about to call me," she said.

"Oathbreaker," Follium said. "There is absolutely nothing worse you could be than someone who would go back on their word. It's why... some of us don't like humans. Your kind breaks their promises as fast as you make them."

Follium drained the rest of his coffee, set the cup down, and looked her dead in the eyes. "If he is ever fool enough to bind himself to you and you are unfaithful to him, I *will* throw you off a waterfall. That is a promise, Petra Adelina Bachman."

Petra's mouth dropped open.

"Good morning," Raiker called out as he approached the kitchen from the living room. Petra rearranged her face into a more neutral expression. Raiker eyed the two of them nervously when he walked in.

"What are you two talking about?" he asked.

"The weather," Follium said, and Petra had to concede that he was, in fact, a pretty good liar. "It never rains here."

"Yeah, we got a song about it and everything," Petra said.

Raiker headed for the coffee pot.

"Do I get a good morning kiss?" she asked.

Raiker turned and walked back over to her. He leaned down and kissed her briefly on the lips. Petra smiled and shook her head.

"Better kiss," she demanded.

Raiker grinned and did as he was told, giving her a deep, prolonged kiss that ended with a little sigh. Petra waited until Raiker turned his back to them again to smirk at Follium. Follium glowered at her.

"Well, if you're up, I'm going to get some sleep," Follium announced as he pushed his chair back from the table. "There's a couple more of them on the eastern side now. *Elves.*"

The amount of disdain Follium managed to contain in that last word was even more than he used when he talked about Petra.

"Ugh. *Elves*," Raiker responded in a perfect echo of Follium's tone.

Elves? What do elves look like?

She waited for Follium to retreat up the stairs before she walked out into the living room and pulled back the curtains. There had been six fairies on this side of the house when she had gone to bed last night: two pixies, an anguana, a tree nymph, a fire nymph, and a hobyah. The elves made eight. They looked a bit like wingless glamoured pixies to Petra; painfully handsome human men with pointed ears. Only there seemed to be significant differences in their fashion sense. Every pixie she'd seen ran around wearing next to nothing. The elves wore high collared coats that fell almost to their knees with long sleeves, and pants with boots underneath them. One had jet-black hair that hung to his shoulders in an intricate braid, not a single hair out of place. He wore a silver crown with a diamond that dangled down to the middle of his forehead. The other, taller elf had close-cropped blond hair and a perfectly trimmed goatee. They both bore stern expressions and carried beautifully carved bows and arrows. Petra noted that the pair of pixies outside the house seemed to hold the same disdain for the elves as the pair inside did. They were giving the elves a wide berth, preferring to chat amongst themselves or flirt with the nymphs.

Raiker came up behind her and peered out at them himself. He did a double take when he saw them and his eyes went wide.

"Follium, get down here!" he shouted.

Follium appeared at Raiker's side in an instant, his arakhs drawn. "What's wrong?"

Raiker pointed to the elf with the braid in his hair. "Do you know who that is?" He didn't wait for an answer. "That's Kabshi'l the Clairvoyant."

"Why do I know that name...?" Follium asked.

"Because he's the most powerful psychic in the Unseelie Court."

Follium's eyebrows rose. He stared curiously out the window at the elf.

"Fairies can be psychic?" Petra interjected.

Follium turned and looked at her as if she was slow. "*Humans* can be psychic. Why would you think we're any different?"

Petra made a mental note to circle back to that topic another time.

"He can read minds," Raiker clarified for her. "It's a very rare skill."

Petra looked out at the elf again, and she realized that the almond-shaped diamond on his crown was meant to look like a third eye.

"Whoever's after the Key went to a lot of pains to conceal their identity from you, and me, and all of them out there," Raiker said slowly.

"Best piece of transmittal magic I've ever seen," Follium agreed.

"Me too," Raiker said.

Raiker pointed at Kabshi'l again. "But I'd bet a sack of gold it didn't work on him. That elf might be the only one who knows who the buyer is." He smiled mischievously at Follium. "You still have that bag?"

The magic bag that Follium had stuffed Petra in appeared in his hand, and Petra scowled at it. Follium eyed the grin on Raiker's face with apprehension.

"What are you planning, old friend?" Follium said.

"I'd just like to ask him a couple questions," Raiker replied.

"The two of us cannot fight off—" Follium began to protest, but Raiker cut him off.

"So, we grab him, and we pull him through the wards. The rest won't be able to follow."

"Yes, but we have to step through the wards to grab him. There are eight of them out there, and that's just the ones on this side of the house."

"So, we create a distraction first," Raiker replied.

Follium let out a dramatic sigh of exasperation. "'Create a distraction'? There're 28 fairies surrounding the property! That would have to be one hell of a good distraction."

Petra turned away from the argument, trying to remember where she left her purse. She had a hook for it in the foyer, but it wasn't there.

"28? I thought there were 27," Raiker said.

Petra headed up the stairs, the sound of their bickering fading behind her. She found her purse on the bedroom nightstand, and she rooted around in it until she found her keys at the bottom. On the ring were the keys to her Jetta, her front door, the hotel safe, the lock on the bicycle she almost never used, and the spare to Mrs. Porter's place she'd forgotten to return after cat-sitting for a week while Mrs. Porter was in Bermuda. Petra removed each key from the ring one at a time as she walked back down the stairs.

Raiker was kneeling in the living room with his hands pressed into the floor and Follium was standing over him.

"I'll be damned," Raiker said. "There *is* a hulder down there. How did I miss that?"

"You're an idiot," Follium supplied.

Petra ignored them and stepped out the front door. She walked up the driveway at a brisk pace, the keys clutched in her sweaty palm. The Unseelie reacted immediately to her presence. They began shouting her name all at once, trying to get her to look them in the eye. Petra kept her gaze away from their eyes, fighting the urge to look up.

Raiker and Follium caught up with her just before she reached the edge of the driveway. Their urgent demands that she return to the house added to the cacophony of voices vying for her attention.

"QUIET!" Petra yelled, and surprisingly, at least for a moment, everybody shut up.

"You want the Key, right?" she yelled.

She didn't dare look any higher than Kabshi'l knees, but she watched as those knees began to retreat from the property line.

"Don't!" Kabshi'l shouted. "It's a—"

"Go get it!" Petra yelled and she tossed the handful of keys through the wards and into the street.

The road in front of her erupted into absolute chaos as the fairies dove for the keys. One of the pixies scooped up the door key only to be parted from it a moment later as the anguana wrapped her tail around him and squeezed until he dropped it. The key was then snatched up by the hobyah, who only held onto it for a second before the blond elf shot him in the eye.

Raiker shot her a look that was half anger, half admiration before charging over the property line with his sword held high, Follium hot on his heels. They flew straight for Kabshi'l, who seemed to have already figured out that he was the target. The elf vanished, and Raiker cast something that looked remarkably like a glowing fishhook. The hook reached into the place Kabshi'l had disappeared from and yanked him back.

Before they could grab him, the other elf stepped in to defend his friend, and then Petra's view was blocked as a massive dogwood tree sprouted out of the middle of the road, cracking through the pavement. The tree nymph was crouched on a branch at the top, nearly camouflaged, their hair a curtain of white flowers and their skin the same dark brown as the bark. Petra spotted the glint off the Jetta key in their hand. The nymph smiled at Petra, and then they took the key and licked it.

Suddenly, Petra felt a tug around her abdomen. It was as if there was an invisible rope around her waist. On the other end of the rope was the nymph in the tree, reeling her in. Petra dug her heels in and fought as hard as she could. The nymph was stronger than her, but not by much, and she only succeeded in shifting her a few inches forward.

The nymph let go all at once, and Petra fell over backwards. Without wasting a second of the advantage they'd gained, the nymph cackled and quickly yanked Petra forward. Petra flipped on to her belly and slid towards the edge of the warding. She clawed desperately at the grass for purchase and only succeeded in ripping it out a handful at a time.

"Petra, catch!" Follium yelled.

With a thud, one of Follium's arakhs sunk into the earth just inches away from her. Petra grabbed onto the hilt as she slid past. It acted like a stake and slowed her inexorable slide for a precious few seconds, but then the arakh came free in her hand.

Petra rolled over onto her back, sat up, and brought the arakh down on the empty air where the rope should be just as her feet slid through the warding. The magic rope snapped and Petra fell backwards. She quickly scrambled back away from the edge again, about a split second before the anguana tried to grab her foot.

More fairies had arrived at this side of the yard. Raiker and Follium emerged from the chaos. They flew back into the yard, dodging blasts of magic that ricocheted off the wards. Follium had the now full and wiggling bag slung over his shoulder. Raiker grabbed Petra by the arm as he flew past, pulling her off the ground and up into the air. They landed on the porch, poured in the front door, and collapsed behind it.

Follium flung the sack down off his shoulder. From inside it, Kabshi'l was screaming curses and indignations.

"See," Raiker said, smiling at Follium. "I told you it would work. Just needed a good distraction."

Petra and Raiker burst into giddy laughter. A moment later the sound was drowned out by some kind of small explosion bouncing off the wards.

"You are both completely insane," Follium said.

After making the elf swear many vows that he would behave himself, Follium upended the sack onto Petra's kitchen floor. Raiker conjured a length of glowing orange cord and tied Kabshi'l to one of the kitchen chairs, securing each wrist to the arms and each ankle to the legs. Follium made a point of checking the knots behind Raiker.

Kabshi'l looked a little worse for the wear, and he took a moment to use a glimmer of magic to straighten out his hair, returning the rogue strands to the tight black braid. Behind him, Raiker was using the reflective surface of the refrigerator as a mirror so he could fix his own tousled copper hair.

"Is he basically a pixie without the wings?" Petra asked.

All three fairies glared at her.

"We are *nothing* like elves," Follium said. "Bunch of stuck-up, flightless prudes."

"Better than being perverted, impetuous hedonists," Kabshi'l muttered.

"A little hedonism might do wonders for that stick up your ass. You should try catching an orgy sometime," Raiker suggested.

"Who would invite him?" Follium said with a bark of laughter.

"Okay!" Petra said, throwing her hands up in surrender. "I take it back. Sorry I asked."

Follium and Raiker reeled in their laughter and then turned their attention back to the elf strapped to the chair. Their expressions turned menacing.

"I've never met a psychic before," Raiker said, leaning over Kabshi'l in a manner that the elf didn't seem to appreciate. "Do I even need to ask the question, or do you already know what we want?"

Kabshi'l ignored him and stared quizzically at Petra instead. Something about his gaze put her teeth on edge. His thin, manicured eyebrows rose.

"You're not quite who everyone thinks you are," he said to Petra. "The human who was given the Key died over a year ago."

Raiker and Follium exchanged a worried look. It occurred to Petra that it was possible they hadn't properly thought through their plan to abduct a psychic.

"'*Es tut mir leid Oma, ich werde aber bald zum Abendessen kommen,*'" Kabshi'l recited in perfect German, and Petra clapped her hand to her mouth. "That was the last thing you said to her. But you didn't come over for dinner soon, because your job was so much more important than visiting your grandmother. Imagine what would have happened if Mrs. Porter hadn't stopped by. How long do you think your grandmother's corpse would have rotted on the floor before you bothered to visit her?"

A fresh wave of guilt so powerful it was nauseating washed over Petra. She sunk down into the chair behind her. Raiker looked back at her, alarm and sympathy etched on his face.

"He's vile. Ignore him," Follium advised.

Kabshi'l turned that piercing gaze on Follium and smiled before he spoke again. "He doesn't love you, you know. Not the way he loves her."

"That's enough!" Raiker shouted. His voice echoed off the ceiling tiles. "Tell us who's looking for the Key."

Kabshi'l laughed darkly. "Or you'll what? You don't possess any means to make me give you the answers you seek. I'm not afraid to die. And Seelie don't have the resolve for torture."

"Oh really? You think so?" Follium said, smiling like he knew something Kabshi'l didn't.

"Follium," Raiker said, his voice a warning.

Follium pointed at Raiker. "Look at him and tell me he doesn't have the resolve for torture."

Raiker seemed to sink into himself, his shoulders slumping, his wings folding in, and his gaze drifting down to his feet. Kabshi'l studied him curiously for a few seconds and then his eyes went as wide as the diamond on his forehead.

"You," he said. "You're the child that tortured the Sartori brothers to death."

Petra noted with disgust that Kabshi'l sounded impressed. Follium looked smug, like he was pleased he won the argument. Petra wanted to punch them both. Raiker still hadn't raised his eyes from the ground. He seemed deeply uncomfortable playing this role.

"Tell us who's seeking the Key," Follium said.

Kabshi'l weighed his options.

"No," he said finally. His smile was a taunt that Raiker couldn't see, because Raiker was still staring at his feet. "What are you going to do now, Raiker the Rogue?"

Raiker was quiet for a long time. He exhaled a protracted sigh, and then he raised his eyes and squared his shoulders.

"Petra, please go to your room," he said in a quiet voice. His flaming sword appeared in his hand.

"No," Petra said, standing up.

"My lady, I don't..." Raiker's voice broke. "I don't want you to see me like this. Please."

Kabshi'l's calculated look of calm had begun to betray real worry. But Petra didn't give a damn about that. All she cared about was that shame in Raiker's voice as he prepared to do something unspeakable. Petra approached Raiker slowly. She took his empty hand in hers and then moved to stand in front of him, putting herself between him and Kabshi'l. She kissed his lips lightly.

"You don't have to do this," she said.

"Yes I do," he insisted without much conviction.

Petra rested her hand on the hilt of his sword. "This isn't who you are."

She took the sword from him, and he didn't resist her. Petra let it clatter to the floor, and then slipped her other hand into his. Gratitude and wonder replaced the shame in his eyes. He rested his forehead against hers, breathing deep.

"You only say that because you don't know the things he's done," Kabshi'l said. "Would you like me to tell you?"

Petra let go of Raiker and whirled around. She took a moment to swallow her anger before she spoke to their prisoner.

"Why aren't you afraid of dying?" she asked.

"I am a devout follower of Armaita, the great creator. In death she will raise me to Elysium, and I will spend eternity in paradise," he said with great sincerity.

"Fables and nonsense," Follium muttered.

Most of Petra's life had been fables and nonsense lately. Elf Heaven didn't seem like that much more of a stretch.

She knelt down in front of Kabshi'l. Follium made a move to stop her, but Raiker held him back with a wordless gesture. Petra reached for the elf's left wrist and pulled back the sleeve of his long coat. She got a good look at what she'd only glanced at earlier. There was a thin black tattoo encircling Kabshi'l's wrist, just like the one from the photograph of Oberon.

"What about her?" she asked.

There was something in Kabshi'l's eyes then and Petra course corrected.

"Him," she amended. "What about him?"

Follium moved to the dining room window and looked out. "That blond elf out there? We could grab him too. I bet you'll be a lot more forthcoming if we—"

"That's not him," Petra interrupted.

She remembered the way the other elf was solely focused on grappling for the keys while Kabshi'l had tried to make a break for it. Those two might know each other, but there was hardly loyalty between them, let alone multiple millennia-spanning love.

"How will he feel if you die?" Petra asked.

Kabshi'l hesitated before answering. "He'll understand."

"Bullshit," Petra said. "You won't come home, and for what? You really think this name you don't want to give up is worth your life? Because he won't think that."

"He will bathe in your blood," Kabshi'l spat.

"You'll still be gone," Petra said. "He will still go to bed without you every night. Do you love him?"

"Of course, I love him."

"Then why would you do that to him if you have a choice?"

Kabshi'l was silent.

"Look at me," Petra said. "Use that talent of yours. Because I know what it feels like to lose your family. Look at Raiker, he does too. We know what it's like to be the only one left behind. Is that what you want for him?"

It was hard to tell if he took her suggestion, but he was quiet, and something did cross his expression. Perhaps just a glimmer of empathy.

"Give us the name of the fairy that hired you to steal the Key, and I swear, you can go home to him," Petra said.

Kabshi'l looked from her to Raiker and Follium.

"If you expect me to take a human's word—" he started.

"I swear it," Raiker said. "The moment you give us the name, you can leave here."

Kabshi'l took a long look at his left wrist.

"Duchess Calantha the Charming," he said.

Raiker and Follium reeled as if they had been slapped.

"Wait, I know that name. Who's Calantha?" Petra asked.

"She's *Seelie*," Follium said. "She's Queen Titania's consort."

Follium and Raiker both insisted that they should abstain for as long as they were still under siege, but they both drank the wine that Petra put in front of them anyway. They'd made Kabshi'l swear he was telling the truth and then chucked him back over the line of wards mostly unharmed, although Raiker had made a point of giving him a good kick first. They were all rather happy to see the back of him.

Now they were sitting around Petra's kitchen table, and for what felt like the millionth time Raiker said, "But why would Calantha want the Key?"

It was abundantly clear they hadn't expected one of the good guys to be behind this.

"I don't suppose your leaders are democratically elected?" Petra asked.

The fairies stared at her blankly for a few seconds before seeming to at least grasp the gist of what she was suggesting.

"You think she's trying to overthrow Queen Titania?" Raiker asked.

"The Beast is one of the few things that would pose an actual threat to her," Follium pointed out. "But I *know* Calantha. Well, I knew her back when her standing at Court wasn't quite so lofty. Calantha isn't a revolutionary. Calantha likes parties, and sparkling gowns, and making love until you no longer care that she's spending all your gold."

"I think I know the type," Petra said. "Also, do all fairies play for both teams?"

That earned her another blank look.

"You know what? Never mind. It's not super germane to the discussion," Petra muttered.

"What'd you buy her?" Raiker asked Follium with a smirk.

"Jewelry, dresses... possibly a small island. I don't want to talk about it," Follium said.

Raiker laughed while Follium glowered at him and drank deeply from his wine glass. Petra would have loved a good laugh at Follium's expense, but her thoughts were elsewhere. She was thinking about how years of watching true crime had taught her that it's always the husband. That might be a bit too heteronormative in this case, but she suspected the principle still applied.

"She doesn't have to be a revolutionary to want Titania dead," Petra reasoned. "I mean, she's her girlfriend—"

"'Girlfriend' is a human nonsense word. She's her *consort*," Follium corrected.

"*One* of her consorts," Raiker amended further. "Although I believe Queen Titania does favor her."

"Whatever," Petra said irritably. "How about 'intimate partner violence'? Are those human nonsense words too, or do you also have that problem in Arcadia?"

This time they didn't seem to have any trouble grasping her meaning.

"We would use the word 'violator' to describe someone who would hurt their lover, if their lover is weaker than they are," Raiker said. "Assuming that's what you meant."

Petra nodded.

"But *Calantha* is the weak one," Follium said.

Raiker snorted. "Lady Calantha could probably burn us both to dust without breaking a sweat."

"You know what I meant, smart-ass," Follium said. "Queen Titania could destroy Calantha with just the power in her little finger."

"Unless she had the Beast to even the score," Petra said.

The three of them sat quietly with the implications of that for a long time. The sun was going down and the kitchen was growing dark, with the curtains drawn tight against the many eyes outside.

"We have to warn the Queen," Follium said finally.

"Yes," Raiker agreed. "And soon, before Duchess Calantha figures out that we know and she..."

"Burns us all to dust?" Petra supplied.

Raiker took her hand in his and squeezed it gently. "I won't allow anything to happen to you, my lady."

"He means he'll die *trying* to not let anything happen to you," Follium interjected, and Raiker glared at him. "But if Duchess Calantha the Charming wants us dead, we're dead. No amount of foolhardy determination is going to change that." Follium sighed and then sat up straighter, a determined glint in his eye. "Alright, here's the plan. I'll sneak out past the siege line."

"How?" Raiker interrupted.

"I don't know yet," Follium said.

"So, it's more like half a plan then," Petra said.

Follium banged his fist on the table. "Both of you shut up. I will sneak out. You two stay here and do your level best to make those fairies believe all three of us are still inside. I'll go straight to the palace and request an audience with Queen Titania. A private audience. Not even her guards should hear this. If it's a personal vendetta that's one thing, but if Calantha is planning a coup, she might have co-conspirators. We don't know who we can trust."

Raiker nodded and drained his wine glass. "Good plan. Except for one thing. I'm going, not you."

"Like hell you are," Follium shot back.

"It's too dangerous. I'm not letting you risk your life for me."

"I'm not doing it for you, you narcissistic prick. And anyway, how do you plan getting an audience with the queen?"

"I'll trade in on my mother's good name," Raiker said. "It usually works."

"Not as well my mother's name does."

"Enough!" Petra shouted.

The pixies stopped their heated argument and looked at her. She pulled a quarter out of her pocket.

"Call it in the air. Heads or tails?" Petra said, and flipped the quarter.

"What?" Follium said.

"Heads," Raiker said.

The coin landed on heads.

"Okay," Petra said. "Raiker's going." She took a deep breath. "And I'm going with you."

What followed couldn't precisely be described as a fight. A fight would imply that there had been arguing on both sides. Certainly, Raiker had done quite a lot of arguing. He said it was too dangerous for Petra to go with him. She'd be safer staying at the house with Follium. If Calantha found out why they were there he wouldn't be able to protect her. Petra had simply insisted

that she was going over and over and refused
to be budged. Eventually, Raiker had tried to
get Follium to convince her; apparently because
he was under the rather wrong impression that
she might listen to Follium. That backfired
spectacularly (and surprised the hell out of Petra)
when Follium proceeded to take her side.

"You shouldn't go to Court without an escort,"
he reasoned. "Plus, she's another witness."

Then Raiker and Follium had done quite a
lot of arguing. Eventually, Raiker asked Petra to
step out of the room. When she refused, Raiker
switched to Dryadian and Follium followed suit.
The only word she could understand then was
her own name– a word that seemed to be coming
up at lot.

Petra stalked off to the other side of the kitchen,
but she continued to watch them, wondering
what it was that Raiker didn't want her to hear.
Raiker had stopped yelling. He spoke softly to
Follium, his face full of worry. Follium laughed at
him, and then stopped when he seemed to realize
that whatever Raiker had said, he said it with
complete sincerity. Follium's face ran through
shock, disbelief, and then anger, until he was
shouting at Raiker at the top of his lungs. Raiker
didn't shout back. He looked at Follium with
pleading eyes and continued to speak. And then
Petra caught one of the maybe six words she knew
in Dryadian.

Raiker said "please."

Follium deflated. He shook his head, grumbled,
sighed, and put his face in his hands. But when

he lowered his hands again, he nodded. Raiker threw his arms around him, and the two of them hugged a little longer than Petra liked. They spoke for a few more moments, and then Raiker turned back to Petra.

"You win, my lady," Raiker said. "You can come."

Chapter Twenty-One

Follium strode confidently into the garden. The plastic toy squirt gun Petra had dug out of the garage was held at his side. It had been hot pink when Petra had received it for her seventh birthday. Now it was faded to a dull yellow. But it was loaded, and it still worked.

He raised his hand in a wave to the fairies on the other side of the garden fence. There were three, all fire nymphs, with petite bodies like glass that had been filled with molten lava. The rest of the fairies were around the front and sides of the house, and hopefully that's where they would stay.

"Good evening, dears," Follium said. "Have you ever heard of a Super Soaker?"

They stood and looked at Follium curiously, but they didn't seem actively concerned about the toy in his hand until a blast of water shot through the warding. The pressurized jet hissed into a cloud of steam when in hit their skin, and the nymphs shrieked in indignation. They began to hurl fistfuls of fire in Follium's direction. The wards held fast. Fireballs exploded on impact with the invisible wall and spread out in a cloud of raging hot, white and electric blue flames. It blocked out the view of everything in the garden below.

"Now!" Raiker said, and he and Petra ran out the backdoor.

Raiker got to the fairy ring first. He reached out in front of him and grasped the air with both fists, ripping open the portal. Follium cackled as he continued to spray the screaming nymphs. Raiker clapped him on the shoulder and then dove through the portal, Petra hot on his heels. The door back to Alius shut behind them with a snap.

Petra took a moment to catch her breath and let her eyes adjust after the blinding, fiery light. Raiker stepped a few paces ahead of her, holding out his sword and scanning the woods.

"Do they know we're here?" Petra asked.

"... No" Raiker said after a long pause. "No, I don't think anyone's watching this side." He sheathed his sword and scooped her into his arms. "We need to run before they figure it out."

Raiker raced through the sky, faster than he had ever flown with Petra before. She clung to his neck and closed her eyes against the wind. She opened them again when they landed on Raiker's front porch. Petra breathed a little easier now that they were safely inside the wards.

"Alright," Raiker said as he charged into the house. "I said you could come, but I have conditions."

"Okay..." Petra said slowly.

"Don't talk to anyone unless they talk to you first," Raiker said. "Don't eat or drink anything that's offered to you."

He picked her up and flew to the door opposite his bedroom. Inside was a small guest room. Raiker went to the wardrobe and flung it open.

"Don't stare at anyone."

He pulled a few things out of the wardrobe and laid them on the bed.

"Here, pick a gown," he said.

Petra eyed them suspiciously. "And who do these dresses belong to?"

Raiker laughed and kissed her cheek. "Don't ask questions you don't want the answer to either."

Grumbling a little, Petra looked at the clothes on the bed. All the tops seemed to have somewhat less fabric than she would have liked. Raiker perched on the footboard and watched her appraise her options.

"Also, don't say 'thank you'," he said. "And don't tell anyone your true name—"

"What are you worried is gonna happen at Court exactly?" Petra asked.

"I just don't want anyone to get it in their head to steal you from me."

"Steal me from you?" Petra repeated, her eyes narrowing. "I belong to *myself*, not to you."

Raiker flew off the bed and put his hands on her shoulders, his expression bordering on panic. "Definitely don't say that!" he hissed, "You can't be here unaccompanied. When you're here, you are *mine*, or someone else will make you theirs. Do you understand?"

Petra shoved her way out of the death grip Raiker had on her shoulders and went back to digging through the discards of his former conquests. A light blue gown with a full skirt caught her eye.

Raiker groaned. "You don't comprehend how important this is. It's like..." He seemed to wrack his brain for a moment. "Last week, when you picked up a collar for Shitpoo– Do you remember why you told me you wanted him to wear it? You said that he's cute and friendly. If someone finds him, if they don't think he has an owner, they might decide to keep him."

"I'm the DOG in this analogy?!"

"It's a surprisingly apt metaphor! Please don't be angry. Just tell me you understand."

"Fine!" Petra said, throwing her hands up in defeat. "I'm yours. I got it."

The corners of Raiker's mouth twitched into a smile. He slid his hands down to her hips and pulled her closer.

"Say that again," he requested, looking her up and down and biting his lower lip.

"I'm yours," she said.

"One more time?"

"*No.*" Petra pushed him away, grumbling in German.

Her mood improved significantly after she
put on the dress. The longer she stared at her
reflection the less she cared that the gown had
probably belonged to one of Raiker's 1,429 exes.
The pale blue fabric magically tailored itself
to her shape when she slipped it on. It had a
voluminous skirt that glittered with hundreds of
crystal beads. It was backless, and the strapless
bodice was nearly as insubstantial, with a neckline
down to her navel and crystal-covered blue
fabric just barely concealing her nipples. But no
matter how she moved in it, the fabric stayed in
place, and her breasts stayed (literally) magically
suspended.

Petra stood in front of the full-length mirror in
Raiker's bedroom and stared open mouthed. It
was stunning.

"You need jewelry," Raiker insisted. "Hold on."

Raiker looked good too, in a tight-fitting
doublet that left a lot of skin exposed and
accentuated his waist. Blue cord laced up the
front and around his wings in the back, matching
the cord that ran up the sides of his thigh-high
boots.

He turned from her and began to feel along the
bedroom walls.

"I'm not sure I do," Petra argued as she preened
in front of the mirror. "There is such a thing as
too much sparkle."

"No there isn't," Raiker insisted.

He made an exasperated noise, dropped his
hands, and flew out the open bedroom door.
Petra left the mirror and leaned out of the room.

Raiker was feeling along the walls just below the door.

"What are you doing?" she asked.

Raiker gave her a sheepish look. "Sometimes I get paranoid when I drink and I hide things. And then in the morning I can't remember where I... ah-ha!"

He stopped on a tree branch and pressed his hands into the bark. The air shimmered under his hands and a cubby hole appeared with a hum. He pulled a gold box out of it and flew it back up to her.

"Here," he said. "Pick something."

He opened the box, revealing an unorganized pile of expensive looking jewelry. Petra laughed as she began to dig through it.

"Oh my God. Are these from some ex-girlfriend too, or did you steal them?"

Her laughter trailed off as her hand settled on a diamond pendant shaped like a spider.

"Neither," Raiker said.

He took the spider pendant from her hand and set the box down. Petra stepped back over to the mirror and Raiker stood behind her, fastening the necklace around her neck.

"Now you're perfect," he said, and he planted a kiss on her bare shoulder that made her shiver.

Petra had no argument with that as she took in her reflection and fingered the diamond around her neck, pale blue like the dress.

"It even matches your eyes," Raiker murmured.

"Yeah," Petra said as she ran her hands over the gown. "Ice-blue."

"No, not ice," Raiker said. "Your eyes are the color of the hottest part of a flame."

He spun her around to face him and brushed his lips against her ear as he whispered softly.

"You burn, Petra."

Petra shivered again and kissed him, his lips only an inch away from hers with her heels. He put his arms around her waist and she reached down and moved his hands up to her breasts, moaning softly.

"We have to leave," Raiker insisted with some difficulty.

"We could be quick," Petra suggested.

"Nothing I want to do to you in that dress will be quick," he countered.

Petra hoped that was a promise. Raiker untangled himself from her and turned to the mirror, fixing the teal and copper hair she'd mussed. Petra watched him restyle his hair and then belt his sword around his waist, sliding it into a sheath studded with sapphires. She picked up her own sword, the sober reality of the danger they were in returning to her with a snap.

"Are you ready for this?" he asked her without turning around.

Petra hesitated before she spoke. "I release you from your vow to protect me."

Raiker whirled around, shock and confusion on his face. "Petra... You don't know what you're saying."

"I do," she insisted. "I've been informed."

The confusion stayed on his face for a few
moments more and then shifted to anger "...
Dammit, Follium..." he muttered.

"He's just worried about you. I am too. If
something goes wrong... I don't want you to die
for me. You don't... you don't have to worry about
avenging me if something happens."

Raiker put his head in his hands, messing up his
hair again. "Do you honestly believe that vow was
the only reason I'd risk my life for you?"

"...No," Petra said, "But please don't. You should
have run the other night when that banshee
came. If you have the chance to save yourself,
I want you to take it. I'm not worth it. I mean,
compared to you, I'm gonna die soon anyway,
right? You're supposed to live for thousands of
years still. I'm just—"

"Stop," Raiker said, his voice choked. He pulled
her into a hug so tight it nearly crushed her and
buried his face in her hair. "Stop talking, Petra.
Please."

Petra hugged him back, her own voice equally
unsteady. "I just want you safe, Raiker."

Raiker pulled away and cupped her cheek in his
hand. Tears glimmered in his eyes as he stared
into hers.

"Reylinghae," he said. "My name is Reylinghae."

Now it was Petra's turn to be stunned into
silence. A smile began on her lips and spread
slowly to her cheeks.

"I thought you didn't want to give me that
power over you," she said, laughing a little.

Raiker didn't laugh with her.

"You already have power over me," he said. "I think you did from the moment I met you."

She held onto him tighter, her heart swelling in her chest. He kissed her, his lips soft against hers. They were both breathless when the kiss ended.

Petra rested her forehead against his. "Rey...?"

"Ray-lin-ghey," he said slowly.

"Ray-lin-jay?"

Raiker laughed and kissed her forehead. "Close enough."

The sparkling blue ball gown had made Petra feel like Cinderella back when she was at Raiker's house looking at herself in the mirror. She felt significantly less like a fairy tale princess now, as she was on all fours in the dirt, shaking, sobbing, and vomiting the contents of her stomach. She had thought the experience of "traveling" might be slightly better this go around since she knew what to expect, but her body had other ideas.

"Scheiße. Ich hasse das. Ich bin kein Aschenputtel. Mist Mist Mist," Petra mumbled in between sobs.

Raiker knelt next to her, stroking her hair and murmuring apologies.

They were outside of the castle, around the corner from the main gate, but Petra had barely caught a glimpse of the towering building before she'd collapsed. Raiker had chosen the spot for its seclusion, so that Petra could have some time to compose herself. The small part of her brain that was still firing on all cylinders was grateful that at least no one else could see her falling apart.

A feminine voice called out in Dryadian. Petra glanced up in the direction of the speaker. A female pixie in a slinky silver dress was approaching them. She had diamonds in her bubble gum pink hair.

So much for seclusion.

Petra waved weakly at the stranger and then threw up onto the grass again. The pink-haired pixie tutted and exchanged a few words with Raiker before kneeling down next to Petra.

"You poor thing," she said in accented English. "Here." With a snap of her fingers a flask appeared in her other hand.

"What's in that?" Raiker asked.

"Only ginger elixir. Promise," she replied. "It works wonders when you've overindulged the night before."

Petra accepted the flask and gulped down the liquid. It was spicy and sweet and it settled her stomach almost immediately. She still didn't quite feel ready to stand, but she did graduate to a sitting position.

"Oh, you are exquisite, aren't you?" the pixie said once Petra had had a chance to push her hair back out of her face. Big, lime green eyes looked Petra up and down.

The pixie turned to Raiker and spoke over her. "Does she have any skills?"

"She's an artist," Raiker boasted. "She paints. She also speaks two languages and she's incredibly clever for her age."

"I am not your goddamn show dog," Petra snapped.

The stranger let out a peel of laughter so loud Petra nearly missed Raiker's babbled apologies. "You have some bite, little mayfly. You'll be great fun at Court. There's quite the party today. But you can't go in there looking like this."

The pixie took her hand and pulled her to her feet.

"Just look at what you've done to your lovely dress," she scolded.

There was a fair bit of mud on the skirt now. Petra also suspected that her face and hair looked like hell and that the cold sweat she'd broken out in wasn't doing her body odor any favors either.

With another snap of the pixie's fingers a clutch appeared in her hand. Within two minutes she had fixed Petra's hair, magically removed the mud from her gown, smoothed over her blotchy complexion, and spritzed her with perfume that smelled like lilies.

"There," she declared. "Pretty as a picture." She held up a small mirror so Petra could examine the results.

"Thank you," Petra said.

Petra remembered she wasn't supposed to say that (although Raiker had never explained why) a moment after the words left her mouth. Raiker shot her a look and the other pixie giggled.

"Is she new?" she asked.

"It's only her second time in Arcadia," Raiker said nervously. "She's still learning the rules..."

"I'll tell you what, beautiful girl, you can repay my favor by granting me a dance," the pink-haired pixie said with a smile. "Assuming that's alright with...?"

"Raiker the Rogue," Raiker supplied with a small bow. "Swindler, plunderer, and housebreaker extraordinaire. And yes, that sounds most reasonable, my lady."

Jesus H. Christ is he seriously talking right over me again?

The other pixie raised her eyebrows for just a moment, and then she smiled and returned Raiker's bow with a curtsey.

"It's a pleasure to meet you, Raiker the Rogue. You have the honor of addressing Duchess Calantha the Charming, Consort to Queen Titania." She turned her lime green eyes to Petra. "And what should I call you, beautiful girl?"

Chapter Twenty-Two

P etra kept her face arranged in a perfect mask of calm, but inside her thoughts screamed with panic. *Calantha hired Raiker. Did she recognize his name? Fuck! Of course, she did. If she's keeping tabs on what's going on at my house at all she knows that Raiker and Follium have the place on lock down. If she knows who he is she's probably guessed who I am too. She's still playing it cool because she doesn't know that we know she's the buyer, but—*

Calantha was still waiting expectantly for Petra to offer her a fake name. Petra reached again for her mother's name and swapped out "Bachman" for her cousins' surname.

"Liese Klara Müller," Petra said.

"Charmed," Calantha said.

Calantha had positioned herself between Petra and Raiker, and when Raiker tried to move back to Petra's side she quite conspicuously stepped in his way.

"Forgive us, your grace, but we really should be getting inside now," Raiker said.

"What's your hurry?" Calantha asked. The castle courtyard was surrounded by a solid wall of towering trees. The main entrance was just around the corner from them. Petra calculated what their odds were if they just made a break for the door and they didn't look good.

"We're... here to see the Queen," Raiker said with some hesitation.

"Oh... I'm sure she's not granting any more audiences today," Calantha said. She wasn't a good liar. Her already high voice went up a few notes; her words rushed. "Yes, my love's been positively swamped with petitioners all morning. No sense in hurrying inside only to be turned away."

"Just the same, we should—"

Raiker moved to go to Petra again, but Calantha placed her hand on his chest and cut him off.

"I have a better idea," she said.

They were all alone. No witnesses. Maybe if someone else wandered over here...

Calantha must have been thinking the same thing. She put her other hand on Raiker's hip and hooked her thumb under the waistline of his pants.

"I keep a house on an island not too far away. We could fly from here. You and your human will have considerably more fun with me than you will at the party in there," she said.

"Anyone ever told you that you have a very high opinion of yourself?" Raiker said.

His tone was teasing, flirtatious even, and it would have made Petra mad if not for her suspicion about what Raiker was really up too.

He's stalling.

Petra looked around for something that could help them get away from a fairy with the power to reduce them to dust.

Calantha giggled. "Darling, I'm good enough for the Queen. You will never have it better." Her hand resting on his hip glowed and Raiker gasped. "Besides, the poor mayfly's still so terribly shaken. A glass of wine and a little personal attention would be good for her, don't you think?"

"Ah, there it is," Raiker teased. "Admit it, you don't give two figs about me. You just want me to share her."

They were talking over her again. Calantha's back was turned to Petra and her hands were all over Raiker, all her considerable charms focused on convincing him he'd rather have a ménage à trois on a private island than talk to Titania.

And she's ignoring me.

"Not true," Calantha mock pouted. "I happen to have a fondness for scoundrels, Raiker the Rogue."

Calantha brushed her lips over his. There was a metallic hum as Petra drew the sword at her back. Calantha heard it just in time to whirl around and put her hands up in front of her face. The iron blade sliced through the palm of her hand, drawing a thin line of blood.

No pixie Petra had seen yet had seemed over-thrilled to be forced into their true form, but the deafening scream of horror and indignation Calantha let out as scales appeared on her skin and her perfect face was replaced with a pointed chin and hook nose was something else. Petra backed away from the enraged pixie and tripped, landing hard on the ground. Her magic may have been temporarily gone, but the look in Calantha's moss green eyes said that she had every intention of ripping Petra apart with her bare hands.

Before she could, Raiker conjured a pair of glowing cuffs that clapped onto her wrists and fastened into the ground, pinning her in place. He flew past her, grabbed Petra by the waist, and shot through the air towards the palace entrance.

"How long will that hold her?" Petra shouted over the wind.

There was a loud snap as somewhere behind them the chains holding Calantha severed.

The entrance to the palace courtyard was an ornate gold archway. Two guards in white uniforms stood in front of it. They had drawn their swords, alarmed by Calantha's screams.

"Someone's hurt over there! Hurry!" Petra said as Raiker landed in front of them.

The guards flew off to investigate, and Petra and Raiker darted inside.

"She won't come in here until she can put her glamour back. She's too damn vain. We have to get to the Queen before that," Raiker said, pulling

Petra towards the castle by the hand. He stopped
for just a moment to hug her and kiss her lips.

"You were amazing," he said with a smile.
"Come on."

There was indeed a party inside the courtyard,
with musicians playing strange, beautiful
sounding instruments and buffet tables piled
high with desserts. Rain began to fall overheard,
and the drops pitted off the top of an invisible
ceiling, dripping off like glass. All manner of
flowers grew in a beautiful chaotic jumble of
color.

And in the middle of it all were the fairies.
Hundreds of them dancing and cavorting with
abandon. Pixies in glittering gowns spun in
midair like ballerinas. A pair of flower nymphs
with bright green skin were kissing in a bed
of daisies, nearly blending in with the garden.
There was a squat dwarf chugging a tankard of
beer nearly as big as he was while a gaggle of
water nymphs cheered him on. They passed an
anguana with lizard arms, and Petra panicked
briefly before reminding herself that these
were supposed to be the good guys. Even the
elves looked like they were enjoying the party,
although they stood rather stiffly in a corner and
seemed to be mostly keeping to themselves.

Raiker pulled her through the crowd towards
the castle, acknowledging a few fae with a smile
or a wave, but never stopping. The castle loomed
in front of them, a massive structure formed
from one single live oak tree. Glimpses of lit
rooms shone through the windows that were set

into the larger branches. Fitted into the entrance was a solid gold door twenty feet high. The doors stood open, with more uniformed guards standing sentry on either side.

Raiker gave his name to one of the guards who waived them through the door and into a grand foyer with murals painted on the walls. Several doors and halls, or rather branches, split off from the foyer, but the door they were headed for was directly across from the gold one. It was nearly as tall as the first, only this one was shut firmly and barred by another six guards, and it was made out of...

"Is that diamond?" Petra asked in wonder, marveling at the dazzling refractive stone through which blurred outlines of the throne room could be glimpsed.

Raiker didn't answer her in his rush to give their names to the guards. It took some convincing to get the guards to open the doors– with Raiker dropping his mom's name and swearing several vows that that what they were bringing to the Queen was a matter of life and death. Eventually, they acquiesced, and Raiker and Petra were ushered inside.

There was a carpet of tiny purple flowers running in a long strip from the door to the backless, carved diamond throne on a dais at the other end of the room. The throne room was huge, and it was filled with beautifully dressed courtiers lounging on large pillows nearby their Queen.

Queen Titania herself sat upon her throne. She looked nothing like the Joseph Noel Paton paintings or the movie adaptations of *A Midsummer Night's Dream* Petra had seen. She was black, with skin so dark it reflected the purple in her gown. Her long hair was pulled up in an intricate braid on top of her head, framed by a glittering amethyst crown that glowed softly. Her dress had been made to look like wisteria blooms, or perhaps it was made from wisteria blooms, with a huge skirt and a high-collared bodice. Her purple eyes fixed on Petra when they walked in. Petra felt curiously drawn in by her gaze, entranced by the Seelie Queen's beauty and intimidated by her imperious presence.

"Presenting Raiker the Rogue, swindler, plunderer, and housebreaker extraordinaire, son of Desidae the Spider Charmer, escorting the human Liese Klara Müller," the guard announced before turning back to them. "You have the honor of addressing our most magnificent Royal Highness Queen Titania the Almighty, ruler of the Seelie Court, rightful leader of all of Arcadia, Alius, and the unknown universe, accompanied today by her Royal Highness Princess Valfarren..."

Petra had been so drawn in by those purple eyes she'd hardly noticed the pixie seated on a smaller throne slightly behind and to the right of Titania's. Princess Valfarren looked at lot like her mother, which Petra supposed was more of an affectation than genetics. Petra studied the Princess's face as the guard rattled off her many titles. Her expression was a mask that betrayed neither interest nor boredom with the proceedings.

Raiker waited until the guard finished speaking and shut the door behind them to silently step forward and Petra followed his lead. He bowed and Petra curtsied to the queen first, then to the Princess, and then they knelt in front of the throne. Raiker kept his head down until Titania spoke.

"Desidae's son... Didn't I banish you?" she asked.

She had a powerful, deep voice that would have had no trouble commanding the attention of everyone in the room even if she weren't the queen.

Raiker flushed. "No, you... you most generously granted me a pardon for my crimes, your grace."

Titania turned her head to the courtier standing closest to her throne, who flipped frantically through a massive book before nodding in affirmation.

"Hmm. That's right. You may rise," Titania said.

Raiker bounded to his feet first and offered Petra his hand, helping her up.

"Ah. You've brought me a gift," Titania said to Raiker, smiling in approval.

She stood from her throne and flew forward on her gossamer wings, landing right in front of them. "If this is some blatant attempt to curry my favor, you should know that it's working."

Titania reached out and tucked an errant blonde curl behind Petra's ear, stroking her face as she did. It was only then that Petra realized the gift in question was her.

To his credit, Raiker's smile never wavered, but it had become rather fixed. Petra wasn't sure how well she was maintaining her own poker face as she watched Titania flit around her in a circle, looking her up and down.

"She's lovely," Titania murmured. "And so tall."

Titania stood a few inches shorter than Petra, looking up at her face.

"Female humans are normally much more diminutive than this, aren't they?" she asked. She rose up on her wings just high enough that Petra was the one looking up at her.

"They are, your royal highness," the elf with the book answered her.

Titania trailed her fingers down Petra's arm, and Petra narrowly resisted the urge to pull away. Up close, she could see the slim black tattooed line encircling Titania's right wrist. It looked just like the one Petra had seen in the photograph of Oberon, or the one that Kabshi'l had, except that Titania's had a single slash through it. Perhaps it indicated Oberon's passing, and that Titania was free to hit on whoever she wanted.

Whether they wanted it or not. Petra tried to turn to Raiker for help, but Titania put her hand on her cheek, holding her still.

"And such pretty blue eyes. Does she do any tricks?" Titania asked.

"She's... she's actually, um..." Raiker stammered and seemed to wilt as the queen turned her gaze on him. "She's mine. I didn't bring her for you."

Petra would have breathed a sigh of relief, but she didn't quite dare make a sound. Raiker knelt in front of the Queen again, prostrating himself in penance and babbling atonements as fast as he could spit them out.

"But I offer my sincerest apologies for neglecting to bring you a gift, your highness. Rest assured, when I return again, it will be with a present worthy of your—"

"Come now, child. Don't be impertinent," Titania chided him. "Surely you wouldn't deny your Queen this tiny indulgence?"

"I would never dream of denying my most beautiful and powerful Queen anything she desires. If you were to ask me for the stars themselves, I would fetch them back for you or perish trying."

Titania seemed slightly mollified by his flattery, but she hadn't stopped touching Petra either. Her fingers wound her way through Petra's hair and her piercing violet eyes roved her body appraisingly.

"But this human," Raiker continued, "She's unwilling to part with my company."

"Unwilling?" Titania repeated, and then for the first time since they walked into her throne room, Titania addressed Petra directly.

"Is this true?"

Petra chanced a glance at Raiker, who gave her the subtlest of nods.

"It's true," Petra said, and then after a moment's hesitation added, "Your royal highness."

Titania's eyes narrowed. Petra strongly suspected that this was someone who had not heard the word "no" for several hundred years at least. The hand, which had moments ago been lightly caressing the curve of her neck, now tightened on her shoulder, a grip that was just this side of being painful.

"She doesn't mean to insult you," Raiker said. "You know how humans are." He managed an almost convincing laugh. "Once you bed them, they can get so irrationally attached. I couldn't be rid of her now if I tried."

Petra had just decided that she was going to slap Raiker the first chance she got, but then Titania relaxed her grip on her shoulder and smiled.

"One night with me and she'd forget you'd ever existed," Titania said.

"There is not a doubt in my mind that is true, my glorious Queen," Raiker said. "But she'd never consent to being given away, and I wouldn't want to cause her any... undue distress."

Titania sighed and stopped petting Petra's hair. "No, we wouldn't want that." The Queen turned and settled back into her seat on her diamond throne. "If she's not a gift, why have you brought her to me?"

There was some kind of commotion then outside of the door. Voices shouting in the foyer. Titania raised her eyebrows in mild interest and glanced in the direction of the guards at the closed door. Raiker cast a worried glance that direction as well before addressing Titania in a rush.

"Your grace, might I request a private audience?" he said. "It's urgent."

The courtier next to Titania snickered. "What call could the likes of you possibly have to—?"

But he fell silent as Titania lifted her hand.

"You may have your private audience, little one," Titania said.

Several mouths dropped open, but there were no outright objections as Princess Valfarren and the courtiers grabbed their drinks and headed for the exit. The guards opened the doors to let them pass. Calantha's voice cut through the crowd. "Out of my way!"

The crowd parted and Calantha flew in, her glamour now restored. She shot Petra and Raiker a death glare as she flew past. She landed on the dais, just in front of the Queen's feet, and dropped into a low curtsey.

"Where did you wander off to, my love?" Titania asked, beckoning Calantha forward. She tugged Calantha into her lap and kissed her. The kiss went on for an uncomfortable amount of time, with lots of wandering hands and soft moans.

While they carried on, Petra looked at Raiker and mouthed the words, *What do we do?*

Raiker held up both hands in a helpless gesture.

"My guards should have told you I'm giving a private audience," Titania said.

The guards in question stood awkwardly by the door, like they weren't sure if they should exit or keep holding it for Calantha.

"They did," Calantha said, stroking Titania's cheek. "I didn't think it applied to me. You never send me away."

Titania caught Calantha's hand in hers and Calantha flinched.

"Too bold, little one," Titania cautioned in a dangerous voice. She stood suddenly, spilling Calantha out of her lap. "I ordered my courtroom cleared."

Calantha landed on her feet and knelt low, her gaze on the floor. "I beg your forgiveness, your royal highness." She chanced raising her head. "Might I ask for a word with you before..."

She trailed off after a look from the queen.

"Forgive me," Calantha begged again.

With a last look at Raiker and Petra, Calantha left the courtroom. The guards pulled the diamond doors closed behind her.

"I assume you believe you have a good reason for this," the Queen said with a slight smirk as soon as they were alone.

Raiker nodded and swallowed hard before finding his voice.

"Yes, my Queen," he said. "We have reason to believe that Duchess Calantha the Charming intends to harm you."

Titania only laughed.

"My Calantha? Harm me?" she repeated. "I don't think she has the spine or the poor sense to try."

Petra couldn't help but notice, Titania did not mention Calantha not having a *reason*.

"She's been consorting with Unseelie and other... shall we say disreputable types like myself," Raiker continued. "She's offered a substantial sum of gold to whichever fairy can bring her the Key."

Titania's smile faded and her eyes narrowed. "You said you had an urgent matter to discuss and you waste my time with children's' stories?"

"It's not a story," Petra interjected.

Raiker shot her a look that plainly said she should not have spoken up.

"Oh. The mayfly has an opinion," Titania said. "Please, enlighten us with your views on the situation, dear."

Petra had every intention of doing just that, but before she could speak Raiker started babbling apologies again, only ceasing when Titania commanded him to be silent.

"You never answered me before," Titania said. "If she's not a gift, why is it you've brought this impertinent monkey here?"

There was a glimmer of a moment in which Petra believed Raiker might object to Titania calling her an impertinent monkey, and then it passed.

"We know the Key is real, because it was written that Petra Adelina Bachman has the Key," he began.

Titania stood and stared at Petra, her violet eyes wide.

"That's Petra?" she asked.

"Yes," Raiker said, and then quickly amended, "Well, actually she's—"

Titania raised her hand and Raiker instantly fell silent. She stepped down from the dais her throne sat upon and slowly approached Petra. Her violet eyes flamed orange and Petra took an involuntary, stumbling step backwards.

"And you brought her here," Titania said, her voice shaking. "You brought this... filthy... oathbreaking... harlot here?"

"W-What?" Raiker said, torn between fear and confusion. In a blink Titania closed the remaining distance between them and grabbed Petra by the throat. She held her up above her head with one hand, hovering in midair while Petra dangled and clawed ineffectually at the fingers crushing her windpipe.

"*Petra Adelina Bachman, WHERE IS MY KEY?!*"

Chapter Twenty-Three

All the times Raiker or Follium had successfully pushed Petra it had felt like a pleasant suggestion. An idea that their magic had tricked her brain into thinking it was something she wanted to do. It still felt like her decision, she just happened to be deciding what they wanted.

There was no freewill left when Titania pushed her. No fighting it. All she could do, all she could think was to obey. The only trouble, or at least what felt like the most pressing issue at the moment, was that she couldn't tell Titania she didn't know where her Key was because she couldn't breathe. She tried anyway, forcing the words out of her mouth as best she could and succeeding only in making a few breathy choking noises.

Raiker yelled and ran at Titania. With a wave of the Queen's hand his body flew backwards and slammed into the wall. There was a thud and a crack as his head hit, but the noise sounded wrong, like someone had turned down the volume in the room. Petra's vision began to gray around the edges. Raiker's eyes were shut. His head was bleeding. He wasn't moving. And still that was much less important than answering Titania's question.

I don't know. I don't know. I don't know.

Titania let go of her throat and Petra fell to the ground, landing hard on her knees.

She sucked in a precious breath of air and immediately used it to say, "I don't know."

Her words came out hoarse and brought on a fit of coughing, but they were at least audible. Speaking them released her mind from Titania's iron grip. Her ability to focus on other things returned. She turned to look at Raiker just in time to see his eyes flutter open again. Her vision was clearing and the sound was beginning to return as the blood rushed back to her head.

"How can you not know?" Titania demanded.

It wasn't a push this time, and Petra was too busy coughing to answer anyway.

"Oberon gave it to you. He thought he could hide it from me. Did you lose it?"

"I didn't lose it," Petra managed. "I'm not—"

Titania kicked her hard in the sternum. Petra screamed so loud it nearly drowned out the sound of her ribs breaking.

"Don't hurt her!" Raiker shouted. Blood ran down his face, and when he tried to stand, he fell over. "Please, don't—"

"*Quiet,*" Titania commanded.

Raiker's mouth opened to speak again, but no sound came out.

"Did you think I didn't know about you?" Titania asked Petra, her voice a dangerous whisper.

Petra didn't answer. She was sobbing softly and clutching her abdomen against the pain. Every inhalation burned all the way down her throat, and stabbed sharply as her lungs expanded against her broken ribs.

"*Look at me when I'm talking to you, mayfly!*" Titania screamed.

Petra looked up into those flaming orange eyes. She didn't have a choice.

"You weren't the first, you know," Titania said. "There was nothing special about you at all. You weren't even the first human whore Oberon got with child. Tell me, did you know he was bound to me when you let him take you on your back in the dirt like a flightless worm? You're all a bunch of liars and oathbreakers. What did it matter to you that he'd made vows to me? It certainly didn't matter to him."

"I didn't..." Petra's mind was reeling. "That wasn't—"

"STOP LYING TO ME!" she shrieked.

She turned her back to Petra and began to pace the throne room, agitated and ranting. "I thought I'd feel better when I killed them, but it didn't make any difference."

Petra caught Raiker's eye from across the room and mouthed the word, *run*, but Raiker only shook his head.

"I had to be so careful. Had to make them look like accidents," Titania rambled. "I could have been facing an uprising if anyone found out I was executing humans. Banished from my own court." She laughed a disturbing, deranged laugh that made Petra's hair stand on end. Petra tore her eyes away from Raiker and focused again on what Titania was saying. A horrible, creeping realization began to dawn in her mind.

"Who did you kill?" Petra asked.

Titania turned to her and smiled, a maniacal gleam in her eyes. "Perhaps it's good that the little thief brought you here. Had to be so clever about it. Secretive. Maybe it would have been more satisfying if I could have seen the look on your face. If I could have ripped her apart right in front of you."

"Who...?" Petra's voice broke. "Who did you kill?"

Titania knelt down next to Petra, hovering an inch away from her face.

"Oberon's bastards," she said. "All his half-breed mutt children. The living ones at least."

The deer came out of nowhere. That was what the witnesses told the police. What the police told me and Oma. The deer ran out in the road, and Mama tried to swerve around it and she hit a tree. She hit a tree and she died. Strange to see a deer in the middle of the day like that, that was what they said.

"What was yours called again?" Titania asked. She smirked. "Oh right. Liese. That's the name you gave at the door, isn't it? Liese Klara."

The deer came out of nowhere. The deer came out of nowhere and it took away my mama.

Titania chuckled. "Such a shame she had to die. She was so very pretty. Lillian Greene's bastard was pretty too, in his day. Tell me, Petra, now that I can speak plainly, how does it feel knowing I murdered your daughter?"

Just a freak accident that's what they said. Nobody's fault. No one to blame but God.

Raiker found his voice again. "Not her daughter, her mother. My Queen, she isn't—"

"*Quiet,*" Titania snapped without looking at him, and Raiker fell silent.

Oma called Mama her wunder. Her miracle. She said she found out she was pregnant just after Opa died. That God saw she couldn't bear to be alone and so He sent her a miracle. And then He took Mama back to heaven early, because sometimes miracles don't last, but we should be grateful for them anyway. That's what Oma said, even when I cried and told Oma it wasn't fair.

But it wasn't God that took my mama away.

Petra screamed and lunged at Titania. She barely succeeded in touching her before the Queen sent her flying across the room. Petra landed badly and felt her arm break. She slid the last few feet across the throne room until her head collided with the hard diamond door. Dazed and broken, she noticed dimly that one knock off Manolo Blahnik heel had fallen off her foot and was lying by Titania's feet.

"Still not enough," Titania muttered. "That's why I need my Key back. Oberon never once broke his vows to me with another fae. No fairy would ever touch that oathbreaker. But humans don't care about honor. Humans lie, and breed, and consume. They don't care about anything. Oberon thought he could stop me. He tried to hide my Key and then he killed himself rather than face me. But I will get my Key back. Calantha has over a hundred fairies searching for it now. I will find it and when I do, I will burn every last human and all of Alius with them. The Beast will devour you all."

She smiled like a child excited for Christmas morning.

"*Now tell me where you left my Key,*" she commanded.

Petra would've stood if she were able. She managed to lift her head off the ground at least and she spit out a mouthful of blood.

"Go fuck yourself, your highness" Petra said.

Titania's mouth dropped open in a perfect "o" of surprise.

"Oh, I am going to enjoy this," Titania said with relish.

She flew towards Petra slowly, and a glowing amethyst scepter appeared in her hand. *No, not a scepter*, Petra realized, eyeing the pointed tip. *A spear.*

Raiker moved from the wall and put himself between Petra and Titania. He knelt down on one knee, begging, but he kept his eyes on Titania, and one hand on the hilt of his sword.

"Please, your majesty," he begged. "She's not who you think she is. Please spare her. I'll do anything."

Titania pointed her spear at his throat, and he winced as the point grazed his Adam's apple.

"I told you to be quiet," she said. "You disobeyed an order from your Queen, little one. That doesn't come without consequence."

"I don't care what happens to me," he said. "Just don't hurt her, please."

"Raiker, don't..." Petra said.

"Hush, my lady," he said.

Titania laughed and lowered her spear.

"How sweet," she said. "You may rise. Don't worry, little one. I'm not going to hurt her."

Raiker stood hesitantly, sensing a trap. Titania put her hand on his shoulder and spun him around to face Petra.

"You're going to," Titania said.

"What?"

"You're going to draw your sword and kill her. I want to see the look in her eyes when you betray her. And once you do, you will swear to me that you will never speak of the things you heard here today. And then you can fly out of those doors. I won't stop you. I promise."

Petra and Raiker locked eyes from across the room.

"*No*," he said vehemently, shaking his head.

"Raiker... it's okay," Petra said, sounding so much braver than she felt. "Just... do what she says and get out of here, please."

"Petra, stop—" his voice choked with a sob, "Stop talking."

Titania giggled. "Listen to her, child. That whore of a mayfly is making more sense than you ever have in your whole pitiful life. Now do it, or I will make you do it."

"Please don't die for me, Raiker," Petra said, crying.

He curled into himself, his wings closed and his shoulders sagging. He stared at Petra helplessly, and Petra knew then that there was no convincing him to leave here without her. And there was no fighting Titania. Titania was going to win.

"My Queen, I can't live with this. Don't make me do this," Raiker begged.

The Queen had run out of patience. She grabbed the top set of his folded wings by the tips, pinning them shut together. Her other hand clamped down on the veins running along the top and she pulled hard to the left. There was a horrible snapping sound and Raiker shrieked. Petra screamed with him, in wordless fear and rage. Raiker fell to his hands and knees, shaking all over, and slowly unfolded his broken wings. The tips were bent at a right angle and blood poured out of the cracks, pooling in the carpet of purple flowers at his feet. For one desperate moment, he tried to fly, screaming from the pain of it, but trying anyway. His wings made a discordant, rattling buzz and failed to lift him off the ground.

Petra tried to go to him, but Titania pushed her back against the door with a flick of her hand, hard enough to knock the wind from her lungs. The Queen stepped in front of Raiker's sobbing form and lifted up his chin with one hand. He squeezed his eyes shut.

"*Open your eyes*," Titania commanded.

He complied instantly, his beautiful copper eyes wide, fearful, and locked on to hers.

"*Draw your sword*," she said.

Raiker reached for the hilt of his sword and pulled it from its sheath.

"*Kill her*."

Raiker stood. He raised his sword. Titania moved out of his way and he took a step forward. Then another. Petra's back was against the door, and she pressed into it further almost involuntarily, as if she could melt through it and run. Briefly, she considered drawing the sword at her back, but she couldn't bring herself to raise it against him. She knew she couldn't possibly win that fight anyway, even as badly as he was hurt. He left a trail of blood behind him as he continued to walk forward.

Her body shook, staring at that flaming sword and dreading the inevitable. She closed her eyes, and she could still see the glow of it behind her eyelids as he came closer. He was almost next to her now, within striking distance, and she forced herself to open her eyes and look at him. He needed to know that she knew this wasn't his fault. That he'd never hurt her if he had a choice.

"I love you, Reylinghae," she said as he held the sword over her.

He hesitated.

He hesitated.

"I love you, Reylinghae," she said again in a rush. "I should have told you sooner. I was scared." Petra grabbed on to his other hand, holding tightly. "I love you so much it fucking terrifies me. I want to be bound to you."

Fear replaced the cold intensity in Raiker's eyes. He lowered his sword just a bit, so that the blade was pointed at her throat instead of preparing to cleave her head in two.

Titania snickered. "That is not going to work."

Petra ignored her and babbled through tears. "I know you, Reylinghae, and this isn't who you are. You're not a killer. You've got more compassion in your little finger than most people have in their whole bodies." She reached her trembling hand out to the hand holding the sword. She rested hers on top of his, squeezing lightly, and he didn't resist her. "You make me feel like I have family again, Reylingae. I could be your family, and you could be mine, and I'll... I'll paint butterflies for our kids, like your mom used to do because you love them. Because she loved you, Reylinghae. And I love you."

Raiker's arm shook, and then with a roar of effort he threw his sword across the room. It sunk into the wall with a *twang.*

Titania's hold broken, Raiker grabbed Petra and pulled her into his arms.

"I love you too," he said. "I'm so sorry."

Petra hushed his apologies with a kiss. They were still kissing when Titania ripped them apart, grabbing Raiker by the wings with a scream of fury and tossing him across the room. He landed just behind her throne with a thud. A moment later he bounded to his feet again. He licked the blood from his split lip and smiled. That roguish, playful, devastatingly beautiful smile of his.

He sat down on Titania's throne and stretched languorously, his broken wings unfolding behind him.

"Hmm. It's not very comfortable, is it?" he mused.

"Get down from there!" Titania hissed.

"Or what?" he teased. "You'll make me? You couldn't make me hurt Petra. I think you're a little off your game today, your grace."

"Oh, I can make you hurt her," Titania growled. "I just need to break you some more first."

"Gods, it's cold too," Raiker said, fluttering off with a dramatized shudder. "Is that why Oberon broke his vows? He'd rather fuck warm humans than come home to his frigid bitch queen? Your cunt must be colder than a snowball on the south pole from sitting on this thing all day."

"How dare you!" Titania shrieked. Her voice echoed through the empty throne room. "Who do you think you are that you can talk to your queen this way?!"

Raiker held out his hand, and the sword that was sunk into the wall reappeared in it. He grasped the hilt tightly.

"I am Raiker the Rogue, swindler, plunderer, and housebreaker extraordinaire. The only beloved child of Desidae the Spider Charmer. Petra Adelina Bachman is my love and she is under my protection. You will not touch her again."

Titania launched herself into the air and conjured a ball of light the size of a globe. She flung it at Raiker. Raiker swung his sword like a great bat, knocking it back in her direction with a bark of laughter. His sword shattered from the impact. Titania didn't move from its path as the orb hurtled her way. She waved her hands just before it connected. The ball disintegrated in a cloud of blue smoke.

Raiker took advantage of her moment of distraction by darting from one end of the room to the other, sliding to a stop right in front of Petra.

He flashed her a grin and Petra couldn't help but grin back.

The moment passed and Titania attacked again. This time he repelled it with a glowing orange shield. He knelt behind it, feeding in more magic to repair it as it splintered continuously. His glamour vanished with a pop.

"How long do you honestly think you can keep that up?" Titania said with a dark laugh.

"Long enough," Raiker said, as he repaired the shield once more.

Flames spouted from Titania's hands, ricocheting off the shield. Raiker cried out as he fought her off. That roguish smile was still there in spite of the obvious pain on his face.

"Come on," he taunted. "Can't you do any better than that?"

Apparently, she could. With another shriek the fire doubled, and Raiker gasped from the effort of holding it back. Blood began to pour from his ears. His hands still holding the shield, and his life fading before her eyes, Raiker turned his head back to Petra.

"I'm sorry we didn't get more time," he said.

The door behind Petra opened and she fell backwards into the foyer. A pixie guard dressed in white loomed over her.

"Time to go, Petra," the guard said.

And before she could say anything, he grabbed her by the arm, pulling her away from Raiker.

Chapter Twenty-Four

P etra screamed as her arm wrenched out of its
socket. The pixie flew fast, faster than Petra's
body could handle, the G-force rippling her skin.
They were out of the foyer in seconds and then
out of the courtyard. The pain in her shoulder
seemed suddenly insignificant as her molecules
ripped apart. The next second they were in the
woods and she collapsed shaking onto the grass,
staring down at a red and white mushroom. The
guard wrenched open the air around the fairy
ring, tossed her rudely through the opening, and
then darted through himself.

Petra landed in the patch of green clover that
grew inside the Feenring in her backyard and
heard the portal snap shut behind them. She
threw up into the clover, reliving the taste of

Calantha's ginger elixir, and looked up at the guard weakly.

The unfamiliar pixie stood in front of the spot where the door to Arcadia had closed. He clutched an arakh tightly in each hand, as if he expected it to open again at any moment and danger to come through. Those weapons looked familiar.

"F-Follium?" Petra asked.

The guard turned to her briefly and nodded.

"How did you know—?" A fresh wave of nausea hit her and she was unable to complete the question.

"I came when he called for me," Follium answered. He shook his head and sighed. "Gods deliver me, I always do..."

With a last nervous look at the space where the door had shut, Follium sheathed his arakhs and turned to Petra.

Petra was trying, and mostly failing, to quell the shaking in her limbs and pull herself back to her feet. She succeeded only in sitting up. It was hard to focus on anything that wasn't the screaming pain from her broken bones. She let out a small gasp of relief when Follium put his hands on her chest and knit her cracked ribs back together. Then, as she struggled to regain some of her senses, she groaned and pushed his hand away.

"Hold still," Follium snapped.

He reached for her dislocated shoulder and Petra shoved him away again.

"*Petra Adelina Bachman, hold still*!" he commanded.

The suggestion held only for moments before Petra's mind batted it away.

"No," she managed weakly.

Scowling, Follium grabbed her roughly and pinned her arms in his iron grip. Petra felt her shoulder slip back into place with a soft pop.

"Save your magic," she protested.

"I don't think we've been followed," he said. "And I'm no match for Queen Titania if she shows up anyway. I might as well... Raiker would've been angry with me if I let you suffer longer than necessary. So will you stop struggling?"

"No," Petra said.

Whether it was because Follium was healing her or because the effects of traveling back to the fairy ring were beginning to wear off, she found some of her strength returning; the resolve creeping back into her voice.

"You have to go back for him," she said as she yanked her, now unbroken, arm away.

"There's nothing to go back for," Follium said.

"Stop that!" Petra sobbed. "Stop talking about him like he's already... You don't know that he's..."

Can't say it.

"No, I don't know that he's dead. I *hope* he is, because if he isn't that means she's still hurting him," Follium said.

"Coward!" Petra spat. "You fucking coward!"

Follium grabbed her by the shoulders hard enough to bruise her skin and roared into her face. "You think I wouldn't go back for him if I

thought there was even a fraction of a chance?!
Now, BE STILL!"

Petra slumped, defeated, and allowed Follium
to continue healing her. The tears fell steadily
down her face and into her lap, her sobs the only
sound as Follium worked in silence.

"She's going to kill everyone if we don't stop
her," Petra spoke up. "I mean, all the humans."

Follium's hand froze, hovering an inch above
her fractured clavicle.

"She... She can't have really meant that," he
mumbled.

"She did," Petra insisted. "It's what she wants the
Key for."

Follium met her eyes, as if he were searching for
any hint that she could be lying or exaggerating,
and finding none, he returned to working in
silence.

"We have to stop her," Petra said again.

"We can't," he answered quietly. "We'd need an
army to go against Queen Titania."

"But if we don't—"

"I'll destroy it. The Key is still here somewhere.
We'll find it eventually, and when we do, I will
crush that damnable thing into dust."

His hands moved over her one bare foot and the
deep purple bruise vanished from her skin.

"And that's problem solved then?" Petra said.
"She's still Queen, and we just hope she doesn't
find a different way to commit genocide?"

"Yes," Follium said shortly.

Petra's bruises, cuts, and breaks gone, Follium
stood and began to shift his glamour back from

the pale-skinned royal guard into his usual, barrel-chested form. Outside of the garden, the Unseelie fire nymphs eyed them with wary interest.

"There has to be something we can do," Petra pleaded. "Someone who could help us. Maybe if the rest of the Seelie Court knew what she was planning or maybe if we found the Key we could—"

"There is nothing we can do."

"You mean there's nothing you're willing to try."

Follium turned his back to her and let out a long breath, clenching his fists tightly at his sides.

Slowly, Petra climbed to her feet, trying to stop the quivering in her knees. She slipped off her other shoe, standing barefoot in the fairy ring.

"Open the door then," she said, her voice projecting far more resolve than she actually felt.

Follium whirled to face her. "What?"

"If you won't go back for him, I will. Open the door."

"I'm not going to let you kill yourself."

"I have to try," Petra insisted. "And what do you care? You don't even like me. Just open the door!"

"You're right. I don't like you. But I promised Raiker I'd protect you if he couldn't."

The revelation stunned Petra into silence for a few seconds before she found her voice again.

"Fine," she said. "Then I release you from your vow to protect—"

"You can't release me! I promised him, you IDIOT CHILD!" Angry tears sprung into Follium's eyes as he glared down at Petra. "I'm going to find the Key and destroy it, and until then you will STAY HERE, inside the wards, where you can't get anyone else killed! And if I have to chain you down to make that happen, I will! DO YOU UNDERSTAND?!"

Petra sank back onto the grass, sobs choking her voice.

"I didn't..." she sobbed. "He's not dead... He can't be dead."

Follium turned and stalked into the house, slamming the back door behind him hard enough to shatter the glass window. Petra was left alone, curled up in the fairy ring behind the closed door to Arcadia, sobbing into the skirt of her fire-blue dress. It wasn't until her sobs finally quieted that she heard the sound of Follium upstairs in her old bedroom. He was crying too.

She didn't sleep at first. The ordinarily cozy double bed felt impossibly big without him in it. She usually slept right in the middle when she slept alone, but now Petra found herself gravitating towards the right side of the bed without meaning to, leaving the left side horribly vacant. It was cold too, even with Shitpoo snoozing by her feet and every quilt in the house piled on top of her. Eventually she moved to the ratty, paint-flecked armchair in her garage/studio, and it was there that sleep finally, mercifully, claimed her.

And once it had, it didn't want to let go. Petra slept, and slept, and slept. It was hard to say for how long. Raiker had stolen the little digital clock radio that normally sat on Opa's workbench months ago, and the small windows at the top of the garage doors only told her when it was night and day. She woke occasionally, once to the sounds of heavy footsteps and crashing in the master bedroom over her head. For a moment, she considered the possibility that the noises might not just be Follium tearing her house apart looking for the Key. They could mean that an Unseelie was in the house. They could mean danger. But the motivation needed to get up and check was beyond her, and so she closed her eyes again.

Besides, she knew that when she was sleeping, she might dream of him.

They weren't all good dreams. In fact, most of them were not. Her dreams were confused things full of screams, and blood, and a deer frozen in the path of a blue minivan; a deer with eyes the color of wisteria blossoms. Only it was her driving the van, and somehow it was also her watching the van as some inexorable force pushed it off of the road and into the tree; pushed, not driven, and it was her wide eyes watching the glass windshield shatter inward as the hood bent towards her and it was her watching the same glass scatter on the pavement at her feet, as she stood there helplessly, with one shoe off and one shoe on, and closed her eyes so that she didn't have to see any more.

When she opened them again, she was back in her studio, safe and warm, a pencil resting comfortably in her hand as she sat in front of her easel.

"That's really good, Petralein," Liese said as she leaned over her shoulder to look at the sketches. "You're going to be so talented when you grow up. I can't wait to see it."

His eyes were hard to capture, at least in black and white. Petra's pencil moved over the paper, sketching out the almond shape of Raiker's wide, expressive eyes. It wouldn't be until she started painting that she could hope to emulate the way the light made the ever-shifting color of his irises sparkle, or how they completed that cocky smile of his. She could see that smile in his eyes even when she couldn't see his lips.

"Why aren't you painting? You said you were going to paint me," he said.

"I will," Petra said. "I'm doing a few studies first, maybe take some pictures, and then I'll paint from those."

Raiker stretched and then settled back into his pose; lounging naked on a pile of pillows on the floor of the garage, propped up on one elbow with his gossamer wings spread out behind him.

"But why?" he asked. "I'm right here. Why not just paint from looking at me?"

Petra glanced up from her sketchbook and smirked. "Because you will never hold still long enough."

Raiker's lips contorted into a pout. "That's not true. I can be still. Watch."

He froze, and Petra scrutinized his eyes again before turning back to her sketchpad.

"What are your studies of?" he asked, craning his neck as if he could somehow see around the back of the easel.

Petra rolled her eyes and reviewed the sketches she'd done so far. "Your eyes, your cheekbones, the points on your ears, the way your waist curves in from your hips... your penis."

Raiker giggled. "It's adorable how you can't even say that word without blushing."

"Shut up," Petra said as she smiled and felt still more color rush into her cheeks.

She glanced back to make sure Mama wasn't still standing there behind her, but she was gone. She must have gone to work...

"So, what is your artistic opinion of my penis?"

Petra kept her eyes on her sketchpad, unable to meet his gaze.

"I think it's perfect," she said. "All of your body is perfect." She frowned slightly as she appraised the drawings in front of her. "It's weird."

"Well, that's certainly not the adjective I was hoping for," Raiker said, sounding putout enough that Petra immediately felt guilty.

"Sorry," she said, turning away from her easel to address him directly. "I just meant... because your body isn't real. Your glamour is completely symmetrical. It's gorgeous, but it's... unnatural."

"You're symmetrical," Raiker countered, still pouting.

"Not perfectly. Not if you look hard enough. But the more I look at you the more I see this mirror image."

Raiker was still frowning, but seemed at least partly mollified by her explanation.

"Except your wings," she added. "You don't glamour those."

"Are you telling me my wings aren't symmetrical?" Raiker said skeptically.

Petra pointed to his lower right wing. "That one's bigger than the opposite one."

"It is not. Let me see that."

Raiker stood up and Petra snorted and threw down her pencil in exasperation. He leaned over her to look at the drawings she'd made of his wings. His brow scrunched as he studied them.

"Well now I can't unsee it," he said.

Petra laughed and gave the hand on her shoulder a reassuring squeeze.

"Imperfections are beautiful," she said. "Your wings are the most beautiful thing I've ever seen."

"Are they still?"

His voice came out small and hurt. He wasn't behind her anymore. He was back in front of her easel, posing again, with tears on his face. There was blood soaked into the pillows on the floor; blood that had poured from the cracks in his broken wings.

"Do you think I should glamour them now? Are my imperfections still beautiful?"

Petra drew in a deep breath, trying to quiet the sob in her voice before she answered him.

"*Yes*," she said.

Raiker smiled sadly, as if he didn't quite believe her. "If only we'd really done this, my love. You have so many photographs of your mother and your grandmother. What do you have of me?"

Petra looked at her easel in dismay. The sketchpad was blank.

"No studies, no photographs, no paintings. Is that why you're dreaming of me, my love? Of all the little details of my body? Can you remember what I look like?"

"Yes," Petra said.

He began to fade in front of her, his face slowly disappearing. "For how long?"

It was Shitpoo who woke her this time, and just about the only thing that could compel her to leave the chair was the knowledge that if she didn't answer his frantic, whining pleas she was going to have to clean dog pee off the floor, and that sounded infinitely more exhausting. She made her way to the door into the foyer, groaning as the cramps worked their way out of her legs.

She supposed she should be sad, but what she felt now was more akin to numbness. That may have been why she didn't lose her mind when she opened the door and saw the state of her living room. For all of Raiker's proclamations about being a thief, this was the first time the place truly looked like it had been robbed. Every single thing in her living room that could be turned over, moved, or emptied had been, and most of it had been done with little regard to the fragility of the objects in question. The couch was flipped over and shoved against the opposite wall, its cushions tossed into the kitchen. All the movies in the cabinet under the TV had been pulled out and strewn around the room, even the old VHS tapes from the back. All 19 of her mom's James Bond movies. Her well-worn copies of *Thumbelina* and *Ferngully*. Most of them had since been stepped on. That was just as well because it was unlikely that the TV, currently resting on its face, would ever work again anyway. She stopped to pick up the photograph of Oma and Liese in the hospital, newborn Petra clutched in her mother's arms. After staring at the image of their happy, smiling faces for a moment, she tossed it back to the floor herself, and went to grab Shitpoo's leash.

She only made it as far as the porch before Follium appeared and yanked her back inside.

"We are surrounded by Unseelie! What the hell do you think you're doing?!" he shouted as he slammed the front door shut again.

Petra pulled her arm back out of his grasp. Before she could answer, Shitpoo spared her the trouble, raising one leg and spraying a stream of urine on to Follium's boots. Follium leapt back in disgust.

"Good boy," Petra said.

Follium scowled.

"You can't just keep me in here," she said.

"I think you'll find that I can."

"Fine. You can walk the dog then. I don't care."

She turned and strode away from him, stepping carefully around the puddle of dog piss. Follium let out a string of curses only half under his breath. The words "reckless bitch" was among them.

"Yeah. Okay. You know what?" Petra said, turning to face him again. "I did what you asked. I told him he didn't have to protect me anymore. He chose to stay anyway. I get that blaming me makes this easier for you, but you're just gonna have to find another way to deal with that."

She didn't wait to hear his response. She didn't care to hear it. Petra turned and walked back into the garage, settling into her armchair again.

And she went back to sleep.

Eventually, she did leave the garage, if only because Follium barged in and demanded that he search that room next.

"It won't be in here," Petra protested without much conviction. "All this stuff is mine."

Follium remained unconvinced. He looked around the room wildly and seized on the old workbench against the wall.

"That looks older than you," he said.

"Well, yeah. That was my Opa's, but..."

No. That's not right, is it?

Follium tapped his foot impatiently.

"But...?" he asked.

Should I stop calling him my Opa?

Petra tried to focus. "But it's mostly newer stuff in there. Oma swapped out most of Opa's—"

Günter's. Should I call him Günter?

"—old hand tools for the electric kind a long time ago. Besides, you really think the Key's going to be disguised as a power drill?"

"How should I know? What's a power drill?"

My Opa was the King of the goddamn fairies.

Petra shook her head to clear it and threw up her hands in half-hearted defeat. "Whatever. Knock yourself out."

She carefully made her way through the tossed living room and into the kitchen, which she was surprised to find not only clean, but in use. There was a pot of something earthy simmering on the stove and a lump of dough rising under a tea towel. In the fridge she found a covered bowl of pasta with cheese sauce and more fresh fruits and vegetables than she suspected that refrigerator had seen since Oma died.

Everybody processes grief differently.

When Liese died, Oma spent so much time baking she barely left the kitchen. At first, she had said it was to prepare for the funeral, but then after the funeral was over, she didn't stop. Add that to the piles of casseroles and cookies their friends and neighbors were constantly bringing by, and the boxes of *Springerle* and *Pfeffernuss* that family kept mailing over from Templin, and Oma and Petra had so much food they ran out of room in the refrigerator. And still Oma kept baking...

Petra had thought it was great. All her favorite cousins came to visit and play with her, she didn't have to go to school, she was only loosely supervised, and she was drowning in cookies. The fact that her mama was dead was difficult to grasp at six, and it was a good, sugar-fueled week before that notion really began to sink in. She'd play on her swing in the backyard and listen for the sound of the minivan pulling into the drive, and slowly that horrible thought, the one the grownups had been trying to explain, had clicked into place. There would be no minivan sound. Mama wasn't coming home from work ever again. And then she'd sat in her swing and cried, and stared in through the kitchen window, watching Oma bake *Blachinda.*

Oma had died in that kitchen, not baking this time, but drinking her morning coffee. And at age 26, Petra understood the concept of death just fine, but her initial gut reaction still veered to disbelief. The conversation she'd just had on the phone with a frantic Mrs. Porter couldn't possibly have actually happened. So, she'd hung up the phone, turned back to her computer, and stared blankly at the screen until Beth asked if she was on drugs. Petra had replied, quite calmly, that her grandmother was dead, and then she began to cry and couldn't stop.

Beth, Del, Brad– they had tried to comfort her, everyone had really, and all with the same platitudes about Oma having lived a good, long life and it being her time. Only Petra remained unconvinced that Oma's life had been good. The woman had grown up during World War II, lost her husband and her daughter far too young.

The father of her child too.

Though some part of Petra knew it was selfish, it was difficult to accept that it was "her time" when Petra still needed her. And even if she had believed those platitudes, they did nothing, *nothing* to assuage the crippling guilt she felt for letting the woman that raised her die alone on the kitchen floor.

"Es tut mir leid Oma, ich werde aber bald zum Abendessen kommen."

Petra's stomach turned, staring at the bowl of pasta, and she shut the fridge and left the kitchen without eating anything.

Did Oma bake when Günter died too? Did she turn to Oberon because she was grieving? Or was she sleeping with Oberon already?

Petra couldn't think of anything she wanted to do less than sleep with a strange man. She just wanted Raiker back. She wanted his arms around her again.

Shitpoo ran into the kitchen and scuttled to a stop at her feet, his big eyes wide with the expectation of refrigerator scraps. Petra sat down on the floor and scooped the little dog into her arms, cradling him against her chest. She buried her face in his fur and cried.

Days passed and grief began to mingle with unbearable tedium. Petra cleaned the house. She paced. She watched from the window as Follium walked Shitpoo in the backyard. She searched for the Key without much enthusiasm. She stopped just short of clawing at the walls, but it was a near miss.

Earlier in the week the thought of going back to work, of resuming "normal" life, would have been intolerable. But by the time Sunday arrived, the day before her unpaid leave of absence was supposed to come to an end, work was starting to sound better than another day in this house without Raiker. Almost anything was starting to sound better.

She found Follium in the kitchen, grinding hazelnuts by hand, as if he hadn't already made so much food that about a quarter of it was rotting in the fridge. Petra watched him sprinkle the nuts over chocolate bread dough and began kneading them in.

"What?" he asked without turning around.

Getting any more than a single syllable out of Follium was a challenge lately, but then, Petra hadn't been feeling particularly loquacious herself.

"I need to go back to work," she said.

Follium snorted as he aggressively kneaded the dough. "You do see them out there, right?"

Petra followed his gaze to the kitchen window. The fire nymphs in the neighbor's tree had been joined by a hobyah and diminutive female elf bearing an elegant rapier and a disinterested expression. Even their adversaries were beginning to find the siege boring.

"Okay, but—" she began.

"You leave here, you die, and then I'll die avenging you. And I've no intention of dying today."

Follium flung the dough at the counter, sending up a little mushroom cloud of flour dust.

"Why don't you just pick which one of them you think you can take and hand me over?" Petra snapped. She moved to stand next to him and pointed to the elf out the window. "That one looks small-ish."

Something that might possibly have been concern crossed Follium's expression.

"You don't mean that..." he said.

Petra shrugged. "Why not? Everybody else in this house has died."

Follium opened his mouth to speak, and there was pity in his eyes. But whatever he had initially meant to say to Petra he seemed to think better of, and after a moment he turned back to his dumplings and managed only to half-grumble, "There are better uses for your energy than feeling sorry for yourself."

She'd had no reason to expect any better, but his answer made her see red anyway.

"Oh, forgive me for hoping for the tiniest bit of empathy from the only other person who knows exactly what I'm feeling!" Petra yelled.

The volume of her voice momentarily stunned him into silence.

"...I'm not a 'person,'" he finally muttered. "That's a human—"

"Fuck you, you pedantic asshole!" She cried as the energy required for rage seemed to desert her. "He's gone," she said between sobs. "We loved him, and he's gone."

Her eyes were on the little spray of pink roses in the garden as the tears ran down her face. When she looked at Follium again she could see tears on his face as well. Impulsively, she turned and hugged him. He rested his hand on the back of her neck and held on tight as she cried into his chest. It was Petra that eventually pulled away, and then they both took a small step back and looked at each other awkwardly.

"You loved him for a few moons," Follium said. "I loved him for—"

"Grief isn't a contest," Petra shot back, but her retort was more playful now than angry.

"We were the same age, you know," Follium said with a sad smile. "I can't remember a time when I didn't know him." He chuckled. "And he was exactly that arrogant at five-years-old as he was at 2,000."

Petra laughed as her tears continued to fall.

"Always had that bleeding heart too," Follium continued. "He used to bring home every wounded animal he found in the woods. Even the ones that were so obviously beyond anything Desidae could do to fix them. And he'd cry like... There must be a hundred little graves in the woods behind his house. Birds and chipmunks and butterflies..."

Shitpoo wandered into the kitchen and sat expectantly at Follium's feet, waiting for scraps. Follium tossed him a piece of hazelnut and scratched him behind the ears.

"You're lucky he only got you the one dog," he said. "If you'd have kept him here any longer there'd have been a pack of them."

Petra laughed and Shitpoo rolled over, exposing his black fuzzy belly.

There was a crack from the backyard, and Petra turned to the window just in time to see the broken branch fall to the ground on the neighbor's side of the fence. It had cracked, because the elf's eviscerated body had fallen on it as she fell from the tree, and the slim branch had collapsed beneath the corpse's weight. Petra's eyes darted from the broken branch up to the higher branches. They were splattered with blood. The remains of the fire nymphs and the hobyah were nearly unrecognizable.

"Get away from the window!" Follium barked as he drew the arakhs at his side.

Petra spun wildly to the window on the far wall and then to the one over the dining room table, finding similar carnage at every turn. A moment ago, they had been under siege, and now they were surrounded on all sides by corpses.

"What's happening?" Petra said.

Another crack, this one much greater than the sound of the branch breaking, resounded through the house as the warding exploded in a shower of glowing shards.

Follium grabbed Petra and pulled her behind him as he put his back to the corner. She was eye level with the bottom of his shoulder blades, and shoved so far into the corner she could hardly see around him.

That is until he suddenly dropped his weapons and knelt, bowing his head in deference to the fairy now sitting at her kitchen table.

Titania locked her eyes on Petra's and smiled.

Chapter Twenty-Five

P etra grabbed one of the arakhs off the ground and lunged for the chair as fast as she could. Follium was faster. Still kneeling, he clamped his hand on to her wrist and yanked her back, twisting until she dropped the weapon with a small yelp of pain.

"Kneel before your Queen and be silent," Titania commanded, and instantly Petra did, her knees hitting the tile floor and her mouth snapping shut.

Titania chuckled. She was dressed in light purple again, this time trading the over-sized gown for a slim, flowing dress and boots. The delicate color was offset by the spray of fresh blood on her bodice.

"Is she always this puerile?" Titania asked.

Follium had loosened his grip on Petra's wrist, but he had not released it, and Petra could feel his hand shaking.

"She's... she's grieving, your grace. I beg you excuse her conduct. She's not in her right mind."

"Grief does make us all a bit mad, doesn't it?" Titania said, speaking directly to Petra. "Your little thief knows all about that."

Knows. She said, "knows," not "knew."

"It was quite the exertion, knocking down your wards. Fetch me some wine, will you, Follium?"

Follium stood to obey, but he hesitated before turning his back to the Queen. "...This human is under my protection..."

"Then you're a fool," she said.

For just a second, Follium's eyes darted to his arakhs.

"And you are very fortunate I haven't come here to hurt her today," Titania finished.

Follium breathed a small sigh of relief and scurried to the pantry in search of wine.

"He's very talkative when his tongue isn't bound, your thief. You should have told me who you really are. If I had known that you were Petra's granddaughter, I wouldn't have been quite so... Well, my quarrel was not with you."

Shitpoo crept past Petra, eyeing Titania and emitting a low growl. Petra tried to stop him, or at least tell him to stay, but with her arms and tongue frozen all she could do was watch. Titania smiled at Shitpoo and wordlessly called him to her with a crook of her finger. He stopped growling and hopped obediently onto her lap.

"I did know about you. I tried to count them all once, all of Oberon's living human descendants. So many generations. I simply had to draw a line somewhere."

Petra's heart pounded in her chest and a tear fell as she watched Titania lift Shitpoo off her lap and hold him up with both hands.

"And killing your mother and Lillian Greene's son and the other dozen or so bastards was risk enough. If I'd have started in on the grandchildren I never would have stopped"

Titania began to chant softly. As she did Shitpoo's black fur began to stand on end and then to glow a bright, electric blue. She set him back down on the ground, and he shot away at top speed. His claws skidded madly on the tile as he tore through the kitchen, running around in circles. He darted from the kitchen into the living room. Petra saw him run towards the couch out of the corner of her eye, and then he left her field of vision.

Follium returned and offered the Queen a crystal goblet filled with Two-buck Chuck. Titania took a large, undignified gulp and then gave a small sigh of relief before taking another. There was a fine mist of sweat on her forehead catching the glow of the chandelier overhead.

She's tired. She's powerful, but even her tank runs out eventually.

Petra's eyes darted to the arakh lying a few inches away from her immobilized hand. Titania didn't notice, but Follium did. He glared down at Petra and shook his head ever so slightly. From the other room there was the soft thud of a small object colliding with a wood door, followed by the sound of Shitpoo whining.

"Would you get that door for him?" Titania asked.

Bearing a somewhat confused expression, Follium walked out of the kitchen.

"What was his name?" Titania wondered aloud. "Lillian's boy. Edwin? No... Eddie. He went by Eddie. Eddie Empyrean. That was the human name Oberon assumed, 'Empyrean'. Gods, he was an ass."

There was the faint sound of a door opening and then Shitpoo's claws skidding across the garage floor. A moment later he moved on from the garage and bounded up the stairs. The old house creaked and groaned as he ran through the upstairs bedrooms.

Follium returned to the kitchen just as Titania finished her wine, and he wordlessly refilled her glass.

"Did you know you had an Uncle Eddie?" Titania asked.

When Petra didn't answer the Queen clicked her tongue irritably.

"*You may speak,*" she said.

"No," said Petra. Her tongue had come unstuck, but her limbs remained firmly rooted in a bowed position. "My grandma told everybody that her late husband was my mom's dad."

Titania scoffed at her answer.

"Liars and oathbreakers," she muttered darkly. "The world is going to be better off without humans in it."

"Is Raiker alive?" Petra asked.

Titania acknowledged her question with a small smile and then turned back to her wine without answering it.

"Titania, just tell—"

"If you don't start addressing me with the deference I am owed, I'm going to have to... ah."

Titania smiled and broke off as Shitpoo ran back into the kitchen. Her smile turned to a frown as he slid to a stop at her feet. He shook as if he was trying to shake off water. It was Titania's spell he shook off instead, his fur changing from that glowing blue back to black. He yawned widely and curled up on the floor, falling asleep on the spot.

"It isn't here..." Titania said. "Where did she take it if she didn't hide it here?"

Months of tearing the house apart for the Key and Titania had ended the search in about four minutes.

The queen flew across the kitchen and grabbed Petra by the hair, pulling her up until her bare feet dangled an inch off the floor. Petra clenched her teeth against the pain and tried her damnedest not to cry out.

"Answer me!" Titania demanded. "It's not anywhere on the property. Where else would your grandmother have taken it?"

"Goodwill?" Petra offered. "She could have pawned it or thrown it down a storm drain or chucked it off Mt. Baldy for all I know!"

Titania let go of her hair in disgust, and Petra crashed back to the floor. Follium was by her side a moment later, frantically checking for injuries. His hands shook as he ran his thumb over the purple bruise on her knee, and his eyes shifted from it to Titania. She watched him with a smirk.

"Do you feel compelled to strike your Queen now, Follium the Fool?" she asked.

Follium thought hard before answering. "I think... the injury is small enough to be considered insignificant, and I'm certain its infliction was an accident, your grace. It would be obstinance, not honor, if I were to repay the injury in kind."

Titania chuckled. "You're smarter than I thought you were. Perhaps even smart enough to heed my advice."

Petra found that she could move again, but Follium kept his hand on her bruised knee. The arakh was a foot away, and she didn't think she'd make it more than a few inches before he pinned her down.

"Is he alive?" Petra asked again.

"Quiet, little one. The adults are talking," Titania said before turning back to Follium. "I'm going to tell Calantha to withdraw her offer for the Key, at least until I have a better lead on where it is. That should stop anyone from continuing to pester this human. She'll be safe. Unless of course you're fool enough to tell anyone that I was the one seeking out the Key, or why. You have the sense to keep that information to yourself and see to it that Petra does, don't you?"

Follium nodded. "Yes, your grace."

"Because if either of you tell anyone, or if you utter anything else that may reflect unfavorably on my character, the injuries I will inflict on her will not be insignificant, and they will not be by accident. Do you understand?"

"Perfectly, your royal highness."

Follium took a small steadying breath and then left Petra's side, walking slowly until he was standing in front of Titania. He knelt at her feet.

"If you'll forgive my boldness, my Queen, I would like to ask a small favor," he said.

Titania's eyebrows shot up to her amethyst crown. "You are in no position to ask favors of me."

"Yes, my Queen. But..."

Her formidable glare strongly suggested he should stop speaking, but he pressed on.

"I just want to know if he's alive."

Titania used the point of her spear to raise Follium's chin until he was looking up at her. Petra wasn't sure when exactly the weapon had appeared in her hand.

"Tell me, Follium the Fool," she purred in a dangerous undertone, "For what purpose do you believe I might be keeping him alive? I have the information I needed from him, and he has no value as a hostage." Her voice dropped to a purr. "Do you imagine that I'm punishing him? Is that what you're accusing your Queen of?"

Follium chose not to answer.

"What is it that you're picturing?" she asked. "Some lightless, secret dungeon, and your little thief chained to the floor, wailing like a child over his broken wings? And me, taking my pleasure in his pain? Do you think he cries for you to come and save him?"

Tears fell steadily down Follium's face.

"Well, you're wrong," she said with a smile. "He only ever cries for her."

Petra lunged for the arakh on the floor and ran at Titania with a wordless scream of rage. She wasn't thinking about the odds of the Queen ever allowing the blade to connect. She only knew she needed to hurt her. She needed to try.

She didn't make it within three feet of Titania. It wasn't the Queen that stopped her, it was Follium, with a backhand that slammed her down to the floor. Her vision exploded in shades of orange and white and the pain shot through her head, not strong enough to knock her out, but well enough to stun her senseless. Through the grogginess, she registered the sound of Titania laughing.

"Can I trust you to manage one human, or is keeping her in line beyond your abilities?" she asked.

"I-I can, my Queen. She won't be a problem," Follium said.

With another chuckle, Titania vanished.

"I'm sorry," Follium said as soon as she was gone.

"No, you're not," Petra mumbled.

She sat up slowly, her hand clapped over her swollen eye.

"I can fix it," he offered.

"No."

She stood on unsteady legs and examined her reflection in the refrigerator door. The red mark stood out prominently on her pale skin.

"No, I'm gonna wear this one," she said.

"Don't be stupid."

Follium reached his hand towards her face and Petra slapped him.

"Do not fucking touch me ever again," she said.

Follium backed away from her, looking much more angry than sorry now. He retrieved and sheathed his arakhs while Petra busied herself making an ice pack.

"He's alive," she said after they had both been silent for some time.

"It doesn't mean anything," he said.

"It means we could save him."

"No, it doesn't, Petra. This isn't better, knowing he's alive. His suffering is not worth your ridiculous false hope!"

He groaned and put his face in his hands. "I'm leaving. I'll check on you occasionally. You'll be fine. Go back to work. Go back to your life. You'll be... I'm going to go find a tavern and drink until I can't remember anything. Maybe you should do the same."

"That's your advice?" Petra said, lowering the ice pack so she could glare at him out of both eyes. "Just forget him?"

He shrugged. "You can't do anything else."

With a last guilty look at Petra's face, Follium vanished, leaving her alone.

Chapter Twenty-Six

M onday morning dawned cold and cloudy, with uncharacteristic rain falling heavy from the Southern California sky. Petra woke to a house that was empty for the first time in a very long time.

She got up. She took a shower. She put on makeup, taking some time to attempt to cover up the burgundy-colored bruise around her eye and largely failing at the task.

"I fell down the stairs," she rehearsed to the mirror.

Not even her reflection was convinced.

She eschewed Follium's fresh baked bread in favor of a stale bagel out of a bag, which she ate standing over the kitchen sink. Either Titania had cleaned up the mess she'd made or, more likely, Follium had done it. There were no more fairy bodies out the kitchen window. No living ones either. Without a buyer for the Key, no new mercenaries had appeared to replace the last batch.

Out in the garden, the flowers were starting to wilt.

Mrs. Mason had already agreed to walk Shitpoo while she was at work. Petra left her house key in the hollow of the live oak tree before she got in her car. She drove the same route she took every day. She sat in the same traffic. She heard the same mundane patter on the radio.

The hotel was quiet when she arrived, with only Sylvia manning the front desk and the back offices still empty. Sylvia greeted her with a "welcome back" and a warm smile that faltered when she saw the bruise. She accepted Petra's line about falling down the stairs without much conviction.

Petra sat at her desk. Logged into her computer. Looked over the notes Beth had left her about everything she had missed in the past two weeks. All the things she needed to do today.

Revenue report.
Occupancy report.
Rooming list.
Return phone calls.
Sit at this desk until well past dark, then go home to my empty house and drink cheap wine until I pass out.
Rinse and repeat.

Absentmindedly, she sketched a dragonfly wing in ballpoint pen on the bottom of her to do list.

Were the cells of his wings rounded like that? Or more square?

"I didn't know you draw."

Petra jumped at the sound of Sylvia's voice, the pen scrawling a line of blue across the wing.

"I used to," Petra said.

"You should still. That's good," Sylvia insisted.

"Thanks. I guess I have been drawing a little more lately. I..."

Does this make me your muse?

The blue line vivisecting the wing was almost exactly where Titania had snapped it in half.

Petra crumpled the paper with one hand and looked up at Sylvia. She was shifting her weight from one foot to the other.

"Uh... You know, I wanted to ask you something, but we can do this later if um..." Sylvia trailed off as her eyes darted to Petra's bruised face again. "Boss lady, are you sure you only fell down the stairs?"

"We can talk now," Petra said. "What's up?"

Sylvia hesitated a full five seconds apparently deciding to let it go.

"I was wondering if we had any openings in maintenance or maybe housekeeping? My cousin, Marko, got laid off, and if he doesn't find something soon, they're gonna yank his green card."

"Uh..." Petra considered it for a moment. "Not really, but we could use another front desk agent."

"Yeah..." Sylvia cringed and chuckled. She pulled something up on her phone and handed it to Petra. "How do you feel about visible tattoos?"

Petra snorted when she glanced at the picture. Marko was huge, looked like at he lived at the gym, and had visible tattoos on just about every inch of his skin. She handed back the phone.

"Maybe I can convince Beth to hire security," Petra suggested.

"Don't let the muscles fool you. He's a big teddy bear."

"Sorry, I can't help."

Sylvia shrugged and slipped the phone back into her pocket. "I'm sure he'll find something." She smiled mischievously. "But you know, since you're not hiring him... he doesn't really know anyone here and he wanted to do Disneyland. Maybe you could take him?"

Sensing the "no" before Petra had a chance to respond, Sylvia quickly launched into a list of Marko's attributes.

"He's really sweet and funny and smokin' hot and he plays the violin and his English is... coming along."

"No, he, um, he sounds great, but I'm not... I..." Petra stammered.

"You seeing someone already?" Sylvia offered.

She wanted to say yes, but that wasn't really the answer.

"I was," she said finally, the past tense catching in her throat, "But he's... he's gone." The tears that always seemed so close to the surface lately spilled over, and Petra sobbed. "Raiker's gone."

Sylvia gasped. "You mean 'gone' as in... he died?"

Petra was crying too hard to respond, but that was answer enough anyway. Sylvia rushed over to her and pulled her into a hug, murmuring condolences and apologies.

"I don't even have a picture of him," Petra finally said when her sobs had quieted some. "We weren't together very long and I just never... I'm forgetting what he looked like already."

Sylvia pulled away slightly so she could look at Petra. "Wait, you said 'Raiker', right? You mean that guy who brought you flowers? The cute one with the blue hair and the top hat?"

Petra's mouth dropped open with the realization. "He came to the front desk..."

"He's on the security footage."

Petra sat back down in her chair and quickly turned to the computer. Her hand shook as she reached for the mouse and nearly knocked over her coffee.

"Here, I got it," Sylvia said, kneeling next to the desk and taking over.

"It was the morning," Petra said. "It would have been July um..."

"Oh! I know!" Sylvia said. She left the security program and clicked on the reservation system. "That was the same day 'Sharon fucking Holly' checked in," she said with air quotes and a giggle. "I remember because you were hiding at the coffee shop so everyone would stop asking questions about that guy, and then I had to deal with that Karen by myself."

Sylvia did a quick search for Sharon Holly's past reservations and found that she had checked in on July 2nd. She switched back to the security footage and queued up that date, starting at seven a.m. and fast forwarding. Petra watched herself come in that morning at triple speed, then Hope arriving to help Sylvia with check outs. Guests checking out. Sharon Holly pitching a fit.

"Stop!" Petra said, but Sylvia was already slowing the video to real time.

Petra watched on the computer screen as Raiker swaggered into the hotel in his top hat and tails. His eyes were copper colored that day and his hair was bright teal. He gave Hope and Sylvia one of those heart-melting smiles and bowed as he introduced himself. Fresh tears fell down Petra's face, but this time they were accompanied by a smile.

Hope took the bouquet of wildflowers from Raiker and she and Sylvia disappeared into the office with them. He set his cane down across the front desk and drummed his long fingers on the marble surface as he waited. After casting a furtive glance at the door, he reached in his pocket and pulled out a compact mirror. He rearranged his hair until he was satisfied with it and then quickly returned the mirror to his pocket, resuming his casual pose at the desk.

Petra laughed and reached her hand up to the screen, touching her finger to the image of his face.

Wordlessly, Sylvia clicked over to Petra's email, attaching the video file and firing it off.

"*Thank you,*" Petra said.

Sylvia squeezed her hand and pulled the video up again.

"No problem, boss lady."

On the screen, Petra walked out of her office in a blood-red pencil skirt. Raiker smiled when he saw her, and it wasn't the same smile he had given Hope and Sylvia. That one was just for her.

The office door opened and Beth walked in, pausing in the doorway at the scene in front of her: Sylvia kneeling next to the desk and Petra crying and smiling all at once, absorbed in the images in front of her.

"Petra, are you okay?" Beth asked, setting down her breakfast burrito. "What's going on?"

On the screen Petra watched her own face turn as red as her skirt. She grabbed Raiker by the hand and dragged him out of frame, leaving Sylvia and Hope behind to giggle and exchange curious whispers.

What was it he said to me? Something about being naked, and I was pissed, but also kinda really wanted to see him naked again. He knew it too. He always looked at me like he could see right through me.

"Petra?" Beth said again.

Looks, not looked, because he's not gone. He's alive, and he never gave up on saving me even when I begged him not to. I can't give up on him.

"Uh, maybe we should give her minute. She's going through some stuff," Sylvia said.

"No," Petra said suddenly, her eyes shooting up from the screen to focus on Beth. "No, I'm okay. But I need to talk to you about something."

"Okay, Bachman" Beth said, a little confused by the intensity of Petra's gaze. "What's up?"

"I quit," Petra said.

Chapter Twenty-Seven

"Hey! You're tracking in mud!" the cashier shouted.

Petra froze and looked down at her mud-caked hiking boots, then slowly turned to look at the set of footprints she'd created; a straight line from her car parked by the gas pump, through the door, and three paces into the Shell station.

"Shit. Sorry," Petra mumbled.

She backtracked out the door again, taking care to step only where she had stepped before. Now safely outside, Petra sat down on the curb and removed the black army surplus boots, swearing again as she realized the mud had somehow found its way to the bottom of her left sock as well. A closer examination of the left boot revealed a small hole worn down next to the tread.

She ditched her left sock too and then padded into the convenience store wearing only the right one, the floor cold against her bare foot. The teenage cashier snorted.

"What the hell happened to you anyway?" he asked.

Petra looked herself up and down. There was quite a bit more mud on the hem of her pants and a decent-sized gash on her upper arm. She'd tried to stop the bleeding as best as she could with her sweatshirt (now stained and tied around her waist), but it had still streaked down to her elbow and dried there.

"Hiking," she said. "I wandered off the path a bit."

Gloria came darting into the convenience store, leaving a trail of tiny mud prints in between Petra's larger ones. Petra swooped over and picked the girl up.

"We've been looking for fairy rings!" Gloria told the cashier excitedly. "Tante says it's for an art project and Mom says Tante's full of shit."

"Uh... cool..." the cashier said uncertainly.

Petra threw Gloria over her shoulder and paid cash for five gallons of gas. Gloria giggled as Petra carried her back out of the store. Del tromped over to the door, just as covered in mud they were.

"Did you go potty?" Del asked as Petra set the giggling child back on her feet.

"I forgot..." Gloria admitted.

Del took the girl by the hand and led her back into the store, cursing under her breath. Del's muddy footprints joined the rest, and the cashier glared like he wished he could set them all on fire with his mind.

Petra slunk away from the door and back over to her rusty Chevy Celebrity. She leaned against the faded matte blue paint and checked her phone while the gas pumped. There were four missed calls in the last five hours, most of which looked like bill collectors or robo calls, but she decided to return the one from Beth.

"I need some extra banquet help on the 17th. Interested?" Beth asked.

"Maybe," Petra said.

She opened her passenger door and retrieved her overstuffed backpack from the backseat, cradling the phone on her shoulder while she searched for her planner.

"What kind of banquet?" Petra asked.

"Quinceañera."

Petra sighed.

"I know," Beth said. "Not the best tips. But there'll be really great home cooked food and tres leches cake."

Petra's stomach grumbled just thinking about tres leches cake. Mexican food did sound a lot better than another night of ramen noodles.

The sounds of her stomach were drowned out by an engine rumbling. An all too familiar red Mustang pulled up at the pump across from hers. Brad climbed out of the driver's seat and pushed his Ray-Bans up onto his head. There was a moment right before he spotted her where Petra seriously considered ducking into her car and pretending she hadn't seen him. But then he was waving. Petra withdrew her hand from the backpack and waved back, and somehow managed to drop the backpack in the process. The contents scattered in a shower of papers and stray water bottles. Cursing silently while Beth continued to sell her on the merits of working the Quinceañera, Petra knelt down to pick up her planner, now easy to spot amongst the unfurled piles of stuff.

Brad rushed over and started scooping photographs, maps, and notebooks up off the pavement. Petra mouthed the words *thank you* and held up a finger before turning to her planner.

She flipped to her calendar. On the 16th she was painting a mural at the new daycare center on Hillcrest, and on the 18th she and Del were taking Gloria to the Griffith Observatory (Gloria's latest ambition was to become an exobiologist), but the 17th was still open. Before she told Beth that, she turned to her ledger in the back of the planner. December was actually shaping up to be a pretty good month. She was within $50 of her expenses, and she could probably break even if she took the bus a few more times this month. If things got desperate, she could always take another weird commission. Last month a woman had found her Etsy and paid Petra $200 to paint a portrait of her cat on a coffee mug. Occasionally, her real paintings sold on Etsy too, but that wasn't a reliable source of income.

"Sorry, I can't work that day," she said.

"Can't work, or don't want to?" Beth asked.

She may have turned Beth down a few too many times at this point.

"Okay. Don't want to," Petra admitted. "I'm sorry. I'm just—"

"Really busy," Beth finished for her. "I know. I wish you'd tell me about this mystery project of yours."

Petra muttered her apologies and goodbyes as quickly as she could and hung up. Brad was looking at the stack of papers clutched in his hand. On the top of the stack was a copy of an old photograph– the senior Petra Adelina Bachman sitting on the couch, smiling and holding a newborn Liese. The curtains were pulled back on the window behind them, revealing a blown glass hummingbird feeder. The birdfeeder was circled in black Sharpie, and another circle was drawn around the patterned silk ottoman Oma was resting her feet on.

"Thanks," Petra said, holding out her hand, "I'll take those."

Brad ignored her outstretched hand and flipped through the stack of photographs, notes, and maps.

"What is all this?" he asked. "They look like serial killer notes."

"Uh… antiquing," she said.

"Antiquing?" Brad repeated with a snort of disbelief.

Petra snatched the papers back and scrambled to scoop the rest up off the pavement. "Just tracking down some of my Oma's old stuff. I think she sold some things when my mom got pregnant."

Brad picked up a map of Joshua Tree National Park. It was crisscrossed with hand drawn lines and X's.

"And the maps? The hiking gear?" he asked.

"Unrelated. Well, tangentially related. Actually" —Petra grabbed the map and stuffed it into her backpack— "none of your business."

"Ouch," Brad said, scowling. "Forgive me for taking an interest."

He stood up and left Petra to shove the remaining papers into her backpack.

"I'm sorry," Petra conceded. "I'm just tired and the 105 was nuts."

"Apology accepted," he said with a half-smile.

Brad held out his hand and Petra hesitated before taking it, allowing him to help her to her feet.

"Thanks for your help," Petra said. "It was good seeing you."

She was almost sincere when she said it too. Petra tossed her backpack on the passenger seat next to Gloria's booster.

"Hey, wait," Brad said. "I should, um... Just wait right here for a sec."

Petra shut the Chevy's door again and waited while Brad darted back to his car. He retrieved a small gift bag from the locked glove box and walked back over. He fidgeted with the hem of his shirt with his other hand.

"I should have given this back a long time ago," he started. "I think I drove by your house like, six or eight times, but the first time you weren't home and I thought somebody would snatch it if I left it on the porch, and the time after that weirdo you were screwing was there." He scowled. "How is Raiker the Rogue?"

Petra smirked. "How are your teeth?"

Brad self-consciously ran his tongue over his convincing-looking fake teeth.

"Uh, anyway... here," he finished, handing her the bag.

Petra reached in and pulled out a velvet-covered jewelry gift box, the big kind a new necklace might come in. She flipped it open. Nestled inside was a gold locket studded with a single ruby. "Petra" was engraved on the front in flowing cursive letters, but of course it wasn't Petra herself the locket had been engraved for, it was for—

"Oma's locket," Petra said, her mouth dropping open in surprise. Surprise lasted about 1.2 seconds, and then her next emotion kicked into gear. "You stole my Oma's locket?!!" Petra screamed.

"Borrowed it, sort of," Brad said, as he wisely stepped out of range of Petra's arms. "And before you say anything, I already talked to the jeweler and he swore he could put it back exactly the way it was. His card's in the bag."

"Put it— What?" Petra said.

She removed the locket from the gift box. At a glance, it looked exactly the same, but when she held it, she realized it was heavier. Fatter.

Caught between confusion and rage, Petra opened the locket. There was the familiar picture of her, her Oma, and her mom on the left, and the picture of her Opa—

Günter

—on the right. Only now there were slots for another two pictures. The locket had been carefully expanded, the hinges replaced and an additional thin, gold panel added to the middle. It turned smoothly like pages in a book, a photo album in miniature, and the delicate latch had also been swapped out for something slightly larger, so that the locket still snapped open and shut with a click. There were no pictures in the two added frames. Only little ovals of glass.

Momentarily lost for words, Petra finally managed to blurt out, "Why?"

Color crept into Brad's cheeks.

"Look, you're so paranoid about losing that thing, you hardly ever wear it. I didn't think you'd notice it was missing," he said.

"It's been missing for *over half a year*!" Petra shouted. "You didn't think I'd notice that?!"

"I wasn't planning on keeping it for half a year. I was planning on..." The blush had now extended to his ears. "I put in a picture of us," he said. "And I got you an engagement ring with an ruby to match. I had this whole thing I was gonna say about becoming part of your family and leaving a space blank for... for a picture of our kids someday and... and I was embarrassed, okay? I know you were probably freaking out thinking you'd lost it or fairies stole it or something. I should've given it back way before now."

Brad had never been terribly comfortable with silence. His fidgeting intensified while Petra stared at the locket, lost in thought. She wasn't thinking about Brad's confession. She was thinking about how Oma had told her that her Opa had given her the locket, and now she was wondering exactly which Opa it was Oma had been talking about.

She was thinking about how the locket wasn't in the house when Titania searched it.

Gloria bounded back to the car, Del trailing behind.

"Oh, hey Del," Brad said. "How have you been?"

Del laughed. "Dude, you know we don't have to pretend to like each other anymore, right?"

She brushed past him and went to buckle Gloria into her seat. Brad called her a bitch only half under his breath.

Petra barely registered any of the conversation around her. Her gaze was still fixed on the locket.

"Did you know there's another picture in there?" Brad asked.

That got a reaction. Petra's eyes shot up from the locket to Brad.

"What?" she said.

"There's a picture of some guy. Here."

Brad took the open locket from her hand and carefully pried open the glass encasing Günter's picture. Tucked into the same little frame was another picture, hidden behind the first.

Petra knew whose face she would see well before Brad handed her the tiny oval-shaped photograph, but she gasped when she looked at it anyway. Oberon was leaning against the live oak tree and smiling for the camera, this time captured in faded color. On the back of the photograph was the word "heulen" in Oma's handwriting.

"It means, 'wail', right?" Brad said.

"No. I mean, I guess it does, but it's, um, it's the noise a wolf makes," Petra mumbled back, distracted.

"Does that mean something to you?"

Oma! Da ist eine Wolf in der Treppe eingeschlossen!

Petra grabbed the rest of the locket back from Brad and snapped it all together again. She gave him a quick hug that he was too surprised to return.

"Thanks for this. I gotta go," she said in a rush.

"Uh, yeah. No prob—"

She slammed the car door shut, cutting off the rest of his words, checked that everyone was buckled, and peeled out of the parking lot.

Somehow, Petra managed to drive under the limit and keep up a stream of idle chatter as she drove back to Del's apartment. As soon as her passengers were out of the car, she floored it. She raced down side streets and nearly flew through a red light when she found herself staring down at the locket in her cup holder instead of watching where she was going.

I ruled it out. I thought that anguana or some other fairy stole it, and it couldn't be the Key then because Titania wouldn't still be looking for it.

Brad wasn't wrong about her almost never wearing the locket. Oma had worn it all the time. She was wearing it in nearly every photograph Petra found. Every picture from around the time Liese was born at least.

"Dein Opa hat es mir gegeben," she'd always said. "Your grandfather gave it to me." And all this time there was his picture, hidden away. Maybe if I'd worn it more, I would have found it. The picture, or the clue scribbled on the back. The message she left for just me.

The car skidded to a screeching halt in the driveway and Petra bounded out of it, racing to her front door with the locket clutched tightly in her hand. Shitpoo greeted her at the door, yipping excitedly at her ankles as she ran for the stairs.

"Is there a reason you're in a hurry?"

Petra jumped, her heart pounding in her chest. Follium was sitting on her couch, drinking a glass of water.

"Verdammtes feenhaftes Arschloch! Phones! We've had 'em here for 150 years now! Learn how to use one, and stop showing up at my house like this! Mist!" Petra yelled as she put her hand over her rapidly beating heart.

She slipped the locket into her pocket with the other hand.

Follium ignored her swearing, his eyes fixed on the dried blood on her arm. He quickly crossed the room and grabbed her arm. Petra held still while he healed her and then twitched her arm away, not wanting him to touch her any longer than necessary.

"Who did this to you?" he demanded.

"Big guy. Very dangerous. Goes by the name 'prickly pear cactus'," she said, rolling her eyes.

"That's not funny."

Petra sat down on the bottom step and Shitpoo hopped onto her lap. Follium stood over her. Petra wondered if he did that on purpose, positioning himself so that she had to crane her neck to meet his eyes. She chose to look at her dog instead, giving Shitpoo a good scratch behind the ears. Her heart rate seemed disinclined to go back to a resting pace, but she tried not to let the panic show in her expression. Shitpoo seemed to pick up on her mood, whining softly and then aggressively snuggling to comfort her.

"Are you going to tell me where you've been all day?" Follium asked.

"Nope."

Follium let out an exasperated sigh. "Are you still looking for the Key?"

Her heart rate picked up speed again.

"Of course, I'm still looking," she said without looking at him. "The fate of the entire human race is at stake. Don't you think this is maybe a little more than a one-man job?"

Follium tisked and Petra corrected herself before he could say it.

"It's an expression, Follium. I know you're not a 'man'. Jesus."

"Well, have you found anything?"

Petra hesitated a fraction longer than she should of, but her voice was clear and confident when it came out. "Maybe. I tracked this humming bird feeder to an antique store in Claremont, but the lady won't tell me who she sold it to. I bet you could convince her."

Petra retrieved the picture of the glass birdfeeder from her car and wrote the address for the antique shop on the back. Follium snorted when he saw the photo.

"At least that will be easy to break," he said as he stuffed the picture into his pocket.

Without quite meaning to, Petra put her hand on her own pocket, feeling the small lump of metal concealed there.

Follium finished his water before he left, leaving the empty glass on the coffee table. Petra watched him through the kitchen window as he opened the fairy ring in the garden. He stepped through the open portal, and after a last glance back at her through the window, shut it firmly behind him.

Petra ran for the kitchen and then back to the stairs. She took them two at a time until she reached the third step from the top, the one that always squeaked when she stepped on it.

No, not a squeak, a heulen. Like a wolf.

She must have been young when it happened, because she didn't remember the story herself, but Oma had loved to tell it. Petra had run to her grandmother in a panic, shouting that there was a wolf in the stairs.

"A wolf? On the stairs?" Oma had repeated.

"No, *in*, Oma," Petra had insisted.

Petra had grabbed her by the hand and dragged her to the third stair from the top, so that she could hear the *"heulen treppe"*. She was absolutely convinced there was a wolf under that step, and wasn't satisfied until Oma went to get Opa's hammer and pried the board up, revealing a small empty space, but no wolf. Crisis thus averted, Oma had hammered the board tightly back into place, eliminating the *heulen*.

A week later Petra had brought her the hammer, and asked Oma if she could put the heulen back. She missed the sound.

Petra didn't have Opa's hammer now, but she did have the big knife from the butcher block in the kitchen. She wedged it under the loose board and pushed with all her might, until the tip of the knife snapped off but the board did come loose. There was still no wolf, but wedged into that tiny space was a letter. A letter that began, *"Mein liebes Petralein"*.

"My dear little Petra,
There are things I should have told you, and if you're reading this now, that means I never did, and I'm so sorry. When you were young, I thought this was too much to burden a child with, and when you were older, I thought as an adult you would never believe me. All I can do is hope that you'll believe what I've written here, and forgive me for the secrets I kept.

My husband and I tried to start a family for nearly a decade. I lost the last baby just after I lost him. I prayed for God to send me an angel. To give me the child we'd wanted for so long. I prayed for a miracle.

It wasn't God that answered my prayers..."

Petra read the rest of the letter. Then she read it again. And when she'd finished reading it a third time, she had a plan.

Chapter Twenty-Eight

I n the past three months, Petra had traveled to
every National Park within driving distance,
starting with the ones with the highest number of
missing persons and unexplained deaths. Every
year, about 1,600 people go missing while visiting
National Parks. Of the ones that are found, some
of them tell strange stories. They don't remember
why they left the path or what happened to
them during the days and weeks they were lost.
They disappear from wide open spaces where no
rational person could get lost. Or they starve, not
because they were out of food, but because they
inexplicably decided to abandon their rations. Or
their water. Or their clothes.

Sometimes these people say they were
abducted by aliens.

But in the older reports, the missing person stories from a hundred years ago or more, those people usually said they were taken by the fairies.

Petra had visited the places where missing hikers were found, the last places they were seen before they vanished, and the places where their bodies had been located. She scoured the internet for reports of UFO sightings and mysterious lights, and she visited those places too. She paid particular attention to the stories of the hikers who were never seen again, retreading the same ground the Park Rangers fruitlessly searched.

But Petra had a better handle on what they should have been looking for. She was looking for mushrooms growing in a perfect ring.

The one she'd found at Joshua Tree National Park stood out to her because of just how out of place it seemed with the environment. Joshua Tree was a stark desert landscape where even the light seemed dusty brown, punctuated by rock outcrops and green cacti. The titular Joshua trees that studded the area were short, spiky, and unfriendly looking. Lichens sometimes grew on shaded rocks and tree bark, but there were no mushrooms to be seen anywhere. By all accounts, mushrooms shouldn't grow in these conditions.

Except for the place that they did, three miles northeast of the Lost Horse Loop hiking trail. This one was smaller than the fairy ring in her backyard, with a circle just big enough to stand in. Petra had visited this spot twice now, and she hadn't seen anything that would confirm without a doubt that this was a fairy ring. But the botanical strangeness of its presence alone had her mostly sold on this being her best bet, and the fact that 15 hikers had gone missing near the Lost Horse Loop didn't hurt either.

11 of those hikers had been found; disoriented, but alive. Three vanished. One dead.

Petra only hoped her name wouldn't be added to that list.

The circular portal in her backyard always opened as a two-dimensional door to the east and west, with barely a line visible if you looked at it from the northern or southern side. Hoping that held true for all fairy rings, Petra unloaded her backpack and set up her chair on the south side of the mushrooms, where she might be a little less visible. Inside the ring, she popped up a collapsible bowl and poured in a cup of heavy cream. She scattered all of her gold and silver jewelry around the bowl for good measure.

All of her jewelry, that is, except for Oma's locket, which was around her neck and tucked into her shirt, the metal resting against her skin. She wore Desidae's spider pendant too, the diamond sitting just a little higher than her locket.

Petra waited.

And waited.

And waited.

As the sun began to set, the temperature in the desert began to lower with it. Petra retrieved her jacket and a thermos full of coffee from the backpack. It didn't take long for the hot coffee and California winter jacket to feel woefully inadequate. Petra tried to check the weather on her phone, but there was no signal in this area. She knew that already, but the instinct to turn to the smartphone was too strong. There was a reason she had brought paper maps and a compass. She had a blanket too, lying behind the lawn chair. Petra resisted the urge to use it. It was better served concealing what was underneath it.

With full dark setting in, Petra retrieved the kerosene lantern from her bag and fired it up. Having the lantern lit was almost worse. Before she had been able to see the trees in the distance, illuminated by moonlight. Now her night vision was shot, and she couldn't see a thing outside the three-foot radius of light.

The wind started to pick up. It built steadily into a heulen so loud it drowned out the sound of the coyotes. It cut through Petra's thin jacket and whipped the exposed skin on her face and hands. Petra knelt to root through her backpack for her gloves, shifting through the contents by lantern light. Her search was abruptly cut off when the lantern fell over and shattered, plunging the area into darkness. Petra swore and fumbled for her phone, the flashlight app being about the only useful thing left on it.

Before she could turn it on, another source of light suddenly appeared. The portal in the fairy ring opened with a flash and then snapped shut a second later. She couldn't see anything inside the fairy ring, but she could hear something moving there. A shuffling, scraping noise, and the sound of the jewelry clanging together softly.

Hoping that whatever it was couldn't see her any better than she could see it, Petra pulled the sword from her back with both hands and brought it down in the middle of the ring. For a split second she was sure she had missed, as the sword whistled down through the open air without connecting with anything. And then it did connect, with something only about a foot off the ground. She'd hit the fairy with the flat side of the sword, not the edge. If she killed it, she'd be back at square one, not to mention bring about who knows what consequences. But by striking it she hoped she'd knock out its magic just long enough to gain an advantage, maybe even stun the thing if she got lucky.

The fairy had definitely not been stunned.

"THE FOOK KINDA GREETING BE THIS?!" the diminutive fairy yelled in a nearly incomprehensible Irish accent.

Petra dove behind her chair and grabbed the bag she had hidden under the blanket. Her eyes had adjusted just enough to make out the fairy's silhouette, and she lunged for it, landing almost face down in the dirt with the opening of Follium's magic bag slamming down over the top of the thing. The fairy kicked, screamed, and swore some more, but Petra managed to pull the bag shut and flip it around, using the slack to tie a big knot at the top.

She stood, panting, and held the bag up by one hand. The shape of the tiny fairy almost vanished in the large burlap sack. It couldn't have weighed more than five pounds, and with the bag depriving him of his magic, Petra had the physical advantage in spades.

Although nothing in the fairy's demeanor suggested that was the case.

"PUT ME DOWN AFORE I STRIKE YE DOWN YA BLEEDIN' SHITE! I'll SLIT YE GOB TA FANNY AND DANCE IN YER INSIDES! YOU DINNA KEN WHO YE'RE DEALN' WITH!"

The fairy's stature didn't seem to have much impact on the booming quality of his voice.

"You finished?" Petra asked.

"YER DAMNED FER BREATHIN' YA FILTHY BEASTIE! WHAT MANNER ER THING ARE YE TA SNATCH UP A FAIRY WHEN HE'S TAKIN' OFFERING?! YOU'VE NO SHAME T'ALL! I OUGHTTA BEAT SOME MANNERS INTA YA!"

"Okay," Petra said. "Go ahead. How's your magic working in there?"

The fairy grumbled and swore a few more times. Petra sat down on the ground with the bag at her feet, keeping a tight hold on the knot. The fabric moved as the fairy strained and pushed against it, testing the bounds of the magic burlap and finding it unyielding.

"Armaita's mercy! How'd ye come ta have such a bag as this?" he asked.

"I stole it," Petra answered. "It was woven by Calceo the Clever. You're not getting out unless I let you out. And I will let you out, if you swear to do what I ask. If you don't, I'm gonna leave this bag somewhere where the animals will find you a lot faster than any fairy will."

As if to emphasize her threat, the howling coyotes in the distance got louder. The fairy made a few more attempts at magicking or straight up shoving his way out of the bag. Petra waited quietly for him to give up.

"I've a sum 'o gold 'neath the ground near here," he eventually offered.

And I thought Raiker was a bad liar.

"I'm not interested in your money," Petra said. "I need you to open the fairy ring and take me to Queen Titania's palace."

He snorted. "Bloomin' waste of a wish. Whatcha be needin' me fer that? Canna ye just..." he trailed off as the comprehension dawned, then let out a string of curse words and bark of laughter at his own expense.

"Tell ye what, lassie," he said. "Ye promise not ta ever tell a soul I wassa 'nough a eejit ta get nabbed by a fookin' human, I'll take ye anywhere ye want."

"Deal," Petra said. "Swear it first."

The fairy cleared his throat before rattling off his vow. "I, Leighin the Explorer, swear that if ye release me from this infernal bag, I will take ye to my queen, and—"

"You will take me to Queen Titania," Petra corrected.

Leighin the Explorer was quiet for several seconds and then he began to laugh. It was an unnerving sound that started as a chuckle and grew to a full-bodied, foul-natured shriek that raised a line of goose bumps on Petra's arms.

"Shame ye caught me out on that," Leighin said. "I'd'uv loved ta seen what sorta sport Queen Mab would'a made of ya."

Petra wasn't at all sure she would fare much better with Queen Titania, but she swallowed her apprehension. When she spoke again, it was in a tone of assertiveness and deadly calm. "Another trick like that, and you're dead."

"Ye need me, lassie. Yer not about ta kill me," Leighin countered.

"I caught you easy enough. You're replaceable."

He must have believed her, because when he spoke his vow again, it was without any traps or deceits as far as Petra could decipher. She ran the words back over in her head several times before finally undoing the knot and upending the bag. Leighin tumbled out, and Petra got her first proper look at the fairy by the light of her cell phone. The tiny figure wasn't ugly by any stretch, but his rugged features suggested he either didn't glamour his looks or couldn't. He fluttered off the ground on shiny black wings and dusted off the sleeves of his velveteen coat.

"What business have ye with the Seelie Queen anyway?" he asked.

Petra took a moment to consider if she was going to answer the question. Leighin reached for the air in front of him and pulled open the fairy ring, creating a portal big enough for Petra to pass through. Arcadia was dark on the other side of it, and much like the coyotes on her side, something was howling in the night.

"I'm going to kill her," Petra said.

Leighin looked Petra up and down and snorted. "Good fookin' luck with that." He gestured to the open door. "After you, lassie."

Chapter Twenty-Nine

Leighin left her on a trail in the woods about a mile from the palace, insisting that he wouldn't dare get any closer. Petra's limbs were still shaking from Traveling here, her violently emptied stomach churning. It was colder here than it had been in the desert; the grass crystalized with frost. The sun began to rise as she walked, casting dappled green light on the trail.

The trail ended at the entrance to the courtyard. It was empty. Two fairies, a dwarf and an elf, dressed in the white uniform of Titania's guards, blocked the entrance. The dwarf carried a deadly looking hammer, the surface area as big as Petra's head, and the elf had a rapier sheathed at her side. Petra squared her shoulders and marched up to them.

"Are you lost, human?" the elf asked.

"My name is Petra Adelina Bachman. I'm here to request an audience with Queen Titania," she said.

The guards exchanged a look of barely contained amusement.

"Who let you out at this hour?" the dwarf said.

"Excuse me?" Petra said.

"Whom do you belong to?"

Raiker. I belong to Raiker. And if I ever see him again, I swear I'll say it as many times as he wants me to.

"If you just give Titania my name—" Petra said.

"Her royal highness does not see petitioners at this hour, and even if she did a human can't ask an audience. Now where is the fairy you belong to?" the dwarf demanded.

"I bet she's been abandoned," the elf said. "Look at her, she's dirty and freezing. Obviously, no one's caring for her."

"*I'd* like to care for her," said the dwarf with a lecherous grin.

Petra scowled and slapped his hand as he reached for her.

"I'm not abandoned," she said. "I belong to—"

"She belongs to me," a high, feminine voice called out.

The guards whirled to look behind them and came face-to-face with Calantha the Charming. She was barefoot in a nightgown that perfectly matched her bubblegum-pink hair. She gave the guards a tight smile that betrayed something dangerous behind her eyes.

The dwarf swallowed hard and looked from Petra to Calantha with a panicked expression.

"Your ladyship," he said. "I never meant any offense by—"

"I'm sure you didn't," Calantha replied.

She bent down to the dwarf's eye level, took his face in her hands, and planted a chaste kiss on his lips. There was a soft pop, and where the guard once stood was a little green frog, croaking frantically and hopping on top of his oversized hammer. The other guard stared at her compatriot with wide eyes.

"Come along now, lovely," Calantha said, extending one delicate hand out to Petra.

Petra shut her open mouth and, not possessing a better plan, took the hand that was offered to her. Calantha walked briskly through the courtyard, pulling Petra along with her as she spoke in a rapid undertone.

"Listen, when my Queen says, 'Fly,' I say, 'How far?', alright? She told me to bring her the Key, and I didn't get to the position I'm in by asking a lot of questions. I didn't know what the Key was, or what she wanted it for, and I didn't want to know."

"But you know now?" Petra interrupted.

Calantha shushed her as they passed the second set of guards and entered the palace foyer. Instead of walking towards the throne room, Calantha hung a right and pulled Petra down a hallway and into a small, darkened alcove. Her voice dropped further still.

"I know she killed every single fairy I had looking for the Key," she said. "I know Raiker isn't the first fairy who went into her throne room and never came out again. You shouldn't be able to Travel inside the bounds of the palace, but if anyone can do it, she can. I don't know what she does with them, but my love has a formidable temper and some..." her wings folded in behind her, body language betraying that calculated facade, "...peculiar predilections," she finished.

"What's that supposed to mean?" Petra asked.

Calantha nervously fingered the robin's egg-sized diamond dangling between her breasts, and then seemed to think better of elaborating.

"It means... it means I don't think we're meant to live as long as she has." Her words had taken on a slightly unhinged desperation. "Look, just don't tell me what you're doing here. You wanted in, and I got you in. The Queen is in her throne room, and there are no sentries on the door at this hour. I'm going back to my chamber. You never saw me, and I never helped you, understood?"

"Understood," Petra said. "Thank you, Calantha."

"You owe me rather more than a dance now, beautiful girl." Calantha kissed her cheek and then fled down the hallway, disappearing around the corner.

Petra took a deep breath and then walked off in the other direction, back towards the foyer. Every footstep sounded too loud as she walked closer to the great set of diamond doors. No one else walked in. No one stopped her as she pulled them open with shaking hands.

The doors swung open with surprising, perhaps even magical, ease. On the other end of the huge throne room Titania sat on one of the pillows near her throne, wrapped in a silk robe and nursing a cup of tea. Her crown lay on the pillow next to her.

She looked up when the door opened and her eyebrows raised. The Queen quickly stood up and returned the amethyst crown to her head.

"I'm going to have every last one of my guards beaten. How in the stars did you get in here unannounced?" Titania asked, sounding more curious than angry.

Petra shut the doors behind her and walked towards the queen.

"I'm here to bargain," Petra said.

Titania chuckled. "You should know by now that bargaining with fairies is a dangerous business, little one. And what could you possibly have to..."

Titania trailed off as she realized what bargaining chip Petra must have.

"Is he still alive?" Petra asked, holding her breath as she waited for the answer.

But Titania wasn't going to volunteer that information. With a wave of her hand her robe was replaced with a voluminous gown. She sat down on her throne just as her scepter appeared in her hand. The Queen waved Petra over, waiting in silence until Petra stood just below the dais. She motioned for Petra to bow, her smile expectant. Gritting her teeth, Petra knelt in front of the throne.

"Suppose that he is," Titania said. "What's this bargain you've come to offer me?"

"If Raiker is alive," Petra said, "you give him back to me. You let us walk out of here, and never bring harm upon us, or our descendants, ever again. You let us be. And in exchange for that"—Petra looked up and met Titania's violet eyes—"I promise, I will put the Key in your hand."

Titania regarded her curiously.

"*Are you lying to me, little one?*" she said, leaving Petra no option but to answer honestly.

"No," Petra said. "I really have it, and I really will hand it over to you." She stood and glared up at the Queen before adding, "I swear it on my mother's grave."

Titania chuckled and shook her head. "You know what the Key does. I've told you what I plan to do with it. You would doom your entire race if it meant you could be with your love?"

Petra let her silence answer for her.

"Well child, you've gone a long way towards confirming that humans aren't worth the air they breathe," Titania said.

"I don't care what you think," Petra said. "Just please give him back to me."

The Queen regarded her for a few moments.

"Petra Adelina Bachman," Titania said, "You have a deal."

"Swear it," Petra said.

"I, Titania the Almighty, give my oath that if you hand over my Key, I will let you and Raiker walk out of this palace, and never again bring harm to either of you, or any of your half-breed descendants."

She stood from her throne and laughed. "'I will put the Key in your hand.' You must think you're very clever, little mayfly. Tell me, how exactly do you plan to take it back once you hand it to me?"

Petra fought to keep her expression neutral. "We had a deal."

"Yes, yes. Although, our deal was contingent on your little thief being alive. I suppose I ought to check..."

Petra held her breath as Titania flew from the dais to the wall behind it. The Queen reached her hand out to the wall. A heavy, stone door appeared there at her touch. The room behind it was dark, too dark to see inside as Titania stepped in. Petra strained her eyes and took a few, tentative steps closer. She backed up again as the Queen reemerged, flying out of the room holding Raiker aloft by one arm. Titania dropped him roughly to the ground in front of the throne.

His glamour was gone, but those were definitely his sad eyes that were looking up at Petra. He wasn't restrained. He didn't need to be. He was too weak to fight back anymore. Every inch of his skin was either bruised black or sliced open, his blood dripping onto Titania's rug. He was still dressed in the vest and pants he'd worn to Court the day she'd lost him, but they were shredded to rags and ill-fitting on his smaller, real body. Or perhaps his clothes were hanging off him because he'd been starved. Petra had seen his true form so few times it was hard to remember, but she didn't think his ribs usually jutted out like that. Worst of all, his wings looked as though a giant hand had grabbed them and squeezed tight. They were a crushed mess of cracked veins and rent scales.

"Raiker!"

Petra ran to the crumpled figure on the floor, and Titania made no move to stop her. She put her hand on his cheek, lifting his wounded brown eyes towards hers. He shuddered when she touched him and pulled away as far as his broken, beaten limbs would allow him to.

"Raiker..." Petra said, her voice faltering. "Raiker, it's me... It's Petra... I came back for you..."

Raiker only shook his head and began to sob softly. Petra turned her gaze back to Titania.

"What have you done to him?" she demanded, angry tears in her eyes.

Titania snickered and shrugged her shoulders, utterly unconcerned. "He disobeyed his Queen. That doesn't come without consequence."

Petra reached for him again, resting her hand on his shoulder.

"No," he moaned weakly. "No more tricks, please..."

"It's not a trick, little one," Titania said. "She's really here this time."

Raiker only cried harder and curled further into himself.

"Promise," Titania added.

Raiker stiffened and then looked up at Petra, the faintest glimmer of hope in his eyes.

"Petra... you're here," he said, as if he hardly dared believe it.

"I'm here," Petra said, throwing her arms around him and holding on as tightly as she could without hurting him.

Her lips found his as he clung to her so tight it hurt. At another time, perhaps she might have registered how alien the fine scales on his body felt or hesitated at the touch of the short claws on his hands, but right then, finally kissing him again, Petra barely noticed.

After a few seconds passed he broke the kiss and pushed her away, terror replacing the hope and relief that was in his eyes.

"No," he said, "No, no, no. What are you doing here? Petra, you have to go. Run! Get out of here!"

"It's okay. We'll be okay," she hushed him. "We're gonna walk out of here together."

"Not before you hold up your end," Titania reminded her.

Titania held out her hand.

"Petra, what have you done? What did you promise her?" Raiker said.

Petra kissed his forehead. "Don't worry."

"This pathetic human you've fallen so madly in love with just traded your life for the lives of seven and a half billion people," Titania informed him. "When you said she was irrationally attached to you, you weren't joking."

"W-What?" Raiker said. "She wouldn't..."

Petra stood up and stepped away from him, not meeting his eyes.

"Petra..." Raiker begged. "Petra, you can't—"

"Too late to talk her out of it now," Titania said before turning her attention back to Petra. "We have a deal."

Petra's hands shook as she reached behind her neck to undo the clasp on the locket. She held it up by the end of the chain and let it drop into Titania's outstretched hand, the chain pooling on her palm. Grinning broadly, Titania placed her other hand on top of it and slid it over the locket. Where Oma's ruby-studded locket had been there was now a carved ruby key.

Titania laughed and ran her finger down its length.

"Oh, how I missed you," she whispered.

Titania grasped the Key and flew over their heads, landing in the center of the room. Petra rushed back to Raiker's side.

"Can you stand?" she asked him.

Raiker made no move to even try. "Petra, what have you done?" he sobbed.

Titania started to chant and then to sing, the low rhythm of her voice the only sound save for Raiker's sobs. The volume of her voice rose and the throne room began to shake. Portraits rattled off the walls and great cracks shot through the floor. Petra knelt next to Raiker and threw her arms over him, shielding his neck as if from an earthquake.

The tremors intensified as Titania's voice reached an impossible volume. The air in front of her ripped in two, and everything went eerily still. Behind the rip was a void of pure, unending blackness, save for a huge glowing red box with a lock on the front. The box was at least two stories tall and just as wide. The cavernous throne room was barely big enough to contain it. Titania stepped into that void and placed the Key in the lock. She turned it and then pulled the Key back out, standing back as the red Cage melted away.

A paw emerged first—big as a boulder, its crimson fur ending in long claws. That first step shook the room again. Three more elongated paws followed, and then the rest of the creature. It was bigger than the cage that had contained it. Once released, it grew larger still, stretching out as far as the room would allow. It howled, an unearthly sound that split Petra's ears. The Beast looked like a gigantic red wolf, with three lupine heads, a fanged serpent for a tail, and hellfire burning in its many eyes.

As the Beast siffed the air, the cage behind it began to melt. A puddle of liquid ruby that looked horribly like blood formed, then began to twist and reshape. The liquid snaked out and encircled each of the Beast's necks, making four ruby collars for each of the four violently snapping heads.

The rift Titania had sung into existence closed as if it had never been there. Titania stood in front of the Beast, gazing up at it fearlessly with the Key clutched in her hand.

"I have work for you again, my dear one," she said. "I need you to go to Alius and raze the humans from this earth."

The Beast growled and scraped one clawed paw across the floor, shredding the tree bark beneath it.

"Destroy them the way you destroyed the antea," she said.

One of the wolf heads eyed the Key in Titania's hand, snorted and let out another low growl. The other two wolf heads and the serpent on its tail turned and looked at Petra.

"Go now," Titania said.

Worry was just beginning to creep into her voice. The head that was eyeing the Key pushed at it with its nose and snapped its teeth. Titania jumped and flew backwards involuntarily.

"I have the Key. Why aren't you listening to me?" she said.

"Because it's mine," Petra said. She stood in front of Raiker, putting herself between him and the Queen as Titania slowly turned to face them. "Oberon gave it to me."

Petra held out her hand and focused on the Key Titania was clutching. It vanished from the Queen's hand and reappeared in Petra's. Petra felt the cold stone against her skin. The thought crossed her mind that she missed the locket, and the second she did it became the locket again. Petra smiled and fastened the chain back around her neck.

"Oberon gave it to you," Titania repeated, her voice shaking with disbelief.

"He knew what you were planning, after you found out about the affairs. It wasn't enough to just hide the Key from you. He had to make it so you couldn't use it anymore. It's not really a Key, is it? It's more like a leash."

All eight of the Beast's eyes were on Petra now. Focused. Awaiting orders.

"It took a lot of magic to tie the Key to a name. Oberon didn't kill himself, not on purpose. But he warned my Oma, he knew the spell might kill him, but he had to try. He disguised it, and he gave it to her to hide it. And then he used every last bit of his magic and his life force working the spell that tied it to her name. My name. He died saving the human race from you." Petra smiled. "My grandfather was a hero."

"Your grandfather was an oathbreaking, unfaithful, duplicitous, ass!" Titania spat.

Petra shrugged. "Yeah, he was that too."

Titania shook with rage, staring at the locket around her neck.

"'Petra Adelina Bachman has the Key'," Titania quoted. "I should have known. It wouldn't be written like that unless..." She put her hands to her temples, thinking hard. "He gave it to his human whore, and it should have reverted back to belonging to whoever held it when she died, but it went to you instead..." Titania's head snapped back up. "If I killed you, I could take it back."

Petra held her ground, unafraid. "You swore an oath that you wouldn't."

Titania was stunned into silence, her mouth dropping open. She began to laugh, a bitter, half-crazed laugh.

"I did, didn't I?" she said. Titania sunk down to her knees, as if she were deflating, her purple gown pooling around her. Tears streaked her face. "I suppose you think I might strike you down now anyway." She smiled. "But I won't... I'm better than him... I always was."

The Beast lurked behind Titania, still watching Petra. And without having to say a word, Petra gave the order.

Titania made no move to save herself as the Beast stepped towards her, its great paws shaking the ground with a resounding boom. She knew, perhaps better than most, just how little point there would be in fighting it. She didn't even turn to face it. She sat, and she waited for death to inevitably come and claim her at last. Petra held Raiker's hand in hers and closed her eyes just before it happened. She only heard the crunch of its great teeth.

Queen Titania the Almighty didn't so much as whimper.

Chapter Thirty

Epilogue

He was in his own bed. He knew that even with his eyes closed. The quilt felt familiar, comfortable on his skin. It smelled like home— like morning glories and evergreen. Raiker slowly opened his eyes and for a moment he stared at the sitting room wall in confusion. His gaze drifted up from the wall to the bedroom door high above his head. Someone had moved his bed down into the sitting room.

He rolled over slowly, still groggy and confused. It hurt to move, but not so much that he couldn't do it.

Not like it had before.

His head now angled towards the kitchen, he could see Petra sitting at the table. She was reading *A Midsummer Night's Dream* and sipping tea from his favorite purple mug. Her long hair cascaded down her back, a torrent of golden curls with just a single strand of silver catching the light overhead. The silver hair was probably not long for this world. He suspected she plucked them out, that perhaps she was even fearful of his reaction to these signs of aging, but he sort of liked them. He liked the way they shined. Raiker watched her tuck one of those curls behind her ear and smile at something funny in the play; her blue eyes alight with mirth.

"Am I dreaming, my love?" he asked.

Petra jumped at his voice and put the book down. "You're awake!"

"Am I not meant to be?"

"Your doctors— Sorry, healers said it might be another day or two before you woke up. They've been keeping you sedated while they..."

Petra kept talking, but Raiker was finding it hard to focus.

Healers. I needed healers. I remember Petra crying. Screaming for someone to help me as the guards rushed in because I was bleeding. I was...

Raiker sat up in bed with a start. He let out a gasp as his wings hummed to life and lifted him up off the bed and into the air. It hurt to fly, the way it had hurt to roll over. His wings ached and the effort of it was making his head swim.

But he was flying.

He grinned and laughed and groaned from the pain and cried all at once. And then he realized that Petra was yelling at him and trying to grab on to his ankles and yank him back down. He allowed her to pull him back onto the bed. He sank into it, exhausted.

"I can fly," he said, overjoyed.

"Yeah, but you're not supposed to yet," Petra said. "Your healers said no flying, no magic, no sex, and no walking any more than you need to."

Raiker laughed. "Gods, am I allowed any fun at—"

He stopped as his eyes fell on his upper left wing. There was a small cluster of gray close to the wing tip. A patch of the clear, iridescent cells of his wings had turned light gray and opaque. A marred spot a little bigger than his fist. The veins running around those cells were no longer bright copper-colored, but a dark, unhealthy brown. On further inspection, he noticed with growing horror that it wasn't the only spot like it, just the biggest one. Here and there, all over his wings, were more patches of gray.

Petra took his hand. "They healed most of the damage, but they said there were cells that the circulation was cut off for too long, and without blood those cells..."

"Died," Raiker finished in a small voice.

"Yes," Petra confirmed.

Raiker tried to hold the tears back. He tore his gaze away from those ugly gray spots and focused on Petra's face instead.

"But I can fly," he said.

"You can fly," Petra repeated. "You should be able to fly just as well as you could before. You just need to rest awhile."

He swallowed hard, focusing on the positives and forcing the tears down. "Suppose I could glamour them..."

"I wish you wouldn't."

"They're ugly, Petra."

"No," she insisted. Petra let her hand trail lightly across his wing. "You earned these scars saving my life. I think they're beautiful."

The tears spilled over then. She kissed him softly and held him in her arms. He grasped on to her, breathing in the scent of her skin and wanting nothing more than to never have to let go of her again.

"You saved my life too," he said. "You came back for me."

"I'm so sorry I didn't come sooner."

She was sobbing now too. He hushed her and kissed her again, drying her tears. She reached up to touch his cheek and wiped his away as well, leaving her hand resting on the curve of his cheek bone.

Raiker sat up and touched his other cheek, then looked down and examined the rest of his body.

"Who did my glamour?" he asked.

The front door opened and Follium walked in, carrying Shitpoo in his arms.

"You're awake!" Follium said, that broad, familiar smile lighting up his face.

Shitpoo also greeted him with enthusiasm, bounding out of Follium's arms and hopping onto the bed.

"Do I have you to thank for this, old friend?" Raiker asked.

"No, you were too..." Follium faltered. "It was a bit beyond my abilities to heal you after..."

"He meant his glamour," Petra supplied.

"Oh, that," Follium grinned. "That was simple. I've only been staring at that form for almost 3,000 years."

Raiker petted the little dog in his lap with one hand while he continued to examine his face with the other. He frowned.

"My nose is too small," he said.

"HA!" Petra shouted, so loud that Shitpoo jumped. "I told you!"

Follium grumbled and tossed Petra a coin, which she caught and held aloft triumphantly. "Fine, you were right."

"Oh, I knew I was right, but I wouldn't mind hearing you say it a few more times."

Raiker chuckled at the exchange. He felt more awake now, his mind coming back into focus and shaking off the effects of the sleeping potion. He could feel the subtle, familiar energy of the morning glories on the walls again. And something else... something in the corner of the room by the stove.

Something powerful.

The more he focused on it, the more obvious its presence became. He couldn't quite believe he hadn't noticed it before. He could feel Follium's magic too, a sort of glow emanating from his body, warm, like a flame. But if Follium's magic was a candle, this thing was a bolt of lightning.

The source of the strange energy stepped out from behind the stove. It looked like a large, skinny dog, reddish-orange in color and trotting around the kitchen on spindly limbs. It turned its brown eyes to him and Raiker felt it reach out. Its magic crawled over his skin.

Raiker tried to back away and succeeded only in banging into the headboard. "That is not a dog!"

"No, she's not," Petra said. "Cerbi, be nice."

The crawling feeling stopped, and "Cerbi" curled up on the floor.

"You... that's the..." Raiker stammered.

"I told her she looked scary and that's what she did. I think she looks cute as a greyhound," Petra said.

"You think the Beast of the apocalypse is cute?"

Petra shrugged and held out her hand. The Beast obediently walked over and allowed Petra to scratch her behind the ears. Shitpoo curled further into Raiker's lap and whined.

Follium laughed. "Don't worry. You'll get used to it. Took me at least a fortnight before my heart stopped pounding out of my chest just looking at that thing."

Follium reached into his pocket and handed Petra something shiny.

"More gifts?" she said.

Petra held up a silver pendant encrusted with rubies to the light. Raiker's eyes went from the pendant in Petra's hand to the wall next to the door, where piles of gifts sat, mostly unopened.

"Another from the Queen," said Follium.

Raiker's heart skipped a beat and Petra rushed to clarify.

"Queen *Valfarren*. Titania's daughter."

"You slept right through the Princess's coronation." Follium said. "Truth be told, I think they rushed the coronation a bit. Didn't want to give anyone a lot of time to question who ought to be in charge now."

"*Should* she be in charge?" Raiker said. "Princess Valfarren's barely more than a child."

"She's my age," Petra pointed out sharply.

"She's, ah, I only meant by fairy standards she's, well..." Raiker floundered, trying to steer the conversation into safer territory. A memory and a realization came back to him with a gasp, "Gods in heaven, you murdered the Queen of the Seelie Court! How are you not clapped in iron?!"

Petra flinched. "Believe me they wanted to."

"She had the blood rights," Follium chimed in. "Queen Titania murdered her mother." He chuckled. "The Beast didn't hurt either."

Petra ran a hand through the Beast's fur. "The royal guards weren't in the best position to argue."

"And... and now Queen Valfarren is sending you gifts?" Raiker asked, feeling as though he was missing something. Expensive jewelry seemed a strange way to react to a someone ordering their pet to eat your mother.

"Everyone is sending her gifts," Follium said. "Jewels, wine, trees, food, offers to father her children—"

"Offers to *what*?!" Raiker repeated.

Follium laughed. "Careful there, old friend. You almost sound jealous. You've been spending too much time with humans."

"I'm not jealous, I'm confused," Raiker said. He turned back to Petra. "Why are you entertaining offers to father your children?"

Petra's temper flamed in her blue eyes.

"I mean, why are fairies offering to father your children?" he quickly amended.

Her fury cooled slightly. "Because of Cerbi," she said. "The Key's tied to my name and my bloodline until I die. Then it's up for grabs again."

"Has anyone threatened you?" he asked.

"Well..."

When Petra trailed off uncomfortably Raiker turned to Follium for answers instead. Follium held up four fingers.

"And Cerbi made very short work of them all," Follium added. "I don't believe anyone on this earth poses an actual threat to her."

"And I like it that way," Petra said. She grabbed Raiker's hand and held on tight. "I think we've lived through enough for this lifetime. I'm not letting anyone hurt me or anyone I love ever again."

As if in agreement, Cerbi barked. Raiker resisted the urge to back away from her.

"Queen Valfarren wants me to move into the palace and live there till I die, so she can grab up the Key then," Petra said.

"Better her than Mab," Follium said.

"I don't trust any of them," Petra said. "Valfarren seems okay, but I don't know her, and her mom was übergeschnappt. For all I know she is too."

Raiker was beginning to understand. "But you could pass the name on, the way your grandmother did."

"Yeah," Petra said. "And my kids can pass it to their kids and their kids pass it to their kids until there's enough Petra Adelina Bachmans running around that no one person or fairy ever has that much power ever again. And I should probably do it sooner, rather than later, just in case I choke on an apple and die or something."

"Alright," Raiker said. "But you're mine."

Follium laughed. "You are so jealous."

"I am not jealous! I just think it's ridiculous that other fae are even offering, when if anyone's going to father her children, it'll be — Stop laughing at me!"

Petra squeezed his hand.

"Follium, could you give us a minute?" she asked.

Follium nodded. He leaned over the bed and scooped Shitpoo up from Raiker's lap. Then, much to Raiker's surprise, he kissed Petra on the cheek.

"You do remember his healers said no sex?" he teased.

"I remember. Go!" Petra said as she waved him off.

Follium headed for the door. "Come on, Shitpoo. And this time, will you please actually relieve yourself and not just sniff every tree in Arcadia..."

He stepped out the door, leaving them alone. Petra looked apprehensive, sad even, and Raiker was beginning to worry about what she would say next. She'd pulled away from him, sitting with her hands in her lap.

"You... Do you not want children?" he asked.

"No, I do," she said.

She stared down at her hands.

"... Do you not want them with me?" he asked.

Petra looked up at him. "I wasn't sure how to ask you. I wasn't sure I even *should* ask you."

"Petra, I don't under—"

"Because our kids would be human," she said. "I can't ask you to have babies with me if you know that you'll outlive them."

Raiker closed the distance between them and pulled her into his arms. He ran his fingers through her hair and tried to swallow the lump in his throat.

"I'll be there to watch over them when you're gone," he said softly. "And I'll watch over our grandchildren after them, and then our great-grandchildren." He chuckled and kissed her forehead. "Generations of Petra Adelina Bachmans, and no doubt all of them as stubborn as you are. I believe I'm going to be very busy."

Petra laughed and kissed him. There were tears on her face.

"Are you sure?" she said.

"My love, I've never been more sure of anything."

He could feel his eyelids drooping again. Maybe he really wasn't supposed to have woken up for a couple more days. Echoing his thoughts, Petra pulled him down on the bed, curling up with her head resting on the pillow next to him. He put his hand on her hip.

"Just how long until we can get to making these babies?" he asked, yawning.

"Another three weeks at least."

Raiker frowned and closed his eyes. "We'll see about that," he mumbled.

He was home, and he was safe, and Petra was here, *really here,* in his arms. He didn't want to miss another second with her, but he was so tired...

"Raiker?"

"Hmm?"

"Can we get married first?"

Raiker opened his eyes. "Anything you want, my love. Although, you might tell me what that means exactly."

"We exchange rings— at a ceremony. We swear vows."

"What kind of vows?"

"To have and to hold, to love and to cherish, for better or for worse, till death... till death do us part."

Raiker smiled and closed his eyes again. "That sounds a lot like binding."

He wondered if when she'd said rings she meant a tattooed ring like binding, or if she meant jewelry. He opened his mouth to ask her and yawned again.

"Get some sleep," she whispered. "I'll be right here when you wake up."

Acknowledgements

Acknowledgements

I'm in the habit of periodically deciding I'm a talentless hack. So when I say there are people without which this book would have never been completed, I mean it quite literally. Thank you to my husband, Brandon Owens, for pushing me to pursue a career in writing even when it wasn't paying the bills. Thank you to Chelsea Jenkins, for every time you asked me to come over to drink wine and discuss my book. Thank you to Todd Reynolds, for penning the first piece of *Fairy Thief* fanfic. And thank you to Brittany Curry, for telling me this was your very favorite book and thus furnishing me with a lifetime's worth of serotonin.

Extra special thanks goes out to all my other beta readers- Evan Tillet, Ana Figel, Jonathan Hope, Adara Huls, Elizabeth Gilson, Stephanie Harkness Moxley, Kim Plyler, Savannah Mercer,

Alana Hoare, and basically half of Theatre of Dare.

To Lora Kellogg, Ashley Johnson, Jeniece McDonald, my brother– Chris Frazier, and all the old iPoly crew– thanks for being my loyal readers way before anyone else was.

A somewhat strange thanks goes to the boy I used to nanny for, Carter Jeffreys. Back when I was a quarter through this book, and I'd given up on it entirely, my husband convinced me to pull it out and read some chapters aloud. I had to censor myself with the 9-year-old in the same room playing video games, but he wasn't really paying attention to me anyway. Until he was. The more I read, the more Carter began to listen. Next thing I know he's staring at me with rapt attention, begging for more chapters. I figured if my book could pull a 9-year-old away from his video games, I must be on to something. So thank you Carter for inspiring me to keep writing *The Fairy Thief*, and please get your mom's permission before you read it.

But writing is only half the battle, and I'd be remiss if I didn't thank all the people who helped me transform this book from a mess of a manuscript into a published novel. To Kristi Morgan– even though you weren't ultimately able to publish my book, you were the first publisher out of the 115 I queried to give me a shot. To my brilliant editor Amanda Clarke, *The Fairy Thief* wouldn't have been half the novel it is without your insight (and I'm sorry for all the things I said when you told me to gut the first act).

Danke sehr to Nev Warren for translating my bad German and teaching me some very cool swear words. And thanks to Aamna Shahid of Etheric Tales for giving me a cover more beautiful than I ever dreamed of.

Finally, thank you to my 4th grade teacher, Ms. Bachman, for telling me I could be a writer someday. I'll never forget it.

Katrina Mae Leuzinger lives in the beautiful Outer Banks of North Carolina with her husband and their fearsome small blond child. When she's not writing urban fantasy novels, she works as a local journalist, makes a spectacle of herself in her community theater, and buys more books than she will ever read. Follow her shenanigans at www.KatrinaMaeLeuzinger.com.